The Collected Supernatural and Weird Fiction of Guy de Maupassant Volume 1

The Collected
Supernatural and Weird
Fiction of
Guy de Maupassant
Volume 1

Including Two Novelettes
'Little Louise Roque' and 'Mad'
and Forty-Four Short Stories
of the Strange and Unusual

Guy de Maupassant

LEONAUR

The Collected
Supernatural and Weird
Fiction of
Guy de Maupassant
Volume 1
Including Two Novelettes
'Little Louise Roque' and 'Mad'
and Forty-Four Short Stories
of the Strange and Unusual
by Guy de Maupassant

FIRST EDITION

Leonaur is an imprint
of Oakpast Ltd

ISBN: 978-0-85706-437-0 (hardcover)
ISBN: 978-0-85706-438-7 (softcover)

http://www.leonaur.com

Contents

The Golden Braid   7

At Sea   14

Beside a Dead Man   20

Coco   25

No Quarter   30

The Traveller's Story   38

A Jolly Fellow   45

Letter Found on a Corpse   54

Legend of Mont St. Michel   61

Little Louise Roque   66

Mad   104

Francis   137

Magnetism   143

On the River   148

The Spectre   154

Mother Savage   161

The Blind Man   169

The Devil   174

He?   182

The Diary of a Madman   190

The Englishman   198

The Englishman of Etretat   205

The Inn 209

The Mad Woman 223

"The Terror" 227

The Unknown 234

The White Wolf 240

A Fishing Excursion 246

Was it a Dream? 252

Who Knows? 258

A Strange Traffic 273

A New Year's Gift 279

A Sister's Confession 286

Abandoned 291

Bellflower 300

Denis 306

The Horla 313

The Parrot 340

The Man With The Dogs 347

Ghosts 354

The Spasm 361

The Penguins' Rock 368

The White Lady 373

Violated 379

Minuet 384

Am I Insane? 389

The Golden Braid

A.k.a. A Tress of Hair / The Head of Hair / One Phase of Love

The walls of the cell were bare and whitewashed. A narrow, barred window, so high that it could not easily be reached, lighted this little room; the crazy man, seated on a straw chair, looked at us with a fixed eye, vague and haunting. He was thin, with wrinkled cheeks and almost white hair that one would think had grown white in a few months. His clothes seemed too large for his dried-up limbs, his shrunken chest, and hollow body. One felt that this man had been ravaged by his thoughts, by a thought, as fruit is by a worm. His madness, his idea, was there in his head, obstinate, harassing, devouring. It was eating his body, little by little. It, the Invisible, the Impalpable, Immaterial Idea was eating into his flesh, drying up his blood, snuffing out his very life.

What a mystery, that this man whom a Dream was sending to his grave! This Possessed One inspired terror and pity and infinite compassion! What weird dream, fatal and horrible, lived under that brow lined by deep, moving furrows?

Said the physician:

"He has terrible furious spells; he's one of the most strangest lunatics that has ever come under my observation. He is afflicted with erotic and morbid mania. He's a sort of necrophile. He has written a diary which clearly shows the malady of his mind. His folly becomes almost palpable, so to speak. If you care to, you may look over this strange document."

I followed the doctor into his office and he handed me the

diary of this poor, demented wretch.

"Read it," said he, "and then tell me what you think of it." Here is what was written in the diary:

Until the age of thirty-four I lived quietly, without one love affair. Life seemed very good to me very simple, and very easy. I was wealthy. I liked so many things, that I had a passion for none. How good it is to live! Every morning I woke up happy and did the things I liked to do. And I went to bed satisfied with the hope of the next day and the peaceful future to look forward to.

I had had several mistresses without ever having felt the frenzy of desire, or the ardent love that sometimes comes after possession. It is good to live that way. It is perhaps better to love, but then, love is frightful. And yet, those who love in a commonplace way, must experience great happiness, but not such happiness as mine, for love came to me in the strangest manner.

As I was wealthy, I indulged my taste for antiquities of all sorts; and I often thought of the unknown hands that had touched these things, of the eyes that had admired them, of the hearts that had loved them, for one certainly loves inanimate objects! I often remained hours and hours looking at a little watch of the past century. It was so dainty and pretty, with its enamel and its wrought gold! And it ticked as it did on the day when a woman, captivated by the precious jewel, went into the shop and bought it.

This little watch had not stopped going, had never ceased its mechanical life, nor the tic-tac begun a hundred years ago. Who was the first to wear it under her kerchief, the heart of the watch beating against the heart of the woman? What hand had held it lightly clasped in its tapering fingers, had turned it over and over and wiped the porcelain shepherds tarnished by the moisture of the skin? Whose eyes had scanned its flowered face for the expected, beloved and divine hour?

How I should have liked to have known her, the woman

who had owned that rare and exquisite jewel! She is dead! I am possessed by the desire of the women of the past. I love through the ages, all those who have loved The stories of past loves fill me with regrets. Oh! beauty, youth, hope and smiles! Should not these be eternal! How I have wept for whole nights over the poor women of yesterday, so beautiful, so tender, so sweet, whose arms opened to their lovers and who are now dead! Kisses are immortal! They hover from lip to lip, from century to century, from age to age! Mankind gathers them, transmits them and dies.

The past attracts me, the present awes me, because the future means death. I regret all things of the past and I weep over all the people who have lived; I would like to stay the hand of Time But the hours flit by, constantly stealing a little from my lifetime and giving me annihilation of tomorrow. And I will never live again.

But I am not to be pitied. For I found The One I was looking for; and through her, I tasted heavenly delights.

One bright morning I was loafing around Paris, happy and light-hearted, looking into all the shop-windows. All of a sudden I noticed a beautiful Italian cabinet of the seventeenth century. It was a rare and beautiful piece of workmanship. I attributed it to a Venetian artist by the name of Vitelli, who was quite celebrated in his time. I passed on.

Why did the recollection of that cabinet haunt me with such insistence that it made me retrace my steps? I stopped once more in front of the curiosity-shop and felt the temptation to purchase the cabinet.

What a stranger thing temptation is! You look at a thing and, little by little, it seduces you, troubles you, takes possession of you as would a woman's face.

Its charm envelopes you, a weird charm which proceeds from its colour, its shape and its own particular physiognomy, and you already love it, desire it, yearn for it. The fever of possession is upon you, weak at first, as if it were timid, but stronger and stronger as time goes on, until it becomes a raging passion.

And the dealers seem to read in your eyes the secret and irresistible longing that is in you.

I bought the cabinet and had it sent home immediately. I had it placed it in my bedroom.

Oh! I pity all those who do not know the honeymoon that a collecton spends with the antiquity he has purchased. He caresses it with his hand and eye as if it were of flesh; he hovers around it continually and never stops thinking of it. Its cherished remembrance follows him about, in the streets, in society, everywhere; and when he comes home, he runs and looks at it before taking off his hat.

Really, for a week I adored that cabinet. I opened its drawers and its doors, handled it with delight and tasted all the joys of possession.

One night, while I was feeling a panel, I discovered that there was some secret device about the cabinet. My heart began to beat and I spent the whole night trying to solve the mystery.

I succeeded the following day, when I inserted the blade of a knife in a crack of the wood. A board slid back and I saw, lying on black velvet, a marvellous braid of golden hair.

Yes, a big braid of golden hair, almost Titian-coloured, that was tied with a golden cord.

I was bewildered and I trembled from head to foot! An almost imperceptible perfume, so old that it seemed like the ghost of itself, emanated from the drawer and the weird relic.

I lifted it gently, almost religiously, from its resting place. It unrolled and touched the floor, it was so thick and brilliant, so light and serpentine, that it looked like the flaming tail of a comet.

A strange emotion clutched my throat. What was this find?

When and how had this braid been hidden in that drawer? What adventure or drama was behind this discovery?

Who had cut this hair? Had it been a lover, when parting forever from his mistress? Or a husband, animated by a spirit of revenge? Or, had it been the fair owner herself, in a fit of despair?

Was she about to enter a convent when she had thrust that treasure into the drawer, to be a sort of token to the living world? Was she, young and fair, to be nailed in her coffin, and had her lover kept that glorious adornment, the only thing about her that was not destined to perish in the earth, the only thing that he might worship and caress in his hours of despair?

Was it not strange that this golden hair was untarnished, when not bit of the body from whence it had sprung, remained?

It ran through my fingers, caressed my skin with a gentle touch of a dead person. I felt so troubled that I almost wept. I held the braid a long, long time in my hand and it seemed to me as if something of its owner's soul had remained within its meshes. Then I laid it away carefully on the worn velvet, closed the drawer, and went out to take a long walk and be alone with my dreams.

I walked a long time, filled with emotion and sadness, the same one feels after a love kiss. It seemed to me as if I had lived before, as if I had known the owner of the golden hair.

When I got home, an irresistible longing came over me to look at the braid. I took it out of the drawer and instantly a long shudder ran through my frame.

For a few days, I remained in my usual state of mind, although the thought of the golden braid never left me. Whenever I was home, I had to look at it and touch it. I would unlock the drawer with the same emotion I would have felt had it been the door of my beloved's chamber. In my heart and in my hands was a continual, peculiar, sensual yearning to feel the golden flood of this dead hair on my skin. Then, after I had satisfied my longing and had closed the drawer again, I still felt its presence, as if it had been a living, breathing thing imprisoned in the cabinet; I felt its presence and desired it anew; I felt anew the longing to take it out, to touch it and animate myself through its delightful, cool, silky contact.

A month or two, I don't remember exactly, went by. The braid haunted me; I was happy and tormented at the same time, as if I were expecting the fulfilment of my desires.

I used to lock myself in my room to be alone with it, to feel it on my skin, to bite it, kiss it, roll my face in it. I drowned my lips in it and my eyes, so that the light of day would come to me through its golden mazes.

I loved it! Yes, I loved it. I could not live without it, could not remain away from it an hour.

And I waited. . . . . waited for what? I did not know. For *Her*. One night I awoke with the sensation that somebody was in my room.

Of course I was alone. But I could not go to sleep again and as I tossed about without finding rest, I got up to look at the braid. It seemed softer to me, more animated than usual. Do the dead return? The kisses I rained upon it almost made me faint with ecstasy and I carried it to bed with me and glued my lips to it as to a beloved mistress.

The dead come back. For *She* came to me. Yes, I saw her, held her, possessed her as she was in this life, tall, blonde, plump, with cool breasts, and with lyre-shaped hips, and my kisses travelled from her throat to her little feet, following all the divine curves of her body.

Yes, I possessed her, every day and every night. She came to me every night, the Beautiful, Adorable, Mysterious, Unknown One.

My happiness was so great that I was unable to conceal it. When I was with her I felt a superhuman bliss, a strange joy at being able to possess the Invisible, the Immaterial,

Death itself, so to speak. No lover ever tasted such ardent, terrible delights!.

I was unable to conceal my bliss. I loved her so that I would not anywhere without her and I took her every-where with me.

I showed her around town as my wife, I took her to the theatres in private boxes as my mistress.

But they saw her . . . . .they guessed my secret . . . .they tore her from me. . . . . and they threw me into prison, like a malefactor. They took her away from me. . . . .Oh! misery!

Here the manuscript ended. And just as I looked at the physician with bewildered eyes, a frightful cry, a howl of helpless rage and exasperated desire rang through the asylum.

"Listen to him," said the physician, "We have to give that obscene lunatic a shower bath five times a day. Other men besides Sergeant Bertrand, have loved dead women."

Filled with pity, horror and astonishment, I stammered:

"But. . . .the braid. . . .did it really exist?"

The doctor rose, opened a closet filled with bottles and instruments, and grabbing a braid of blonde hair, flung it across the room to me. It flew into my lap like a golden bird.

I shuddered as I felt its soft, caressing touch on my hands. And my heart throbbed with disgust, as when one comes in contact with the accessories of a crime, with covetousness as when one experiences the temptation of something both mysterious and degrading.

The physician shrugged his shoulders and remarked:

"Really the mind of man is capable of anything."

At Sea

The following paragraphs recently appeared in the papers:

Boulogne-Sur-Mer, January 22.— Our correspondent writes:
A fearful accident has thrown our sea-faring population, which has suffered so much in the last two years, into the greatest consternation. The fishing smack commanded by Captain Javel, on entering the harbour was wrecked on the rocks of the harbour breakwater.
In spite of the efforts of the life boat and the shooting of life lines from the shore four sailors and the cabin boy were lost.
The rough weather continues. Fresh disasters are anticipated.

Who is this Captain Javel? Is he the brother of the one-armed man?

If the poor man tossed about in the waves and dead, perhaps, beneath his wrecked boat, is the one I am thinking of, he took part, just eighteen years ago, in another tragedy, terrible and simple as are all these fearful tragedies of the sea.

Javel, senior, was then master of a trawling smack.

The trawling smack is the ideal fishing boat. So solidly built that it fears no weather, with a round bottom, tossed about unceasingly on the waves like a cork, always on top, always thrashed by the harsh salt winds of the English Channel, it ploughs the sea unweariedly with bellying sail, dragging along at its side a huge trawling net, which scours the depths of the ocean, and detaches and gathers in all the animals asleep in the rocks, the flat fish glued to the sand, the heavy crabs with their curved claws, and the lobsters with their pointed moustaches.

When the breeze is fresh and the sea choppy, the boat starts in to trawl. The net is fastened all along a big log of wood clamped with iron and is let down by two ropes on pulleys at either end of the boat. And the boat, driven by the wind and the tide, draws along this apparatus which ransacks and plunders the depths of the sea.

Javel had on board his younger brother, four sailors and a cabin boy. He had set sail from Boulogne on a beautiful day to go trawling.

But presently a wind sprang up, and a hurricane obliged the smack to run to shore. She gained the English coast, but the high sea broke against the rocks and dashed on the beach, making it impossible to go into port, filling all the harbour entrances with foam and noise and danger.

The smack started off again, riding on the waves, tossed, shaken, dripping, buffeted by masses of water, but game in spite of everything; accustomed to this boisterous weather, which sometimes kept it roving between the two neighbouring countries without its being able to make port in either.

At length the hurricane calmed down just as they were in the open, and although the sea was still high the captain gave orders to cast the net.

So it was lifted overboard, and two men in the bows and two in the stern began to unwind the ropes that held it. It suddenly touched bottom, but a big wave made the boat heel, and Javel, junior, who was in the bows directing the lowering of the net, staggered, and his arm was caught in the rope which the shock had slipped from the pulley for an instant. He made a desperate effort to raise the rope with the other hand, but the net was down and the taut rope did not give.

The man cried out in agony. They all ran to his aid. His brother left the rudder. They all seized the rope, trying to free the arm it was bruising. But in vain. "We must cut it," said a sailor, and he took from his pocket a big knife, which, with two strokes, could save young Javel's arm.

But if the rope were cut the trawling net would be lost, and this net was worth money, a great deal of money, fifteen hundred francs. And it belonged to Javel, senior, who was tenacious of his property.

"No, do not cut, wait, I will luff," he cried, in great distress. And he ran to the helm and turned the rudder. But the boat scarcely obeyed it, being impeded by the net which kept it from going forward, and prevented also by the force of the tide and the wind.

Javel, junior, had sunk on his knees, his teeth clenched, his eyes haggard. He did not utter a word. His brother came back to him, in dread of the sailor's knife.

"Wait, wait," he said. "We will let down the anchor."

They cast anchor, and then began to turn the capstan to loosen the moorings of the net. They loosened them at length and disengaged the imprisoned arm, in its bloody woollen sleeve.

Young Javel seemed like an idiot. They took off his jersey and saw a horrible sight, a mass of flesh from which the blood spurted as if from a pump. Then the young man looked at his arm and murmured: "*Foutu*" (done for).

Then, as the blood was making a pool on the deck of the boat, one of the sailors cried: "He will bleed to death, we must bind the vein."

So they took a cord, a thick, brown, tarry cord, and twisting it around the arm above the wound, tightened it with all their might. The blood ceased to spurt by slow degrees, and, presently, stopped altogether.

Young Javel rose, his arm hanging at his side. He took hold of it with the other hand, raised it, turned it over, shook it. It was all mashed, the bones broken, the muscles alone holding it together. He looked at it sadly, reflectively. Then he sat down on a folded sail and his comrades advised him to keep wetting the arm constantly to prevent it from mortifying.

They placed a pail of water beside him, and every few minutes he dipped a glass into it and bathed the frightful wound, letting the clear water trickle on to it.

"You would be better in the cabin," said his brother. He went down, but came up again in an hour, not caring to be alone. And, besides, he preferred the fresh air. He sat down again on his sail and began to bathe his arm.

They made a good haul. The broad fish with their white bellies lay beside him, quivering in the throes of death; he looked at them as he continued to bathe his crushed flesh.

As they were about to return to Boulogne the wind sprang up anew, and the little boat resumed its mad course, bounding and tumbling about, shaking up the poor wounded man.

Night came on. The sea ran high until dawn. As the sun rose the English coast was again visible, but, as the weather had abated a little, they turned back towards the French coast, tacking as they went.

Towards evening Javel, junior, called his comrades and showed them some black spots, all the horrible tokens of mortification in the portion of the arm below the broken bones.

The sailors examined it, giving their opinion.

"That might be the 'Black,'" thought one.

"He should put salt water on it," said another.

They brought some salt water and poured it on the wound. The injured man became livid, ground his teeth and writhed a little, but did not exclaim.

Then, as soon as the smarting had abated, he said to his brother:

"Give me your knife."

The brother handed it to him.

"Hold my arm up, quite straight, and pull it."

They did as he asked them.

Then he began to cut off his arm. He cut gently, carefully, severing al the tendons with this blade that was sharp as a razor. And, presently, there was only a stump left. He gave a deep sigh and said:

"It had to be done. It was done for."

He seemed relieved and breathed loud. He then began again to pour water on the stump of arm that remained.

The sea was still rough and they could not make the shore.

When the day broke, Javel, junior, took the severed portion of his arm and examined it for a long time. Gangrene had set in. His comrades also examined it and handed it from one to the other, feeling it, turning it over, and sniffing at it.

"You must throw that into the sea at once," said his brother.

But Javel, junior, got angry.

"Oh, no! Oh, no! I don't want to. It belongs to me, does it not, as it is my arm?"

And he took and placed it between his feet.

"It will putrefy, just the same," said the older brother. Then an idea came to the injured man. In order to preserve the fish when the boat was long at sea, they packed it in salt, in barrels. He asked:

"Why can I not put it in pickle?"

"Why, that's a fact," exclaimed the others.

Then they emptied one of the barrels, which was full from the haul of the last few days; and right at the bottom of the barrel they laid the detached arm. They covered it with salt, and then put back the fish one by one.

One of the sailors said by way of joke:

"I hope we do not sell it at auction."

And everyone laughed, except the two Javels.

The wind was still boisterous. They tacked within sight of Boulogne until the following morning at ten o'clock. Young Javel continued to bathe his wound. From time to time he rose and walked from one end to the other of the boat.

His brother, who was at the tiller, followed him with glances, and shook his head.

At last they ran into harbour.

The doctor examined the wound and pronounced it to be in good condition. He dressed it properly and ordered the patient to rest. But Javel would not go to bed until he got back his severed arm, and he returned at once to the dock to look for the barrel which he had marked with a cross.

It was emptied before him and he seized the arm, which was well preserved in the pickle, had shrunk and was freshened. He wrapped it up in a towel he had brought for the purpose and took it home.

His wife and children looked for a long time at this fragment of their father, feeling the fingers, and removing the grains of salt that were under the nails. Then they sent for a carpenter to make a little coffin.

The next day the entire crew of the trawling smack followed the funeral of the detached arm. The two brothers, side by side, led the procession; the parish beadle carried the corpse under his arm.

Javel, junior, gave up the sea. He obtained a small position on the dock, and when he subsequently talked about his accident, he would say confidentially to his auditors:

"If my brother had been willing to cut away the net, I should still have my arm, that is sure. But he was thinking only of his property."

Beside a Dead Man

A.k.a. Beside Schopenhauer's Corpse / The Smile of Schopenhauer

He was slowly dying, as consumptives die. I saw him each day, about two o'clock, sitting beneath the hotel windows on a bench in the promenade, looking out on the calm sea. He remained for some time without moving, in the heat of the sun, gazing mournfully at the Mediterranean. Every now and then, he cast a glance at the lofty mountains with beclouded summits that shut in Mentone; then, with a very slow movement, he would cross his long legs, so thin that they seemed like two bones, around which fluttered the cloth of his trousers, and he would open a book, always the same book. And then he did not stir any more, but read on, read on with his eye and his mind; all his wasting body seemed to read, all his soul plunged, lost, disappeared, in this book, up to the hour when the cool air made him cough a little. Then, he got up and re-entered the hotel.

He was a tall German, with fair beard, who breakfasted and dined in his own room, and spoke to nobody.

A vague, curiosity attracted me to him. One day, I sat down by his side, having taken up a book, too, to keep up appearances, a volume of Musset's poems.

And I began to look through *Rolla*.

Suddenly, my neighbour said to me, in good French:

"Do you know German, *monsieur*?"

"Not at all, *monsieur*."

"I am sorry for that. Since chance has thrown us side by side, I could have lent you, I could have shown you, an inestimable thing—this book which I hold in my hand."

"What is it, pray?"

"It is a copy of my master, Schopenhauer, annotated with his own hand. All the margins, as you may see, are covered with his handwriting."

I took the book from him reverently, and I gazed at these forms incomprehensible to me, but which revealed the immortal thoughts of the greatest shatterer of dreams who had ever dwelt on earth.

And Musset's verses arose in my memory:

Hast thou found out, Voltaire, that it is bliss to die,
And does thy hideous smile over thy bleached bones fly?

And involuntarily I compared the childish sarcasm, the religious sarcasm of Voltaire with the irresistible irony of the German philosopher whose influence is henceforth ineffaceable.

Let us protest and let us be angry, let us be indignant, or let us be enthusiastic, Schopenhauer has marked humanity with the seal of his disdain and of his disenchantment.

A disabused pleasure-seeker, he overthrew beliefs, hopes, poetic ideals and chimeras, destroyed the aspirations, ravaged the confidence of souls, killed love, dragged down the chivalrous worship of women, crushed the illusions of hearts, and accomplished the most gigantic task ever attempted by scepticism. He spared nothing with his mocking spirit, and exhausted everything. And even today those who execrate him seem to carry in their own souls particles of his thought.

"So, then, you were intimately acquainted with Schopenhauer?" I said to the German.

He smiled sadly.

"Up to the time of his death, *monsieur.*"

And he spoke to me about the philosopher and told me about the almost supernatural impression which this strange being made on all who came near him.

He gave me an account of the interview of the old iconoclast with a French politician, a doctrinaire Republican, who wanted to get a glimpse of this man, and found him in a noisy tavern, seated in the midst of his disciples, dry, wrinkled, laughing with an unforgettable laugh, attacking and tearing to pieces ideas and beliefs with a single word, as a dog tears with one bite of his teeth the tissues with which he plays.

He repeated for me the comment of this Frenchman as he went away, astonished and terrified: "I thought I had spent an hour with the devil."

Then he added:

"He had, indeed, *monsieur*, a frightful smile, which terrified us even after his death. I can tell you an anecdote about it that is not generally known, if it would interest you."

And he began, in a languid voice, interrupted by frequent fits of coughing.

"Schopenhauer had just died, and it was arranged that we should watch, in turn, two by two, till morning.

"He was lying in a large apartment, very simple, vast and gloomy. Two wax candles were burning on the stand by the bedside.

"It was midnight when I went on watch, together with one of our comrades. The two friends whom we replaced had left the apartment, and we came and sat down at the foot of the bed.

"The face was not changed. It was laughing. That pucker which we knew so well lingered still around the corners of the lips, and it seemed to us that he was about to open his eyes, to move and to speak. His thought, or rather his thoughts, enveloped us. We felt ourselves more than ever in the atmosphere of his genius, absorbed, possessed by him. His domination seemed to be even more sovereign now that he was dead. A feeling of mystery was blended with the power of this incomparable spirit.

"The bodies of these men disappear, but they themselves remain; and in the night which follows the cessation of their heart's pulsation I assure you, *monsieur*, they are terrifying.

"And in hushed tones we talked about him, recalling to mind

22

certain sayings, certain formulas of his, those startling maxims which are like jets of flame flung, in a few words, into the darkness of the Unknown Life.

"'It seems to me that he is going to speak,' said my comrade. And we stared with uneasiness bordering on fear at the motionless face, with its eternal laugh. Gradually, we began to feel ill at ease, oppressed, on the point of fainting. I faltered:

"'I don't know what is the matter with me, but, I assure you I am not well.'

"And at that moment we noticed that there was an unpleasant odour from the corpse.

"Then, my comrade suggested that we should go into the adjoining room, and leave the door open; and I assented to his proposal.

"I took one of the wax candles which burned on the stand, and I left the second behind. Then we went and sat down at the other end of the adjoining apartment, in such a position that we could see the bed and the corpse, clearly revealed by the light.

"But he still held possession of us. One would have said that his immaterial essence, liberated, free, all-powerful and dominating, was flitting around us. And sometimes, too, the dreadful odour of the decomposed body came toward us and penetrated us, sickening and indefinable.

"Suddenly a shiver passed through our bones: a sound, a slight sound, came from the death-chamber. Immediately we fixed our glances on him, and we saw, yes, *monsieur*, we saw distinctly, both of us, something white pass across the bed, fall on the carpet, and vanish under an armchair.

"We were on our feet before we had time to think of anything, distracted by stupefying terror, ready to run away. Then we stared at each other. We were horribly pale. Our hearts throbbed fiercely enough to have raised the clothing on our chests. I was the first to speak:

"'Did you see?'

"'Yes, I saw.'

"'Can it be that he is not dead?'

"'Why, when the body is putrefying?'

"'What are we to do?'

"My companion said in a hesitating tone:

"'We must go and look.'

"I took our wax candle and entered first, glancing into all the dark corners in the large apartment. Nothing was moving now, and I approached the bed. But I stood transfixed with stupor and fright:

"Schopenhauer was no longer laughing! He was grinning in a horrible fashion, with his lips pressed together and deep hollows in his cheeks. I stammered out:

"'He is not dead!'

"But the terrible odour ascended to my nose and stifled me. And I no longer moved, but kept staring fixedly at him, terrified as if in the presence of an apparition. Then my companion, having seized the other wax candle, bent forward. Next, he touched my arm without uttering a word. I followed his glance, and saw on the ground, under the armchair by the side of the bed, standing out white on the dark carpet, and open as if to bite, Schopenhauer's set of artificial teeth.

"The work of decomposition, loosening the jaws, had made it jump out of the mouth.

"I was really frightened that day, *monsieur*."

And as the sun was sinking toward the glittering sea, the consumptive German rose from his seat, gave me a parting bow, and retired into the hotel.

Coco

Throughout the whole countryside the Lucas farm, was known as "the Manor." No one knew why. The peasants doubtless attached to this word, "Manor," a meaning of wealth and of splendour, for this farm was undoubtedly the largest, richest and the best managed in the whole neighbourhood.

The immense court, surrounded by five rows of magnificent trees, which sheltered the delicate apple trees from the harsh wind of the plain, inclosed in its confines long brick buildings used for storing fodder and grain, beautiful stables built of hard stone and made to accommodate thirty horses, and a red brick residence which looked like a little *chateau*.

Thanks for the good care taken, the manure heaps were as little offensive as such things can be; the watch-dogs lived in kennels, and countless poultry paraded through the tall grass.

Every day, at noon, fifteen persons, masters, farmhands and the women folks, seated themselves around the long kitchen table where the soup was brought in steaming in a large, blue-flowered bowl.

The beasts-horses, cows, pigs and sheep-were fat, well fed and clean. Maitre Lucas, a tall man who was getting stout, would go round three times a day, overseeing everything and thinking of everything.

A very old white horse, which the mistress wished to keep until its natural death, because she had brought it up and had always used it, and also because it recalled many happy memories, was housed, through sheer kindness of heart, at the end of the stable.

A young scamp about fifteen years old, Isidore Duval by name, and called, for convenience, Zidore, took care of this pensioner, gave him his measure of oats and fodder in winter, and in summer was supposed to change his pasturing place four times a day, so that he might have plenty of fresh grass.

The animal, almost crippled, lifted with difficulty his legs, large at the knees and swollen above the hoofs. His coat, which was no longer curried, looked like white hair, and his long eyelashes gave to his eyes a sad expression.

When Zidore took the animal to pasture, he had to pull on the rope with all his might, because it walked so slowly; and the youth, bent over and out of breath, would swear at it, exasperated at having to care for this old nag.

The farmhands, noticing the young rascal's anger against Coco, were amused and would continually talk of the horse to Zidore, in order to exasperate him. His comrades would make sport with him. In the village he was called Coco-Zidore.

The boy would fume, feeling an unholy desire to revenge himself on the horse. He was a thin, long-legged, dirty child, with thick, coarse, bristly red hair. He seemed only half-witted, and stuttered as though ideas were unable to form in his thick, brute-like mind.

For a long time he had been unable to understand why Coco should be kept, indignant at seeing things wasted on this useless beast. Since the horse could no longer work, it seemed to him unjust that he should be fed; he revolted at the idea of wasting oats, oats which were so expensive, on this paralyzed old plug. And often, in spite of the orders of Maitre Lucas, he would economize on the nag's food, only giving him half measure. Hatred grew in his confused, childlike mind, the hatred of a stingy, mean, fierce, brutal and cowardly peasant.

When summer came he had to move the animal about in the pasture. It was some distance away. The rascal, angrier every morning, would start, with his dragging step, across the wheat fields. The men working in the fields would shout to him, jokingly:

"Hey, Zidore, remember me to Coco."

He would not answer; but on the way he would break off a switch, and, as soon as he had moved the old horse, he would let it begin grazing; then, treacherously sneaking up behind it, he would slash its legs. The animal would try to escape, to kick, to get away from the blows, and run around in a circle about its rope, as though it had been inclosed in a circus ring. And the boy would slash away furiously, running along behind, his teeth clenched in anger.

Then he would go away slowly, without turning round, while the horse watched him disappear, his ribs sticking out, panting as a result of his unusual exertions. Not until the blue blouse of the young peasant was out of sight would he lower his thin white head to the grass.

As the nights were now warm, Coco was allowed to sleep out of doors, in the field behind the little wood. Zidore alone went to see him. The boy threw stones at him to amuse himself. He would sit down on an embankment about ten feet away and would stay there about half an hour, from time to time throwing a sharp stone at the old horse, which remained standing tied before his enemy, watching him continually and not daring to eat before he was gone.

This one thought persisted in the mind of the young scamp: "Why feed this horse, which is no longer good for anything?" It seemed to him that this old nag was stealing the food of the others, the goods of man and God, that he was even robbing him, Zidore, who was working.

Then, little by little, each day, the boy began to shorten the length of rope which allowed the horse to graze.

The hungry animal was growing thinner, and starving. Too feeble to break his bonds, he would stretch his head out toward the tall, green, tempting grass, so near that he could smell, and yet so far that he could not touch it.

But one morning Zidore had an idea: it was, not to move Coco any more. He was tired of walking so far for that old skeleton. He came, however, in order to enjoy his vengeance. The beast watched him anxiously. He did not beat him that day. He walked around him with his hands in his pockets. He even pretended to change his place, but he sank the stake in exactly the same hole, and went away overjoyed with his invention.

The horse, seeing him leave, neighed to call him back; but the rascal began to run, leaving him alone, entirely alone in his field, well tied down and without a blade of grass within reach.

Starving, he tried to reach the grass which he could touch with the end of his nose. He got on his knees, stretching out his neck and his long, drooling lips. All in vain. The old animal spent the whole day in useless, terrible efforts. The sight of all that green food, which stretched out on all sides of him, served to increase the gnawing pangs of hunger.

The scamp did not return that day. He wandered through the woods in search of nests.

The next day he appeared upon the scene again. Coco, exhausted, had lain down. When he saw the boy, he got up, expecting at last to have his place changed.

But the little peasant did not even touch the mallet, which was lying on the ground. He came nearer, looked at the animal, threw at his head a clump of earth which flattened out against the white hair, and he started off again, whistling.

The horse remained standing as long as he could see him; then, knowing that his attempts to reach the near-by grass would be hopeless, he once more lay down on his side and closed his eyes.

The following day Zidore did not come.

When he did come at last, he found Coco still stretched out; he saw that he was dead.

Then he remained standing, looking at him, pleased with what he had done, surprised that it should already be all over. He touched him with his foot, lifted one of his legs and then let it drop, sat on him and remained there, his eyes fixed on the grass, thinking of nothing. He returned to the farm, but did not mention the accident, because he wished to wander about at the hours when he used to change the horse's pasture. He went to see him the next day. At his approach some crows flew away. Countless flies were walking over the body and were buzzing around it. When he returned home, he announced the event. The animal was so old that nobody was surprised. The master said to two of the men:

"Take your shovels and dig a hole right where he is."

The men buried the horse at the place where he had died of hunger. And the grass grew thick, green and vigorous, fed by the poor body.

No Quarter

A.k.a. Father Milon / Old Milon

The broad sunlight threw its burning rays on the fields, and under this shower of flame life burst forth in glowing vegetation from the earth. As far as the eye could see, the soil was green; and the sky was blue to the verge of the horizon. The Norman farms scattered through the plain seemed at a distance like little woods inclosed each in a circle of thin beech-trees. Coming closer, on opening the worm-eaten stile, one fancied that he saw a giant garden, for all the old apple-trees, as knotted as the peasants, were in blossom. The weather-beaten black trunks, crooked, twisted, ranged along the inclosure, displayed beneath the sky their glittering domes, rosy and white.

The sweet perfume of their blossoms mingled with the heavy odours of the open stables and with the fumes of the steaming dunghill, covered with hens and their chickens. It was midday. The family sat at dinner in the shadow of the pear-tree planted before the door—the father, the mother, the four children, the two maidservants, and the three farm labourers. They scarcely uttered a word. Their fare consisted of soup and of a stew composed of potatoes mashed up in lard.

From time to time one of the maidservants rose up, and went to the cellar to fetch a pitcher of cider.

The husband, a big fellow of about forty, stared at a vine-tree, quite exposed to view, which stood close to the farmhouse, twining like a serpent under the shutters the entire length of the wall.

He said, after a long silence:

"The father's vine-tree is blossoming early this year. Perhaps it will bear good fruit."

The peasant's wife also turned round, and gazed at the tree without speaking.

This vine-tree was planted exactly in the place where the father of the peasant had been shot.

It was during the war of 1870. The Prussians were in occupation of the entire country. General Faidherbe, with the Army of the North, was at their head.

Now the Prussian staff had taken up its quarters in this farm-house. The old peasant who owned it, Père Milon, received them, and gave them the best treatment he could.

For a whole month the German vanguard remained on the lookout in the village. The French were posted ten leagues away without moving, and yet, each night, some of the *uhlans* disappeared.

All the isolated scouts, those who were sent out on patrol, whenever they started in groups of two or three, never came back.

They were picked up dead in the morning in a field, near a farmyard, in a ditch. Their horses even were found lying on the roads with their throats cut by a sabre stroke. These murders seemed to have been accomplished by the same men, who could not be discovered.

The country was terrorized. Peasants were shot on mere information, women were imprisoned, attempts were made to obtain revelations from children by fear.

But, one morning, Père Milon was found stretched in his stable with a gash across his face.

Two *uhlans* ripped open were seen lying three kilometres away from the farmhouse. One of them still grasped in his hand his blood-stained weapon. He had fought and defended himself.

A council of war having been immediately constituted, in the open air, in front of the farmhouse, the old man was brought before it.

He was sixty-eight years old. He was small, thin, a little crooked, with long hands resembling the claws of a crab. His faded hair, scanty and slight, like the down on a young duck, allowed his scalp to be plainly seen. The brown, crimpled skin of his neck showed the big veins which sank under his jaws and reappeared at his temples. He was regarded in the district as a miser and a hard man in business transactions.

He was placed standing between four soldiers in front of the kitchen table, which had been carried out of the house for the purpose. Five officers and the Colonel sat facing him. The Colonel was the first to speak.

"Père Milon," he said, in French, "since we came here we have had nothing to say of you but praise. You have always been obliging, and even considerate toward us. But today a terrible accusation rests on you, and the matter must be cleared up. How did you get the wound on your face?"

The peasant gave no reply.

The Colonel went on:

"Your silence condemns you, Père Milon. But I want you to answer me, do you understand? Do you know who has killed the two *uhlans* who were found this morning near the cross-roads?"

The old man said in a clear voice:

"It was I!"

The Colonel, surprised, remained silent for a second, looking steadfully at the prisoner. Père Milon maintained his impassive demeanour, his air of rustic stupidity, with downcast eyes, as if he were talking to his *curé*. There was only one thing that could reveal his internal agitation, the way in which he slowly swallowed his saliva with a visible effort, as if he were choking.

The old peasant's family—his son Jean, his daughter-in-law, and two little children stood ten paces behind, scared and dismayed.

The Colonel continued:

"Do you know also who killed all the scouts of our army

whom we have found every morning, for the past month, lying here and there in the fields?"

The old man answered with the same brutal impassiveness:

"It was I!"

"It is you, then, that killed them all?"

"All of them—yes, it was I."

"You alone?"

"I alone."

"Tell me the way you managed to do it?"

This time the peasant appeared to be affected; the necessity of speaking at some length incommoded him.

"I know myself. I did it the way I found easiest."

The Colonel proceeded:

"I warn you, you must tell me everything. You will do well, therefore, to make up your mind about it at once. How did you begin it?"

The peasant cast an uneasy glance toward his family, who remained in a listening attitude behind him. He hesitated for another second or so, then all of a sudden he came to a resolution on the matter.

"I came home one night about ten o'clock, and the next day you were here. You and your soldiers gave me fifty crowns for forage with a cow and two sheep. Said I to myself: 'As long as I get twenty crowns out of them, I'll sell them the value of it.' But then I had other things in my heart, which I'll tell you about now. I came across one of your cavalrymen smoking his pipe near my dike, just behind my barn. I went and took my scythe off the hook, and I came back with short steps from behind, while he lay there without hearing anything. And I cut off his head with one stroke, like a feather, while he only said 'Oof!' You have only to look at the bottom of the pond; you'll find him there in a coal bag with a big stone tied to it.

"I got an idea into my head. I took all he had on him from his boots to his cap, and I hid them in the bake-house in the Martin wood behind the farmyard."

The old man stopped. The officers, speechless, looked at one another. The examination was resumed, and this is what they were told.

Once he had accomplished this murder, the peasant lived with only one thought: "To kill the Prussians!" He hated them with the sly and ferocious hatred of a countryman who was at the same time covetous and patriotic. He had got an idea into his head, as he put it. He waited for a few days.

He was allowed to go and come freely, to go out and return just as he pleased, as long as he displayed humility, submissiveness, and complaisance toward the conquerors.

Now, every evening he saw the cavalrymen bearing dispatches leaving the farmhouse; and he went out, one night, after discovering the name of the village to which they were going, and after picking up by associating with the soldiers the few words of German he needed.

He made his way through his farmyard, slipped into the wood, reached the bake-house, penetrated to the end of the long passage, and having found the clothes of the soldier which he had hidden there, he put them on. Then he went prowling about the fields, creeping along, keeping to the slopes so as to avoid observation, listening to the least sounds, restless as a poacher.

When he believed the time had arrived he took up his position at the roadside, and hid himself in a clump of brushwood. He still waited. At length, near midnight, he heard the galloping of a horse's hoofs on the hard soil of the road. The old man put his ear to the ground to make sure that only one cavalryman was approaching; then he got ready.

The *uhlan* came on at a very quick pace, carrying some dispatches. He rode forward with watchful eyes and strained ears. As soon as he was no more than ten paces away, Père Milon dragged himself across the road, groaning: "*Hilfe! Hilfe!*" ("Help! help!").

The cavalryman drew up, recognized a German soldier dismounted, believed that he was wounded, leaped down from his horse, drew near the prostrate man, never suspecting anything, and, as he stooped over the stranger, he received in the middle of the stomach the long, curved blade of the sabre. He sank down without any death throes, merely quivering with a few last shudders.

Then the Norman, radiant with the mute joy of an old peasant, rose up, and merely to please himself, cut the dead soldier's throat. After that, he dragged the corpse to the dike and threw it in.

The horse was quietly waiting for its rider. Père Milon got on the saddle and started across the plain at the gallop.

At the end of an hour, he perceived two more *uhlans* approaching the staff-quarters side by side. He rode straight toward them, crying: "*Hilfe! hilfe!*" The Prussians let him come on, recognizing the uniform without any distrust.

And like a cannon ball the old man shot between the two, bringing both of them to the ground with his sabre and a revolver. The next thing he did was to cut the throats of the horses— the German horses! Then, softly he re-entered the bake-house and hid the horse he had ridden himself in the dark passage. There he took off the uniform, put on once more his own old clothes, and going to his bed, slept till morning.

For four days, he did not stir out, awaiting the close of the open inquiry as to the cause of the soldiers' deaths; but, on the fifth day, he started out again, and by a similar stratagem killed two more soldiers.

Thenceforth, he never stopped. Each night he wandered about, prowled through the country at random, cutting down some Prussians, sometimes here, sometimes there, galloping through the deserted fields under the moonlight, a lost *uhlan*, a hunter of men. Then, when he had finished his task, leaving behind him corpses lying along the roads, the old horseman went to the bake-house where he concealed both the animal and the uniform. About midday he calmly returned to the spot to give the horse a feed of oats and some water, and he took every care of the animal, exacting therefore the hardest work.

But, the night before his arrest, one of the soldiers he attacked put himself on his guard, and cut the old peasant's face with a slash of a sabre.

He had, however, killed both of them. He had even managed to go back and hide his horse and put on his everyday garb, but, when he reached the stable, he was overcome by weakness and was not able to make his way into the house.

He had been found lying on the straw, his face covered with blood.

When he had finished his story, he suddenly lifted his head and glanced proudly at the Prussian officers.

The Colonel, tugging at his moustache, asked:

"Have you anything more to say?"

"No, nothing more; we are quits. I killed sixteen, not one more, not one less."

"You know you have to die?"

"I ask for no quarter!"

"Have you been a soldier?"

"Yes, I served at one time. And 'tis you killed my father, who was a soldier of the first Emperor, not to speak of my youngest son François, whom you killed last month near Evreux. I owed this to you, and I've paid you back. 'Tis tit for tat!"

The officers stared at one another.

The old man went on:

"Eight for my father, eight for my son—that pays it off I sought for no quarrel with you. I don't know you! I only know where you came from. You came to my house here and ordered me about as if the house was yours. I have had my revenge, and I'm glad of it!"

And stiffening up his old frame, he folded his arms in the attitude of a humble hero.

The Prussians held a long conference. A captain, who had also lost a son the month before defended the brave old farmer.

Then the Colonel rose up, and, advancing toward Père Milon, he said, lowering his voice:

"Listen, old man! There is perhaps one way of saving your life—it is—"

But the old peasant was not listening to him, and, fixing his eyes directly on the German officer, while the wind made the scanty hair move to and fro on his skull, he made a frightful grimace, which shrivelled up his pinched countenance scarred by the sabre-stroke, and, puffing out his chest, he spat, with all his strength, right into the Prussian's face.

The Colonel, stupefied, raised his hand, and for the second time the peasant spat in his face.

All the officers sprang to their feet and yelled out orders at the same time.

In less than a minute the old man, still as impassive as ever, was stuck up against the wall and shot, while he cast a smile at Jean, his eldest son, and then at his daughter-in-law and the two children, who were staring with terror at the scene.

The Traveller's Story
A.k.a. Fear

We went up on the bridge again after dinner. The Mediterranean before us had not a ripple on its whole surface, in which a great, calm moon was reflected. The huge steamer sped along, throwing to the heavens sown with stars a great serpent of black smoke. And behind us the whitened water, agitated by the rapid passing of the heavy ship, seemed to be in torture, beaten into froth by the screw, and changed from its smooth splendour where it lay quiet under the rays of the brilliant moon.

We were there, several of us, silent, admiring, our eyes turned toward Africa, whither we were bound. The commander, smoking a cigar as he stood among us, suddenly took up the conversation of the dinner-table:

"Yes, I did have some fears that day. My ship had been six hours with that rocking in the hold, beaten by the sea. Happily, we were picked up toward evening, by an English collier that had spied us."

Then a great man of burly figure and grave aspect, one of those men who seem to have come from some unknown and distant country, from the midst of incessant dangers, whose tranquil eye, in its profundity, appears to hold in some way the foreign landscapes he has seen,—one of those men who give the impression of possessing great courage, spoke for the first time:

"You say, commander, that you were afraid. I cannot believe that. You deceive yourself in the word, and in the sensation you experienced. An energetic man is never afraid in the face of pressing danger. He is moved, excited, anxious, but fear is another thing."

The commander, laughing, replied: "Nonsense! I tell you frankly that I was afraid."

Then the man with the bronze tint said in a slow manner:

"Allow me to explain myself! Fear (and the hardiest men can experience fear) is something frightful, an atrocious sensation, like the decomposition of the soul, a frightful spasm of thought and of the heart, of which the mere remembrance sends a shiver of agony through the frame. But this is not felt when one is brave, nor before an attack, nor before inevitable death, nor before any of all the known forms of peril; it is felt in abnormal circumstances, under certain mysterious influences, in the face of vague dangers. True fear is something like a reminiscence of fantastic terrors of other times. A man who believes in spirits, and who imagines that he sees a spectre in the night, should understand fear in all its horror.

"As for me, I have understood what fear is, in broad day. It was about ten years ago. I also felt it again last winter, one night in December.

"Yet I have taken many chances, had many adventures that seemed mortal. I have often fought, I have been left for dead by robbers. I have been condemned as an insurgent, in America; doomed to be hanged, and thrown into the sea from the bridge of a ship in China. Each time I believed myself lost, but undertook to make the best of it immediately, without grief or even regret.

"But fear—that is something else.

"I had a presentiment in Africa—although presentiment is a daughter of the north—the sun dissipates it like a fog. Notice that well, gentlemen. Among the Orientals, life counts for nothing. They are always resigned to meet death. Nights are clear and free from the disquieting shadows which haunt the brains of the people of cold countries. In the Orient they understand panic, but they are ignorant of fear.

"Well here is what happened to me on African soil:

"I had crossed the great dunes in the south of Ouargla. That is one of the strangest countries in the world. You are familiar with level sand, the true sand of the interminable shore of the sea. Well, figure to yourselves the ocean itself sand, and in the midst of a hurricane; imagine a silent tempest of motionless waves in yellow dust. They are as high as mountains, these unequal waves, differing from each other, and raised suddenly, like unchained billows, but greater still, and streaked like water waves. Upon this furious sea, mute, immovable, the sun of the south turns its implacable and direct flame, devouring it. It is necessary to climb these waves of golden ashes, to redescend, to climb again, to climb incessantly, without repose and without shade. Horses puff, sinking to their knees, and slipping in, they go down the other side of these surprising little hills.

"We were two friends, followed by eight *spahis* and four camels with their drivers. We could no longer speak, as we were suffocated with heat and fatigue and parched with thirst, like this burning desert. Suddenly one of our men uttered a kind of cry. All stopped, and we remained motionless, surprised by an inexplicable phenomenon, known only to travellers in these lost countries.

"Somewhere, near us, in an indeterminate direction, a drum was beating, the mysterious drum of the dunes. It was heard distinctly, at first vibrating loudly, then more feebly, stopping, then taking up its fantastic rolling again.

"The Arabs, much frightened, looked at one another, and one said in his own language: 'Death is upon us.'

"Just then, suddenly, my companion, my friend, almost my brother, fell on his head from his horse, overcome with sunstroke. And for the next two hours, during which I tried in vain to save him, that unseizable drum filled my ears with its monotonous noise, intermittent and incomprehensible.

"I felt slipping into my bones a fear, true fear, hideous fear, in the face of my dead friend, well-beloved, in this hole, burning up in the sun, between four mountains of sand, where an unknown echo brought to us the rapid beating of a drum, two hundred miles from any French village.

"That day, I understood what it was to have fear; and I understood it still better on one other occasion."

The commander interrupted the speaker: "Pardon, sir, but this drum? What was it?"

The traveller answered: "That I do not know. No one knew. The officers, often surprised by this singular noise, attributed it generally to a great echo, multiplied, swelled immeasurably by the little valleys of the dunes, caused by particles of sand being carried in the wind and hurled against a bunch of dried herbs; because they always noticed that the phenomenon was produced in the neighbourhood of plants dried in the sun, and hard as parchment. This drum, then, was a kind of mirage of sound. That is all. But I learned that later.

"Now I come to my second emotion.

"This came to me last winter, in a forest in the northeast of France. The night fell two hours earlier than usual, the sky was so cloudy. I had for a guide a peasant, who walked at my side through a little road, under an arch of pines, through which the unchained wind howled dismally. Between the hilltops I could see clouds scurrying away in line, lost clouds, which seemed to be fleeing before some fright. Sometimes, under a powerful whirlwind, the whole forest bowed in the same breath with a groan of suffering. And the cold took me by force, in spite of my rapid walk and heavy clothing.

"We were going to take supper and sleep at the house of a forest guide whose house was not far from the place where we were. I was going there to hunt.

"My guide would sometimes raise his eyes and mutter: 'Bad weather!' Then he spoke of the people to whose house we were going. The father had killed a poacher, two years before, and since then he had seemed sombre, as if haunted by a memory. His two sons were married and lived with him.

"The shadows were profound. I could see nothing before me, nor about me; and the branches of the trees, clashing against each other, filled the night with confusion. Finally I perceived a light, and soon my companion knocked on a door. The sharp cries of women responded. Then the voice of a man, a strangled voice, asked: 'Who is there?' My guide gave our names. We entered. It was a picture never to be forgotten.

"An old man with white hair and a mad expression of the eye, awaited us in the middle of the kitchen with a loaded gun in his hand, while two great fellows, armed with hatchets, guarded the door. I distinguished in the dark corner two women on their knees, their faces turned against the wall.

"They explained it. The old man put up his gun and ordered them to prepare my room; then, as the women did not budge, he said brusquely:

"'You see, sir, I killed a man here, two years ago tonight. Last year he came back to me. I am expecting him this evening.'

"Then he added, in a tone that made me laugh;

"'So, we are not quite easy.'

"I reassured him as best I could, happy to have come just at this time and to assist at the spectacle of this superstitious terror. I told stories, and succeeded in calming them all somewhat.

"Near the entrance was an old dog, whiskered and nearly blind, one of those dogs that resemble people we know, asleep, with his nose in his paws.

"Outside, the raging tempest was beating against the little house, and through a small hole, a kind of Judas-place, near the door, I suddenly saw, by a sharp flash of lightning, a clump of great trees overturned by the wind.

"In spite of my efforts, I felt sure that a profound terror held these people, and each time that I ceased to speak, all ears seemed to be listening to something in the distance. Weary of trying to dispel these imbecile fears, I asked permission to go to bed, when the old guard suddenly made a bound from his chair, seized his gun again, and stuttered, in a far-away voice:

"'Here he is! Here he is! I'm waiting for him!'

"The two women fell upon their knees in their corners, concealing their faces, and the sons took up their hatchets. 1 was trying to appease them again when the sleeping dog awoke suddenly, and, raising his head, stretching his neck, and looking toward the fire with eyes almost closed, began to utter the most lugubrious howls, of the sort that give a start to travellers in the country at night. All eyes were turned toward him; he remained motionless, resting upon his paws, as if haunted by a vision.

"He was howling at something invisible, unknown, frightful, no doubt, because his hair was bristling. The guide, now livid, cried out:

"He feels him! He feels him! He was there when I killed him!'

"And the two excited women began to howl with the dog.

"In spite of myself, a great shiver ran down between my shoulders. The sight of the terrified animal in that place, at that hour, in the midst of those benighted people, was frightful.

"For an hour, the dog howled without ceasing; his wails sounded as if he were in agony from a dream. And fear, ungovernable fear, entered my being. Fear of what? Did I know what? It was fear, and that was all.

"We remained motionless, livid, in expectation of some frightful event, with listening ear and beating heart, starting at the least noise. And the dog began to go about the room, touching the walls, and growling. That beast nearly made us mad!

"The peasant who had brought me threw himself upon the animal, in a kind of paroxysm of furious terror, and opening the door, with a little push threw it outside.

"He was then silent, and all of us remained plunged in a silence more terrifying still. Suddenly we all started with surprise. A form glittered on the wall, the outside wall toward the forest; then it passed against the door, which it seemed to touch with hesitating hand; then we heard nothing for two minutes, which almost drove us out of our senses; then it returned, always rubbing against the wall; and it scratched lightly, as a child does with his nail; then suddenly a head appeared against the glass, a white head, with luminous eyes like those of a deer. And there came from his mouth an indistinct sound, a plaintive murmur.

"Then a fearful noise resounded through the kitchen. The

old guide had shot. And immediately the sons hurried to block up the door, putting against it the great table and bringing the side-table to its assistance.

"And I swear to you that from the fracas of that gunshot, which I had not expected, I had such an agony of heart and soul and body that I felt myself swooning, ready to die of fear.

"We remained there until light, incapable of moving, not saying a word, stiff with indescribable fright.

"They did not dare take down the barricade until, through a crevice in the door, they saw a ray of daylight.

"At the foot of the wall, opposite the door, the old dog lay, his mouth pierced with a ball.

"He had gone out of the yard, crossing through a hole under the fence."

The man with the bronzed visage was silent; but he added soon:

"That night I ran into no danger; but I would rather encounter all the hours that have brought me the greatest peril than that one minute of the shooting at the shaggy head of the old dog."

A Jolly Fellow

A.k.a. Saint Anthony

They called him Saint Anthony, because his name was Anthony, and also, perhaps because he was a joyous good liver, fond
of joking, powerful at eating and drinking, and had a vigorous
hand with servants, although he was more than sixty years old.
He was a tall peasant of the country of Caux, of high colour,
great in chest and girth, and was perched upon long legs that
seemed too thin for the weight of his body. A widower, he lived
alone with his maid and his two menservants on his farm, which
he directed in sly, jovial fashion, careful of his interests, attending
to business affairs, the breeding of the cattle, and the cultivation
of the land. His two sons and three daughters, married to advantage, lived in the neighbourhood, and came, once a month, to
dine with their father. His vigour was known in all the country
about; people said, as if it were a proverb: "He is as strong as Saint
Anthony."

When the Prussian invasion occurred. Saint Anthony, at the
inn, promised to eat an army, for, like a true Norman, he was a
romancer, and a little of a coward and a blusterer. He brought
his heavy fist down on the wooden table, making it jump, while
the cups and glasses danced, and he cried out, with red face and
cunning eye, in the false anger of the jovial fellow: "In Heaven's
name! Will it be necessary to eat some of them?" He counted
on the Prussians not coming any farther than Tanneville; but
when he learned that they were at Rautot, he would not go out
of his house, and he watched without ceasing through the little

window of his kitchen, expecting every moment to see the glint of bayonets.

One morning, as he was eating soup with his servants, the door opened and the mayor of the commune. Master Chicot, appeared, followed by a soldier, wearing on his head a black cap set off with a point of copper. Saint Anthony arose with a bound; everybody looked at him, expecting to see him cut the Prussian in pieces; but he contented himself with shaking hands with the mayor, who said to him:

"Here's one of 'em for you to take care of. Saint Anthony. They came in the night. I haven't been surly with them, seeing they talk of shooting and burning if the least thing happens. You are warned. Give him something to eat. He seems a good lad. I am going to the other houses to seek quarters for the rest of them. There is enough for everybody."

And he went out.

Father Anthony looked at his Prussian and grew pale. He was a great boy, fat and white, with blue eyes and blond hair, bearded up to the cheek-bones, and he seemed stupid and timid, like a good child. The Norman rogue comprehended him immediately as he thought, and, reassured, made him a sign to sit down. Then he asked: "Will you have some soup?"

The stranger did not understand. Anthony then made an audacious move, and, pushing a full plate under the nose of his unexpected guest, he said: "There, eat that, you big pig!"

The soldier responded: "*Ja,*" and began to eat ravenously, while the farmer, triumphant, feeling his power recognized, winked his eye at his servants, who made strange faces and had a great desire to laugh but were restrained by fear.

When the Prussian had cleared his plate. Saint Anthony served him another, the contents of which disappeared like the first, but he recoiled before the third helping, which the farmer tried by force to make him eat, repeating: "Come, now, put that inside of you. You shall grow fat, or I'll know the reason why, my pig!"

And the soldier, comprehending nothing except that he was urged to eat all he wanted, laughed with a contented air, making a sign that he was full.

Then Saint Anthony, suddenly becoming familiar, tapped him on the front, saying: "He has enough in his paunch, has my pig!" But upon this he doubled himself with laughter, growing red enough for an attack of apoplexy, and was unable to speak for a moment. An idea had seized him which suffocated him with laughter: "That's it! That's it!" he cried, "Saint Anthony and his pig! I am Saint Anthony and this is my pig!" And the three servants laughed loudly in their turn.

The old man was so pleased with his jest that he ordered the maid to bring some brandy, of the ten-year-old brand, with which he regaled everybody. They drank with the Prussian, who smacked his lips as a bit of delicate flattery, in order to indicate that he found it delicious. And Saint Anthony cried out in his face: "Yes! This is something fine! You don't find anything like it at home, my

After this, father Anthony never went out without his Prussian. He had found his opportunity. It was vengeance to him, the vengeance of a great rogue. And all the people of the countryside, who were trembling with fear, laughed until in torture, behind the backs of their conquerors, at the face of Saint Anthony and his pig. Indeed, as a joke, they thought it had not its equal. He had only to say a few things like this: "Go along, pig! Go!" in order to provoke convulsions of merriment.

He would go among his neighbours every afternoon with his German, their arms around each other, and would present him with a gay air, tapping him on the shoulder and saying: "See! Here is my pig! Look at him and tell me if you think he is getting fat, this here animal!"

And the peasants fairly bubbled with laughter—he was such a wag, this rogue of an Anthony!

"I'll sell him to you, Casar," he would say, "for three *pistoles*."

"I take him, Anthony, and invite you to come and have some of the pudding."

"Me," said Anthony, "what I want is some of the feet."

"Punch his body and see how fat he is!" said Casar.

And everybody would wink slyly, not laughing too much, however, for fear the Prussian might surmise finally that they were mocking him. Anthony alone, growing bolder every day, would pinch the calves of his legs, crying out: "Nothing but fat!" or strike him on the back and shout: "There's some good bacon!" Then the old man, capable of lifting an anvil, would seize him in his arms and raise him up in the air, declaring: "He weighs six hundred and not a bit of waste!"

He got into the habit of offering his pig something to eat wherever they went. It was the great pleasure, the great diversion of every day. "Give him whatever you like," he would say, "he will swallow it." And when they would inquire if the man wished some bread and butter, potatoes, cold mutton, or venison, Anthony would say to him: "Here you are now, it's your choice!"

The soldier, stupid and gentle, ate for politeness, enchanted with so much attention; he would make himself sick rather than refuse; and he was growing fat truly, too stout for his uniform, which fairly delighted Saint Anthony, who kept telling him: "You know, my pig, it's pretty soon going to be necessary for you to have a new cage."

They became apparently the best friends in the world. And when the old man went on business into the surrounding country, the Prussian accompanied him of his own accord, for the sole pleasure of being with him.

The weather was very rigorous; it had frozen hard; the terrible winter of 1870 seemed to throw all plagues together upon France Father Anthony, who looked out for things ahead and took advantage of opportunities, foreseeing that he would need manure for his spring work, bought some of a neighbour who found himself in straits; he arranged to go each evening with his cart and bring it home, a load at a time. And so, toward evening of each day, he was to be seen on the way to Haules's farm, half a mile distant, always accompanied by his pig. And everybody ran along with them, as they go on Sunday to a grand mass, for each day was a feast-day for feeding the animal.

But the time came when the soldier began to be suspicious. And, when they laughed too much he rolled his eyes as if disturbed, and sometimes they sent forth a spark of anger.

One evening, when he had eaten to the extent of his capacity, he refused to swallow another morsel, and undertook to start up and go away. But Saint Anthony stopped him with a blow on the wrist and, placing his two hands on the Prussian's shoulders, he sat him down again so hard that the chair cracked under him.

A perfect tempest of gaiety followed; and Anthony, radiant, picked up his pig, rubbing the wounded spot, with the semblance of healing it. Then he declared: "Since you won't eat, you shall drink, by jiminy!" And somebody went to the alehouse for brandy.

The soldier rolled his eyes in wicked fashion; but he drank, nevertheless, as much as they wished; and Saint Anthony held his head, to the great amusement of his assistants.

The Norman, red as a tomato, with fiery eye, filled the glasses, drinking and guying him with "To your sweetheart!" And the Prussian, without a word, encompassed glass after glass of these bumpers of cognac.

It was a struggle, a battle, a defence! In Heaven s name! who could drink the most? They could take no more, either of them, when the bottle was drained, but neither was conquered. They were neck and neck, and that was all. It would be necessary to start over the next day.

They went out stumbling, and started homeward beside the cart filled with manure, which two horses dragged slowly along. The snow began to fall, and the night, without a moon, seemed to shed a sad light over this death of the plains. The cold took hold of the two men, increasing their drunkenness, and Saint Anthony, discontented at not having triumphed, amused himself with pushing his pig by the shoulder, trying to make him fall over into the ditch. The man evaded the attacks by retreat; and each time he would mutter some German words in an irritated tone, which made the farmer laugh heartily. Finally, the Prussian became angry; and just at the moment when Anthony gave him another push, he responded with a terrible blow of the fist which made the old colossus totter.

Then, inflamed with brandy, the old fellow seized the man by the arms and shook him for some seconds, as if he had been a child, and then threw him with all his might to the other side of the road. Content with his execution, he folded his arms and laughed in good earnest.

But the soldier got up quickly, bareheaded, his cap having rolled off, and, drawing his sword, made a plunge for father Anthony. When the farmer saw this he seized his great fork of yellow holly, strong and supple as a beef tendon.

The Prussian came on with his head lowered, weapon in front of him, sure of killing his foe. But the old man, grasping with firm hand the blade whose point was aimed to pierce his body, turned it aside, and struck his enemy such a sharp blow upon the temple, with the point of the fork, that he fell at his feet. Then the peasant looked at his fallen foe frightened, stupefied with astonishment, seeing the body shaken with spasms at first, and then lying motionless upon its face. He stooped, turned him over and looked at him a long time. The man's eyes were closed, and a little stream of blood was running from a hole in the forehead. In spite of the darkness, father Anthony could distinguish the brown spot of blood on the snow.

He remained there, bewildered, while his cart went on at the horses' regular step. What was to be done? He would shoot him! Then the Prussians would burn his place and work ruin throughout the country! But what should he do? What should he do? How conceal the body, conceal the death, deceive the Prussians? He could hear voices in the distance, in the silence of the snowstorm. Then he became excited, and, seizing the cap, he put it on the man's head again; and, taking him by the back, he raised him up, ran, overtook his team, and threw the body on the manure. Once at home, he could think what to do.

He went along with short steps, racking his brain but unable to decide anything. He understood the matter and felt sure that he was lost. Finally he came to his house. A bright light shone through a dormer window; his servant was not yet asleep. Then he made his wagon back quickly to the edge of a hole in the field. He thought by overturning the load the body would fall underneath, in the ditch; and he tipped the cart over. As he had thought, the man was buried under the manure. Anthony evened off the heap with his fork, and stuck it in the ground at the side. He called his manservant, ordered him to put the horses in the stable, and went to his chamber.

He went to bed, reflecting continually upon what he had done, but no helpful idea came to him, and his fear increased when he was quiet in bed. The Prussians would shoot him! The sweat of fear started out upon him; his teeth chattered; he got up, shivering so that he could scarcely hold his clothes to get into them. He went down into the kitchen, took a bottle of liquor from the sideboard, and went back to his chamber. He drank two large glasses of liquor in succession, adding a new drunkenness to the old one, without calming the agony of his soul. He felt that he had made a pretty mess of it this time!

He walked the floor to and fro, seeking a ruse or explanation for his wickedness. And from time to time he would rinse his mouth with a draught of the ten-year-old cognac to put some heart into his body. But he could think of nothing, nothing. Toward midnight, his watchdog, a kind of half wolf, which he called "Devour," began the howl of death. Father Anthony trembled to the marrow. And each time that the beast began his long, mournful wail again, a shiver of fear would run along the spine of the old man.

He had fallen upon a chair, with weak knees; he was besotted, unable to do more, expecting that Devour would continue his wailing, and his nerves were played upon by every form of fear that could set them vibrating. The clock downstairs struck five. The dog was still howling, and the farmer was becoming mad. He got up and started to unchain the animal, so that he might no longer listen to it. He went downstairs, opened the door, and went out into the night.

The snow was falling still. All was white. The farm buildings were great, black spots. As he approached the kennel, the dog pulled on his chain. He loosed him. Then, Devour made a bound, stopped short, with hair bristling, paws trembling, smelling the air, his nose turned toward the manure heap.

Saint Anthony trembled from head to foot, muttering: "What's the matter with you, dirty beast?" And he advanced some steps, casting a penetrating eye through the uncertain shadows, the undefined shadows of the courtyard. Then he saw the form of a man seated on his manure-heap!

He looked at the figure, and gasped with horror, motionless. But suddenly he perceived near him the handle of his fork stuck in the earth. He pulled it from the soil, and, in one of those transports of fear which make cowardly men more bold, he rushed on with it, to see who the man was.

It was he, the Prussian, soiled from his bed of manure, the warmth of which had revived him and partly brought him back to his senses. He had seated himself mechanically, and was resting there upon the snow which had powdered him well, over the filth and blood, still besotted by drunkenness, stunned by the blow, and exhausted from his wounds.

He perceived Anthony and, too much stupefied to understand anything, he made a movement as if to rise. The old man, as soon as he recognized him, fumed like a wild beast. He sputtered: "Ah! pig I pig! you are not dead! you have come to denounce me right away—Wait—wait!" And throwing himself upon the German, he raised his four-pointed fork like a lance and brought it down, with all the force of his two arms, in the man's breast, even to the handle. The soldier turned over on his back with a long death-sigh, while the old farmer drew the weapon from the wound and replunged it in the body, blow upon blow, striking like a madman, stamping with his feet upon the head and the rest of the body, which was still palpitating, and from which the blood spouted in great jets.

Then he stopped, overcome with the violence of his effort, breathing the air in great draughts, appeased by the accomplishment of his deed.

As the cocks began to crow in the poultry-yard, and the day was dawning, he set himself to work to bury the man. He dug into the manure-heap, until he came to earth, then dug still deeper, working in a disorderly fashion, with furious force in his arms and his whole body. When the trench was long enough, he rolled the dead body into it with the fork, replaced the earth, kicking it about until It was level, put the manure over it again, and smiled to see the snow thicken and complete his work, wholly covering all traces with its white veil.

Then he stuck his fork into the manure again and returned to the house. His bottle was still half full upon the table. He emptied it with a gulp, threw himself upon the bed, and slept profoundly.

He awoke sobered, his mind calm and active, capable of judging the case and foreseeing results. At the end of an hour, he was scouring the country asking everybody the whereabouts of the soldier. He went to the officers, to find out, he said, why they had taken his man away.

As the Prussians knew nothing of the peculiar situation between the two men, they were not suspicious; and Anthony even directed the search, affirming that the Prussian had gone running after some petticoat nearly every evening.

An old refugee policeman, who kept an inn in a neighbouring village, and who had a pretty daughter, was arrested on suspicion of being the murderer, and was shot.

Letter Found on a Corpse

A.k.a. Found on a Drowned Man / The Drowned Man

You ask me, *Madame*, whether I am laughing at you? You cannot believe that a man has never been smitten with love. Well, no, I have never loved, never! What is the cause of this? I really cannot tell. Never have I been under the influence of that sort of intoxication of the heart which we call love! Never have I lived in that dream, in that exaltation, in that state of madness into which the image of a woman casts us. I have never been pursued, haunted, roused to fever heat, lifted up to Paradise by the thought of meeting, or by the possession of, a being who had suddenly become for me more desirable than any good fortune, more beautiful than any other creature, more important than the whole world! I have never wept, I have never suffered on account of any of you. I have not passed my nights thinking of one woman without closing my eyes. I have no experience of waking up with the thought and the memory of her shedding their illumination on me. I have never known the wild desperation of hope when she was about to come, or the divine sadness of regret when she parted with me, leaving behind her in the room a delicate odour of violet-powder.

I have never been in love.

I too, have often asked myself why is this. And truly I can scarcely tell. Nevertheless, I have found some reasons for it; but they are of a metaphysical character, and perhaps you will not be able to appreciate them.

I suppose I sit too much in judgement on women to submit much to their fascination. I ask you to forgive me for this remark. I am going to explain what I mean. In every creature there is a moral being and a physical being. In order to love, it would be necessary for me to find a harmony between these two beings which I have never found. One has always too great a predominance over the other, sometimes the moral, sometimes the physical.

The intellect which we have a right to require in a woman, in order to love her, is not the same as virile intellect. It is more and it is less. A woman must have a mind open, delicate, sensitive, refined, impressionable. She has no need of either power or initiative in thought, but she must have kindness, elegance, tenderness, coquetry, and that faculty of assimilation which, in a little while, raises her to an equality with him who shares her life. Her greatest quality must be tact, that subtle sense which is to the mind what touch is to the body. It reveals to her a thousand little things, contours, angles, and forms in the intellectual life.

Very frequently pretty women have not intellect to correspond with their personal charms. Now the slightest lack of harmony strikes me and pains me at the first glance. In friendship, this is not of importance. Friendship is a compact in which one fairly divides defects and merits. We may judge of friends, whether man or woman, take into account the good they possess, neglect the evil that is in them, and appreciate their value exactly, while giving ourselves up to an intimate sympathy of a deep and fascinating character.

In order to love, one must be blind, surrender oneself absolutely, see nothing, reason from nothing, understand nothing. One must adore the weakness as well as the beauty of the beloved object, renounce all judgment, all reflection, all perspicacity.

I am incapable of such blindness, and rebel against a seductiveness not founded on reason. This is not all. I have such a high and subtle idea of harmony that nothing can ever realize my ideal. But you will call me a madman. Listen to me. A woman, in my opinion, may have an exquisite soul and a charming body without that body and that soul being in perfect accord with one another. I mean that persons who have noses made in a certain shape are not to be expected to think in a certain fashion. The fat have no right to make use of the same words and phrases as the thin. You, who have blue eyes, *Madame*, cannot look at life, and judge of things and events as if you had black eyes. The shades of your eyes should correspond, by a sort of fatality, with the shades of your thought. In perceiving these things I have the scent of a bloodhound. Laugh if you like, but it is so.

And yet I imagined that I was in love for an hour, for a day. I had foolishly yielded to the influence of surrounding circumstances. I allowed myself to be beguiled by the mirage of an aurora. Would you like to hear this short history?

I met, one evening, a pretty, enthusiastic woman who wanted, for the purpose of humouring a poetic fancy, to spend a night with me in a boat on a river. I would have preferred—but, no matter, I consented.

It was in the month of June. My fair companion chose a moonlight night in order to excite her imagination all the better.

We had dined at a riverside inn, and then we set out in the boat about ten o'clock. I thought it a rather foolish kind of adventure; but as my companion pleased me I did not bother myself too much about this. I sat down on the seat facing her, seized the oars, and off we started.

I could not deny that the scene was picturesque. We glided past a wooded isle full of nightingales, and the current carried us rapidly over the river covered with silvery ripples. The grasshoppers uttered their shrill, monotonous cry; the frogs croaked in the grass by the river's bank, and the lapping of the water as it flowed on made around us a kind of confused, almost imperceptible murmur, disquieting, which gave us a vague sensation of mysterious fear.

The sweet charm of warm nights and of streams glittering in the moonlight penetrated us. It seemed bliss to live and to float thus, to dream and to feel by one's side a young woman sympathetic and beautiful.

I was somewhat affected, somewhat agitated, somewhat intoxicated by the pale brightness of the night and the consciousness of my proximity to a lovely woman.

"Come and sit beside me," she said.

I obeyed. She went on:

"Recite some verses for me."

This appeared to me rather too much. I declined; she persisted. She certainly wanted to have the utmost pleasure, the whole orchestra of sentiment, from the moon to the rhymes of poets. In the end, I had to yield, and, as if in mockery, I recited for her a charming little poem by Louis Bouilhet, of which the following are a few strophes:

I hate the poet who with tearful eye
Murmurs some name while gazing tow'rds a star,
Who sees no magic in the earth or sky,
Unless Lizette or Ninon be not far.

The bard who in all Nature nothing sees
Divine, unless a petticoat he ties
Amorously to the branches of the trees,
Or nightcap to the grass, is scarcely wise.

He has not heard the eternal's thunder tone,
The voice of Nature in her various moods,
He cannot tread the dim ravines alone,
And of no woman dream 'mid whispering woods.

I expected some reproaches. Nothing of the sort. She murmured:

"How true it is!"

I remained stupefied. Had she understood?

Our boat was gradually drawing nearer to the bank, and got entangled under a willow which impeded its progress. I drew my arm around my companion's waist, and very gently moved my lips toward her neck. But she repulsed me with an abrupt, angry movement:

"Have done, pray! You are rude!"

I tried to draw her toward me. She resisted, caught hold of

the tree, and nearly upset us both into the water. I deemed it the prudent course to cease my importunities.

She said:

"I would rather have you capsized. I feel so happy. I want to dream—that is so nice." Then, in a slightly malicious tone, she added:

"Have you, then, already forgotten the verses you recited for me just now?"

She was right. I became silent.

She went on:

"Come! rowl!

And I plied the oars once more. I began to find the night long and to see the absurdity of my conduct. My companion said to me:

"Will you make me a promise?"

"Yes. What is it?"

"To remain quiet, well-behaved, and discreet, if I permit you—"

"What? Say what you mean!"

"Here is what I mean! I want to lie down on my back in the bottom of the boat with you by my side. But I forbid you to touch me, to embrace me—in short to—to caress me."

I promised. She warned me:

"If you move, I'll capsize the boat."

And then we lay down side by side, our eyes turned toward the sky, while the boat glided slowly through the water. We were rocked by the gentle movements of the shallop. The light sounds of the night came to us more distinctly in the bottom of the boat, sometimes causing us to start. And I felt springing up within me a strange, poignant emotion, an infinite tenderness, something like an irresistible impulse to open my arms in order to embrace, to open my heart in order to love, to give myself, to give my thoughts, my body, my life, my entire being to someone.

My companion murmured, like one in a dream:

"Where are we? Where are we going? It seems to me that I am quitting the earth. How sweet it is! Ah! if you loved me—a little!"

My heart began to throb. I had no answer to give. It seemed to me that I loved her. I had no longer any violent desire. I felt happy there by her side, and that was enough for me.

And thus we remained for a long, long time without stirring. We caught each other's hands; some delightful force rendered us motionless, an unknown force stronger than ourselves, an alliance, chaste, intimate, absolute, of our persons lying there side by side which belonged to without touching each other. What was this? How do I know? Love, perhaps.

Little by little, the dawn appeared. It was three o'clock in the morning. Slowly, a great brightness spread over the sky. The boat knocked against something. I rose up. We had come close to a tiny islet.

But I remained ravished, in a state of ecstasy. In front of us stretched the shining firmament, red, rosy, violet, spotted with fiery clouds resembling golden vapours. The river was glowing with purple, and three houses on one side of it seemed to be burning.

I bent toward my companion. I was going to say: "Oh! look!" But I held my tongue, quite dazed, and I could no longer see anything except her. She, too, was rosy, with the rosy flesh tints with which must have mingled a little the hue of the sky. Her tresses were rosy; her eyes were rosy; her teeth were rosy; her dress, her laces, her smile, all were rosy. And in truth I believed, so overpowering was the illusion, that the aurora was there before me.

She rose softly to her feet, holding out her lips to me; and I moved toward her, trembling, delirious, feeling indeed that I was going to kiss Heaven, to kiss happiness, to kiss a dream which had become a woman, to kiss an ideal which had descended into human flesh.

She said to me: "You have a caterpillar in your hair." And suddenly I felt myself becoming as sad as if I had lost all hope in life.

That is all, *Madame*. It is puerile, silly, stupid. But I am sure that since that day it would be impossible for me to love. And yet—who can tell?

(The young man upon whom this letter was found was yesterday taken out of the Seine between Bougival and Marly. An obliging bargeman, who had searched the pockets in order to ascertain the name of the deceased, brought this paper to the author.)

Legend of Mont St. Michel

I had first seen this fairy-like castle from Cancale It had looked to me like a confused mass, like a gray shadow rising in the foggy sky. I saw it again from Avranches at sunset. The immense stretch of sand was red, the horizon was red, the whole boundless bay was red; alone, the castle growing out there in the distance like a weird, fantastic manor, like a dream palace, strange and beautiful—this alone remained almost black in the brilliancy of the dying day.

The following morning at dawn I went toward it across the sands. My eyes fastened on this, gigantic jewel, as big as a mountain, cut like a cameo, and as dainty as lace. The nearer I approached the greater my admiration grew, for nothing in the world could be more wonderful or more perfect.

As surprised as if I had discovered the habitation of a god, I wandered through those halls supported by frail or massive columns, raising my eyes in wonder to those spires which looked like rockets starting for the sky, and to that incredible crowd of towers, of gargoyles, of slender and charming ornaments, a regular fireworks of stone, granite lace, a masterpiece of colossal and delicate architecture.

As I was looking up in ecstasy a Lower Normandy peasant came up to me and told me the story of the great quarrel between Saint Michael and the devil.

A sceptical genius has said: "God made man in his image and man has returned the compliment."

This saying is an eternal truth, and it would be very curious to write the history of the local divinity on every continent, as well as the history of the patron saints in each one of our provinces. The negro has his ferocious man-eating idols; the polygamous Mahometan fills his paradise with women; the Greeks, like a practical people, have deified all the passions.

Every village in France is under the influence of some protecting saint, modelled according to the characteristics of the inhabitants.

Saint Michael watches over Lower Normandy, Saint Michael, the radiant and victorious angel, the sword-carrier, the hero of Heaven, the victorious, the conqueror of Satan.

But this is how the Lower Normandy peasant, cunning, underhanded, and tricky, understands and tells of the struggle between the great Saint and the Devil.

To escape from the malice of his neighbour, the Demon, Saint Michael built himself, in the open ocean, this habitation worthy of an archangel; and only such a saint could build a residence of such magnificence.

But as he still feared the approaches of the Wicked One, he surrounded his domains by quicksands, more treacherous even than water.

The Devil lived in a humble cottage on the hill, but he owned all the salt marshes, the rich lands where grow the finest crops, the wooded valleys and all the fertile hills of the country, but the Saint a ruled only over the sands. Therefore Satan was rich, whereas Saint Michael was as poor as a church mouse.

After a few years of fasting the Saint grew tired of this state of affairs and began to think of some compromise with the Devil, but the matter was by no means easy, as Satan kept a good hold on his crops.

He thought the thing over for about six months; then one morning he set out for land. The Demon was eating his soup in front of his door when he saw the Saint. He immediately rushed toward him, kissed the hem of his sleeve, invited him in and offered him refreshments.

Saint Michael drank a bowl of milk and then began: "I have

come here to propose to you a good bargain."

The Devil, candid and trustful, answered:

"Very well."

"Here it is. Give me all your lands."

Satan, growing alarmed, wished to speak "But—"

The Saint continued: "Listen first. Give me all your lands. I will take care of all the work, the ploughing, the sowing, the fertilizing, everything, and we will share the crops equally. How does that suit you?"

The Devil, who was naturally lazy, accepted. He only asked in addition for a few of those delicious *surmullets* which can be caught around the solitary mountain. Saint Michael promised the fish.

They shook hands and spat to show that it was a bargain, and the Saint continued: "Here, so that you will have nothing to complain of, choose that part of the crops which you prefer: that which will be above ground or in the ground." Satan cried out: "I choose all that will be above ground."

"It's a bargain!" said the Saint. And he went away.

Six months later, all over the immense domain of the Devil, one could see nothing but carrots, turnips, onions, salsify, all the plants whose juicy roots are good and savoury and whose useless leaves are good for nothing but for feeding animals.

Satan wished to break the contract, calling Saint Michael a swindler.

But the Saint, who had developed quite a taste for agriculture, went back to see the Devil and said:

"Really, I hadn't thought of that at all; it was just an accident, no fault of mine. And to make things fair with you, this year I'll let you take everything that is under the ground."

"Very well," answered Satan.

The following spring all the Evil Spirit's lands were covered with golden wheat, oats as big as beans, flax, magnificent *colza*, red clover, peas, cabbage, artichokes, everything that blossoms into grains or fruit in the sunlight.

Once more Satan received nothing, and this time he completely lost his temper. He took back his fields and remained deaf to all the fresh propositions of his neighbour.

A whole year rolled by. From the top of his lonely manor Saint Michael looked at the distant and fertile lands and watched the Devil direct the work, take in his crops and thresh the wheat. And he grew angry, exasperated at his powerlessness. As he was no longer able to deceive Satan, he decided to wreak vengeance on him, and he went out to invite him to dinner for the following Monday.

"You have been very unfortunate in your dealings with me," he said; "I know it, but I don't want any ill feeling between us, and I expect you to dine with me. I'll give you some good things to eat."

Satan, who was as greedy as he was lazy, accepted eagerly. On the day which had been decided on, he donned his finest clothes and set out for the castle.

Saint Michael sat him down to a magnificent meal. First there was a *vol-au-vent*, full of cocks' crests and kidneys, with meat-balls, then two big *surmullets* with cream sauce, a turkey stuffed with chestnuts soaked in wine, some salt-marsh lamb as tender as possible, vegetables which melted in the mouth and nice warm cake which was brought on smoking and spreading a delicious odour of butter.

They drank hard and sparkling cider and red wine both flat and sparkling, and after each course more room was made with some old apple brandy.

The Devil drank and ate to his heart's content; in fact he took so much that he found himself inconvenienced.

Then Saint Michael arose in anger and cried in a voice like thunder: "What! before me, rascal! You dare—before me—"

Satan, terrified, ran away, and the saint, seizing a stick, pursued him. They ran through the halls, turning around the pillars, running up the staircases, galloping along the cornices, jumping from gargoyle to gargoyle. The poor Demon, who was woefully ill, was running about madly and soiling the Saint's home. At last he found himself at the top of the last terrace, from which could be seen the immense bay, with its distant cities, sands and pastures. He could no longer escape, and the Saint came up behind him and gave him a furious kick, which shot him through space like a cannonball.

He shot through the air like a javelin and fell heavily before the town of Mortain. His horns and claws stuck deep into the rock, which keeps through eternity the traces of this fall of Satan's.

He stood up again, limping, crippled until the end of time, and as he looked at this fatal castle in the distance, standing out against the setting sun, he understood well that he would always be vanquished in this unequal struggle, and he went away limping, heading for distant countries, leaving to his enemy his fields, his hills, his valleys and his marshes.

And this is how Saint Michael, the patron saint of Normandy, vanquished the Devil.

Another people would have dreamed of this battle in an entirely different manner.

Little Louise Roque
A.k.a. The Case of Louise Roque

1

Mederic Rompel, the postman, familiarly called by the country people "Mederi," started at his usual hour from the posthouse at Rouy-le-Tors. Having passed through the little town, striding like an old trooper, he cut across the meadows of Villaumes in order to reach the bank of the Brindelle, which led him along the water's edge to the village of Carvelin, where his distribution commenced. He travelled quickly, following the course of the narrow river, which frothed, murmured, and boiled along its bed of grass under the arching willow-trees.

The big stones, impeding the flow of water, created around them a sort of aqueous necktie ending in a knot of foam. In some places, there were cascades a foot wide, often invisible, which made under the leaves, under the tendrils, under a roof of verdure, a noise at once angry and gentle. Further on, the banks widened out, and you saw a small, placid lake where trout were swimming in the midst of all that green vegetation which keeps undulating in the depths of tranquil streams.

Mederic went on without a halt, seeing nothing, and with only one thought in his mind: "My first letter is for the Poivron family; then I have one for M. Renardet; so I must cross the wood."

His blue blouse, fastened round his waist by a black leathern belt, moved in quick, regular fashion above the green hedge of willow-trees; and his stick of stout holly kept time with the steady march of his feet.

He crossed the Brindelle over a bridge formed of a single tree thrown lengthwise, with a rope attached to two stakes driven into the river banks as its only balustrade.

The wood, which belonged to M. Renardet, the mayor of Carvelin, and the largest landowner in the district, consisted of a number of huge old trees, straight as pillars, and extended for about half a league along the left bank of the stream which served as a boundary for this immense arch of foliage. Alongside the water there were large shrubs warmed by the sun: but under the trees you found nothing but moss, thick, soft, plastic moss, which exhaled into the stagnant air a light odour of loam and withered branches.

Mederic slackened his pace, took off his black cap trimmed with red lace, and wiped his forehead, for it was by this time hot in the meadows, though not yet eight o'clock in the morning.

He had just recovered from the effects of the heat, and had accelerated his pace when he noticed at the foot of a tree a knife, a child's small knife. As he picked it up, he discovered a thimble, and then a needlecase, not far away.

Having found these objects, he thought: "I'll intrust them to the mayor," and resumed his journey. But now he kept his eyes open, expecting to find something else.

All of a sudden, he drew up stiffly as if he had run up against a wooden bar. Ten paces in front of him on the moss, lay stretched on her back a little girl, quite naked. She was about twelve years old. Her arms were hanging down, her legs parted, and her face covered with a handkerchief. There were little spots of blood on her thighs.

Mederic now advanced on tiptoe, as if afraid to make a noise; he apprehended some danger, and glanced toward the spot uneasily.

What was this ? No doubt, she was asleep. Then, he reflected that a person does not go to sleep thus, naked, at half past seven in the morning under cool trees. Then she must be dead; and he must be face to face with a crime. At this thought, a cold shiver ran through his frame, although he was an old soldier. And then a murder was such a rare thing in the country—and above all the murder of a child—that he could not believe his eyes. But she had no wound—nothing save these blood drops on her legs. How, then, had she been killed?

He stopped when quite near her and stared at her, while leaning on his stick. Certainly, he knew her, as he knew all the inhabitants of the district; but, not being able to get a look at her face, he could not guess her name. He stooped forward in order to take off the handkerchief which covered her face; then paused with outstretched hand, restrained by an idea that occurred to him.

Had he the right to disarrange anything in the condition of the corpse before the magisterial investigation? He pictured justice to himself as a general whom nothing escapes, who attaches as much importance to a lost button as to a stab of a knife in the stomach. Perhaps under this handkerchief evidence to support a capital charge could be found; in fact if there were sufficient proof there to secure a conviction, it might lose its value if touched by an awkward hand.

Then he straightened up with the intention of hastening toward the mayor's residence, but again another thought held him back. If the little girl was still alive, by any chance—he could not leave her lying there in this way. He sank on his knees very gently, a yard away from her, through precaution, and stretched his hand toward her feet. The flesh was icy cold, with that terrible coldness which makes dead flesh frightful, and leaves us no longer in doubt. The letter-carrier, as he touched her, felt his heart leap to his mouth, as he said himself afterward, and his lips were parched with dry saliva. Rising up abruptly he rushed off through the trees to M. Renardet's house.

He hurried on in double-quick time, with his stick under his arm, his hands clenched, and his head thrust forward, and his leathern bag, filled with letters and newspapers, flapping regularly at his side.

The mayor's residence was at the end of the wood, which he

used as a park, and one side of it was washed by a little lagoon formed at this spot by the Brindelle.

It was a big, square house of gray stone, very old. It had stood many a siege in former days, and at the end of it was a huge tower, twenty metres high, built in the water. From the top of this fortress the entire country around could be seen in olden times. It was called the Fox's Tower, without anyone knowing exactly why; and from this appellation, no doubt, had come the name Renardet, borne by the owners of this fief, which had remained in the same family, it was said, for more than two hundred years. For the Renardets formed part of that upper middle class which is all but noble and was met with so often in the provinces before the Revolution.

The postman dashed into the kitchen where the servants were taking breakfast, and exclaimed:

"Is the mayor up? I want to speak to him at once."

Mederic was recognized as a man of weight and authority, and it was soon understood that something serious had happened.

As soon as word was brought to M. Renardet, he ordered the postman to be sent up to him. Pale and out of breath, with his cap in his hand, Mederic found the mayor seated in front of a long table covered with scattered papers.

He was a big, tall man, heavy and red-faced, strong as an ox, and greatly liked in the district, though of an excessively violent disposition. Very nearly forty years old, and a widower for the past six months, he lived on his estate like a country gentleman. His choleric temperament had often brought him into trouble, from which the magistrates of Rouy-le-Tors, like indulgent and prudent friends, had extricated him.

Had he not one day thrown the conductor of the diligence from the top of his seat because the latter had nearly crushed his retriever, Micmac? Had he not broken the ribs of a gamekeeper, who had abused him for having passed through a neighbour's property with a gun in his hand? Had he not even caught by the collar the sub-prefect, who stopped in the village in the course

of an administrative round described by M. Renardet as an elec-
tioneering tour; for he was against the government, according
to his family tradition?

The mayor asked:

"What's the matter now, Mederic?"

"I have found a little girl dead in your wood."

Renardet rose up, with his face the colour of brick.

"A little girl, do you say?"

"Yes, *M'sieu'*, a little girl, quite naked, on her back, with blood
on her, dead—quite dead!"

The mayor gave vent to an oath:

"By God, I'd make a bet 'tis little Louise Roque! I have just
learned that she did not go home to her mother last night.
Where did you find her?"

The postman pointed out where the place was, gave full details, and offered to conduct the mayor to the spot.

But Renardet became brusque:

"No, I don't need you. Send the steward, the mayor's secretary, and the doctor immediately to me, and resume your rounds.
Quick, go quick, and tell them to meet me in the wood."

The letter-carrier, a man used to discipline, obeyed and withdrew, angry and grieved at not being able to be present at the
investigation.

The mayor, in his turn, prepared to go out. He took his hat,
a big soft hat, and paused for a few seconds on the threshold of
his abode. In front of him stretched a wide lawn in which three
large patches were conspicuous—three large beds of flowers in
full bloom, one facing the house and the others at either side
of it. Further on, rose skyward the principal trees in the wood,
while at the left, above the spot where the Brindelle widened
into a pool, could be seen long meadows, an entirely flat green
sweep of country, cut by dykes and monster-like willows, twisted
dwarf-trees, always cut short, having on their thick squat trunks
a quivering tuft of branches.

To the right, behind the stables, the outhouses, and the buildings connected with the property, might be seen the village,

which was prosperous, being mainly inhabited by raisers of oxen.

Renardet slowly descended the steps in front of his house, and, turning to the left, gained the water's edge, which he followed at a slow pace, his hands behind his back. He went on, with bent head, and from time to time he glanced round in search of the persons for whom he had sent.

When he stood beneath the trees, he stopped, took off his hat, and wiped his forehead as Mederic had done; for the burning sun was shedding its fiery rain upon the ground. Then the mayor resumed his journey, stopped once more, and retraced his steps. Suddenly stooping down, he steeped his handkerchief in the stream that glided at his feet and stretched it round his head, under his hat. Drops of water flowed along his temples, over his purple ears, over his strong red neck, and trickled, one after the other, under his white shirt-collar.

As yet nobody had appeared; he began tapping with his foot, then he called out: "Hallo! Hallo!"

A voice at his right answered: "Hallo! Hallo!" and the doctor appeared under the trees. He was a thin little man, an ex-military surgeon, who passed in the neighbourhood for a very skilful practitioner. He limped, having been wounded while in the service, and had to use a stick to assist him in walking.

Next came the steward and the mayor's secretary, who, having been sent for at the same time, arrived together. They seemed scared, as they hurried forward, out of breath, walking and trotting in turn in order to hasten, and moving their arms up and down so vigorously that they seemed to do more work with them than with their legs.

Renardet said to the doctor:

"You know what the trouble is about?"

"Yes, a child found dead in the wood by Mederic."

"That's quite correct. Come on."

They walked on side by side, followed by the two men. Their steps made no noise on the moss, their eyes were gazing downward right in front of them.

The doctor hastened his steps, interested by the discovery. As soon as they were near the corpse, he bent down to examine it without touching it. He had put on a pair of glasses, as you do when you are looking at some curious object; then he turned round very quietly and said, without rising up:

"Violated and assassinated, as we shall prove presently. This little girl, moreover, is almost a woman—look at her throat."

Her two breasts, already nearly full-developed, fell over her chest, relaxed by death. The doctor lightly drew away the handkerchief which covered her face. It was almost black, frightful to look at, the tongue protruding, the eyes bloodshot. He went on:

"Faith, she was strangled the moment the deed was done."

He felt her neck:

"Strangled with the hands without leaving any special trace, neither the mark of the nails nor the imprint of the fingers. Quite right. It is little Louise Roque, sure enough!"

He delicately replaced the handkerchief:

"There's nothing for me to do. She's been dead for the last hour at least. We must give notice of the matter to the authorities."

Renardet, standing up, with his hands behind his back, kept staring with a stony look at the little body exposed to view on the grass. He murmured:

"What a wretch! We must find the clothes."

The doctor felt the hands, the arms, the legs. He said:

"She must have been bathing, no doubt. They ought to be at the water's edge."

The mayor thereupon gave directions:

"Do you, Principe [this was his secretary], go and look for those clothes for me along the river. Do you, Maxime [this was the steward], hurry on toward Rouy-le-Tors, and bring on here to me the examining magistrate with the *gendarmes*. They must be here within an hour. You understand."

The two men quickly departed, and Renardet said to the doctor:

"What miscreant has been able to do such a deed in this part of the country."

The doctor murmured:

"Who knows? Everyone is capable of that! Everyone in particular and nobody in general. However, it must be some prowler, some workman out of employment. As we live under a Republic, we must expect to meet this sort of miscreant along the roads."

Both of them were Bonapartists. The mayor went on:

"Yes, it could only be a stranger, a passer-by, a vagabond without heart or home."

The doctor added with the shadow of a smile on his face:

"And without a wife. Having neither a good supper nor a good bed, he procured the rest for himself. You can't tell how many men there may be in the world capable of a crime at a given moment. Did you know that this little girl had disappeared?"

And with the end of his stick he touched one after the other the stiffened fingers of the corpse, resting on them as on the keys of a piano.

"Yes, the mother came last night to look for me about nine o'clock, the child not having come home for supper up to seven. We went to try and find her along the roads up to midnight, but we did not think of the wood. However, we needed daylight to carry out a search with a practical result."

"Will you have a cigar?" said the doctor.

"Thanks, I don't care to smoke. It gives me a turn to look at this."

They remained standing in front of the young girl's body, pale and still, on the dark background of moss. A big fly was walking along one of the thighs, it stopped at the blood-stains, went on again, always rising higher, ran along the side with his lively, jerky movements, climbed up one of the breasts, then came back again to explore the other. The two men silently watched this wandering black speck. The doctor said:

"How tantalizing it is, a fly on the skin! The ladies of the last

73

century had good reason to paste them on their faces. Why has the fashion gone out?"

But the mayor seemed not to hear, plunged as he was in deep thought.

All of a sudden he turned around, surprised by a shrill noise. A woman in a cap and a blue apron rushed up through the trees. It was the mother, La Roque. As soon as she saw Renardet she began to shriek:

"My little girl, Where's my little girl?" in such a distracted manner that she did not glance down at the ground. Suddenly, she saw the corpse, stopped short, clasped her hands, and raised both her arms while she uttered a sharp, heartrending cry—the cry of a mutilated animal. Then, she rushed toward the body, fell on her knees, and snatched away the handkerchief that covered the face. When she saw that frightful countenance, black and convulsed, she recoiled with a shudder, then pressed her face against the ground, giving vent to terrible and continuous choking screams, her mouth close to the thick moss.

Her tall, thin frame, to which her clothes clung tightly, was palpitating, shaken with convulsions. They could see her bony ankles and withered limbs covered with thick blue stockings, shivering horribly. Unconsciously she dug at the soil with her crooked fingers as if to make a grave in which to hide herself.

The doctor pityingly said in a low tone :

"Poor old woman!"

Renardet felt a strange rumbling in his stomach; then he gave vent to a sort of loud sneeze that issued at the same time through nose and mouth; and, drawing his handkerchief from his pocket, began to weep copiously, coughing, sobbing noisily, wiping his face, and stammering:

"Damn—damn—damned pig to do this! I would like to see him guillotined!"

But Principe reappeared, with his hands empty. He murmured:

"I have found nothing, *M'sieu', le Maire*, nothing at all anywhere."

The mayor, scared, replied in a thick voice, drowned in tears:
"What is it you could not find?"

"The little girl's clothes."

"Well—well—look again, and find them—or you'll have to answer to me."

The man, knowing that the mayor would not brook opposition, set forth again with hesitating steps, casting on the corpse horrified and timid glances.

Distant voices arose under the trees, a confused sound, the noise of an approaching crowd; for Mederic had, in the course of his rounds, carried the news from door to door. The people of the neighbourhood, stupefied at first, had gone gossiping from their own firesides into the street, and from one threshold to another. Then they gathered together. They talked over, discussed, and commented on the event for some minutes, and they had now come to see it for themselves.

They arrived in groups, a little faltering and uneasy through fear of the first impression of such a scene on their minds. When they saw the body they stopped, not daring to advance, and speaking low. Then they grew bold, went on a few steps, stopped again, advanced once more, and soon formed around the dead girl, her mother, the doctor, and Renardet, a thick circle, agitated and noisy, which swayed forward under the sudden pushes of the last comers. And now they touched the corpse. Some of them even bent down to feel it with their fingers. The doctor kept them back. But the mayor, waking abruptly out of his torpor, broke into a rage, and, seizing Dr. Labarbe's stick, flung himself on his townspeople, stammering:

"Clear out—clear out—you pack of brutes—clear out!"

And in a second the crowd of sightseers had fallen back two hundred metres.

La Roque was lifted up, turned round, and placed in a sitting posture; she remained weeping with her hands clasped over her face.

The occurrence was discussed among the crowd; and young lads, with eager eyes, curiously scrutinized the nude body of the girl. Renardet perceived this, and, abruptly taking off his vest, flung it over the little girl, who was entirely lost to view under the wide garment.

The spectators drew quietly nearer. The wood was filled with people, and a continuous hum of voices rose up under the tangled foliage of the tall trees.

The mayor, in his shirt-sleeves, remained standing, with his stick in his hands, in a fighting attitude. He seemed exasperated by this curiosity on the part of the people, and kept repeating:

"If one of you comes nearer, I'll break his head just as I would a dog's."

The peasants were greatly afraid of him. They held back. Dr. Labarbe, who was smoking, sat down beside La Roque, and spoke to her in order to distract her attention. The old woman soon removed her hands from her face, and replied with a flood of tearful words, pouring forth her grief in rapid sentences. She told the whole story of her life, her marriage, the death of her man—a bull-sticker, who had been gored to death—the infancy of her daughter, her wretched existence as a widow without resources and with a child to support. She had only this one, her little Louise, and the child had been killed—killed in this wood. All of a sudden, she felt anxious to see it again, and dragging herself on her knees toward the corpse, she raised up one corner of the garment that covered it; then she let it fall again, and began wailing once more. The crowd remained silent, eagerly watching the mother's gestures.

But all of a sudden there was a swaying of the crowd, and a cry of "*The gendarmes! The gendarmes!*"

Two *gendarmes* appeared in the distance, coming on at a rapid trot, escorting their captain and a little gentleman with red whiskers, who was bobbing up and down like a monkey on a big white mare.

The steward had found M. Putoin, the examining magistrate, just at the moment when he was mounting to take his daily ride, for he posed as a good horseman, to the great amusement of the officers.

He dismounted along with the captain, and pressed the hands of the mayor and the doctor, casting a ferret-like glance on the linen vest which swelled above the body lying underneath.

When he was thoroughly acquainted with the facts, he first gave orders to get rid of the public, whom the *gendarmes* drove out of the wood, but who soon reappeared in the meadow, and formed a line, a long line of excited and moving heads all along the Brindelle, on the other side of the stream.

The doctor in his turn gave explanations of which Renardet took a note in his memorandum book. All the evidence was given, taken down, and commented on without leading to any discovery. Maxime, too, came back without having found any trace of the clothes.

This surprised everybody; no one could explain it on the theory of theft, since these rags were not worth twenty *sous*; so this theory was inadmissible.

The examining magistrate, the mayor, the captain, and the doctor set to work by searching in pairs, putting aside the smallest branches along the water.

Renardet said to the judge:

"How does it happen that this wretch should conceal or carry away the clothes, and should then leave the body exposed in the open air and visible to everyone?"

The other, sly and knowing, answered:

"Perhaps a dodge? This crime has been committed either by a brute or by a crafty blackguard. In any case, we'll easily succeed in finding him."

The rolling of a vehicle made them turn their heads. It was the deputy magistrate, another doctor, and the registrar of the court who had arrived in their turn. They resumed their searches, all chatting in an animated fashion.

Renardet said suddenly:

"Do you know that I am expecting you to lunch with me?"

Everyone smilingly accepted the invitation, and the examining magistrate, finding that the case of little Louise Roque was quite enough to bother about for one day, turned toward the mayor:

"I can have the body brought to your house, can I not? You have a room in which you can keep it for me till this evening."

The other got confused, and stammered:

"Yes—no—no. To tell the truth, I prefer that it should not come into my house on account of—on account of my servants who are already talking about ghosts in—in my tower, in the Fox's Tower. You know—I could no longer keep a single one. No—I prefer not to have it in my house."

The magistrate began to smile:

"Good! I am going to get it carried off at once to Rouy, for the legal examination."

Turning toward the doctor:

"I can make use of your trap, can I not?"

"Yes, certainly."

Everybody came back to the place where the corpse lay. La Roque, now seated beside her daughter, had caught hold of her head, and was staring right before her, with a wandering listless eye.

The two doctors endeavoured to lead her away, so that she might not witness the dead girl's removal; but she understood at once what they wanted to do, and, flinging herself on the body, she seized it in both arms. Lying on top of the corpse, she exclaimed:

"You shall not have it—'tis mine—'tis mine now. They have killed her for me, and I want to keep her—you shall not have her!"

All the men, affected and not knowing how to act, remained standing around her. Renardet fell on his knees, and said to her:

"Listen, La Roque, it is necessary—in order to find out who killed her. Without this it could not be found out. We must make a search for him in order to punish him. When we have found him, we'll give her up to you. I promise you this."

This explanation shook the woman's mind, and a feeling of hatred manifested itself in her distracted glance.

"So then they'll take him?"

"Yes, I promise you that."

She rose up, deciding to let them do as they liked; but when the captain remarked:"'Tis surprising that her clothes cannot be found," a new idea, which she had not previously thought of, abruptly found an entrance into her brain, and she asked:

"Where are her clothes? They're mine. I want them. Where have they been put?"

They explained to her that they had not been found, then she called out for them with desperate obstinacy and with repeated moans:

"They're mine—I want them. Where are they? I want them!"

The more they tried to calm her, the more she sobbed, and persisted in her demands. She no longer wanted the body, she insisted on having the clothes, as much perhaps through the unconscious cupidity of a wretched being to whom a piece of silver represents a fortune, as through maternal tenderness.

And when the little body, rolled up in blankets which had been brought out from Renardet's house, had disappeared in the vehicle, the old woman, standing under the trees, held up by the mayor and the captain, exclaimed:

"I have nothing, nothing, nothing in the world, not even her little cap—her little cap."

The *curé* had just arrived, a young priest already growing stout. He took it on himself to carry off La Roque, and they went away together toward the village. The mother's grief was modified under the sugary words of the clergyman, who promised her a thousand compensations. But she incessantly kept repeating:"If I had only her little cap."

This idea now dominated every other.

Before they were out of hearing Renardet exclaimed:

"You will lunch with us. *Monsieur l'Abbé*—in an hour's time?"

The priest turned his head round, and replied:

"With pleasure, *Monsieur le Maire*. I'll be with you at twelve."

And they all directed their steps toward the house, whose gray front and large tower, built on the edge of the Brindelle, could be seen through the branches.

The meal lasted a long time. They talked about the crime and everybody was of the same opinion. It had been committed by some tramp passing there by chance while the little girl was bathing.

Then the magistrates returned to Rouy, announcing that they would return next day at an early hour. The doctor and the *curé* went to their respective homes, while Renardet, after a long walk through the meadows, returned to the wood, where he remained walking till nightfall with slow steps, his hands behind his back.

He went to bed early, and was still asleep next morning when the examining magistrate entered his room. He rubbed his hands together with a self-satisfied air. He said:

"Ha! ha! Still sleeping? Well, my dear fellow, we have news this morning."

The mayor sat up on his bed.

"What, pray?"

"Oh! Something strange. You remember well how the mother yesterday clamoured for some memento of her daughter, especially her little cap? Well, on opening her door this morning, she found on the threshold her child's two little wooden shoes. This proves that the crime was perpetrated by someone from the district, someone who felt pity for her. Besides, the postman Mederic found and brought me the thimble, the scissors, and the needlecase of the dead girl. So then the man in carrying off the clothes in order to hide them, must have let fall the articles which were in the pocket. As for me, I attach special importance to the wooden shoes, as they indicate a certain moral culture and a faculty for tenderness on the part of the assassin. We will therefore, if you have no objection, pass in review together the principal inhabitants of your district."

The mayor got up. He rang for hot water to shave with, and said:

"With pleasure, but it will take rather a long time, so let us begin at once."

M. Putoin sat astride on a chair, thus pursuing even in a room, his mania for horsemanship. Renardet now covered his chin with a white lather while he looked at himself in the glass; then he sharpened his razor on the strop and went on:

"The principal inhabitant of Carvelin bears the name of Joseph Renardet, mayor, a rich landowner, a rough man who beats guards and coachmen—"

The examining magistrate burst out laughing:

"That's enough; let us pass on to the next."

"The second in importance is ill. Pelledent, his deputy, a rearer of oxen, an equally rich landowner, a crafty peasant, very sly, very close-fisted on every question of money, but incapable in my opinion of having perpetrated such a crime."

M. Putoin said:

"Let us pass on."

Then, while continuing to shave and wash himself, Renardet went on with the moral inspection of all the inhabitants of Carvelin. After two hours' discussion, their suspicions were fixed on three individuals who had hitherto borne a shady reputation—a poacher named Cavalle, a fisher for chub and crayfish named Paquet, and a bull-sticker named Clovis.

2

The search for the perpetrator of the crime lasted all the summer, but he was not discovered. Those who were suspected and those who were arrested easily proved their innocence, and the authorities were compelled to abandon the attempt to capture the criminal.

But the murder seemed to have moved the entire country in a singular fashion. It left a disquietude, a vague fear, a sensation of mysterious terror, springing not merely from the impossibility of discovering any trace of the assassin, but above all from that strange finding of the wooden shoes in front of La Roque's door on the day after the crime. The certainty that the murderer had assisted at the investigation and that he was doubtless still living in the village, left a gloomy impression on every mind, and hung over the neighbourhood like a constant menace.

The wood, besides, had become a dreaded spot, a place to be avoided, and supposed to be haunted.

Formerly, the inhabitants used to come and lounge there every Sunday afternoon. They used to sit down on the moss at the foot of the huge trees, or walk along the water's edge watching the trout gliding under the green undergrowth. The boys used to play bowls, hide-and-seek, and other games in certain places where they had upturned, smoothed out, and levelled the soil, and the girls, in rows of four or five, used to trip along holding one another by the arms, and screaming out with their shrill voices ballads which grated on the ear, disturbed the tranquil air with discord and set the teeth on edge like vinegar. Now nobody ventured into and under the towering trees, as if afraid of finding there some corpse lying on the ground.

Autumn arrived; the leaves began to fall. They fell day and night from the tall trees, whirling round and round to the ground; and the sky could be seen through the bare branches. Sometimes when a gust of wind swept over the tree-tops, the slow, continuous rain suddenly grew heavier, and became a hoarsely growling storm, which drenched the moss with thick yellow water that made the ground swampy and yielding.

And the almost imperceptible murmur, the floating, ceaseless whisper, gentle and sad, of this rainfall seemed like a low wail, and the continually falling leaves, like tears, big tears shed by the tall mournful trees, which were weeping, as it were, day and night over the close of the year, over the ending of warm dawns and soft twilights, over the ending of hot breezes and bright suns, and also perhaps over the crime which they had seen committed under the shade of their branches, over the girl violated and killed at their feet. They wept in the silence of the desolate empty wood, the abandoned, dreaded wood, where the soul, the childish soul of the dead little girl must have been wandering all alone.

The Brindelle, swollen by the storms, rushed on more quickly, yellow and angry, between its dry banks, lined with thin, bare willow-hedges.

Renardet suddenly resumed his walks under the trees. Every day, at sunset, he came out of his house, descended the front steps slowly, and entered the wood, in a dreamy fashion with his hands in his pockets. For a long time he would pace over the damp, soft moss, while a legion of rooks, rushing to the spot from all the neighbouring haunts in order to rest in the tall summits, spread themselves through space, like an immense mourning veil floating in the wind, uttering violent and sinister screams. Sometimes they would perch on the tangled branches dotting with black spots the red sky, the sky crimsoned with autumn twilight. Then, all of a sudden, they would set off again, croaking frightfully and trailing once more above the wood the long darkness of their flight. Then they would swoop down, at last, on the highest tree-tops, and gradually their cawings would die away, while advancing night merged their black plumes into the blackness of space.

Renardet was still strolling slowly under the trees; then, when the darkness prevented him from walking any longer, he went back to the house, sank all of a heap into his armchair in front of the glowing hearth and dried his feet at the fire.

Now, one morning, an important bit of news was circulated around the district: the mayor was getting his wood cut down.

Twenty woodcutters were already at work. They had commenced at the corner nearest to the house, and they worked rapidly in the master's presence.

At first the loppers climbed up the trunk. Tied to it by a rope collar, they clung round it in the beginning with both arms, then, lifting one leg, struck the tree hard with the edge of a steel instrument attached to each foot. The edge penetrated the wood and remained stuck in it; and the man rose up as if on a step in order to strike with the steel attached to the other foot, and then once more supported himself till he could lift his first foot again.

With every upward movement was slipped higher the rope

collar which fastened him to the tree. Over his loins hung and glittered the steel hatchet. He kept continually climbing in easy fashion like some parasite attacking a giant, mounting slowly up the immense trunk, embracing it and spurring it in order to decapitate it.

As soon as he reached the lowest branches, he stopped, detached from his side the sharp axe, and struck. Slowly, methodically, he chopped at the limb close to the trunk. Suddenly the branch cracked, gave way, bent, tore itself off, and fell, grazing the neighbouring trees in its fall. Then it crashed down on the ground with a great sound of broken wood, and its slighter branches quivered for a long time.

The soil was covered with fragments which other men cut in their turn, bound in bundles, and piled in heaps, while the trees which were still left standing looked like enormous posts, gigantic forms amputated and shorn by the keen steel axes of the cutters.

When the lopper had finished his task, he left at the top of the straight slender shaft of the tree the rope collar which he had brought up with him, descending again with spur-like prods along the discrowned trunk, which the woodcutters below attacked at the base, striking it with heavy blows which resounded through all the rest of the wood.

When the base of the tree seemed pierced deeply enough, some men commenced dragging, to the accompaniment of a signal cry in which all joined harmoniously, at the rope attached to the top. All of a sudden, the immense column cracked and tumbled to the earth with the dull sound and shock of a distant cannon-shot. Each day the wood grew thinner, losing its trees one by one as an army loses its soldiers.

Renardet no longer walked up and down. He remained from morning till night, contemplating, motionless, with his hands behind his back, the slow death of his wood. When a tree fell, he placed his foot on it as if it were a corpse. Then he raised his eyes to the next with a kind of secret, calm impatience, as if he expected or hoped for something at the end of this massacre.

Meanwhile, they were approaching the place where little Louise Roque had been found. At length, they came to it—one evening, at the hour of twilight.

As it was dark, the sky being overcast, the wood- cutters wanted to stop their work, putting off till next day the fall of an enormous beech-tree. But Renardet objected to this, insisting that even at this late hour they should lop and cut down this giant, which had overshadowed and seen the crime.

When the lopper had laid it bare, had finished its toilet for the guillotine, and the woodcutters had sapped its base, five men commenced hauling at the rope attached to the top.

The tree resisted; its powerful trunk, although cut half-way through, was as rigid as iron. The workmen, altogether, with a sort of regular jump, strained at the rope, stooping down to the ground, and they gave vent to a cry with lungs out of breath, so as to indicate and direct their efforts.

Two woodcutters stood close to the giant, with axes in their grip, like two executioners ready to strike once more, and Renardet, motionless, with his hand on the bark, awaited the fall with an uneasy, nervous feeling.

One of the men said to him:

"You're too near. *Monsieur le Maire.* When it falls, it may hurt you."

He did not reply and did not recoil. He seemed ready to catch the beech-tree in his open arms in order to cast it on the ground like a wrestler.

All at once, at the foot of the tall column of wood there was a shudder which seemed to run to the top, like a painful shiver; it bent slightly, ready to fall, but still resisted. The men, in a state of excitement, stiffened their arms, renewed their efforts with greater vigour, and, just as the tree, breaking, came crashing down, Renardet suddenly made a forward step, then stopped, his shoulders raised to receive the irresistible shock, the mortal blow which would crush him to the earth.

But the beech-tree, having deviated a little, only grazed against his loins, throwing him on his face five metres away.

The workmen rushed forward to lift him up. He had already risen to his knees, stupefied, with wandering eyes, and passing his hand across his forehead, as if he were awaking out of an attack of madness.

When he had got to his feet once more, the men, astonished, questioned him, not being able to understand what he had done. He replied, in faltering tones, that he had had for a moment a fit of abstraction, or rather a return to the days of his childhood, that he imagined he had to pass under that tree, just as street-boys rush in front of vehicles driving rapidly past, that he had played at danger, that, for the past eight days, he felt this desire growing stronger within him, asking himself whether, every time a tree was cracking, was on the point of falling, he could pass beneath it without being touched. It was a piece of stupidity, he confessed; but everyone has these moments of insanity, these temptations to boyish folly.

He made this explanation in a slow tone, searching for his words and speaking in a stupefied fashion.

Then he went off, saying:

"'Till tomorrow, my friends—till tomorrow."

As soon as he had reached his study, he sat down before his table, which his lamp, covered with a shade, lighted up brightly, and, clasping his hands over his forehead, began to cry.

He remained crying for a long time, then wiped his eyes, raised his head, and looked at the clock. It was not yet six o'clock.

He thought:

"I have time before dinner."

And he went to the door and locked it. He then came back, and sat down before his table. He pulled out a drawer in the middle of it, and taking from it a revolver, laid it down over his papers, under the glare of the sun. The barrel of the firearm glittered, and cast reflections which resembled flames.

Renardet gazed at it for some time with the uneasy glance of a drunken man; then he rose and began to pace up and down the room.

He walked from one end of the apartment to the other,

stopped from time to time and started to pace up and down again a moment afterward. Suddenly, he opened the door of his dressing-room, steeped a towel in the water-jug and moistened his forehead, as he had done on the morning of the crime.

Then he began to walk up and down once more. Each time he passed the table the gleaming revolver attracted his glance, and tempted his hand; but he kept watching the clock, thinking:

"I have still time."

It struck half past six. Then he took up the revolver, opened his mouth wide with a frightful grimace, and stuck the barrel into it, as if he wanted to swallow it. He remained in this position for some seconds without moving, his finger on the lock; then, suddenly, seized with a shudder of horror, he dropped the pistol on the carpet, and fell back on his armchair, sobbing:

"I can't. I dare not! My God! My God! How can I have the courage to kill myself?"

There was a knock at the door. He rose up in a stupefied condition. A servant said:

"*Monsieur's* dinner is ready."

He replied: "All right. I'm going down."

He picked up the revolver, locked it up again in the drawer, then looked at himself in the glass over the mantelpiece to see whether his face did not look too much troubled. It was as red as usual, a little redder perhaps. That was all. He went down, and seated himself before the table.

He ate slowly, like a man who wants to drag on the meal, who does not want to be alone with himself.

Then he smoked several pipes in the dining-room while the plates were being removed. After that, he went back to his room.

As soon as he was alone, he looked under his bed, opened all his cupboards, explored every corner, rummaged through all the furniture. Then he lighted the tapers over the mantelpiece, and, turning round several times, ran his eye all over the apartment in an anguish of terror that made his face lose its colour, for he knew well that he was going to see her, as he did every night—little Louise Roque, the little girl he had violated and afterward strangled.

Every night the odious vision came back again. First, it sounded in his ears like the snorting that is made by a thrashing machine or the distant passage of a train over a bridge. Then he commenced to pant, to feel suffocated, and had to unbutton his shirt-collar and loosen his belt. He moved about to make his blood circulate, he tried to read, he attempted to sing. It was in vain. His thoughts, in spite of himself, went back to the day of the murder, made him go through it again in all its most secret details, with all the violent emotions he had experienced from first to last.

He had felt on rising up that morning, the morning of the horrible day, a little vertigo and dizziness which he attributed to the heat, so that he remained in his room till the time came for lunch.

After the meal he had taken a *siesta*, then, toward the close of the afternoon, he had gone out to breathe the fresh, soothing breeze under the trees in the wood.

But, as soon as he was outside, the heavy scorching air of the plain oppressed him more. The sun, still high in the heavens, poured out on the parched, dry, and thirsty soil, floods of ardent light. Not a breath of wind stirred the leaves. Beasts and birds, even the grasshoppers, were silent. Renardet reached the tall trees, and began to walk over the moss where the Brindelle sent forth a slight, cool vapour under the immense roof of trees. But he felt ill at ease.

It seemed to him that an unknown, invisible hand was squeezing his neck, and he could scarcely think rationally, having usually few ideas in his head. For the last three months, only one thought haunted him, the thought of marrying again. He suffered from living alone, suffered from it morally and physically. Accustomed for ten years past to feeling a woman near him, habituated to her presence every moment, to her embrace each successive day, he had need, an imperious and perplexing need of incessant contact with her and the regular touch of her lips. Since Madame Renardet's death, he had suffered continually without knowing why, had suffered from not feeling her dress brush against his legs every day, and, above all, from no longer being able to grow calm and languid in her arms. He had been scarcely six months a widower, and he had already been looking out through the district for some young girl or some widow he might marry when his period of mourning was at an end.

He had a chaste soul, but it was lodged in a vigorous Herculean body, and carnal images began to disturb his sleep and his vigils. He drove them away; they came back again; and he murmured from time to time, smiling at himself:

"Here I am, like St. Antony."

Having had this morning several besetting visions, the desire suddenly came into his breast to bathe in the Brindelle in order to refresh himself and reduce his feverishness.

He knew, a little further on, of a large deep spot where the people of the neighbourhood came sometimes to take a dip in summer. He went there.

Thick willow-trees hid this clear pool of water where the current rested and went to sleep for a little while before starting on its way again. Renardet, as he appeared, thought he heard a light sound, a faint plash which was not that of the stream or the banks. He softly put aside the leaves and looked. A little girl, quite naked in the transparent water, was beating the waves with both hands, dancing about in them a little, and dipping herself with pretty movements. She was not a child nor was she yet a woman. She was plump and well formed, yet had an air of youthful precocity, as of one who had grown rapidly, and who was now almost ripe. He no longer moved, overcome with surprise, with a pang of desire, holding his breath with a strange, poignant emotion. He remained there, his heart beating as if one of his sensual dreams had just been realized; as if an impure fairy had conjured up before him this young creature, this little rustic Venus born of the river foam, who was making his heart beat faster.

Suddenly the little girl came out of the water, and without seeing him came over to where he stood looking for her clothes in order to dress herself. While she was gradually approaching him with little hesitating steps, through fear of the sharp pointed stones, he felt himself pushed toward her by an irresistible force, by a bestial transport of passion, which stirred up all his carnality, stupefied his soul, and made him tremble from head to foot.

She remained standing some seconds behind the willow-tree which concealed him from view. Then, losing his reason entirely, he opened the branches, rushed on her, and seized her in his arms. She fell, too scared to offer any resistance, too much terror-stricken to cry out, and he possessed her without understanding what he was doing.

He woke up from his crime, as one wakes out of a nightmare. The child burst out weeping.

He said:

"Hold your tongue! Hold your tongue! I'll give you money."

But she did not hear him, she went on sobbing.

He went on:

"Come now, hold your tongue! Do hold your tongue. Keep quiet."

She still kept shrieking, writhing in the effort to get away from him. He suddenly realized that he was ruined, and he caught her by the neck to stop her from uttering these heartrending, dreadful screams. As she continued to struggle with the desperate strength of a being who is flying from death, he pressed his enormous hands on that little throat swollen with cries. In a few seconds he had strangled her, so furiously did he grip her, yet not intending to kill but only to silence her.

Then he rose up overwhelmed with horror.

She lay before him with her face bleeding and blackened. He was going to rush away when there sprang up in his agitated soul the mysterious and undefined instinct that guides all beings in the hour of danger.

It was necessary to throw the body into the water; but he did not; another impulse drove him toward the clothes, of which he made a thin parcel. Then, as he had a piece of twine, he tied it up and hid it in a deep portion of the stream, under the trunk of a tree, the foot of which was immersed in the Brindelle.

Then he went off at a rapid pace, reached the meadows, took a wide turn in order to show himself to peasants who dwelt some distance away on the opposite side of the district, and came back to dine at the usual hour, telling his servants all that was supposed to have happened during his walk.

He slept, however, that night—slept with a heavy, brutish sleep, such as the sleep of persons condemned to death must occasionally be. He opened his eyes at the first glimmer of dawn, and waited, tortured by the fear of having his crime discovered, for his usual waking hour.

Then he would have to be present at all the stages of the inquiry as to the cause of death. He did so after the fashion of a somnambulist, in a hallucination which showed him things and human beings in a sort of dream, in a cloud of intoxication, with that dubious sense of unreality which perplexes the mind at times of the greatest catastrophes.

The only thing that pierced his heart was La Roque's cry of anguish. At that moment he felt inclined to cast himself at the old woman's feet, and to exclaim:

"'Tis I."

But he restrained himself. He went back, However, during the night, to fish up the dead girl's wooden shoes, in order to carry them to her mother's threshold.

As long as the inquiry lasted, so long as it was necessary to guide and aid justice, he was calm, master of himself, sly and smiling. He discussed quietly with the magistrates all the suppositions that passed through their minds, combated their opinions, and demolished their arguments. He even took a keen and mournful pleasure in disturbing their investigations, in confuting their ideas, in showing the innocence of those whom they suspected.

But from the day when the investigation came to a close,

he became gradually nervous, more excitable than he had been before, although he mastered his irritability. Sudden noises made him jump up with fear; he shuddered at the slightest thing, trembled sometimes from head to foot when a fly alighted on his forehead. Then he was seized with an imperious desire for motion, which compelled him to keep continually on foot, and made him remain up whole nights walking to and fro in his own room.

It was not that he was goaded by remorse. His brutal mind did not lend itself to any shade of sentiment or of moral terror. A man of energy and even of violence, born to make war, to ravage conquered countries, and to massacre the vanquished, full of the savage instincts of the hunter and the fighter, he scarcely took count of human life. Though he respected the Church through policy, he believed neither in God nor in the devil, expecting consequently in another life neither chastisement nor recompense for his acts. As his sole creed, he retained a vague philosophy composed of all the ideas of the encyclopaedists of the last century. He regarded religion as a moral sanction of the law, both one and the other having been invented by men to regulate social relations.

To kill anyone in a duel, or in a battle, or in a quarrel, or by accident, or for the sake of revenge, or even through bravado, would have seemed to him an amusing and clever thing, and would not have left more impression on his mind than a shot fired at a hare; but he had experienced a profound emotion at the murder of this child. He had, in the first place, perpetrated it in the distraction of an irresistible gust of passion, in a sort of sensual tempest that had overpowered his reason. And he had cherished in his heart, cherished in his flesh, cherished on his lips, cherished even to the very tips of his murderous fingers, a kind of bestial love, as well as a feeling of horror and grief, toward this little girl he had surprised and basely killed. Every moment his thoughts returned to that horrible scene, and, though he endeavoured to drive away the picture from his mind, though he put it aside with terror, with disgust, he felt it surging through his soul, moving about in him, waiting incessantly for the moment to reappear.

Then, in the night, he was afraid, afraid of the shadows falling around him. He did not yet know why the darkness seemed frightful to him; but he instinctively feared it, felt that it was peopled with terrors. The bright daylight did not lend itself to fears. Things and beings were seen there; there only natural things and beings which could exhibit themselves in the light of day could be met. But the night, the impenetrable night, thicker than walls, and empty, the infinite night, so black, so vast, in which one might brush against frightful things, the night when one feels that mysterious terror is wandering, prowling about, appeared to him to conceal an unknown danger, close and menacing.

What was it?

He knew it ere long. As he sat in his armchair, rather late, one evening when he could not sleep, he thought he saw the curtain of his window move. He waited, in an uneasy state of mind, with beating heart. The drapery did not stir, then, all of a sudden it moved once more. He did not venture to rise up; he no longer ventured to breathe, and yet he was brave. He had often fought, and he would have liked to catch thieves in his house.

Was it true that this curtain did move? he asked himself, fearing that his eyes had deceived him. It was, moreover, such a slight thing, a gentle flutter of lace, a kind of trembling in its folds, less than such an undulation as is caused by the wind.

Renardet sat still, with staring eyes, and out-stretched neck. Then he sprang to his feet abruptly, ashamed of his fear, took four steps, seized the drapery with both hands, and pulled it wide apart. At first, he saw nothing but darkened glass, resembling plates of glittering ink. The night, the vast, impenetrable night stretched out before him as far as the invisible horizon. He remained standing in front of the illimitable shadow, and suddenly perceived a light, a moving light, which seemed some distance away.

Then he put his face close to the windowpane, thinking that a person looking for crayfish might be poaching in the Brindelle, for it was past midnight. The light rose up at the edge of the stream, under the trees. As he was not yet able to see clearly, Renardet placed his hands over his eyes. Suddenly this light became an illumination, and he beheld little Louise Roque naked and bleeding on the moss. He recoiled frozen with horror, sank into his chair, and fell backward. He remained there some minutes, his soul in distress; then he sat up and began to reflect. He had had a hallucination—that was all: a hallucination due to the fact that a marauder of the night was walking with a lantern in his hand near the water's edge. What was there astonishing, besides, in the circumstance that the recollection of his crime should sometimes bring before him the vision of the dead girl?

He rose up, swallowed a glass of wine, and sat down again. He thought:

"What am I to do if this come back?"

And it did come back; he felt it; he was sure of it. Already his glance was drawn toward the window; it called him; it attracted him. In order to avoid looking at it, he turned aside his chair. Then, he took a book and tried to read; but it seemed to him that he presently heard something stirring behind him, and he swung round his armchair on one foot.

The curtain still moved—unquestionably, it did move this time; he could no longer have any doubt about it. He rushed forward and seized it in his grasp so violently that he knocked it down with its fastener. Then, he eagerly pressed his face against the glass. He saw nothing. All was black without; and he breathed with the delight of a man whose life has just been saved.

Then he went back to his chair, and sat down again; but almost immediately he felt a longing to look out through the window once more. Since the curtain had fallen, the space in front of him made a sort of dark patch, fascinating and terrible, on the obscure landscape. In order not to yield to this dangerous temptation, he took off his clothes, extinguished the lamp, and lay down, shutting his eyes.

Lying on his back motionless, his skin hot and moist, he awaited sleep. Suddenly a great gleam of light flashed across his eyelids. He opened them believing that his dwelling was on fire. All was black as before, and he leaned on his elbow in order to try to distinguish his window, which had still for him an unconquerable attraction. By dint of straining his eyes, he could perceive some stars, and he arose, groped his way across the room, discovered the panes with his outstretched hands, and placed his forehead close to them. There below, under the trees, the body of the little girl glittered like phosphorus, lighting up the surrounding darkness.

Renardet uttered a cry and rushed toward his bed, where he lay till morning, his head hidden under the pillow.

From that moment, his life became intolerable. He passed his days in apprehension of each succeeding night; and each night the vision came back again.

As soon as he had locked himself up in his room, he strove to struggle; but in vain. An irresistible force lifted him up and pushed him against the glass, as if to call the phantom, and ere long he saw it lying in the spot where the crime was committed, lying with arms and legs outspread, just in the way the body had been found.

Then the dead girl rose up and came toward him with little steps just as the child had done when she came out of the river. She advanced quietly, passing straight across the grass, and over the border of withered flowers. Then she rose up into the air toward Renardet's window. She came toward him, as she had come on the day of the crime. And the man recoiled before the apparition—he retreated to his bed, and sank down upon it, knowing well that the little one had entered the room, and that she now was standing behind the curtain, which presently moved. And until daybreak, he kept staring at this curtain, with a fixed glance, ever waiting to see his victim depart.

But she did not show herself anymore; she remained there behind the curtain which quivered tremulously now and then.

And Renardet, his fingers clinging to the bedclothes, squeezed them as he had squeezed the throat of little Louise Roque.

He heard the clock striking the hours; and in the stillness the pendulum kept time with the loud beatings of his heart. And he suffered, the wretched man, more than any man had ever suffered before.

Then, as soon as a white streak of light on the ceiling announced the approaching day, he felt himself free, alone at last, alone in his room; and then he went to sleep. He slept some hours—a restless, feverish sleep in which he retraced in dreams the horrible vision of the night just past.

When, later on, he went down to breakfast, he felt exhausted as if after prodigious fatigue; and he scarcely ate anything, haunted as he was by the fear of what he had seen the night before.

He knew, however, that it was not an apparition—that the dead do not come back, and that his sick soul, possessed by one thought alone, by an indelible remembrance, was the only cause of his punishment, was the only evoker of that awful image, brought back by it to life, called up by it and raised by it before his eyes, in which the ineffaceable resemblance remained imprinted. But he knew, too, that he could not cure it, that he could never escape from the savage persecution of his memory; and he resolved to die, rather than endure these tortures any longer.

Then, he pondered how he would kill himself. He wished for some simple and natural death which would preclude the idea of suicide. For he clung to his reputation, to the name bequeathed to him by his ancestors; and if there were any suspicion as the cause of his death, people's thoughts might be perhaps directed toward the mysterious crime, toward the murderer who could not be found, and they would not hesitate to accuse him.

A strange idea came into his head, that of letting himself be crushed by the tree at the foot of which he had assassinated little Louise Roque. So he determined to have the wood cut down and to simulate an accident. But the beech-tree refused to smash his ribs.

Returning to his house, a prey to utter despair, he had snatched up his revolver, and then he did not dare to fire it.

The dinner bell summoned him. He could eat nothing, and

went upstairs again. But he did not know what he was going to do. Now that he had escaped the first time, he felt himself a coward. Presently, he would be ready, fortified, decided, master of his courage and of his resolution ; just now, he was weak, and feared death as much as he did the dead girl.

He faltered out to himself:

"I will not venture it again—I will not venture it." Then he glanced with terror, first at the revolver on the table, and next at the curtain which hid his window. It seemed to him, moreover, that something horrible would occur as soon as his life was ended. Something? What? A meeting with her, perhaps! She was watching for him; she was waiting for him; she was calling him; and her object was to seize him in her turn, to exhibit herself to him every night so that she might draw him toward the doom that would avenge her, and lead him to death. He began to cry like a child, repeating: "I will not venture it again—I will not venture it," Then, he fell on his knees, and murmured: "My God! my God!" without believing, nevertheless, in God. He no longer dared, in fact, to look out through his window where he knew the apparition was visible, nor at the table where his revolver gleamed.

When he had risen up, he said:

"This cannot last; there must be an end of it."

The sound of his voice in the silent room made a shiver of fear pass through his limbs, but, as he could not come to a decision, as he felt certain that his finger would always refuse to pull the trigger of his revolver, he turned round to hide his head under the bedclothes, and to plunge into reflection.

He would have to find some way in which he could force himself to die, to invent some device against himself, which would not permit of any hesitation on his part, any delay, any possible regrets. He began to envy condemned criminals who are led to the scaffold surrounded by soldiers. Oh! if he could only beg of someone to shoot him; if he could, confessing the state of his soul, confessing his crime to a sure friend who would never divulge it, obtain from him death.

But from whom could he ask this terrible service ? From whom? He cast about for one among his friends whom he knew intimately. The doctor ? No, he would talk about it afterward, most certainly. And suddenly a fantastic idea entered his mind. He would write to the examining magistrate, who was on terms of close friendship with him and would denounce himself as the perpetrator of the crime. He would in this letter confess everything, revealing how his soul had been tortured, how he had resolved to die, how he had hesitated about carrying out his resolution, and what means he had employed to strengthen his failing courage.

And in the name of their old friendship he would implore of the other to destroy the letter as soon as he had ascertained that the culprit had inflicted justice on himself. Renardet could rely on this magistrate; he knew him to be sure, discreet, incapable of even an idle word. He was one of those men who have an inflexible conscience, governed, directed, regulated by their reason alone.

Scarcely had he formed this project when a strange feeling of joy took possession of his heart. He was calm now. He would write his letter slowly, then at daybreak he would deposit it in the box nailed to the wall in his office, then he would ascend his tower to watch for the postman's arrival, and when the man in the blue blouse came in sight, he would cast himself headlong on to the rocks on which the foundations rested. First he would take care to be seen by the workmen who were cutting down his wood. He would then climb to the parapet some distance up which bore the flagstaff displayed on file days. He would smash this pole with a shake and precipitate it along with him.

Who would suspect that it was not an accident? And he would be dashed to pieces, having regard to his weight and the height of the tower.

Presently he got out of bed, went over to the table, and began to write. He omitted nothing, not a single detail of the crime, not a single detail of the torments of his heart, and he ended by announcing that he had passed sentence on himself—that he was going to execute the criminal—and begged of his friend, his old friend, to be careful that there should never be any stain on his memory.

When he had finished his letter, he saw that the day had dawned.

He closed it, sealed it, and wrote the address; then he descended with light steps, hurried toward the little white box fastened to the wall in the corner of the farmhouse, and when he had thrown into it the fatal paper which made his hand tremble, he came back quickly, shot the bolts of the great door, and climbed up to his tower to wait for the passing of the postman, who would convey his death sentence.

He felt self-possessed, now. Liberated! Saved!

A cold dry wind, an icy wind, passed across his face. He inhaled it eagerly, with open mouth, drinking in its chilling kiss. The sky was red, with a burning red, the red of winter, and all the plain whitened with frost glistened under the first rays of the sun, as if it had been powdered with bruised glass.

Renardet, standing up, with his head bare, gazed at the vast tract of country before him, the meadow to the left, and to the right the village whose chimneys were beginning to smoke with the preparations for the morning meal. At his feet he saw the Brindelle flowing toward the rocks, where he would soon be crushed to death. He felt himself reborn on that beautiful frosty morning, full of strength, full of life. The light bathed him and penetrated him like a newborn hope. A thousand recollections assailed him, recollections of similar mornings, of rapid walks, the hard earth which rang under his footsteps, of happy chases on the edges of pools where wild ducks sleep. All the good things that he loved, the good things of existence rushed into memory, penetrated him with fresh desires, awakened all the vigorous appetites of his active, powerful body.

And he was about to die? Why? He was going to kill himself stupidly, because he was afraid of a shadow—afraid of nothing? He was still rich and in the prime of life! What folly! All he wanted was distraction, absence, a voyage in order to forget.

This night even he had not seen the little girl because his mind was preoccupied, and so had wandered toward some other subject. Perhaps he would not see her anymore ? And even if she still haunted him in his house, certainly she would not follow him elsewhere! The earth was wide, the future was long.

Why die?

His glance travelled across the meadows, and he perceived a blue spot in the path which wound alongside of the Brindelle. It was Mederic coming to bring letters from the town and to carry away those of the village.

Renardet got a start, a sensation of pain shot through his breast, and he rushed toward the winding staircase to get back his letter, to demand it back from the postman. Little did it matter to him now whether he was seen. He hurried across the grass moistened by the light frost of the previous night, and he arrived in front of the box in the corner of the farmhouse exactly at the same time as the letter-carrier.

The latter had opened the little wooden door, and drew forth the papers deposited there by the inhabitants of the locality.

Renardet said to him:

"Good morrow, Mederic."

"Good morrow, *M'sieu' le Maire*."

"I say, Mederic, I threw a letter into the box that I want back again. I came to ask you to give it back to me."

"That's all right, *M'sieu' le Maire*—you'll get it."

And the postman raised his eyes. He stood petrified at the sight of Renardet's face. The mayor's cheeks were purple, his eyes were glaring with black circles round them as if they were sunk in his head, his hair was all tangled, his beard untrimmed, his necktie unfastened. It was evident that he had not gone to bed.

The postman asked:

"Are you ill, *M'sieu' le Maire?*"

The other, suddenly comprehending that his appearance must be unusual, lost countenance, and faltered:

"Oh! no—oh! no. Only I jumped out of bed to ask you for

this letter. I was asleep. You understand?"

Said Mederic: "What letter?"

"The one you are going to give back to me."

Mederic now began to hesitate. The mayor's attitude did not strike him as natural. There was perhaps a secret in that letter, a political secret. He knew Renardet was not a Republican, and he knew all the tricks and chicaneries employed at elections.

He asked:

"To whom is it addressed, this letter of yours?"

"To M. Putoin, the examining magistrate—you know my friend, M. Putoin, well!"

The postman searched through the papers, and found the one asked for. Then he began looking at it, turning it round and round between his fingers, much perplexed, much troubled by the fear of committing a grave offense or of making an enemy for himself of the mayor.

Seeing his hesitation, Renardet made a movement for the purpose of seizing the letter and snatching it away from him. This abrupt action convinced Mederic that some important secret was at stake and made him resolve to do his duty, cost what it might.

So he flung the letter into his bag and fastened it up, with the reply:

"No, I can't, *M'sieu' le Maire*. From the moment it is addressed and sent to the magistrate, I can't."

A dreadful pang wrung Renardet's heart, and he murmured:

"Why, you know me well. You are even able to recognize my handwriting. I tell you I want that paper."

"I can't."

" Look here, Mederic, you know that I'm incapable of deceiving you—I tell you I want it."

"No, I can't."

A tremor of rage passed through Renardet's soul.

"Damn it all, take care! You know that I don't go in for chaffing, and that I could get you out of your job, my good fellow, and without much delay either. And then, I am the mayor of the district, after all; and I now order you to give me back that paper."

The postman answered firmly:

"No, I can't, *M'sieu' le Maire*."

Thereupon, Renardet, losing his head, caught hold of the postman's arms in order to take away his bag; but, freeing himself by a strong effort, and springing backward, the letter-carrier raised his big holly stick. Without losing his temper, he said emphatically:

"Don't touch me, *M'sieu' le Maire*, or I'll strike. Take care, I'm only doing my duty!"

Feeling that he was lost, Renardet suddenly became humble, gentle, appealing to him like a crying child:

"Look here, look here, my friend, give me back that letter, and I'll recompense you—I'll give you money. Stop! Stop! I'll give you a hundred *francs*, you understand—a hundred *francs!*"

The postman turned on his heel and started on his journey.

Renardet followed him, out of breath, faltering:

"Mederic, Mederic, listen! I'll give you a thousand *francs*, you understand—a thousand *francs*."

The postman still went on without giving any answer.

Renardet went on:

"I'll make your fortune, you understand—whatever you wish—fifty thousand *francs*—fifty thousand *francs* for that letter! What does it matter to you? You won't? Well, a hundred thousand—I say—a hundred thousand *francs*. Do you understand? A hundred thousand *francs*—a hundred thousand *francs*."

The postman turned back, his face hard, his eye severe:

"Enough of this, or else I'll repeat to the magistrate everything you have just said to me."

Renardet stopped abruptly. It was all over. He turned back and rushed toward his house, running like a hunted animal.

Then, in his turn, Mederic stopped, and watched this flight with stupefaction. He saw the mayor re-entering his own house, and he waited still as if something astonishing was about to happen.

Presently the tall form of Renardet appeared on the summit of the Fox's Tower. He ran round the platform like a madman. Then he seized the flagstaff and shook it furiously without succeeding in breaking it; then, all of a sudden, like a swimmer taking a plunge, he dived into the air with his two hands in front of him.

Mederic rushed forward to give succour. As he crossed the park, he saw the woodcutters going to work. He called out to them, telling them an accident had occurred, and at the foot of the walls they found a bleeding body the head of which was crushed on a rock. The Brindelle surrounded this rock, and over its clear, calm waters, swollen at this point, could be seen a long, thin, red stream of mingled brains and blood.

Mad

This manuscript was found among the papers of Viscount Jacques de X—— who committed suicide a few years ago, in his room in a hotel at Piombières.

1

For days and days, nights and nights, I had dreamed of that first kiss which was to consecrate our engagement, and I knew not on what spot I should put my lips, madly thirsting as they were for her beauty and her youth. Neither on her forehead—that was accustomed to family caresses; nor on her light hair, which mercenary hands had dressed; nor on her eyes, whose turned-up lashes looked like little wings, because that would have made me think of the farewell caress which closes the eyelids of some dead woman whom one has adored. Not on her lovely mouth, which I will not, which I must not possess until that divine moment when Elaine will at last belong to me altogether and for always, but on that delicious little dimple which comes in one of her cheeks when she is happy, when she smiles, and which excited me as much as did her voice of languorous softness, on that evening when our wooing began at the Souverettes'.

Our parents were walking slowly up and down under the chestnut-trees in the garden, and had left us alone altogether for a few minutes. I went up to her and took both her trembling hands into mine, and gently drawing her close to me, I whispered:

"How happy I am, Elaine, and how I love you!" Then I kissed her almost timidly, on the dimple. She trembled, as if from the pain of a burn, blushed deeply and with an affectionate look, she said: "I love you, too, Jacques, and I am very happy!"

That embarrassment, the sudden emotion which revealed the perfect spotlessness of a pure mind, the instinctive recoil of virginity, her childlike innocence, that blush of modesty, delighted me above everything as a presage of happiness. It seemed to me as if I were unworthy of her. I was almost ashamed of bringing and putting into her small, saintlike hands the remains of a damaged heart, a heart polluted by debauchery, a miserable thing which had served as a toy for unworthy mistresses, which was intoxicated with lies, and felt as if it would die of bitterness and disgust.

2

How quickly she has become accustomed to me! How suddenly she has turned into a woman and become metamorphosed. Already she no longer is at all like the artless girl, the sensitive child, to whom I did not know what to say, and whose sudden questions disconcerted me!

She is *coquettish*, and there is seduction in her attitudes, in her gestures, in her laugh, and in her touch. One might think that she was trying her power over me, and that she guesses that I no longer have any will of my own. She does with me whatever she likes, and I am quite incapable of resisting the beautiful charm that emanates from her. I feel carried away by her caressing hands, and so happy that I am at times frightened at the excess of my own felicity.

My life now passes amid the most delicious of punishments. Those afternoons and evenings that we spend together, those unconstrained moments when, sitting on the sofa together, she rests her head on my shoulder, holds my hands, and half shuts her beautiful eyes while we settle what our future life shall be,— when I cover her with kisses and inhale the odour of all those little silky locks that form a halo round her imperial brow,— excite me, unsettle me, kill me. And yet I feel inclined to shed tears when the time comes for us to part, and I really only exist when I am with Elaine.

I can scarcely sleep. I see her rise up in the darkness, delicate, fair, and pink, so supple, so elegant with her small waist and tiny hands and feet, with that graceful head and that look of mockery and of coaxing which lies in her smile, that dawn-like brightness which illumes her brow, that when I think that she is going to become my wife, I feel inclined to sing, and to shout amorous folly into the silence of the night.

Elaine also seems to be at the end of her strength. She has grown languid and nervous; she would like to wipe out the fortnight that we still have to wait, and so little does she hide her longing, that one of her uncles, Colonel d'Orthez, said after dinner the other evening: "By Jove, my children, one would take you for two soldiers who are looking forward to their furlough!"

3

I do not know how I feel, or whence those fears come which have so suddenly assailed me, and taken possession of my whole being like a flight of poisoned arrows. The nearer the day approaches that I am so ardently longing for, on which Elaine will take my name and belong to me, the more anxious, nervous, and tormented by the uncertainty of the morrow I feel.

I love, and I am passionately loved, and few couples start on the unknown journey of a totally new life and enter into matrimony with such hopes, and such an assurance of happiness, as we two.

I have such faith in the girl I am going to marry, and have made her such vows of love, that I should certainly kill myself without a moment's hesitation if anything were to happen to separate us, or to force us to a dignified but irremediable rupture, or if Elaine were seized by some fatal illness. And yet I hesitate, I am afraid, for I know that many others have made shipwreck, have lost their love on the way, have disenchanted their wives and have themselves been disenchanted in those first ecstasies of possession, during that first night of tenderness and of intimacy.

What does Elaine expect in her vague innocence, which has been lessened by the half confidence of married friends, by semi-avowals, by all the kisses of this sort of apprenticeship which is a court of love; what does she expect, what does she hope for? Will her refined, delicate, vibrating nature bend to the painful submission of the initial embrace; will she not rebel against that ardent attack that wounds and pains? Oh! to have to say to oneself that it must come to that, to lower the most ideal of affections, to think that one is risking one's whole future happiness at such a hazardous game, that the merest trifle might make a woman completely ridiculous or hopeful, and cause an idolized woman to laugh or cry!

I do not know a more desirable, a prettier, or more attractive being in the whole world than Elaine. I am worn out by feverish love, I thirst for her lips and I wish every particle of her being to belong to me. I love her ardently, but I would willingly give half that I possess to have got through this ordeal, to be a week older, *and still happy!*

4

My mother-in-law took me aside yesterday, while they were dancing, and with tears in her eyes said in a tremulous voice:

"You are going to possess the most precious object that we own, and the one we love best. I beg you to always spare the slightest unhappiness, and to be kind and gentle toward her. I count on your uprightness and affection to guide her and protect her in this dangerous life in Paris."

And then, giving way to her feelings more and more, she added:

"I do not think that you suppose that I have tried to instruct her in her new duties or to disturb her charming innocence, which has been my work; when two persons worship each other like you two do, a girl learns what she is ignorant of, so quickly and so well!"

I very nearly burst out laughing in her face, for such a theatrical phrase appeared to me both ridiculous and doubtful. So that respectable woman had always been a passive, pliable, inert object, who never had one moment of vibration, of tender emotion in her husband's arms; and I understood why, as I waited at the club, he escaped as soon as possible and made other connections which cost him dear, but in which he found at least some appearance of love.

Oh! to call that supreme bliss of possession a duty, a bliss which makes human beings divine, which transports them far from everything, to term a duty that despotic pain of virginity, which guesses, which waits, which longs for those mysterious, unknown, brief sufferings that contain the germs of future pleasure, the only happiness of which one never tires.

And that piece of advice, at the last moment, which was commonplace and natural, and which I ought to have expected, enervated me and, in spite of myself, plunged me into a state of perplexity from which I could not extricate myself. I remembered those absurd stories which we hear among friends, after a good dinner. What would be that last trial of our love for her and for me, and could that love which then was my whole life come out of the ordeal lessened or increased tenfold? And when I looked at the couch on which Elaine, my adored Elaine, was sitting, with her head half hidden behind the feathers of her fan, she whispered in a rather vexed voice:

"How cross you look, my dear Jacques! Is the fact of your getting married the cause of it? And you have such a mocking look on your face. If the thought of it terrifies you too much, there is still time to say *no!*"

And delighted, bewitched by her caressing looks, I said in a low voice, almost into her small ear:

"I adore you; and these last moments that still separate us from each other seem centuries to me, my dear Elaine!"

5

There were tiresome ceremonies yesterday and today, which I went through almost mechanically.

First, there is the *yes* before the mayor at the civil ceremony, (civil marriages are obligatory in France, though usually followed by the religious rite), like some everyday response in church, which you are in a hurry to get over. It has almost the suggestion of an imperious law, to which you are bound to submit—of a state of bondage, which will, perhaps, be very irksome, since the whole of existence is made up of chances.

And then the service in church, with the decorated altar, the voices of the choir, the solemn music of the organ, the unctuous address of the old priest, who marks his periods and seems quite proud of having prepared Elaine for confirmation, and then the procession to the vestry, the shaking of hands, and the greetings of people whom you scarcely see, and whom you do or do not recognize.

Under the long tulle veil, which almost covered her, with the symbolical orange flowers on her bright, light hair, in her white dress, with her downcast eyes and her graceful figure, Elaine looked to me like a Psyche, whose innocent heart was vowed to love. I felt how vain and artificial all this ceremony was, how little this show counted before *the kiss*, the triumphant, revealing, maddening *kiss*, which rivets the flesh of the wife to the lips and the flesh of the husband, which turns the immaculate youth of the virgin into a woman, and consecrates it to tender caresses, to dreams, and to future ecstasies

6

Elaine loves me as much as I adore her.

She left her parental abode as if she were going to some festivity, without turning round toward all that she had left behind her in the way of affection and recollection, and without even that farewell tear, which the first kiss effaces, on her long turned-up lashes.

She looked like a bird which has escaped from its cage, and does not know where to settle, which beats its wings in the intoxication of the light and warbles incessantly. She repeated her words as if she were rather intoxicated, and her laugh sounded like the cooing of a pigeon. Looking into my eyes, with her eyes full of languor, and her arms round my neck like a bracelet, and with her burning cheek against mine, she suddenly exclaimed:

"My darling, would you not give ten years of your life to have already got to the end of the journey?"

The passionate question so disconcerted me that I did not know what to reply; my brain reeled as if I had been at the edge of a precipice. Did she already know what her mother had not told her? Had she already learned what she ought to have been ignorant of? And had that heart, which I used to compare to "the Vessel of Election," of which the litanies of Our Lady speak, already been damaged?

O white veils that hide the blushes, the half-closed eyes, and the trembling lips of some Psyche! O little hands which you raise in an attitude of prayer toward the lighted and decorated altar! O innocent and charming questions, which delighted me to the depths of my being, and which seemed to me to be an absolute promise of happiness, are you, were you nothing but a lie, and a wonderfully well acted piece of trickery?

But was I not wrong, and an idiot, to allow such thoughts to take possession of me, to poison that deep, absorbing love which was now my only law and my only object, by odious and foolish suggestions? What an abject and miserable nature I must have, for such a simple, affectionate, natural question to disturb me so, when I ought immediately to have replied to Elaine's question, with all the heart that belonged to her:

"Yes, ten or twenty years, because you are my happiness, my desire, my love!"

7

I did not choose to wait until she woke up. I sprang from the bed where Elaine was still sleeping, with her dishevelled hair lying on the lace-edged pillows. Her complexion was almost transparent, her lips were half open, as if she were dreaming, and she seemed so overcome with sleep, that I felt much emotion when I looked at her.

I drank four glasses of diluted champagne, one after the other, as quickly as I could, but it did not quench my thirst. I was fever-ish and would have given anything in the world for something to interest me suddenly, to absorb me and lift me out of that slough in which my heart and my brain were being engulfed, as if in a quicksand. I did not venture to avow to myself what was making me so dejected, what was torturing me and driving me mad with grief, or to scrutinize the muddy bottom of my present thoughts sincerely and courageously, to question myself and to pull myself together.

It would have been so odious, so infamous, to harbour such suspicions unjustly, to accuse that adorable creature who was not yet twenty, whom I loved, and *who seemed to love me*, without having certain proofs, that I felt that I was blushing at the idea that I had any doubt of her innocence. Ah! Why did I marry?

I had a sufficient income to enable me to live as I liked, to pay beautiful women whom I chanced to meet and who pleased me, amused me, and sometimes gave me unexpected proofs of affection, but I had never allowed myself to be caught altogether. In order to keep my heart warm, I had some romantic and sentimental friendships with women in society, some of those delightful flirtations which have an appearance of love, which fill up the idleness of a useless life with a number of unexpected sensations, with small duties, and vague subtle pleasures!

And was I now to be like one of those ships which an un-skilful turn of the helm runs ashore as it is leaving the harbour? What terrible trials were awaiting me, what sorrows and what struggles?

A friend said jestingly to me one night at the club, when I had just broken the bank, a thing which forms an epoch in a player's life:

"If I were in your place, Jacques, I should distrust such runs of luck as that, for one always has to pay for them sooner or later!"

Sooner or later!

I half opened the bedroom door gently. Elaine was in one of those heavy sleeps that follow intoxication. Who could tell whether, when she opened her eyes and called me, surprised at not finding herself in my arms, her whole being would not become languid, and suddenly sink into a state of prostration? I wanted to reason with myself, and to bring myself face to face with those cursed suggestions, as one does with a skittish horse before some object that frightens it—to evoke the recollection of every hour, every minute of that first night of love, and to extract the secret from her.

Elaine's looks and radiant smile were overflowing with happiness, and she had the air of a conqueror who is proud of his triumph, for she was now a *woman* already, and we had *at last been alone* in this modernized country house, which had been redecorated and smartened up to serve as the frame for our affection! She hardly seemed to know what she was saying or doing, and ran from room to room in her light morning dress of mauve crape, without exactly knowing where to sit, and almost dazzled by the light of the lamps that had large shades in the shape of rose leaves over them.

There was no embarrassment, no hesitation, no shamefaced looks, no recoiling from the arms that were stretched out to her, or from the lips that begged; none of those delightful little pieces of awkwardness—which show a virgin soul free from all perversion—in her manner of sitting on my knees, of putting her bare arms round my neck, and of offering me the back of her neck and her lips to kiss. But she laughed nervously, and her supple form trembled when I kissed her passionately on various places, and she said things to me that were suitable for being whispered on the pillows, while a strange languor overshadowed her eyes, and dilated her nostrils.

And suddenly, with a mocking gesture which seemed to bid defiance to a supper that was laid on a small table, cold meat of various kinds, plates of fruit and of cakes, and an ice-pail, from which the neck of a bottle of champagne protruded, she said merrily:

"I am not at all hungry, dear; let us have supper later; what do you say?"

She half turned round to the large bed, which seemed to be quite ready for us, in the shadow of the recess in which it stood, with its two white, untouched, almost solemn pillows. She was not smiling anymore; there was a bluish gleam in her eyes, like that of burning alcohol, and I lost my head. Elaine did not try to escape, and did not utter a complaint.

Oh! that night of torture and delight, that night which ought never to have ended!

I determined that I would be as patient as a policeman who is trying to discover the traces of a crime, that I would investigate the past of this girl, about which I knew nothing. I should be sure to discover some proof, some important reminiscence, some servant who had been her accomplice.

And yet I adored her, my pretty, my divine Elaine, and I would consent to any and everything if only she were what I dreamed, what I wished her to be, if only this nightmare would go and no longer rise up between her and me.

When she woke up, she spoke to me in her coaxing voice. Oh! her kisses, again her kisses, always her kisses, in spite of everything!

Oh! to have believed blindly, to have believed on my knees that she was not lying, that she was not making a mockery of my tenderness, and that she had never belonged, and never would belong, to anyone but me!

8

I wished that I could have transformed myself into one of those crafty, unctuous priests, to whom women confess their most secret faults, to whom they intrust their souls and of whom they frequently ask advice—that Elaine could have come and knelt at the grating of my confessional, where I could press her closely with questions, and gradually extract sincere confidences from her.

As soon as I am by the side of a young or old woman now, I try to give our conversation a ticklish turn. I forget all reserve and I try to make her talk of those jokes which nettle, those words of double meaning which excite, and to lead her up to the only subject that interests and holds me—to find out what she feels in her body as well as in her heart, on that night, when for the first time she has to undergo the nuptial ordeal. Some do not appear to understand me, blush, and leave me as if I were some unpleasant, ill-mannered person and had offended them, or as if I had tried to force open the precious casket in which they keep their sweetest recollections.

Some, on the other hand, understand me only too well, scent something equivocal and ridiculous, though they do not exactly know what, make me go on, and finally get out of the difficulty by some subtle piece of impertinence and a burst of chaffing laughter.

Two or three at most, and these were some of those pretty little upstarts who talk at random, and brag about their vices, and whom one could soon squelch, were one to take the trouble, have related their impressions to me with ironical complaisance, and I found nothing in what they said that reassured me, nor could I discover anything serious, true, or moving in it.

That supreme initiation amused them as much as if it had been a scene from a comedy; the small amount of affection that they felt for the man with whom their existence had been associated grew less and evaporated altogether. They remembered nothing about it except its ridiculous and hateful side, and described it as a sort of pantomime in which they played a bad part. But these did not love and were not adored like Elaine was. They had married either from interest, or that they might not remain old maids—that they might have more liberty and escape from troublesome guardianship.

Foolish dolls, without either heart or head, they had neither that nervous intensity, nor that need for affection, nor that instinct for love which I had discovered in my wife's nature, and which attracted me at the same time that it terrified me.

Besides, who could convince me of my errors, who could dissipate that darkness in which I was lost, what miracle could restore *all* my belief in her again?

9

Elaine felt that I was hiding something from her, that I was not happy. She felt that some threatening obstacle had risen up between us, and that some insupportable suspicion was oppressing me, torturing me, keeping me from her arms, poisoning and disturbing that affection in which I had hoped to find fresh youth, absolute happiness, my dream of dreams.

She never spoke to me about it, however, but seemed to recoil from a definite explanation, which might make shipwreck of her love. She surrounded me with endearing attentions, and appeared to be trying to make my life so pleasant to me that nothing in the world could draw me from it. And she would certainly cure me, if this madness of mine were not, alas! like those wounds which are constantly reopening, and which no balm can heal.

But, at times, I lived again, imagining that her caresses had exorcised me, that I was saved, that doubt was no longer gnawing at my heart, that I was going to adore her again, like I used to adore her. I used to throw myself at her knees and put my lips on her little hands which she abandoned to me, would look at her lovely, limpid eyes—like a piece of a blue sky amid black storm clouds—and whisper, with something like a sob in my throat:

"You love me, do you not, with all your heart, you love me as much as I love you; tell me so again, my dear love; tell me that, and nothing but that!"

And she used to reply eagerly, with a smile of joy on her lips:

"Do you not know it? Do you not see every moment that I love you, that you have taken entire possession of me, and that I only live for you and by you!"

And her kisses would give me new life, and intoxicate me, as when one returns from a long and perilous journey in which one has despaired of ever seeing some loved woman again, and meeting with a frenzied embrace, forgets everything in the divine feeling that one is going to die of happiness.

10

But these clear spots in our sky were only ephemeral, and the cries which accompanied them only grew more bitter and terrible. I knew that Elaine was growing more and more uneasy at the apparent strangeness of my character, that she suffered from it and that it affected her nerves; that the existence to which I was condemning her in spite of myself—all this immoderate love of mine, followed by fits of inexplicable coldness and of low spirits—disconcerted her, so that she was no longer the same, and kept away from me. She could not hide her grief, and was continually worrying me with questions of affectionate pity.

She repeated the same things over and over again, with hateful persistence. Had she vexed me, without knowing it ? Was I already tired of my married life, and did I regret my lost liberty? Had I any private troubles which I had not told her of; heavy debts which I did not know how to pay; was it family matters or some former connection with a woman that I had broken off suddenly, and that now threatened to create a scandal ? Was I being worried by anonymous letters? What was it, in a word; what was it?

My denials only exasperated her, so that she sulked in silence, while her brain worked and her heart grew hard toward me; but could I, as a matter of fact, tell her of the suspicions which were filling my life with gloom and annihilating me? Would it not be odious and vile to accuse her of such a fall, without any proofs or any clew, and would she ever forget such an insult?

I almost envied those unfortunate wretches who had the right to be jealous, who had to fight against a woman's coquetry and light behaviour, and who had to defend their honour against some poacher on the preserves of love. They had a target to aim at; they knew their enemies and knew what they were doing, while I was wandering in a land of terrible mirages, was struggling in the midst of vague suppositions, was causing my own troubles and was enraged with her past, which was, I felt sure, as white and pure as any bridal veil.

Ah! It would be better to blow my brains out, I thought to

myself, than to prolong such a situation! I had had enough of it. I scarcely lived, and I wished to know all that Elaine had done before we became engaged. I wanted to know whether I was the first or the second, and I determined to know it, even if I had to sacrifice years of my life in inquiry, to lower myself to compromising words and acts, to every species of artifice and to spend everything that I possessed!

She might believe whatever she liked, for after all I should only laugh at it. We might have been so happy; so many envied me, and would gladly have consented to take my place!

11

I no longer knew where I was going, but was like a train speeding through a dense fog, disturbing the perfect silence of the sleeping country with puffing and shrill whistles, but all in vain, since the driver cannot distinguish the changing lights of the disks or the signals. Then comes the terrible crash, sending the train off the rails, and piling the carriages into a heap of ruins.

I was afraid of going mad. At times I asked myself whether any of my family had shown signs of mental aberration, and had been locked up in a lunatic asylum—whether the life of constant pleasures that I had led for years, turning night into day and indulging in frequent violent emotions, had not at last affected my brain. If I had believed in anything, or in the science of the occult, which haunts so many restless brains, I should have imagined that some enemy was bewitching me and laying invisible snares for me, suggesting actions quite unworthy of the frank, upright, and well-bred man that I was, and trying to destroy the happiness of which Elaine and I had dreamed.

For a whole week I devoted myself to the hateful business of playing the spy and to the inquiries that were killing me. I had succeeded in discovering the lady's maid who had been in Elaine's service before we were married, a maid whom she loved as a foster sister, who used to accompany Elaine whenever she visited the poor or went for a walk, and used to wake her every morning to do her hair and dress her. She was young, rather pretty, and polished, for Paris had improved her and she knew her difficult business from end to end.

I found out, however, that her virtue was only apparent, especially since she had left Elaine; that she was fond of going to public balls, and that she divided her favours between a man who came from her part of the country, a sergeant in a dragoon regiment, and a footman, and that she spent all her money on horse races and on dress. I felt sure that I should be able to make her talk and get the truth out of her, either by money or cunning; so I asked her to meet me early one morning in a quiet square.

At first she listened to me in astonishment, without replying yes or no, as if she did not understand what I was aiming at, or with what object I was asking her all these questions about her former mistress. But when I offered her a few hundred *francs* to loosen her tongue—I was impatient to get the matter over—and pretended to know that she had managed interviews for Elaine with lovers, that they were known and being followed, that Elaine had been in the habit of frequenting quiet bachelors' quarters, from which she returned late, the sly little wench frowned angrily, shrugged her shoulders, and exclaimed:

"What pigs some men are to have such ideas, and cause such an excellent person as Mademoiselle Elaine any unhappiness. Look here, you disgust me with your bank-notes and your dirty insinuations, and I don't choose to say what you deserve!"

Then she turned her back on me and hurried off, but her insolence, and that indignant reply she had given me, rejoiced me to the depths of my heart, like soothing balm that lulls pain.

I should have liked to have called her back and told her that it was all a joke, that I was devotedly in love with my wife, that I was always on the watch to hear her praised, but she was already out of sight. I felt that I was ridiculous and mean, that I had lowered myself by what I had done, and I swore that I would profit by such a humiliating lesson, and for the future show myself to Elaine as the trusting and ardent husband that she deserved. I thought myself cured, altogether cured.

And yet, I again became a prey to the same bad thoughts, to the same doubts, and persuaded that the girl had lied to me,— just like all women lie when they are on the defensive,—that she had made fun of me, that perhaps *someone* had foreseen this scene and had told her what to say and made sure of her silence, having paid for her complicity. Shall I always knock up against some obstacle, always struggle in this wretched darkness, this mire from which I cannot extricate myself!

12

Nobody knew anything. Neither the Superior of the Convent where she had been brought up until she was sixteen, nor the servants who had waited on her, nor the governesses who had finished her education, could remember that Elaine had been difficult to govern or to teach, or that she had had any other ideas than those of her age. She had certainly shown no precocious *coquetry* or disquieting instincts; she had had no equivocal cousinly intimacies, when if the bridle is relaxed, and one of them has learned at school what love is, the two big children yield to the fatal law of sex, and begin the inevitable eclogue of *Daphnis and Chloe* over again.

However—oh! I felt it too much for it to be nothing but a chimera and a mirage—it was no *virgin* who threw her arms round my neck so lovingly, who returned my first kisses so *deliciously*, who was attracted by my society, who gave no signs of surprise and uttered no complaint, who appeared to forget everything when in my society. No, no, a thousand times no, that could not have been a pure woman.

I should have cast off the intoxication which was bewitching me, and have rushed out of the room where such a lie was being consummated. I ought to have profited by her moments of loving weakness, when she was incapable of collecting her thoughts, and would with tears have confessed an old fault, for which she had not, perhaps, been altogether responsible. Perhaps by my entreaties, or perhaps even by violence, from terror at my furious looks, when my features would have been distorted by rage, and my hands clenched in spite of myself in a gesture of menace and of murder, I might have forced her to open her heart, to show me its defilement, and to tell me her sad love episode.

How do I know whether her colour might not have moved me to pity, whether I should not have wept with her at the heavy cross that we both had to bear, whether I should not have forgiven her and opened my arms wide, so that she might have thrown herself into them as into a peaceful refuge?

Would not any man-about-town, or vicious student on the lookout for innocent girls, have perceived her nervousness, her vice? Would he not have hypnotized her, as it were, by amorous touches, by skilful caresses and reduced her to the absolute passiveness of an animal taken unawares, without any care for the morrow, or what the consequences of such a fault might be?

Or was I completely her dupe and the dupe of a villain? Had she loved, and did she still love, the man who had first possessed her—who had been her first lover? Who could tell me, or come to my aid? Who could give me proof, real, undeniable proof, either that I was an infamous wretch to suspect Elaine, whom I ought to have worshiped with my eyes shut, or that she was guilty, that she had lied, and that I had the right to cast her out of my life and to treat her as a worthless woman!

13

If I had married when young, before wallowing in the mire of Paris, from which you can never cleanse yourself, for heart and body both retain its indelible marks, if I had not been the plaything of a score of mistresses, who disgusted me with belief in any woman, if I had not been weaned from supreme illusions and surfeited with low materialism, should I now have these abominable ideas?

I waited almost until the decline of life before I took the right course and sought refuge in port; before I sought what is pure and virtuous, and heeded the continual advice of those who loved me. I passed too suddenly from the lies, from the ephemeral enjoyments, from the satiety which depraves us, from the vice in which one tries to acquire renewed strength and vigour and to discover some new and unknown sensation, to the pure sentimentalities of an engagement, to the unspeakable delights of a life common to two, to that delicious first and lasting communion which ought to constitute married life.

I had been afraid that somebody else would be beforehand with me and rob me of Elaine's heart, had been fearful of relapsing into my former habits. But if I had possessed moral strength and character enough, in case I had to wait, or even if I had backed out without entering into any engagement and without binding my life to that of the adorable girl whom chance had thrown in my way, it would have been far better. I could have waited, prepared myself, questioned myself, and accustomed myself to that metamorphosis; could have purified myself and forgotten the past in those retreats which precede the solemn ceremony, when pious souls pronounce indissoluble vows.

The reaction had been too sudden and violent for such a convalescent as I. I had worked myself up, and pictured to myself something so white, so virginal, so paradisic, such complete ignorance, such unconquerable modesty and such delicious awkwardness, that Elaine's gaiety, her unconstraint, her fearlessness, and her passionate kisses bewildered me, rousing my suspicions and filling me with anguish.

And yet I know how all, or nearly all, girls are educated in these days, and that the ignorant and simple ones only exist on the stage. I know also that they hear and learn too many things both at home and in society, not to have an intuitive knowledge of the results of love.

Elaine loves me with all her heart, for she has told me so time after time, and she repeats it to me more ardently than ever when I take her into my arms and seem happy. She must have seen that her beauty had, in a manner, converted me; that in order to possess her I had renounced many seductions and a long life of enjoyment; and that, perhaps, she would no longer please me if she were *too much of the little girl*—that she would appear ridiculous to me if she showed her fears by any entreaty, any gesture, or any sigh.

As people in the South say, she would have acted as a brave woman, and boasted, so that no complaint might betray her, would have imparted the wild tenderness of a jealous heart to her kisses, and have attempted a struggle, which would certainly have been useless, against those recollections of mine with which she thought I must be filled, in spite of myself.

I accused myself, so that I might no longer accuse her. I studied my malady; I knew quite well that I was wrong, and indeed I wished to be wrong. I measured the stupidity and the disgrace of such suspicions, but, nevertheless, in spite of everything, they assailed me again, watched me like a spy, and carried me away and consumed me.

Ah! Is there in the whole world, even among the most wretched beggars that are dying of starvation, whom nature crushes in a vise, as it were, or among the victims of misplaced love, anybody who can say that he is more wretched than I?

15

This morning Count de Saulnac, who was lunching here, told us a terrible story of a rape, for which a man is to be tried in a few days.

A charming girl of eighteen grew languid, became so pale and morose, cheeks so wax-like, her eyes so sunken and altogether so anaemic, that her parents grew uneasy and took her to a doctor who lived near them. He examined her carefully, talked vaguely of what was the matter with her, said it was an illness that required assiduous care and attention, and advised the worthy couple to bring the poor girl to him every day for a month.

As they were not well enough off to keep a servant, and each had their work to attend to, the husband as an employee in a public office and his wife as cashier in a milliner's shop, and did not dream of any evil, being further reassured by the charitable, unctuous looks of the doctor, they allowed their daughter to go and consult him by herself.

The old man made much of her, tried to make her get over her shyness, adroitly made her tell him all about her usual life, took a long time in sounding her chest, helped her to dress and undress, in a very paternal way, gave her a potion and was so thoughtful and caressing that the poor girl blushed and felt quite uncomfortable at it all. He soon saw that he could obtain nothing from her innocence, and that she would resist his slightest attempts at improper familiarity. As he was extremely taken with the delicate and attractive girl, and with her charming person, the wretch sent her to sleep with a few magnetic passes, and outraged her.

She awoke without being conscious of what had happened, only feeling rather more listless than usual, as she did when there was thunder in the air. From that time the doctor put longer intervals between her visits, and soon, after having prescribed insignificant remedies for her, he told her that she was cured, and that she need not come and see him anymore. Two months passed, and the girl, who at first had seemed much better and more lively, relapsed into the state of prostration which had so alarmed them, dragged herself about more than walked, and seemed to be sinking under some heavy burden.

As they had not paid the old doctor's bill, and as they were afraid that he would ask them for it if they went to see him again, her father took the girl to Beaujon. He nearly went mad with despair and shame when one of the house-surgeons, without mincing his words, told them in a jesting manner that she was *enceinte*.

Enceinte! What did he mean by that? And by whom?

They were small, thoroughly respectable and upright wage-earners, and this made them heartless. They tormented the poor girl to make her acknowledge her fault and tell them the name of her seducer. It was no use for her to moan, to throw herself at their feet, to tear her hair in desperation, and to swear that no man in the world had even touched her lips. In vain did she exclaim indignantly that it was impossible that such a dreadful thing could be; that the man had made a mistake or was joking with them. In vain did she try to calm them, and to soften them by her entreaties; they turned away, and had only one reply to make:

"His name, his name!"

When she saw that her figure was altering, she was at length convinced, she behaved like an imprisoned animal, did not speak, cowered motionless in the darkest corners, and did not even rebel at the blows which marked her pale, passive face. She carefully thought over every minute in the past few months, and did her utmost to fill up the voids in her memory, and at last she guessed who the guilty person was.

Then, in despair, she scribbled on a scrap of paper:

"I swear to you, my dear parents, that I have nothing to reproach myself with. The old doctor treated me so strangely, that I often felt inclined to run out of the consulting-room. One day he put me to sleep, and perhaps it was he who—"

And not having the courage to finish the lamentable sentence, she went out and drowned herself. The parents had the doctor, who had forgotten all about it, arrested, and in his examination he confessed the crime.

With an evil look on her face, such as I had never seen before, and with vibrating nostrils, Elaine exclaimed in a hard voice:

"To think that such a monster was not sent to the guillotine!"

Can she also have suffered the same thing?

15

But unless Elaine was a monster of wickedness, unless she had no heart, and knew how to lie and to deceive as well as a girl whose only pleasure consists in making all those who are captivated by her play the laughable part of dupes,—unless that mask of youth concealed a most polluted soul,—if there had been any unhappy episode in her life, if she had endured the horrors of violation, and gone through all the misery of desolation, fear, and shame, would not something visible, something intelligible, attacks of low spirits, of gloom, and of disgust with everything have remained, to show the progress of some mysterious malady, a gradual weakening of the brain and the enlargement of an incurable wound?

She would have cried occasionally, would have been absent-minded, confused when spoken to. She would scarcely have taken any interest in anything that happened, either at home or elsewhere. Kisses would have become a torture to her, and would have only excited a fever of revolt in her inanimate being.

I fancy that I can see such a victim of inexorable Destiny, a mentally consumptive woman whose days are numbered, and who knows it. She smiles feebly when anyone tries to get her out of her torpor, to amuse her and to instil a little hope into her soul. Such a victim does not speak, but remains sitting silently at a window for whole days together, making one think that her large, dreamy eyes are looking at strange sights in the depths of the sky, and see a long, attractive highway there. But Elaine, on the contrary, thought of nothing but of amusing herself, of enjoying life and of laughing, adding all the tricks of a girl who has just left school to the seductive grace of a young woman. She carried men away; she was most seductive, and loving seemed to be her life. She thought of nothing but of little *coquettish* acts that made her more adorable, and of those tender innuendoes that triumph over everything, that bring men to their knees and captivate them.

It was thus that I formerly dreamed of the woman who was to be my wife, and this was the manner in which I looked on married life. Now this perpetual joy irritates me like a challenge, like some piece of insolent boasting, and the lips that seek mine, and offer themselves so alluringly and coaxingly to me, sadden and torture me as if they breathed nothing but a Lie.

Ah! If she had been the lover of another man before marriage, if she had belonged to someone else besides me, it could only have been from love, without altogether knowing what she wanted or what she was doing! And, now, because she had acquired a name by marriage, because she had accidentally extricated herself from that misadventure and had won the game, she fancied that I had not perceived anything, that I adored her and was hers absolutely.

How wretched I was! Should I never be able to escape from that night which was growing darker and darker, which was imprisoning me, driving me mad, and raising an increasing and impenetrable barrier between Elaine and me? Would she not, in the end, be the stronger—she whom I loved so dearly? Would not she enfold me in so much love, that at last I should again find my lost happiness as in a calm, sunlit haven? Should I not forget this horrible nightmare when I fell on my knees before her beauty, with a contrite heart and pricked by remorse, happy to give myself to her forever, altogether and more passionately than at the divine period of our betrothal ?

16

Even the sight of our bedroom became painful to me. I was frightened of it; I was uncomfortable there, and felt a kind of repulsion in going there. It seemed to me as if Elaine were repeating a part that someone else had taught her, and I almost hoped that in a moment of forgetfulness she would allow her secret to escape her, and pronounce some name that was not mine. I used to lie awake, with my ears on the alert, in the hope that she might betray herself in her sleep and murmur some revealing word that recalled the past, and my temples would throb and my whole body tremble with excitement.

But when this was over and I saw her sleeping as peacefully as a little girl tired with playing, with parted lips and dishevelled hair, and measured the full extent of the stupidity of my hatred and of the sacrilegious madness of my jealousy, my heart would soften and I would fall into such a state of profound and absolute distress that I might have died of it. Large drops of cold perspiration would course down my cheeks and tears fall from my eyes, and I would get up, so that my sobs might not disturb her rest and wake her.

As this could not continue, however, I told her one day that I felt so exhausted and ill that I should prefer to sleep in my own room. She appeared to believe me, and merely said:

"As you please, my dear!" but her blue eyes suddenly assumed such an anxious, such a grieved look, that I turned my head aside so as not to see them.

17

I was again in the old house—*and without her*—in the old house where Elaine used to spend all her holidays, in that room where the shutters had not been opened since our departure, seven months ago.

Why did I go where the calm of the country, the solitude, and my recollections irritated me and recalled my trouble—where I suffered even more than I did in Paris, and where I thought of Elaine every moment, seeming to see and hear her in a species of hallucination ?

What did her letters that I had taken out of the writing table that she had used as a girl, what did the ball cards which were stuck round the looking- glass in which she used to admire herself formerly, what did her dresses, her dressing gowns, and the dusty furniture whose repose my trembling hands violated tell me? Nothing, and always nothing!

At table, I used to speak with the worthy couple, who had never left the mansion and appeared to look upon themselves as its second masters, with the apparent good nature of a man who was in love with his wife—who wished to speak about her alone, who took an interest in the smallest detail of her childhood and youth. With the jovial familiarity with which peasants talk when a few glasses of white wine have loosened their tongues, they would talk about the girl whom they loved as if she had been their child. At other times I used to question the farmers when they came to settle their accounts.

Had Elaine been restrained like so many girls were; did she like the country, were the peasants fond of her, and had she shown any preference for one or the other? Were many people invited for the shooting, and had she visited much with the other ladies in the neighbourhood?

They drank, with their elbows resting on the table in front of me, uttered her praises in voices as monotonous as a spinning wheel, lost themselves in endless, senseless chatter which made me yawn in spite of myself, telling me her girlish tricks, which certainly did not disclose what I wanted, the traces of that first love, that perilous flirtation, that foolish escapade in which Elaine might have been seduced.

Men and women, old and young, spoke of her with something like devotion. All said how kind and charitable she was, merry as a bird on a bright day; they recalled how she pitied their wretchedness and their troubles, and was still a young girl in spite of her long dresses, fearing nothing, and how even the animals loved her.

She was almost always alone, and was never troubled with any companions; she seemed to shun the house and hide herself in the park when the bell announced some unexpected visit, and when one of her aunts, Madame de Pleissac, said to her one day: "Do you think that you will ever find a husband with your standoffish manners?" she replied with a burst of laughter: "Oh! Very well, then, auntie, I shall do without one!"

She had never given a handle to gossip or to slander, and had not flirted with the best-looking young men in the neighbourhood, any more than she had with the officers who stayed at the chateau during the manoeuvres, or the neighbours who came to see her parents. Some of them, even old men whom years of work had bent like vine-stocks, and had tanned like the leather bottles used by caravans in the East, used to say with tears in their dim eyes:

"Ah! When you married our young lady, we all said that there would not be a happier man in the whole world than you!"

Ought I to have believed them ? Were they not simple, frank souls, ignorant of wiles and of lies, who had no interest in deceiving me, who had lived near Elaine while she was growing up to womanhood, and had been familiar with her?

Could I be the only one who doubted Elaine, the only one who accused her and suspected her, I who loved her so madly, I whose only hope, only desire, only happiness she was ? May Heaven guide me in this wilderness in which I have lost my way, where I am calling for help and where my misery is increasing every day, and grant me the infinite pleasure of being able to enjoy her caresses without evil doubts and to be able to love her as she loves me. And if I must expiate my faults, and this infamous doubt which I am ashamed of not being immediately able to cast from me, if I must pay for my unmerited happiness with usury, I hope that I may be given over to death, provided only that I may belong to her, idolize her, believe in her kisses, believe in her beauty and in her love, for one hour, or for even a few moments!

18

Today I suddenly remembered a funny evening I once spent as a bachelor, at Madame d'Ecoussens, where all of us, some with secret and insurmountable agony, and others with absolute indifference, went into a small room where a female professor of palmistry, who was then in vogue, and whose name I have forgotten, had installed herself.

When it came my turn to sit opposite to her, as if going to confession, she took my hands into her long, slender fingers, felt them, squeezed them, and massaged them, as if they had been a lump of wax which she was about to model into shape.

Severely dressed in black, neither old nor young, with a pensive face, thin lips, and almost copper-coloured eyes, this woman had something commanding, imperious, disturbing about her, and I must confess that my heart beat more violently then usual when she looked at the lines in my left hand through a strong magnifying glass, where the mysterious characters of some satanic design appear, and form a capital M.

She was very interesting, occasionally discovered fragments of my past and gave mysterious hints, as if her looks were following the strange roads of Destiny in those unequal, confused curves. She told me in brief words that I should have and had had some opportunities, that I was wasting my physical, more than my moral, strength in all kinds of love affairs that did not last long, and that the day I really loved or when, to use her expression, I was fairly caught, would be to me the prelude of intense suffering, a real *via crucis* and the beginning of an illness of which I should never be cured. Then, as she examined my line of life, that which surrounds the thick part of the thumb, the lady in black suddenly grew gloomy, frowned, appeared unwilling to continue my horoscope, and said very quickly:

"Your line of life is magnificent, *Monsieur*; you will live to be sixty at least, but take care not to spend your energy too freely or to use it immoderately; beware of strong emotions and of any passionate crisis, for I remark a gap there in the full vigour of your age, and that gap, that incurable malady which I mentioned to you, in the line of your heart—"

I mastered myself, in order not to smile, and took my leave of her, but everything that she foretold has been realized, and I dare not look at that sinister gap which she saw in my line of life—*for that gap can only mean madness!*

Madness, my poor, dear, adored Elaine!

19

I became as bad and spiteful as if the spirit of hatred had possession of me. I envied those whose life was too happy, and who had no cares to trouble them. I could not conceal my pleasure when one of those domestic dramas occurred, in which hearts bleed and are broken, in which odious treachery and bitter sufferings are brought to light.

Divorce proceedings with their miserable episodes, with the wranglings of the lawyers and the unhappiness that they revealed, exposing the vanity of dreams, the tricks of women, the lowness of some minds, the foul animal nature that sits and slumbers in most hearts, attracted me like a delightful play, a piece which rivets one from the first to the last act. I listened greedily to passionate letters, those mad prayers whose secrets some lawyer reads aloud in a mocking tone, and gives out to the bench and to the public, who have come to be amused or to be excited, and to stare at the victims of love.

I followed those romances of adultery which were unfolded chapter by chapter, in the brutal reality of things that had actually occurred, and for the first time I forgot my own unhappiness in them. Sometimes the husband and wife were there, as if they wished to defy each other, to meet in some last encounter, feverishly watching each other, devouring each other with their eyes, hiding their grief and their misery. Sometimes again, the lover or the mistress would be there, would tear their gloves in rage, wishing to defend their love, to bring forward accusations in their turn, tell the advocate that he was lying, threaten and revile him with all the fury raging in them. Friends, however, would restrain them, would whisper something to them in a low voice, press their hands in sympathy, and try to appease them.

It seemed as if I were looking at a heap of ruins, or breathing the odour of an ambulance in which dying men were groaning, and that these unhappy people were assuaging my trouble somewhat by taking a share of it.

I used to read the advertisements in the Agony Columns in the newspapers, where the same exalted phrases used to recur, the same despairing *adieux*, earnest requests for a meeting, echoes of past affection, and vain vows. All this relieved me, vaguely appeased me, and made me think less about myself—that hateful, incurable *ego* whom I longed to destroy!

20

As the heat was very oppressive, and there was not a breath of wind after dinner, Elaine wanted to go for a drive in the Bois de Boulogne. So we drove in the victoria toward the bridge at Suresne.

It was getting late, and the dark drives looked liked deserted labyrinths; cool retreats where one would have liked to have lingered, where the very rustle of the leaves seemed to whisper amorous temptations, where there was seduction in the softness of the air and in the infinite music of the silence.

Occasionally, lights were to be seen among the trees. The crescent of the new moon shone like a half-opened gold bracelet in the quiet sky, and the green sward, the copses, and the small lakes, which gave an uncertain reflection of the surrounding objects, came into sight suddenly, out of the shade, and the intoxicating smell of the hay and of the flower beds rose from the earth as if from a sachet.

We did not speak, but the jolting of the carriage occasionally brought us quite close together, and as if attracted by some irresistible force, I turned to Elaine and saw that her eyes were full of tears, that she was very pale, and my whole body trembled when I looked at her. Suddenly, as if she could not bear the tension any longer, she threw her arms round my neck, and with her lips almost touching mine, she said:

"Why do you not love me any longer? Why do you make me so unhappy? What have I done to you, Jacques?"

She was at my mercy, she was under the charm of one of those moonlight nights which unbrace women's nerves, make them languid, leave them without a will and without any strength, and I thought that she was going to tell me everything and to confess everything to me? I had to steel myself against kissing those sweet coaxing lips, and replied coldly:

"Do you not know, Elaine? Did you not think that sooner or later I should discover everything that you have been trying to hide from me?"

She sat up in terror, repeating as if she were in a daze:

"What have I been trying to hide from you?"

I had said too much, but was bound to go on to the end—to finish, even though I repented of it ever afterward—and amid the noise of the carriage I said in a hoarse voice:

"Is it not your fault if I have become estranged from you, shall not I be the only one to be unhappy, I who loved you so dearly, who believed in you, and whom you have deceived and condemned to take another man's mistress?"

Elaine closed my mouth with my fingers, and panting, with

dilated eyes and with such a pale face that I thought she was go-ing to faint, she said hoarsely:

"Be quiet, be quiet, you are frightening me—frightening me as if you were a madman—"

Her words froze me, and I shivered as if some phantoms were appearing among the trees and showing me the place that had been marked out for me by Destiny. I felt inclined to jump from the carriage and to run to the river which was calling to me from yonder in maternal tones, inviting me to an eternal sleep. But Elaine called out to the coachman:

"We will go home, Firmin; drive as fast as you can!"

We did not exchange another word. During the whole drive Elaine sobbed convulsively, though she tried to hide the sound with her pocket handkerchief, and I understood that it was all finished,—*that I had killed our love.*

21

Yes, all was finished, and stupidly finished, without the deci-sive explanation, through which I should find strength to escape from a hateful yoke, and to repudiate the woman who had al-lured me with false caresses, and no longer ought to bear my name.

It was either that, or else—who knows?—the happiness, the peace, the love which was not troubled by any evil after-thoughts, that absolute love that I dreamed of between Elaine and myself when I asked for her hand, and of which I was still continually dreaming with the despair of a condemned soul far from Paradise, from which I was suffering, and which would kill me.

She had prevented me from speaking; with her trembling hand she had checked that flow of frenzied words which were about to come from my pained heart, those terrible accusations which an imperious, resistless force incited me to utter; and the terrified words which escaped from her pale lips froze me again, and penetrated to my marrow like some piercing wind.

In spite of it all, I was in full possession of my reason; I was not in a passion, and I could not have looked like a fool.

What could she have seen unusual in my eyes that frightened her, what inflections were there in my voice for such an idea suddenly to arise in her brain? Suppose she had not made a mistake, suppose I no longer knew what I was saying nor what I was doing, and really had that terrible malady that she had mentioned, and which I cannot repeat!

It seems now that I can see myself in a mirror of anguish, altogether changed—that my head is a complete void at times. Then it becomes resonant and is struck violent, prolonged blows with a heavy clapper, as if it were a bell. It is filled with tumultuous, deafening vibrations, with loud tocsins, and with monotonous peals succeeded by the silence of the grave.

And the voice of recollection, a voice which tells me Elaine's mysterious history, which speaks to me only of her, which recalls that initial night, that strange night of happiness and of grief, when I doubted her fidelity, when I doubted her heart as well as I did herself, passes slowly through this silence all at once, like the voice of distant music:

"Alas! Suppose she had never fallen!"

22

I must be an object of hatred to her. I left home without writing her a line, without trying to see her, without wishing her goodbye. She may pity me or she may hate me, but she certainly does not love me any longer. I have myself buried that love, for which I would formerly have given my whole life. As she is young and pretty, however, Elaine will soon console herself for these passing troubles with some soul that is the shadow of her own, and will replace me, if she has not done that already, seeking her happiness in adultery.

What are she and her lover plotting? What will they do to prevent me from interfering with them? What snares will they set for me so that I may end my miserable life in some dungeon, from which there is no release?

But that is impossible, it can never be; Elaine belongs to me altogether and forever, she is my property, my chattel, my happiness. I adore her, I want her all to myself, *even though she be guilty*, and I will never leave her again for a moment. I will still cling to her petticoats, I will roll at her feet, and ask her pardon, for I thirst for her kisses and her love.

Tonight in a few hours, I shall be with her, I shall go into *our* room and lie in *our* bed, and I will cover the cheeks of my fair-haired darling with such kisses that she will no longer think me mad. But if she cries out, if she defends herself and spurns me, I shall kill her; I have made up my mind to that

I feel that I shall kill her with the Arab knife that is on one of the console-tables, in our room, among other knickknacks. I see the spot where I shall plunge the sharp blade, in the nape of her neck, which is covered with little, soft, pale, golden curls, of the same colour as the hair of her head. It attracted me so at one time, during the chaste period of our engagement, that I used to wish to bite it. as if it had been a plum. I shall do it someday in the country, just when she is bathed in a ray of sunlight, dazzling in her pink muslin dress—some day on a towing-path, when the nightingales are singing, and the dragon-flies, in their blue and silver splendour, are flying about.

There, there I shall skilfully plunge it in up to the hilt, like those who know how to kill.

23

And after I had killed her, what then?

As the judges would not be able to explain such an extraordinary crime to their satisfaction, they would of course say that I was mad. Medical men would examine me, and would immediately agree that I ought at once to be kept under supervision, taken care of, and placed in a lunatic asylum.

And for years, perhaps,—because I was strong, and because such a vigorous animal as I would survive the calamity intact, although intellect might give way,—I should remain a prey to these *chimeras*, to the fixed idea of her lies, her impurity, and her shame. It would be my one recollection, and I should suffer unceasingly.

I am writing all this perfectly coolly and in full possession of my reason; I have perfect prescience of what my resolve entails, and of this blind rush toward death. I feel that my very minutes are numbered, and that I no longer have anything in my head but fire, except a few particles of what used to be a brain.

Just as a short time ago, I should certainly have murdered Elaine, if she had been with me—when invisible hands seemed to be pushing me toward her, inaudible voices ordering me to commit that murder—it is most probable that I shall have another crisis, and will there be any awakening from that?

Ah! It will be a thousand times better, since Destiny has left me a half-open door, to escape from life before it is too late, before the free, sane, strong man that I am at present becomes the most pitiable, the most destructive, the most dangerous of human wrecks!

May all these notes of my misery fall into Elaine's hands some day, may she read them to the end, pity and absolve me, and for a long time mourn for me!

(Here ends Jacques's journal.)

Francis
A.k.a. Madam Cocotte

We were going out of the asylum when I perceived in one corner of the courtyard a tall, thin man, who was forever calling an imaginary dog. He would call out, with a sweet and tender voice: "Cocotte, my little Cocotte, come here, Cocotte, come here, my beauty," striking his leg, as one does to attract the attention of an animal. I asked the doctor what the matter was with the man. "Oh! that is an interesting case," said he, "he is a coachman named Francis, and he became insane from drowning his dog."

I insisted upon his telling me the story. The most simple and humble things sometimes strike most to our hearts.

And here is the adventure of this man which was known solely to a groom, his comrade.

In the suburbs of Paris lived a rich, middle-class family. Their villa was in the midst of a park, on the bank of the Seine. Their coachman was this Francis, a country boy, a little awkward, but of good heart, simple and easily duped.

When he was returning one evening to his master's house, a dog began to follow him. At first he took no notice of it, but the persistence of the beast in walking on his heels caused him finally to turn around. He looked to see if he knew this dog. No, he had never seen it before.

The dog was frightfully thin and had great hanging dugs. She trotted behind the man with a woeful, famished look, her tail between her legs, her ears close to her head, and stopped when he stopped, starting again when he started.

He tried to drive away this skeleton of a beast: "Get out! If you want to save yourself—Go, now! *Hou! Hou!*" She would run away a few steps and then sit down waiting; then, when the coachman started on again, she followed behind him.

He made believe pick up stones. The animal fled a little way with a great shaking of the flabby *mammillae*, but followed again as soon as the man turned his back.

Then the coachman, Francis, took pity and called her. The dog approached timidly, her back bent in a circle, and all the ribs showing under the skin. The man smoothed these project-ing bones and, moved by pity, for the misery of the beast, said: "Come along, then!" Immediately the tail began to move; she felt the welcome, the adoption; and instead of staying at her new master's heels, she began to run ahead of him.

He installed her on some straw in his stable, then ran to the kitchen in search of bread. When she had eaten her fill, she went to sleep, curled up, ring-like.

The next day the coachman told his master, who allowed him to keep the animal. She was a good beast, intelligent and faithful, affectionate and gentle.

But immediately they discovered in her a terrible fault. She was inflamed with love from one end of the year to the other. In a short time she had made the acquaintance of every dog about the country, and they roamed about the place day and night. With the indifference of a girl, she shared her favours with them, feigning to like each one best, dragging behind her a veritable mob composed of many different models of the barking race, some as large as a fist, others as tall as an ass. She took them to walk through routes with interminable courses, and when she stopped to rest in the shade, they made a circle about her and looked at her with tongues hanging out.

The people of the country considered her a phenomenon; they had never seen anything like it. The veterinary could not understand it.

When she returned to the stable in the evening, the crowd

of dogs made siege for proprietorship. They wormed their way through every crevice in the hedge which inclosed the park, devastated the flower beds, broke down the flowers, dug holes in the urns, exasperating the gardener. They would howl the whole night about the building where their friend lodged, and nothing could persuade them to go away.

In the daytime, they even entered the house. It was an invasion, a plague, a calamity. The people of the house met at any moment, on the staircase, and even in the rooms, little yellow pug dogs with tails decorated, hunting dogs, bulldogs, wolf hounds with filthy skin, vagabonds without life or home, beside some new-world enormities which frightened the children.

All the unknown dogs for ten miles around came, from one knew not where, and lived, no one knew how, disappearing all together.

Nevertheless, Francis adored Cocotte. He had named her Cocotte, "without malice, sure that she merited her name." And he repeated over and over again: "This beast is a person. It only lacks speech."

He had a magnificent collar in red leather made for her, which bore these words, engraved on a copper plate: "Mademoiselle Cocotte, from Francis, the coachman."

She became enormous. She was as fat as she had been thin, her body puffed out, under which hung always the long, swaying *mammillae*. She had fattened suddenly and walked with difficulty, the paws wide apart, after the fashion of people that are too large, the mouth open for breath, wide open as soon as she tried to run.

She showed a phenomenal fecundity, producing, four times a year, a litter of little animals, belonging to all varieties of the canine race. Francis, after having chosen the one he would leave her "to take the milk," would pick up the others in his stable apron and pitilessly throw them into the river.

Soon the cook joined her complaints to those of the gardener. She found dogs under her kitchen range, in the cupboards, and in the coal bin, always fleeing whenever she encountered them.

The master, becoming impatient, ordered Francis to get rid of Cocotte. The man, inconsolable, tried to place her somewhere. No one wanted her. Then he resolved to lose her, and put her in charge of a wagoner who was to leave her in the country the other side of Paris, beyond De Joinville-le-Pont.

That same evening Cocotte was back.

It became necessary to take measures. For the sum of five *francs*, they persuaded a cook on the train to Havre to take her. He was to let her loose when they arrived.

At the end of three days, she appeared again in her stable, harassed, emaciated, exhausted.

The master was merciful, and insisted on nothing further.

But the dogs soon returned in greater numbers than ever, and were more provoking. And as they were giving a great dinner, one evening, a stuffed chicken was carried off by a dog, under the nose of the cook, who dared not dispute the right to it.

This time the master was angry, and calling Francis to him, said hotly: "If you don't kick this beast into the water tomorrow morning, I shall put you out, do you understand?"

The man was undone, but he went up to his room to pack his trunk, preferring to leave the place. Then he reflected that he would not be likely to get in anywhere else, dragging this unwelcome beast behind him; he remembered that he was in a good house, well paid and well fed; and he said to himself that it was not worth while giving up all this for a dog. He enumerated his own interests and finished by resolving to get rid of Cocotte at dawn the next day.

However, he slept badly. At daybreak he was up; and, preparing a strong cord, he went in search of the dog. She arose slowly, shook herself, stretched her limbs, and came to greet her master. Then his courage failed and he began to stroke her tenderly, smoothing her long ears, kissing her on the muzzle, lavishing upon her all the loving names that he knew.

A neighbouring clock struck six; he could no longer hesitate. He opened the door; "Come," said he. The beast wagged her tail, understanding only that she was to go out.

They reached the bank and chose a place where the water seemed deepest. Then he tied one end of the cord to the beautiful leather collar, and taking a great stone, attached it to the other end. Then he seized Cocotte in his arms and kissed her furiously, as one does when he is taking leave of a person. Then he held her tight around the neck, fondling her and calling her "My pretty Cocotte, my little Cocotte," and she responded as best she could, growling with pleasure.

Ten times he tried to throw her in, and each time his heart failed him.

Then, abruptly, he decided to do it, and, with all his force, hurled her as far as possible. She tried at first to swim, as she did when taking a bath, but her head, dragged by the stone, went under again and again. She threw her master a look of despair, a human look, battling, as a person does when drowning. Then, before the whole body sank, the hind paws moved swiftly in the water; then they disappeared also.

For five minutes bubbles of air came to the surface, as if the river had begun to boil. And Francis, haggard, excited, with heart palpitating, believed he saw Cocotte writhing in the slime. And he said to himself, with the simplicity of a peasant: "What does she think of me by this time, that beast?"

He almost became idiotic. He was sick for a month, and each night, saw the dog again. He felt her licking his hands; he heard her bark.

It was necessary to call a physician. Finally he grew better; and his master and mistress took him to their estate near Rouen.

There he was still on the bank of the Seine. He began to take baths. Every morning he went down with the groom to swim across the river.

One day, as they were amusing themselves splashing in the water, Francis suddenly cried out to his companion:

"Look at what is coming toward us. I am going to make you taste a cutlet."

It was an enormous carcass, swelled and stripped of its hair, its paws moving forward in the air, following the current.

Francis approached it, making his jokes:

"What a prize, my boy! My! But it is not fresh! It is not thin, that is sure!"

And he turned about, keeping at a distance from the great, putrefying body.

Then, suddenly, he kept still and looked at it in strange fashion. He approached it again, this time near enough to touch. He examined carefully the collar, took hold of the leg, seized the neck, made it turn over, drew it toward him, and read upon the green copper that still adhered to the discoloured leather: "Mademoiselle Cocotte, from Francis, the coachman,"

The dead dog had found her master, sixty miles from their home!

He uttered a fearful cry, and began to swim with all his might toward the bank, shouting all the way. And when he reached the land, he ran, all bare, through the country. He was mad!

Magnetism

It was at the close of a dinner-party of men, at the hour
of endless cigars and incessant sips of brandy, amid the smoke
and the torpid warmth of digestion, and the slight confusion of
heads generated by such a quantity of eatables and by the ab-
sorption of so many different liquors. Those present were talking about magnetism, about Donato's tricks, and about Doctor
Charcot's experiences. All of a sudden, those men, so sceptical,
so happy-go-lucky, so indifferent to religion of every sort, began
telling stories about strange occurrences, incredible things which
nevertheless had really happened, they contended, falling back
into superstitions, beliefs, clinging to these last remnants of the
marvellous, becoming devotees to this mystery of magnetism,
defending it in the name of science. There was only one person
who smiled, a vigorous young fellow, a great pursuer of girls of
light behaviour, and a hunter also of frisky matrons, in whose
mind there was so much incredulity about everything that he
would not even enter upon a discussion of such matters.

He repeated with a sneer:

"Humbug! humbug! humbug! We need not discuss Donato,
who is merely a very smart juggler. As for M. Charcot, who is
said to be a remarkable man of science, he produces on me the
effect of those story-tellers of the school of Edgar Allan Poe,
who go mad through constantly reflecting on queer cases of
insanity. He has set forth some nervous phenomena, which are
unexplained and inexplicable; he makes his way into that unknown region which men explore every day, and not being able

to comprehend what he sees, he remembers perhaps too well the explanations of certain mysteries given by priests. Besides,. I would like to hear him speaking on these subjects; that would be quite a different thing from your repetition of what he says."

The words of the unbeliever were listened to with a kind of pity, as if he had blasphemed in the midst of an assembly of monks.

One of these gentlemen exclaimed:

"And yet miracles were performed in former days."

But the other replied: "I deny it. Why cannot they be performed any longer?"

Thereupon, each man referred to some fact, or some fantastic presentiment, or some instance of souls communicating with each other across space, or some case of secret influences produced by one being of another. And they asserted, they maintained, that these things had actually occurred, while the sceptic went on repeating energetically: "Humbug! humbug! humbug!"

At last he rose up, threw away his cigar, and with his hands in his pockets said: "Well, I, too, am going to relate to you two stories, and then I will explain them to you. Here they are:

"In the little village of Etretat, the men, who are all seafaring folk, go every year to Newfoundland to fish for cod. Now, one night the little son of one of these fishermen woke up with a start, crying out that his father was dead. The child was quieted, and again he woke up exclaiming that his father was drowned. A month later the news came that his father had, in fact, been swept off the deck of his smack by a billow. The widow then remembered how her son had awaked and spoken of his father's death. Everyone said it was a miracle, and the affair caused a great sensation. The dates were compared, and it was found that the accident and the dream had very nearly coincided, whence they drew the conclusion that they had happened on the same night and at the same hour. And there is the mystery of magnetism."

The story-teller stopped suddenly.

Thereupon, one of those who had heard him, much affected by the narrative, asked:

"And can you explain this?"

"Perfectly, *Monsieur*. I have discovered the secret. The circumstance surprised me and even embarrassed me very much; but I, you see, do not believe on principle. Just as others begin by believing, I begin by doubting; and when I don't at all understand, I continue to deny that there can be any telegraphic communication between souls, certain that my own sagacity will be enough to explain it. Well, I have gone on inquiring into the matter, and I have ended, by dint of questioning all the wives of the absent seamen, in convincing myself that not a week passes without one of themselves or their children dreaming and declaring when they wake that the father was drowned.

"The horrible and continual fear of this accident makes them always talk about it. Now, if one of these frequent predictions coincides, by a very simple chance, with the death of the person referred to, people at once declare it to be a miracle; for they suddenly lose sight of all the other predictions of misfortune that have remained unconfirmed. I have myself known fifty cases where the persons who made the prediction forgot all about it in a week afterward. But if, in fact, the man was dead, then the recollection of the thing is immediately revived, and people will be ready to believe in the intervention of God, according to some, and in magnetism, according to others."

One of the smokers remarked:

"What you say is right enough; but what about your second story?"

"Oh! my second story is a very delicate matter to relate. It is to myself it happened, and so I don't place any great value on my own view of the matter. One is never a good judge in a case where he is one of the parties concerned. At any rate, here it is:

"Among my acquaintances in society there was a young woman on whom I had never bestowed a thought, whom I had never even looked at attentively, never taken any notice of, as the saying is.

"I classed her among the women of no importance, though she was not quite bad-looking: in fact, she appeared to me to possess eyes, a nose, a mouth, some sort of hair—just a colourless type of countenance. She was one of those beings on whom one only thinks by accident, without taking any particular interest in the individual, and who never excites desire.

"Well, one night, as I was writing some letters by my own fireside before going to bed, I was conscious, in the midst of that train of sensual images that sometimes float before one's brain in moments of idle reverie, while I held the pen in my hand, of a kind of light breath passing into my soul, a little shudder of the heart, and immediately, without reason, without any logical connection of thought, I saw distinctly, saw as if I had touched her, saw from head to foot, uncovered, this young woman for whom I had never cared save in the most superficial manner when her name happened to recur to my mind. And all of a sudden I discovered in her a heap of qualities which I had never before observed, a sweet charm, a fascination that made me languish; she awakened in me that sort of amorous uneasiness which sends you in pursuit of a woman. But I did not remain thinking of her long. I went to bed and was soon asleep. And I dreamed.

"You have all had these strange dreams which render you masters of the impossible, which open to you doors that cannot be passed through, unexpected joys, impenetrable arms!

"Which of us in these agitated, exciting palpitating slumbers, has not held, clasped, embraced, possessed with an extraordinary acuteness of sensation, the woman with whom our minds were occupied? And have you ever noticed what superhuman delight these good fortunes of dreams bestow upon us ? Into what mad intoxication they cast you! With what passionate spasms they shake you! With what infinite, caressing, penetrating tenderness they fill your heart for her whom you hold fainting and hot in that adorable and sensual illusion which seems so like reality!

"All this I felt with unforgettable violence. This woman was mine, so much mine that the pleasant warmth of her skin remained between my fingers, the odour of her skin remained in my brain, the taste of her kisses remained on my lips, the sound of her voice lingered in my ears, the touch of her clasp still clung to my side, and the burning charm of her tenderness still gratified my senses long after my exquisite but disappointing awakening.

"And three times the same night I had a renewal of my dream.

"When the day dawned, she beset me, possessed me, haunted my brain and my flesh to such an extent that I no longer remained one second without thinking of her.

"At last, not knowing what to do, I dressed myself and went to see her. As I went up the stairs to her apartment, I was so much overcome by emotion that I trembled and my heart panted; I was seized with vehement desire from head to foot.

"I entered the apartment. She rose up the moment she heard my name pronounced; and suddenly our eyes met in a fixed look of astonishment.

"I sat down.

"I uttered in a faltering tone some common-places which she seemed not to hear. I did not know what to say or to do. Then, abruptly, I flung myself upon her, seizing her with both arms; and my entire dream was accomplished so quickly, so easily, so madly, that I suddenly began to doubt whether I was really awake. She was, after this, my mistress for two years."

"What conclusion do you draw from it?" said a voice.

The story-teller seemed to hesitate.

"The conclusion I draw from it—well, by Jove, the conclusion is that it was just a coincidence! And, in the next place, who can tell? Perhaps it was some glance of hers which I had not noticed and which came back that night to me—one of those mysterious and unconscious evocations of memory which often bring before us things ignored by our own consciousness, unperceived by our minds!"

"Let that be just as you wish it," said one of his table-companions, when the story was finished, "but if you don't believe in magnetism after that, you are an ungrateful fellow, my dear boy!"

On the River

Last summer I rented a cottage on the banks of the Seine, several miles from Paris, and I used to go out to it every evening. After a while, I formed the acquaintance of one of my neighbours, a man between thirty and forty years of age, who really was one of the queerest characters I ever have met. He was an old boating-man, crazy on the subject of boats, and was always either in, or on, or by the water. Surely he must have been born in a boat, and probably he will die in one, some day, while taking a last outing.

One evening, as we were walking along the edge of the river, I asked him to tell me about some of his nautical experiences. Immediately his face lighted up, and he became eloquent, almost poetical, for his heart was full of an all-absorbing, irresistible, devouring passion—a love for the river.

"Ah!" said he, "how many recollections I have of the river that flows at our feet! You street-dwellers have no idea what the river really is. But let a fisherman pronounce the word. To him it means mystery, the unknown, a land of mirage and phantasmagoria, where odd things that have no real existence are seen at night and strange noises are heard; where one trembles without knowing the reason why, as when passing through a cemetery,—and indeed the river is a cemetery without graves.

"Land, for a fisherman, has boundaries, but the river, on moonless nights, appears to him unlimited. A sailor doesn't feel the same way about the sea. The sea is often cruel, but it roars and foams, it gives us fair warning; the river is silent and treacherous. It flows stealthily, without a murmur, and the eternal gentle motion of the water is more awful to me than the big ocean waves.

"Dreamers believe that the deep' hides immense lands of blue, where the drowned roll around among the big fish, in strange forests or in crystal caves. The river has only black depths, where the dead decay in the slime. But it's beautiful when the sun shines on it, and the waters splash softly on the banks covered with whispering reeds.

"In speaking of the ocean the poet says:

Oh! what tragic tales of the vast, blue deep,—
The vast blue deep prayerful mothers fear,—
The sad waves tell, when at night, we hear,
Their ceaseless moanings in our sleep!

"Well, I believe that the stories the slender reeds tell one another in their wee, silvery voices are even more appalling than the ghastly tragedies related by the roaring waves.

"But as you have asked me to relate some of my recollections, I will tell you a strange adventure that happened to me here, about ten years ago.

"Then, as now, I lived in old mother Lafon's house and a chum of mine, Louis Bernet, who since has given up boating, as well as his happy-go-lucky ways, to become a State Councilor, was camping out in the village of C—— , two miles away. We used to take dinner together every day, either at his place or at mine.

"One evening, as I was returning home alone, feeling rather tired, and with difficulty rowing the twelve-foot boat that I always took out at night, I stopped to rest a little while near that point over there, formed by reeds, about two hundred yards in front of the railway bridge. The weather was gorgeous; the moon shed a silvery light on the shining river, and the air was soft and still. The calmness of the surroundings tempted me, and I thought how pleasant it would be to fill my pipe here and smoke. The thought was immediately executed, and, laying hold of the anchor, I dropped it overboard. The boat, which was following the stream, slid to the end of the chain and came to a stop; I settled myself aft on a rug, as comfortably as I could. There was not a sound to be heard nor a movement to be seen, though sometimes I noticed the almost imperceptible rippling of the water on the banks, and watched the highest clumps of reeds, which at times assumed strange shapes that appeared to move.

"The river was perfectly calm, but I was affected by the extraordinary stillness that enveloped me. The frogs and toads, the nocturnal musicians of the swamps, were voiceless. Suddenly, at my right, a frog croaked. I started; it stopped, and all was silent. I resolved to light my pipe for distraction. But, strange to say, though I was an inveterate smoker I failed to enjoy it, and after a few puffs I grew sick and stopped smoking. Then I began to hum an air, but the sound of my voice depressed me.

"At last I lay down in the boat and watched the sky. For a while I remained quiet, but presently the slight pitching of the boat disturbed me. I felt as if it were swaying to and fro from one side of the river to the other, and that an invisible force or being was drawing it slowly to the bottom and then raising it to let it drop again. I was knocked about as if in a storm; I heard strange noises; I jumped up; the water was shining and all was still. Then I knew that my nerves were slightly shaken, and decided to leave the river. I pulled on the chain.

"The boat moved along, but presently I felt some resistance and pulled harder. The anchor refused to come up; it had caught in something at the bottom and remained stuck. I pulled and tugged but to no avail. With the oars I turned the boat around and forced her upstream, in order to alter the position of the anchor. This was all in vain, however, for the anchor did not yield; so in a rage, I began to shake at the chain, which wouldn't budge.

"I sat down discouraged, to ponder over my mishap. It was impossible to break the chain or to separate it from the boat, as it was enormous and was riveted to a piece of wood as big as my arm; but as the weather continued fine, I did not doubt but that some fisherman would come along and rescue me. The accident calmed me so much that I managed to remain quiet and smoke my pipe. I had a bottle of rum with me so I drank two or three glasses of it and began to laugh at my situation. It was so warm that it would not have mattered much had I been obliged to spend all night out of doors.

"Suddenly something jarred slightly against the side of the boat. I started, and a cold sweat broke over me from head to foot. The noise was due to a piece of wood drifting along with the current, but it proved sufficient to disturb my mind, and once more I felt the same strange nervousness creep over me. The anchor remained firm. Exhausted, I seated myself again.

"Meantime the river was covering itself with a white mist that lay close to the water, so that when I stood up neither the stream, nor my feet, nor the boat, were visible to me; l could distinguish only the ends of the reeds and, a little further away, the meadow, ashen in the moonlight, with large black patches formed by groups of Italian poplars reaching toward the sky. I was buried up to my waist in something that looked like a blanket of down of a peculiar whiteness; and all kinds of fantastic visions arose before me, I imagined that someone was trying to crawl into the boat, which I could no longer see and that the river hidden under the thick fog was full of strange creatures that were swimming all around me.

"I felt a horrible depression steal over me, my temples throbbed, my heart beat wildly, and, losing all control over myself, I was ready to plunge overboard and swim to safety. But this idea suddenly filled me with horror. I imagined myself lost in the dense mist, floundering about aimlessly among the reeds and water-plants, unable to find the banks of the river or the boat; and I felt as if I should certainly be drawn by my feet to the bottom of the dark waters. As I really should have had to swim against the current for at least five hundred yards before reaching a spot where I could safely land, it was nine chances to ten that, being unable to see in the fog, I should drown, although I was a fine swimmer.

"I tried to overcome my dread. I determined not to be afraid, but there was something in me besides my will and that something was faint-hearted. I asked myself what there was to fear; my courageous self railed at the other, the timid one; never before had I so fully realized the opposition that exists between the two beings we have in us; the one willing, the other resisting, and each one triumphing in turn. But this foolish and unaccountable fear was growing worse and worse, and was becoming positive terror. I remained motionless, with open eyes and straining ears, waiting. For what? I scarcely knew, but it must have been for something terrible. I believe that had a fish suddenly taken it into its head to jump out of the water, as frequently happens, I should have fallen in a dead faint. However, I managed to keep my senses after a violent effort to control myself. I took my bottle of brandy and again raised it to my lips.

"Suddenly I began to shout at the top of my voice, turning successively toward the four points of the horizon. After my throat had become completely paralyzed with shouting, I listened. A dog was barking in the distance.

"I drank some more rum and lay down in the bottom of the boat. I remained thus at least one hour, perhaps two, without shutting my eyes, visited by nightmares. I did not dare to sit up, though I had an insane desire to do so; I put it off from second to second, saying: 'Now then, I'll get up,' but I was afraid to move. At last I raised myself with infinite care as if my life depended on the slightest sound I might make, and peered over the edge of the boat. I was greeted by the most marvellous, stupendous sight that it is possible to imagine. It was a vision of fairyland, one of those phenomena that travellers in distant countries tell us about, but that we are unable to believe,

"The mist, which two hours ago hung over the water, had lifted and settled on the banks of the stream. It formed on each side an unbroken hill, six or seven yards in height, that shone in the moonlight with the dazzling whiteness of snow. Nothing could be seen but the flashing river, moving between the two white mountains, and overhead a full moon that illuminated the milky-blue sky.

"All the hosts of the water had awakened; the frogs were croaking dismally, while from time to time a toad sent its short, monotonous, and gloomy note to the stars. Strange to say, I was no longer frightened; I was surrounded by a landscape so utterly unreal that the strangest freaks of nature would not have surprised me at all.

"How long this situation lasted I am unable to tell, for I finally dozed off to sleep. When I awoke, the moon was gone and the sky was covered with clouds. The water splashed dismally, the wind was blowing, it was cold and completely dark. I finished the brandy and lay listening to the rustling of the reeds and the murmur of the river. I tried to see, but failed to distinguish the boat or even my hands, although I held them close to my eyes. The darkness, however, was slowly decreasing. Suddenly I thought I saw a shadow glide past me. I shouted to it and a voice responded: it was a fisherman. I called to him and told him of my plight. He brought his boat alongside mine and both began tugging at the chain. The anchor still would not yield.

" A cold, rainy day was setting in, one of those days that bring disaster and sadness. I perceived another boat, which we hailed. The owner added his strength to ours, and little by little the anchor gave way. It came up very slowly, laden with considerable weight. Finally a black heap appeared and we dragged it into my boat. It was the body of an old woman, with a big stone tied around her neck!"

The Spectre

A.k.a The Apparition / A Ghost / The Story of the Law-Suit

In speaking of a recent lawsuit, our conversation had turned on sequestration, and each of us, thereupon, had a story to tell—a story affirmed to be true. We were a party of intimate friends, who had passed a pleasant evening, now drawing to a close, in an old family residence in the Rue de Grenelle. The aged Marquis de la Tour-Samuel, bowed 'neath the weight of eighty-two winters, at last rose, and, leaning on the mantelpiece, said in somewhat trembling tones:

"I also know something strange, so strange that it has been a haunting memory all my life. It is now fifty-six years since the incident occurred, and yet not a month has passed in which I have not see it again in a dream, so great was and is the impression of fear it has left on my mind. For ten minutes I experienced such horrible fright that, ever since, a sort of constant terror has made me tremble at unexpected noises and objects half-seen gloom of night inspire me with a mad desire to take flight. In short, I am afraid of the dark!

"Ah, no! I would not have avowed that before having reached my present age! Now I can say anything. I have never receded before real danger. So at eighty-two years of age, I do not feel compelled to be brave over an imaginary danger.

"That affair upset me so completely, and caused me such lasting and mysterious and terrible uneasiness, that I never spoke of it to anyone. I will now tell it to you exactly as it happened, without any attempt at explanation.

"In July, 1827, I was in garrison at Rouen. One day, as I was walking on the quay, I met a man whom I thought I recognized, without being able to recall exactly who he was. Instinctively I made a movement to stop; the stranger perceived it and at once extended his hand.

"He was a friend to whom I had been deeply attached as a youth. For five years I had not seen him; he seemed to have aged half a century. His hair was quite white and he walked with a stoop as though completely worn out. He apparently comprehended my surprise, for he told me of the misfortune which had shattered his life.

"Having fallen madly in love with a young girl, he had married her, but after a year of more than earthly happiness she died suddenly of heart failure. He left his *château* on the very day of her burial and came to live at Rouen. There he still dwelt, more dead than alive, desperate and solitary, exhausted by grief, and so miserable he thought constantly of suicide.

"'Now that I have found you again,' he said, 'I will ask you to render me an important service. It is to go to my old home and get for me from the desk in my bedroom—our bedroom—some papers which I have greatly need. I cannot send a servant or an agent, as discretion and absolute silence are necessary. As for myself, nothing on earth would induce me to re-enter that house. I will give you the key of the room, which I myself locked on leaving, and the key of my desk—also a note to my gardener, telling him to open the *château* for you. But come and breakfast with me tomorrow and we will arrange all that.'

"I promised to do him the slight favour he asked. For that matter, it was nothing of a trip, his property being but a few miles distant from Rouen and easily reached in an hour on horseback,.

"At ten o'clock the following day I breakfasted, *tête-à-tête*, with my friend, but he scarcely spoke.

"He begged me to pardon him; the thought of the visit I was about to make to that room, the scene of his dead happiness, overwhelmed him, he said. He, indeed, seemed singularly agi-

155

tated and preoccupied, as though undergoing some mysterious mental struggle.

"At length he explained to me exactly what I had to do. It was very simple. I must take two packages of letters and a roll of papers from the first drawer on the right of the desk of which I had the key. He added: 'I need not beg you to refrain from glancing at them.'

"I was wounded at that remark and told him so somewhat sharply. He stammered: 'Forgive me, I suffer so,' and tears came to his eyes.

"At about one o'clock I took leave of him to accomplish my mission.

"'The weather was glorious, and I cantered over the turf, listening to the song of the larks and the rhythmical striking of my sword against my boot. Then I entered the forest and walked my horse. Branches of trees caressed my face as I passed, and now and then I caught a leaf with my teeth, from sheer gladness of heart at being alive and strong on such a radiant day.

"As I approached the *château* I took from my pocket the letter I had for the gardener, and was astonished at finding it sealed. I was so irritated that I was about to turn back without having fulfilled my promise, but reflected that I should thereby display undue susceptibility. My friend's state of mind might easily have caused him to close the envelope without noticing that he did so.

"The manor seemed to have been abandoned for twenty years. The open gate was dropping from its hinges, the walks were overgrown with grass and the flower beds were no longer distinguishable.

"The noise I made by tapping loudly on a shutter brought out an old man from out a door nearby, who seemed stunned with astonishment at seeing me. On receiving my letter, he read it, reread it, turned it over and over, looked me up and down, put the paper in his pocket and finally said:

"'Well, what is it you wish?'

"I replied shortly:

"'You ought to know, since you have just read your master's orders. I wish to enter the *château*.'

"He seemed overcome. 'Then you are going in—in her room?'

"I began to lose patience and said sharply: 'Of course; but is that your affair?'

"He stammered in confusion: 'No—sir—but—but it has not been opened since—since the-death. If you will be kind enough to wait five minutes I will go to—to see if—'

"I interrupted him angrily: 'See here, what do you mean by your tricks? You know very well you cannot enter the room, since I have the key!'

"He no longer objected. 'Then, sir, I will show you the way.'

"'Show me the staircase and leave me. I'll find my way without you.'

"'But—sir—indeed—'

"This time I silenced him effectually, pushed him aside, and went into the house.

"I first traversed the kitchen, then two rooms occupied by the servant and his wife; next, by a wide hall, I reached the stairs, which I mounted, and recognized the door indicated by my friend.

"I easily opened it, and entered. The apartment was so dark that at first I could distinguish nothing. I stopped short, my nostrils penetrated by the disagreeable, mouldy odour of long-unoccupied rooms. Then as my eyes slowly became accustomed to the darkness I saw plainly enough a large and disordered bedroom, the bed without sheets but still retaining its mattresses and pillows, on one of which was a deep impression, as though an elbow or a head had recently rested there.

"The chairs all seemed out of place. I noticed that a door, doubtless that of a closet, had remained half open.

"I first went to the window, which I opened to let in the light, but the fastenings of the shutters had grown so rusty that I could not move them. I even tried to break them with my sword, but without success. As I was growing irritated over my useless efforts and could now see fairly well in the semi-darkness, I renounced the idea of getting more light, and went over to the writing desk.

"Seating myself in an armchair and, letting down the lid of the desk, I opened the designated drawer. It was full to the top. I needed but three packages, which I knew how to recognize, and began searching for them.

"I was straining my eyes in the effort to read the superscriptions when I seemed to hear, or, rather, feel, something rustle back of me. I paid no attention, believing that a draught from the window was moving some drapery. But in a minute or so another movement, almost imperceptible, sent a strangely disagreeable little shiver over my skin. It was so stupid to be affected, even slightly, that self-respect prevented my turning around. I had then found the second package I needed and was about to lay my hand on the third when a long and painful sigh, uttered just over my shoulder, made me bound like a madman from my seat and land several feet away. As I jumped I had turned about, my hand on the hilt of my sword, and, truly, had I not felt it at my side, I should have taken to my heels like a coward.

"A tall woman dressed in white, stood gazing at me from the back of the chair where I had been sitting an instant before.

"Such a shudder ran through all my limbs that I nearly fell backward. No one can understand unless he has felt it, that frightful, unreasoning terror! The mind becomes vague, the heart ceases to beat, the entire body grows as limp as a sponge.

"I do not believe in ghosts, nevertheless I completely gave way to a hideous fear of the dead, and I suffered, more in those few moments than in all the rest of my life from the irresistible anguish of supernatural fright. If she had not spoken I should have died perhaps! But she spoke, she spoke in a sweet, sad voice that set my nerves vibrating. I dare not say that I became master of myself and recovered my reason. No! I was so frightened that I scarcely knew what I was doing; but a certain innate pride, a remnant of soldierly instinct, made me, almost in spite of myself, maintain a creditable countenance.

She said: 'Oh, sir, you can render me a great service.'

"I wanted to reply, but it was impossible for me to pronounce a word. Only a vague sound came from my throat.

She continued: 'Will you? You can save me, cure me. I suffer frightfully. I suffer, oh! how I suffer!' and she slowly seated herself in the armchair, still looking at me.

"'Will you?' she said.

"I replied 'Yes' by a nod, my voice still being paralyzed.

"Then she held out to me a tortoise-shell comb and murmured:

"'Comb my hair, oh! comb my hair; that will cure me; it must be combed. Look at my head—how I suffer; and my hair pulls so!'

"Her hair, unbound, very long and very black, it seemed to me, hung over the back of the chair and touched the floor.

"Why did I receive that comb with a shudder, and why did I take in my hands the long, black hair which gave to my skin a gruesomely cold sensation, as though I were handling snakes? I cannot tell.

"That sensation has remained in my fingers, and I still tremble when I think of it.

"I combed her hair. I handled, I know not how, those icy locks. I twisted, knotted, and plaited, and braided them. She sighed and bowed her head, seeming to be happy. Suddenly she said, 'Thank you!' snatched the comb from my hands and fled by the door that I had noticed ajar.

"Left alone, I experienced for several seconds the horrible agitation of one who awakens from a nightmare. At length I regained my full senses. I ran to the window and with a mighty effort burst open the shutters, letting a flood of light into the room. Immediately I sprang to the door by which she had departed. I found it closed and immovable!

"Then the mad desire to flee came on me like a panic, the panic which soldiers know in battle. I seized the three packets of letters on the open secretary, ran from the room, dashed down the stairs, found myself outside, I know not how, and seeing my horse a few steps off, leaped into the saddle and galloped away.

"I stopped only when I reached Rouen and my lodgings. There I shut myself into my room in to reflect. For an hour I anxiously stove to convince myself that I had been the victim of an hallucination. I was about ready to believe that all I had seen was a vision, an error of my senses, when, as I approached the window, my eyes fell, by chance, upon my breast. Around the buttons of my uniform were entwined a quantity of long, black hairs. One by one, with trembling fingers, I plucked them off and threw them away.

"I then called my orderly, feeling unable to see my friend that day, wishing, also, to reflect more fully upon what I ought to tell him. I had his letters carried to him, for which he gave the messenger a receipt. He asked after me most particularly, and, on being told I was ill—had had a sunstroke—appeared exceedingly anxious. Next morning I went to him, determined to tell him the truth. He had gone out the evening before and had not yet returned. I called again during the day; my friend was still absent. After waiting a week longer without news of him, I advised the authorities and a judicial search was instituted. Not the slightest trace of his whereabouts or manner of disappearance was discovered.

"A minute inspection of the abandoned *château* revealed nothing of a suspicious character. There was no indication that a woman had been concealed there.

"After fruitless researches all further efforts were abandoned, and in the fifty-six years that have elapsed since then I have heard nothing more."

Mother Savage

1

I had not been back to Virelogne for fifteen years. I went there to hunt in the autumn, staying with my friend Serval, who had finally rebuilt his *chateau*, which had been destroyed by the Prussians. I was infinitely fond of that country. It is one of the delicious corners of the world which has a sensuous charm for the eyes. You love them with a physical love. We folk whom Mother Earth attracts, keep certain tender recollections, often keen, for certain springs, certain woods, certain ponds, certain hills, which have softened us like happy events. Sometimes even memory returns toward a forest nook, or a bit of shore, or a blossoming orchard, which had been visited just once, or some happy day, which has remained in our heart like those pictures of women seen in the street, on a spring morning, with a thin transparent costume, and which leave in our soul and flesh an unappeased, unforgettable desire, the sensation of balked happiness.

At Virelogne, I loved the whole region, sowed with little woods, and traversed by brooks which ran through the soil like veins bringing blood to the earth.

We fished in them for crabs, trout, and eels! Divine happiness! We could bathe in certain places and often found woodcock in the tall grass which grew on the banks of those little narrow streams.

I went, light as a goat, watching my two dogs forage in front of me. Serval, a hundred meters away, on my right, was beating up a field of Burgundian grass. I turned the thickets which formed the boundaries of the Sandes forest, and I perceived a hut in ruins.

Suddenly I recollected that I had seen it for the last time in 1869, neat, vine-clad, with chickens before the door. What is sadder than a dead house with its skeleton standing, dilapidated and sinister?

I recalled also that a woman had given me a glass of wine there, on a day of great fatigue, and that Serval had then told me the story of the inhabitants. The father, an old poacher, had been killed by the *gendarmes*. The son, whom I had seen before, was a tall dry lad who likewise passed for a ferocious killer of game. People called them the Savage family.

Was it a name or a nickname? I hailed Serval. He came with his long stork's stride.

I asked him: "What have become of those people?" And he told me this adventure.

2

"When war was declared, the younger Savage, who was then about thirty-three years old, enlisted, leaving his mother alone in the house. People did not pity her very much, the old woman, because they knew that she had money.

"So she stayed all alone in this isolated house, so far from the village, on the edge of the woods. She was not afraid, how-ever, being of the same race as her men, a strong, tall, thin, old woman, who seldom laughed, and with whom no one joked. The women of the fields do not laugh much, anyway. That is the men's business! They have a sad and narrow soul, leading a life which is gloomy and without bright spots.

"The peasant learns a little of the noisy gaiety of the pot-house, but his wife remains serious with a constantly severe ex-pression of countenance. The muscles of her face never learn the motions of laughter.

"Mother Savage continued her ordinary existence in her hut, which was soon covered with snow. She went to the village once a week to get bread and a little meat: then she returned to her cottage. As people spoke of wolves, she carried a gun on her shoulder, her son's gun, rusty, with the stock worn by the rubbing of the band. She was a curious sight, the tall Savage woman, a little bent, walking with slow strides through the snow, the barrel of the weapon extending beyond the black headdress, which imprisoned the white hair that no one had ever seen.

"One day the Prussians arrived. They were distributed among the inhabitants according to the means and resources of each. The old woman, who was known to be rich, had four soldiers billeted upon her.

"They were four big young men with fair flesh, fair beard, and blue eyes, grown stout in spite of the fatigues they had endured, and good fellows, even if they were in a conquered territory. Alone with this old woman, they showed themselves full of consideration for her, sparing her fatigue and expense as far as they could do so. All four might have been seen making their toilette at the well in the morning, in their shirt-sleeves, splashing their pink and white flesh, the flesh of the men of the north, in the water, on cold snowy days, while Mother Savage came and went preparing their soup. Then they might have been observed cleaning the kitchen, polishing the floor, chopping wood, peeling potatoes, washing the clothes, doing all the household duties, like four good sons around their mother.

"But she thought continually of her own son, the old mother, of her tall, thin boy with his crooked nose, brown eyes, and stiff moustache which made a cushion of black hair on his upper lip. She asked each of the soldiers installed at her hearth:

"'Do you know where his French regiment has gone, the Twenty-third Infantry? My boy is in it.'

"They answered: 'No, we don't know anything at all about it.'

"And understanding her grief and worry they, who had mothers at home, rendered her a thousand little services.

"She liked them very well, moreover, her four enemies: for peasants seldom have patriotic hatreds: that only belongs to the superior classes. The humble, those who pay the most because they are poor and because every new burden rests upon them, those who are killed in masses, who form the true food for cannon because they have numbers, those who, in a word, suffer most cruelly the atrocious miseries of the poor, because they are the weakest and the most unresisting, understand little of those *bellicose* ardours, the excitable points of honour and those pretended political combinations which exhaust two nations in six months, the victorious as well as the vanquished.

"They said in the country, speaking of Mother Savage's gendarmes:'There are four who have found a snug berth.'

"Now, one morning, as the old woman was alone in the house, she perceived afar off on the plain a man coming toward her home. Soon she recognized him: it was the postman, charged with distributing letters. He handed her a folded paper, and she drew from their case her spectacles which she used for sewing, and read:

Madame Savage, this notice is to give you sad news. Your son Victor was killed by a cannon-ball yesterday, which virtually cut him in two. I was very near, as we were side by side in the company and he had asked me to tell you the same day if anything happened to him.
I took his watch from his pocket to bring it to you when the war is finished.

I remain your friend,

Cesaire Rivot.

Soldier of the 2nd Class, in the 23rd of Foot

15 C. de M.— 16

"The letter was dated three weeks back.

"She did not weep. She stood motionless, astounded that she did not yet suffer.

"She thought:'Victor is killed!'

"Then little by little the tears came to her eyes and grief overwhelmed her heart. Ideas came to her one by one, frightful, torturing ideas. She would never kiss him again, her big boy, never again. The *gendarmes* had killed the father, the Prussians had killed the son. He had been cut in two by a cannon-ball. And it seemed to her that she saw the thing, the horrible thing: the head falling, the eyes open. while he gnawed the end of his big moustache, as he did in moments of anger.

"What had they done with his body afterward? If they had only sent her boy back to her, as they had her husband, with a bullet in his forehead.

"But she heard a sound of voices. It was the Prussians, who were returning from the village. She quickly hid the letter in her pocket, and received them tranquilly, with her ordinary expression of face, having had time to wipe her eyes.

"They were all four laughing, enchanted, for they were bringing back a fine rabbit, stolen no doubt, and they made a sign to the old woman that they were going to have something good to eat.

"She applied herself at once to the duties of preparing the breakfast; but when it came to killing the rabbit, her heart failed her. And yet it was not the first. One of the soldiers killed it with a blow behind the ears.

"Once the animal was dead, she took the red body out of the skin; but the sight of the blood which she touched, which covered her hands, of the warm blood which she felt getting cold and coagulating, made her tremble from head to foot; and she kept seeing her tall boy cut in two and all bleeding, like this still palpitating animal.

"She sat at the table with her Prussians, but she could not eat, not even a mouthful. They devoured the rabbit without occupying themselves with her. She looked at them aside without speaking, nursing an idea, with her countenance so impassive that they perceived nothing.

"Suddenly she said: 'I don't even know your names, and it is a month since we have been together.' They understood, not without difficulty, what she wished and gave her their names. That was not enough, she made them write them for her on a piece of paper, with the address of their families, and resting her spectacles on her large nose she scanned this unknown handwriting, then she folded the sheet and put it in her pocket, with the letter which told of the death of her son.

"When the meal was finished, she said to the men:

"'I am going to work for you.'

"And she began to carry straw to the garret in which they slept.

"They were astonished at this act. She explained to them that they would be less cold; and they assisted her. They piled the bundles of straw up to the roof, and thus they made for themselves a sort of big room with four walls of forage, warm and sweet-smelling, where they would sleep wonderfully.

"At dinner one of them was disturbed to see that Mother Savage did not eat anything. She asserted that she had cramps. Then she lighted a good fire to warm herself, and the four Germans climbed to their lodging by the ladder which they used every evening.

"As soon as the trapdoor was closed, the old woman took away the ladder, then she noiselessly opened the outside door and returned to get more bundles of straw, with which she filled the kitchen. She went out barefooted in the snow, so softly that the men heard nothing. From time to time she listened to the deep and uneven snores of the four sleep- ing soldiers. When she thought her preparations were sufficient, she threw into the fire one of the bundles of straw, and when it had ignited she piled it on the others, and then went out again and looked.

"A brilliant light illuminated in a few seconds all the interior of the cottage; then it became a frightful brazier, a gigantic, glowing furnace, whose gleams shone through the narrow window and cast a dazzling light upon the snow.

"Then a great cry came from the top of the house; there was a clamour of human shrieks, of heartrending appeals of anguish and terror. Then, the trapdoor having sunk down into the interior, a whirlwind of fire leaped through the attic, pierced the thatched roof, and ascended to the sky like the flame of a great torch; and the whole cottage was burning.

"Nothing more was heard inside but the crackling of the

flames, the crumbling of the walls, and the crashing of the beams. The roof suddenly fell in, and the glowing remnant of the house shot up into the air, amid a cloud of smoke, a great fountain of sparks.

"The white field, lighted up by the fire, glistened like a cloth of silver tinted with red.

"A bell in the distance began to ring. The old Savage woman stood erect before her ruined home, armed with a gun, her son's, for fear one of the men should escape.

"When she saw that her work was finished, she threw the weapon in the fire. A report rang out.

"The people arrived, peasants and Prussians.

"They found the woman sitting on the trunk of a tree, tranquil and satisfied.

"A German officer who could speak French like a Frenchman, asked her:

"'Where are the soldiers?'

"She stretched her thin arm toward the red mass of flames, which were now dying down, and answered in a strong voice:

"'They are in there!'

"All pressed around her. The Prussian asked:

"'How did the fire start?'

"She replied:

"'I set the house on fire.'

"They did not believe her, thinking that the sudden disaster had made her mad. Then, as everybody gathered around and listened, she related the whole thing from one end to the other, from the arrival of the letter to the last cry of the men, burning up with the house. She did not forget a single detail of what she had felt nor what she had done.

"When she had finished she drew two papers from her pocket, and, to distinguish them from the last gleams of the fire, she again put on her spectacles. Then she said, showing one of them: 'This is the death of Victor.' Showing the other, she added, nodding her head toward the red ruins: 'And this is the list of their names, so that someone may write the news home about them.'

"She quietly handed the white sheet to the officer, who took her by the shoulders, and she resumed:

"'You will write how it happened, and you will tell their relatives that it was I who did it, Victoire Simon, the Savage, don't forget.'

"The officer shouted some orders in German, to the soldiers; they seized her, and threw her against the still heated walls of the house. Then a squad of twelve men drew up in a rank opposite her, at a distance of twenty metres. She did not stir. She had understood. She waited.

"An order resounded, which was followed by a long report of muskets. One delayed shot went off all alone, after the others.

"The old woman did not fall. She sank down as if someone had mowed off her legs.

"The Prussian officer approached. She was cut almost in two, and in her shrivelled hand she held her letter, bathed in blood."

My friend Serval added:

"It was by way of reprisal that the Germans destroyed the *chateau* of the district, which belonged to me."

I thought of the poor, fine young men burned there; and of the atrocious heroism of that other mother, shot against the wall.

And I picked up a little pebble, still blackened by the fire.

The Blind Man

How is it that the sunlight gives us such joy? Why does this radiance when it falls on the earth fill us so much with the delight of living? The sky is all blue, the fields are all green, the houses all white; and our ravished eyes drink in those bright colours which bring mirthfulness to our souls. And then there springs up in our hearts a desire to dance, a desire to run, a desire to sing, a happy lightness of thought, a sort of enlarged tenderness; we feel a longing to embrace the sun.

The blind, as they sit in the doorways, impassive in their eternal darkness, remain as calm as ever in the midst of this fresh gaiety, and, not comprehending what is taking place around them, they continue every moment to stop their dogs from gambolling.

When, at the close of the day, they are returning home on the arm of a young brother or a little sister, if the child says: "It was a very fine day!" the other answers: "I could notice that 'twas fine. Lulu wouldn't keep quiet."

I have known one of these men whose life was one of the most cruel martyrdoms that could possibly be conceived.

He was a peasant, the son of a Norman farmer. As long as his father and mother lived, he was more or less taken care of; he suffered little save from his horrible infirmity; but as soon as the old people were gone, a life of atrocious misery commenced for him. A dependent on a sister of his, everybody in the farmhouse treated him as a beggar who is eating the bread of others. At every meal the very food he swallowed was made a subject of reproach against him; he was called a drone, a clown; and although his brother-in-law had taken possession of his portion of the inheritance, the soup was given to him grudgingly—just enough to save him from dying.

His face was very pale and his two big white eyes were like wafers. He remained unmoved in spite of the insults inflicted upon him, so shut up in himself that one could not tell whether he felt them at all.

Moreover, he had never known any tenderness; his mother had always treated him very unkindly, caring scarcely at all for him; for in country places the useless are obnoxious, and the peasants would be glad, like hens, to kill the infirm of their species.

As soon as the soup had been gulped down, he went to the door in summer time and sat down, to the chimney-corner in winter time, and, after that, never stirred till night. He made no gesture, no movement; only his eyelids, quivering from some nervous affection, fell down sometimes over his white sightless orbs. Had he any intellect, any thinking faculty, any consciousness of his own existence? Nobody cared to inquire as to whether he had or no.

For some years things went on in this fashion But his incapacity for doing anything as well as his impassiveness eventually exasperated his relatives, and he became a laughing-stock, a sort of martyred buffoon, a prey given over to native ferocity, to the savage gaiety of the brutes who surrounded him.

It is easy to imagine all the cruel practical jokes inspired by his blindness. And, in order to have some fun in return for feeding him, they now converted his meals into hours of pleasure for the neighbours and of punishment for the helpless creature himself.

The peasants from the nearest houses came to this entertainment; it was talked about from door to door, and every day the kitchen of the farmhouse was full of people. For instance, they put on the table in front of his plate, when he was beginning to take the soup, a cat or a dog. The animal instinctively scented out the man's infirmity, and, softly approaching, commenced eating noiselessly, lapping up the soup daintily; and, when a rather loud licking of the tongue awakened the poor fellow's attention, it would prudently scamper away to avoid the blow of the spoon directed at it by the blind man at random!

Then the spectators, huddled against the walls, burst out laughing, nudged each other, and stamped their feet on the floor. And he, without ever uttering a word, would continue eating with the aid of his right hand, while stretching out his left to protect and defend his plate.

At another time they made him chew corks, bits of wood, leaves, or even filth, which he was unable to distinguish.

After this, they got tired even of these practical jokes; and the brother-in-law, mad at having to support him always, struck him, cuffed him incessantly, laughing at the useless efforts of the other to ward off or return the blows. Then came a new pleasure—the pleasure of smacking his face. And the plough-men, the servant-girls, and even every passing vagabond were every moment giving him cuffs, which caused his eyelashes to twitch spasmodically. He did not know where to hide himself and remained with his arms always held out to guard against people coming too close to him.

At last he was forced to beg.

He was placed somewhere on the highroad on market-days, and, as soon as he heard the sound of footsteps or the rolling of a vehicle, he reached out his hat, stammering:

"Charity, if you please!"

But the peasant is not lavish, and, for whole weeks, he did not bring back a *sou*.

Then he became the victim of furious, pitiless hatred. And this is how he died.

One winter, the ground was covered with snow, and it froze horribly. Now his brother-in-law led him one morning at this season a great distance along the highroad in order that he might solicit alms. The blind man was left there all day, and, when night came on, the brother-in-law told the people of his house that he could find no trace of the mendicant. Then he added:

"Pooh! best not bother about him! He was cold, and got someone to take him away. Never fear! he's not lost. He'll turn up soon enough tomorrow to eat the soup."

Next day he did not come back.

After long hours of waiting, stiffened with the cold, feeling that he was dying, the blind man began to walk. Being unable to find his way along the road, owing to its thick coating of ice, he went on at random, falling into dikes, getting up again, without uttering a sound, his sole object being to find some house where he could take shelter.

But by degrees the descending snow made a numbness steal over him, and his feeble limbs being incapable of carrying him farther, he had to sit down in the middle of an open field. He did not get up again.

The white flakes which kept continually falling buried him, so that his body, quite stiff and stark, disappeared under the incessant accumulation of their rapidly thickening mass; and nothing any longer indicated the place where the corpse was lying.

His relatives made pretence of inquiring about him and searching for him for about a week. They even made a show of weeping.

The winter was severe, and the thaw did not set in quickly. Now, one Sunday, on their way to mass, the farmers noticed a great flight of crows, who were whirling endlessly above the open field, and then, like a shower of black rain, descended in a heap at the same spot, ever going and coming.

The following week these gloomy birds were still there. There was a crowd of them up in the air, as if they had gathered from all corners of the horizon; and they swooped down with a great cawing into the shining snow, which they filled curiously with patches of black, and in which they kept rummaging obstinately. A young fellow went to see what they were doing, and discovered the body of the blind man, already half devoured, mangled. His wan eyes had disappeared, pecked out by the long voracious beaks. And I can never feel the glad radiance of sunlit days without sadly remembering and gloomily pondering over the fate of the beggar so deprived of joy in life that his horrible death was a relief for all those who had known him.

The Devil

The peasant was standing opposite the doctor, by the bedside of the dying old woman, and she, calmly resigned and quite lucid, looked at them and listened to their talking. She was going to die, and she did not rebel at it, for her life was over—she was ninety-two.

The July sun streamed in at the window and through the open door and cast its hot flames on to the uneven brown clay floor, which had been stamped down by four generations of clodhoppers. The smell of the fields came in also, driven by the brisk wind, and parched by the noontide heat. The grasshoppers chirped themselves hoarse, filling the air with their shrill noise, like that of the wooden crickets which are sold to children at fair time.

The doctor raised his voice and said: "Honoré, you cannot leave your mother in this state; she may die at any moment." And the peasant, in great distress, replied: "But I must get in my wheat, for it has been lying on the ground a long time, and the weather is just right for it; what do you say about it, mother?"

And the dying woman, still possessed by her Norman avariciousness, replied *yes* with her eyes and her forehead, and so urged her son to get in his wheat, and to leave her to die alone. But the doctor got angry, and stamping his foot he said: "You are no better than a brute, do you hear, and I will not allow you to do it. Do you understand? And if you must get in your wheat today, go and fetch Rapet's wife and make her look after your mother. I *will* have it. And if you do not obey me, I will let you die like a dog, when you are ill in your turn; do you hear me?"

The peasant, a tall, thin fellow with slow movements, who was tormented by indecision, by his fear of the doctor and his keen love of saving, hesitated, calculated, and stammered out: "How much does La Rapet charge for attending sick people?"

"How should I know?" the doctor cried. "That depends upon how long she is wanted for. Settle it with her, by Jove! But I want her to be here within an hour, do you hear."

So the man made up his mind. "I will go for her," he replied; "don't get angry, doctor."

And the latter left, calling out as he went: "Take care, you know, for I do not joke when I am angry!"

And as soon as they were alone, the peasant turned to his mother, and said in a resigned voice: "I will go and fetch La Rapet, as the man will have it. Don't go off while I am away."

And he went out in his turn.

La Rapet, who was an old washerwoman, watched the dead and the dying of the neighbourhood, and then, as soon as she had sewn her customers into that linen cloth from which they would emerge no more, she went and took up her irons to smooth the linen of the living. Wrinkled like a last year's apple, spiteful, envious, avaricious with a phenomenal avarice, bent double, as if she had been broken in half across the loins, by the constant movement of the iron over the linen, one might have said that she had a kind of monstrous and cynical affection for a death struggle. She never spoke of anything but of the people she had seen die, of the various kinds of deaths at which she had been present, and she related, with the greatest minuteness, details which were always the same, just like a sportsman talks of his shots.

When Honoré Bontemps entered her cottage, he found her preparing the starch for the collars of the village women, and he said: "Good evening; I hope you are pretty well, Mother Rapet."

She turned her head round to look at him and said: "Fairly well, fairly well, and you?"

" Oh! as for me, I am as well as I could wish, but my mother is very sick."

"Your mother?"

"Yes, my mother!"

"What's the matter with her?"

"She is going to turn up her toes, that's what's the matter with her!"

The old woman took her hands out of the water and asked with sudden sympathy: "Is she as bad as all that?"

"The doctor says she will not last till morning."

"Then she certainly is very bad!"

Honoré hesitated, for he wanted to make a few preliminary remarks before coming to his proposal, but as he could hit upon nothing, he made up his mind suddenly.

"How much are you going to ask to stop with her till the end? You know that I am not rich, and I cannot even afford to keep a servant-girl. It is just that which has brought my poor mother to this state, too much work and fatigue! She used to work for ten, in spite of her ninety-two years. You don't find any made of that stuff nowadays!"

La Rapet answered gravely: "There are two prices: Forty *sous* by day and three *francs* by night for the rich, and twenty *sous* by day, and forty by night for the others. You shall pay me the twenty and forty."

But the peasant reflected, for he knew his mother well. He knew how tenacious of life, how vigorous and unyielding she was. He knew, too, that she might last another week, in spite of the doctor's opinion, and so he said resolutely: "No, I would rather you would fix a price until the end. I will take my chance, one way or the other. The doctor says she will die very soon. If that happens, so much the better for you, and so much the worse for me, but if she holds out till tomorrow or longer, so much the better for me and so much the worse for you!"

The nurse looked at the man in astonishment, for she had never treated a death as a speculative job, and she hesitated, tempted by the idea of the possible gain. But almost immediately she suspected that he wanted to juggle her. "I can say nothing until I have seen your mother," she replied.

"Then come with me and see her."

She washed her hands, and went with him immediately. They did not speak on the road; she walked with short, hasty steps, while he strode on with his long legs, as if he were crossing a brook at every step. The cows lying down in the fields, overcome by the heat, raised their heads heavily and lowed feebly at the two passers-by, as if to ask them for some green grass.

When they got near the house, Honoré Bontemps murmured: "Suppose it is all over?" And the unconscious wish that it might be so showed itself in the sound of his voice.

But the old woman was not dead. She was lying on her back, on her wretched bed, her hands covered with a pink cotton counterpane, horribly thin, knotty paws, like some strange animal's, or like crabs' claws, hands closed by rheumatism, fatigue, and the work of nearly a century which she had accomplished.

La Rapet went up to the bed and looked at the dying woman, felt her pulse, tapped her on the chest, listened to her breathing, and asked her questions, so as to hear her speak: then, having looked at her for some time longer, she went out of the room, followed by Honoré. His decided opinion was, that the old woman would not last out the night, and he asked: "Well?"

And the sick-nurse replied: "Well, she may last two days, perhaps three. You will have to give me six *francs*, everything included."

"Six *francs*! six *francs*!" he shouted. "Are you out of your mind? I tell you that she cannot last more than five or six hours!" And they disputed angrily for some time, but as the nurse said she would go home, as the time was slipping away, and as his wheat would not come to the farmyard of its own accord, he agreed to her terms at last:

"Very well, then, that is settled; six *francs* including everything, until the corpse is taken out."

"That is settled, six *francs*."

And he went away, with long strides, to his wheat, which was lying on the ground under the hot sun which ripens the grain, while the sick-nurse returned to the house.

She had brought some work with her, for she worked without stopping by the side of the dead and dying, sometimes for herself, sometimes for the family, who employed her as seamstress also, paying her rather more in that capacity. Suddenly she asked:

"Have you received the last sacrament, Mother Bontemps?"

The old peasant woman said "No" with her head, and La Rapet, who was very devout, got up quickly: "Good heavens, is it possible? I will go and fetch the *curé*"; and she rushed off to the parsonage so quickly, that the urchins in the street thought some accident had happened, when they saw her trotting off like that.

The priest came immediately in his surplice, preceded by a choirboy, who rang a bell to announce the passage of the Host through the parched and quiet country. Some men, working at a distance, took off their large hats and remained motionless until the white vestment had disappeared behind some farm buildings; the women who were making up the sheaves stood up to make the sign of the cross; the frightened black hens ran away along the ditch until they reached a well-known hole through which they suddenly disappeared, while a foal, which was tied up in a meadow, took fright at the sight of the surplice and began to gallop round at the length of its rope, kicking violently. The choirboy, in his red cassock, walked quickly, and the priest, the square *biretta* on his bowed head, followed him, muttering some prayers. Last of all came La Rapet, bent almost double, as if she wished to prostrate herself; she walked with folded hands, as if she were in church.

Honoré saw them pass in the distance, and he asked: "Where is our priest going to?"

And his man, who was more acute, replied: "He is taking the sacrament to your mother, of course!"

The peasant was not surprised and said: "That is quite possible," and went on with his work.

Mother Bontemps confessed, received absolution and extreme unction, and the priest took his departure, leaving the two women alone in the suffocating cottage. La Rapet began to look at the dying woman, and to ask herself whether it could last much longer.

The day was on the wane, and a cooler air came in stronger puffs, making a view of Epinal, which was fastened to the wall by two pins, flap up and down. The scanty window curtains, which had formerly been white, but were now yellow and covered with fly-specks, looked as if they were going to fly off, and seemed to struggle to get away, like the old woman's soul.

Lying motionless, with her eyes open, the old mother seemed to await the death which was so near, and which yet delayed its coming, with perfect in- difference. Her short breath whistled in her throat. It would step altogether soon, and there would be one woman less in the world, one whom nobody would regret.

At nightfall Honoré returned, and when he went up to the bed and saw that his mother was still alive he asked: "How is she?" just as he had done formerly, when she had been sick. Then he sent La Rapet away, saying to her: "Tomorrow morning at five o'clock, without fail."

And she replied: "Tomorrow at five o'clock."

She came at daybreak, and found Honoré eating his soup, which he had made himself, before going to work.

"Well, is your mother dead?" asked the nurse.

"She is rather better, on the contrary," he replied, with a malignant look out of the corner of his eyes. Then he went out.

La Rapet was seized with anxiety, and went up to the dying woman, who was in the same state, lethargic and impassive, her eyes open and her hands clutching the counterpane. The nurse perceived that this might go on thus for two days, four days, eight days, even, and her avaricious mind was seized with fear. She was excited to fury against the cunning fellow who had tricked her, and against the woman who would not die.

Nevertheless, she began to sew and waited with her eyes fixed on the wrinkled face of Mother Bontemps. When Honoré returned to breakfast he seemed quite satisfied, and even in a bantering humour, for he was carrying in his wheat under very favourable circumstances.

La Rapet was getting exasperated; every passing minute now seemed to her so much time and money stolen from her. She felt a mad inclination to choke this old ass, this headstrong old fool, this obstinate old wretch—to stop that short, rapid breath, which was robbing her of her time and money, by squeezing her throat a little. But then she reflected on the danger of doing so, and other thoughts came into her head, so she went up to the bed and said to her: "Have you ever seen the Devil?"

Mother Bontemps whispered: "No."

Then the sick-nurse began to talk and to tell her tales likely to terrify her weak and dying mind. "Some minutes before one dies the Devil appears," she said, "to all. He has a broom in his hand, a saucepan on his head and he utters loud cries. When anybody had seen him, all was over, and that person had only a few moments longer to live"; and she enumerated all those to whom the Devil had appeared that year: Josephine Loisel, Eulalie Ratier, Sophie Padagnau, Seraphine Grospied.

Mother Bontemps, who was at last most disturbed in mind, moved about, wrung her hands, and tried to turn her head to look at the other end of the room. Suddenly La Rapet disappeared at the foot of the bed. She took a sheet out of the cupboard and wrapped herself up in it; then she put the iron pot on to her head, so that its three short bent feet rose up like horns, took a broom in her right hand and a tin pail in her left, which she threw up suddenly, so that it might fall to the ground noisily.

Certainly when it came down, it made a terrible noise. Then, climbing on to a chair, the nurse showed herself, gesticulating and uttering shrill cries into the pot which covered her face, while she menaced the old peasant woman, who was nearly dead, with her broom.

Terrified, with a mad look on her face, the dying woman made a superhuman effort to get up and escape; she even got her shoulders and chest out of bed; then she fell back with a deep sigh. All was over, and La Rapet calmly put everything back into its place; the broom into the corner by the cupboard, the sheet inside it, the pot on to the hearth, the pail on to the floor, and the chair against the wall. Then with a professional air, she closed the dead woman's enormous eyes, put a plate on the bed and poured some holy water into it, dipped the twig of boxwood into it, and kneeling down, she fervently repeated the prayers for the dead, which she knew by heart, as a matter of business.

When Honoré returned in the evening, he found her praying. He calculated immediately that she had made twenty *sous* out of him, for she had only spent three days and one night there, which made five *francs* altogether, instead of the six which he owed her.

He?

(It was in this story that the first gleams of De Maupassant's approaching madness became apparent Thenceforward he began to revel in the strange and terrible, until his malady had seized him wholly. The Diary of a Madman, is in a similar vein).

My dear friend, you cannot understand it by any possible means, you say, and I perfectly believe you. You think I am going mad? It may be so, but not for the reasons which you suppose.

Yes, I am going to get married, and I will tell you what has led me to take that step. My ideas and my convictions have not changed at all. I look upon all legalized co-habitation as utterly stupid, for I am certain that nine husbands out of ten are cuckolds; and they get no more than their deserts for having been idiotic enough to fetter their lives and renounce their freedom in love, the only happy and good thing in the world, and for having clipped the wings of fancy which continually drives us on toward all women. You know what I mean. More than ever I feel that I am incapable of loving one woman alone, because I shall always adore all the others too much. I should like to have a thousand arms, a thousand mouths, and a thousand—*temperaments*, to be able to strain an army of these charming creatures in my embrace at the same moment.

And yet I am going to get married!

I may add that I know very little of the girl who is going to become my wife tomorrow; I have only seen her four or five times. I know that there is nothing unpleasing about her, and that is enough for my purpose. She is small, fair, and stout; so of course the day after tomorrow I shall ardently wish for a tall, dark, thin woman.

She is not rich, and belongs to the middle classes. She is a girl such as you may find by the gross, well adapted for matrimony, without any apparent faults, and with no particularly striking qualities. People say of her: "Mlle. Lajolle is a very nice girl," and tomorrow they will say: "What a very nice woman Madame Raymon is." She belongs, in a word, to that immense number of girls who make very good wives for us till the moment comes when we discover that we happen to prefer all other women to that particular woman we have married.

"Well," you will say to me, "what on earth do you get married for?"

I hardly like to tell you the strange and seemingly improbable reason that urged me on to this senseless act; the fact, however, is that I am frightened of being alone!

I don't know how to tell you or to make you understand me, but my state of mind is so wretched that you will pity me and despise me.

I do not want to be alone any longer at night; I want to feel that there is someone close to me touching me, a being who can speak and say something, no matter what it be.

I wish to be able to awaken somebody by my side, so that I may be able to ask some sudden question, a stupid question even, if I feel inclined, so that I may hear a human voice, and feel that there is some waking soul close to me, someone whose reason is at work—so that when I hastily light the candle I may see some human face by my side—because—because—I am ashamed to confess it—because I am afraid of being alone.

Oh! you don't understand me yet.

I am not afraid of any danger; if a man were to come into the room I should kill him without trembling. I am not afraid of ghosts, nor do I believe in the supernatural. I am not afraid of dead people, for I believe in the total annihilation of every being that disappears from the face of this earth.

Well,—yes, well, it must be told; I am afraid of myself, afraid of that horrible sensation of incomprehensible fear.

You may laugh, if you like. It is terrible and I cannot get over it. I am afraid of the walls, of the furniture, of the familiar objects, which are animated, as far as I am concerned, by a kind of animal life. Above all, I am afraid of my own dreadful thoughts, of my reason, which seems as if it were about to leave me, driven away by a mysterious and invisible agony.

At first I feel a vague uneasiness in my mind which causes a cold shiver to run all over me. I look round, and of course nothing is to be seen, and I wish there were something there, no matter what, as long as it were something tangible: I am frightened, merely because I cannot understand my own terror.

If I speak, I am afraid of my own voice. If I walk, I am afraid of I know not what, behind the door, behind the curtains, in the cupboard, or under my bed, and yet all the time I know there is nothing anywhere, and I turn round suddenly because I am afraid of what is behind me, although there is nothing there, and I know it.

I get agitated; I feel that my fear increases, and so I shut myself up in my own room, get into bed, and hide under the clothes, and there, cowering down rolled into a ball, I close my eyes in despair and remain thus for an indefinite time, remembering that my candle is alight on the table by my bedside, and that I ought to put it out, and yet—I dare not do it!

It is very terrible, is it not, to be like that?

Formerly I felt nothing of all that; I came home quite comfortably, and went up and down in my rooms without anything disturbing my calmness of mind. Had anyone told me that I should be attacked by a malady—for I can call it nothing else— of most improbable fear, such a stupid and terrible malady as it is, I should have laughed outright. I was certainly never afraid of opening the door in the dark; I used to go to bed slowly without locking it, and never got up in the middle of the night to make sure that everything was firmly closed.

It began last year in a very strange manner, on a damp autumn evening. When my servant had left the room, after I had dined, I asked myself what I was going to do. I walked up and down my room for some time, feeling tired without any reason for it, unable to work, and without enough energy to read. A fine rain was falling, and I felt unhappy, a prey to one of those fits of casual despondency which make us feel inclined to cry, or to talk, no matter to whom, so as to shake off our depressing thoughts.

I felt that I was alone and that my rooms seemed to me to be more empty that they had ever been before. I was surrounded by a sensation of infinite and overwhelming solitude. What was I to do? I sat down, but then a kind of nervous impatience agitated my legs, so that I got up and began to walk about again. I was feverish, for my hands, which I had clasped behind me, as one often does when walking slowly, almost seemed to burn one another. Then suddenly a cold shiver ran down my back, and I thought the damp air might have penetrated into my room, so I lit the fire for the first time that year, and sat down again and looked at the flames. But soon I felt that I could not possibly remain quiet. So I got up again and determined to go out, to pull myself together, and to seek a friend to bear me company.

I could not find anyone, so I went on to the *boulevards* to try and meet some acquaintance or other there.

I was wretched everywhere, and the wet pavement glistened in the gaslight, while the oppressive mist of the almost impalpable rain lay heavily over the streets and seemed to obscure the light from the lamps.

I went on slowly, saying to myself, "I shall not find a soul to talk to."

I glanced into several *cafés*, from the Madeleine as far as the Faubourg Poissonière, and saw many unhappy-looking individuals sitting at the tables, who did not seem even to have enough energy left to finish the refreshments they had ordered.

For a long time I wandered aimlessly up and down, and about midnight I started off for home; I was very calm and very tired. My *concierge* (hall-porter) opened the door at once, which was quite unusual for him, and I thought that another lodger had no doubt just come in.

When I go out I always double-lock the door of my room. Now I found it merely closed, which surprised me; but I supposed that some letters had been brought up for me in the course of the evening.

I went in, and found my fire still burning so that it lighted up the room a little. In the act of taking up a candle, I noticed somebody sitting in my armchair by the fire, warming his feet, with his back toward me.

I was not in the slightest degree frightened. I thought very naturally that some friend or other had come to see me. No doubt the porter, whom I had told when I went out, had lent him his own key. In a moment I remembered all the circumstances of my return, how the street door had been opened immediately, and that my own door was only latched, and not locked.

I could see nothing of my friend but his head. He had evidently gone to sleep while waiting for me, so I went up to him to rouse him. I saw him quite clearly; his right arm was hanging down and his legs were crossed, while his head, which was somewhat inclined to the left of the armchair, seemed to indicate that he was asleep. "Who can it be?" I asked myself. I could not see clearly, as the room was rather dark, so I put out my hand to touch him on the shoulder, and it came in contact with the back of the chair. There was nobody there; the seat was empty.

I fairly jumped with fright. For a moment I drew back as if some terrible danger had suddenly appeared in my way; then I turned round again, impelled by some imperious desire to look at the armchair again. I remained standing upright, panting with fear, so upset that I could not collect my thoughts, and ready to drop.

But I am naturally a cool man, and soon recovered myself. I thought: "It is a mere hallucination, that is all," and I immediately began to reflect about this phenomenon. Thoughts fly very quickly at such moments.

I had been suffering from a hallucination, that was an incontestable fact. My mind had been perfectly lucid and had acted regularly and logically, so there was nothing the matter with the brain. It was only my eyes that had been deceived; they had had a vision, one of those visions which lead simple folk to believe in miracles. It was a nervous accident to the optical apparatus, nothing more; the eyes were rather overwrought, perhaps.

I lit my candle, and when I stooped down to the fire in so doing, I noticed that I was trembling, and I raised myself up with a jump, as if somebody had touched me from behind.

I was certainly not by any means reassured.

I walked up and down a little, and hummed a tune or two. Then I double-locked my door, and felt rather reassured; now, at any rate, nobody could come in,

I sat down again, and thought over my adventure for a long time; then I went to bed, and put out my light.

For some minutes all went well; I lay quietly on my back. Then an irresistible desire seized me to look round the room, and I turned on to my side.

My fire was nearly out and the few glowing embers threw a faint light on to the floor by the chair, where I fancied I saw the man sitting again.

I quickly struck a match, but I had been mistaken, for there was nothing there; I got up, however, and hid the chair behind my bed, and tried to get to sleep as the room was now dark. But I had not forgotten myself for more than five minutes when in my dream I saw all the scene which I had witnessed as clearly as if it were reality. I woke up with a start, and, having lit the candle, sat up in bed, without venturing even to try and go to sleep again.

Twice, however, sleep overcame me for a few moments in spite of myself, and twice I saw the same thing again, till I fancied I was going mad. When day broke, however, I thought that I was cured, and slept peacefully till noon.

It was all past and over. I had been feverish, had had the nightmare; I don't know what. I had been ill, in a word, but yet I thought that I was a great fool.

I enjoyed myself thoroughly that evening; I went and dined at a restaurant; afterward I went to the theatre, and then started home. But as I got near the house I was seized by a strange feeling of uneasiness once more; I was afraid of *seeing* him again. I was not afraid of him, not afraid of his presence, in which I did not believe; but I was afraid of being deceived again; I was afraid of some fresh hallucination, afraid lest fear should take possession of me.

For more than an hour I wandered up and down the pavement; then I thought that I was really too foolish, and returned home. I panted so that I could scarcely get upstairs, and remained standing outside my door for more than ten minutes; then suddenly I took courage and pulled myself together. I inserted my key into the lock, and went in with a candle in my hand. I kicked open my half-open bedroom door, and gave a frightened look toward the fireplace; there was nothing there. A—h!

What a relief and what a delight! What a deliverance! I walked up and down briskly and boldly, but I was not altogether reassured, and kept turning round with a jump; the very shadows in the corners disquieted me.

I slept badly, and was constantly disturbed by imaginary noises, but I did not see *him*; no, that was all over.

Since that time I have been afraid of being alone at night. I feel that the spectre is there, close to me, around me; but it has not appeared to me again. And supposing it did, what would it matter, since I do not believe in it and know that it is nothing?

It still worries me, however, because I am constantly thinking of it: *his right arm hanging down and his head inclined to the left like a man who was asleep*—Enough of that, in Heaven's name! I don't want to think about it!

Why, however, am I so persistently possessed with this idea? His feet were close to the fire!

He haunts me; it is very stupid, but so it is. Who and what is HE? I know that he does not exist except in my cowardly imagination, in my fears, and in my agony! There—enough of that!

Yes, it is all very well for me to reason with myself, *to stiffen myself,* so to say; but I cannot remain at home, because I know he is there. I know I shall not see him again; he will not show himself again; that is all over. But he is there all the same in my thoughts. He remains invisible, but that does not prevent his being there. He is behind the doors, in the closed cupboards, in the wardrobe, under the bed, in every dark corner. If I open the door or the cupboard, if I take the candle to look under the bed and throw a light on to the dark places, he is there no longer, but I feel that he is behind me. I turn round, certain that I shall not see him, that I shall never see him again; but he is, none the less, behind me.

It is very stupid, it is dreadful; but what am I to do? I cannot help it.

But if there were two of us in the place, I feel certain that he would not be there any longer, for he is there just because I am alone, simply and solely because I am alone.

The Diary of a Madman

A.k.a. The Madman

When he died he was the head of a high tribunal, an upright magistrate, whose irreproachable life was cited in every court in France. Lawyers, young counsellors, and judges bowed low to mark their profound respect when they looked at his large, pale, thin face lighted up by his flashing dark eyes.

He had spent his life in the pursuit of crime and in the protection of the weak. Swindlers and murderers had no more redoubtable enemy, for he seemed to read their secret thoughts in the depths of their souls, and with a glance of his eye to uncover all their hidden intentions.

So it was that he died at the age of eighty-two, rich in honours, and was followed by the regrets of a nation. Soldiers in red trousers escorted him to his tomb, and men in white cravats voiced their sorrow over his coffin and shed tears that seemed to be genuine.

But glance at this strange document which the distracted notary discovered in the desk where the judge had been in the habit of keeping locked up the records of famous criminals.

Its title was: *Why?*

June 20, 1831.—I have just come from the courtroom. I condemned Blondel to death! Why did this man kill his five children? Why? Often we come across men of this kind who revel in taking life. Yes, this must be a kind of voluptuousness. The greatest of all, perhaps, because does not killing resemble creation more than anything else? To make and to unmake. These two words contain in themselves the history of the universe, all the history of the worlds, everything that is, everything. Why is it so intoxicating to kill?

June 25.—To think that here is a being who lives, who walks, who runs. A being? What is a being? An animated thing which carries within it the principle of motion, and a will governing that motion. It belongs to nothing, this thing. Its feet have no connection with the sod. It is a grain of life that moves on the earth, and this grain of life, come from I know not where, one can destroy as one wills. Then nothing, nothing more. It rots; it's all over with it.

June 26.—Why, then, is it a crime to kill? Yes, why? Contrariwise, in nature it is the law. Every being has a mission to kill; it kills to live, and it lives to kill. The beast kills without ceasing, all day long, every instant of its existence. Man kills without ceasing, in order to nourish himself; as he feels the need too, of killing for pleasure, he invented the chase. The child kills the insects he finds, little birds, all the little animals that come in to his hand. But that does not satisfy the irresistible need of slaughter which is in us. It is not enough to kill beasts; we feel the need, too, of killing man.

Once upon a time they satisfied this need with human sacrifices. Today the necessity of living in society has made a crime of murder. We condemn and punish the murderer. But as we cannot live without yielding to this natural and imperious instinct of death, we solace ourselves, from time to time with wars in which an entire nation slays another nation. It is a debauch of blood, a debauch with which armies become infatuated and which intoxicates civilians also, women and children who read the highly coloured accounts of massacres as they sit in the evening around the lamp.

One might imagine that those who are destined to take part in the butcheries of their fellow-men would be despised? No, they are overwhelmed with honours. They are dressed in gold and brilliant clothes; they wear plumes on their heads, ornaments on their breasts; and they give them crosses, rewards, titles of all kinds. They are proud, respected, loved by the women, acclaimed by the crowd, just because their mission is to shed human blood! They drag along the pavement their instruments of death, which the black-clad passer-by looks at with envy, because to kill is the great law which nature has put into the heart of every being. There is nothing finer and more honourable than to kill!

June 30.—To kill is the law, because Nature loves eternal youth. She seems to cry out through all her unconscious acts: "Quick! quick! quick!" The more she destroys, the more she recreates.

July 2.—A being—what is a human being? Everything and nothing. By his thought he is the reflection of the universe. By his memory and his science he is a digest of the world whose history he carries within him. The mirror of things and the mirror of deeds, every human being becomes a little universe within the universe.

But travel; look at the races as they swarm, and man becomes of no importance, is nothing now, nothing. Get into a boat and put a distance between you and the shore crowded with people, and soon you see nothing but the coastline. The imperceptible creature disappears, so small and insignificant is he. Traverse Europe in an express train and look out of its window. Men, men, everywhere are men, innumerable, unknown, who swarm over the fields, who swarm In the streets—stupid peasants who have just enough Intelligence to turn up the sod, hideous women who know just enough to make soup for the male and to bring forth children.

Go to the Indies, go to China, and you will still see millions of creatures struggling, who are born and who die without leaving behind them more of a trace than an ant that has been crushed on the highway. Go to the country of the blacks sheltered in mud huts, to the land of white Arabs living under brown tents that flap in the wind, and you will come to understand that the

Individual human being is nothing, nothing—the race is all that counts. What is one being, one particular being of a wandering desert tribe? And these people, who are sages in their way, do not worry themselves about death. The man does not count with them. One kills one's enemy—that is war. In olden times that was done from castle to castle, from province to province.

Yes, travel around the world and look at the innumerable and unknown humans swarm. Unknown? Ah! it *is* on that word that the problem hinges. To kill is a crime because we have numbered human beings. When they are born we inscribe their names, we baptize them. The law takes hold upon them. There it is! The being who has not been registered does not count; kill him in the fens or in the desert, kill him on the mountains or in the plain. What does it matter? Nature loves death; She does not punish!

What is sacred is the civil authority. There we have it. That's what looks after man. The human being is sacred because he is registered by the civil authority. Respect the civil authority, the legal god. Down on your knees!

The state may kill, since it has the right to modify the civil authority. When it has slaughtered two hundred thousand men in a war it wipes them off its register, it cancels them by the hand of its recorders. It is over. But we, who may not change by one iota the writings of the town clerk, we must respect life. Civil Authority, thou glorious Divinity which reignest in the temples of municipalities, I salute thee! Thou art stronger than nature. Hah! Hah!

July 3.—What a strange and savoury pleasure it must be to kill, to have there before one a living, thinking creature and to make a little hole in it, only a little hole, to watch flow from it that red thing we call blood which makes life, and then to have before one nothing but flesh, pulpy, cold, inert, void of thought!

Aug, 5.—I, who have spent my life judging, condemning, killing by means of words which I enunciated, killing by the guillotine those who had killed with a knife, I, I, myself . . . suppose I should do what all those murderers did whom I punished, I, I . . . Who would find it out?

Aug. 10.—Who would ever know it? Would any one suspect me, me, particularly if I chose a creature whom I had no interest in putting an end to?

Aug. 15.—Temptation. Temptation has entered Into me like a crawling worm. It crawls; It advances; It wanders through my entire body, into my spirit which thinks of only one thing—killing; into my eyes that experience the urge of looking upon blood, of watching things die; into my ears filled all the time with something strange, horrible, rending, and maddening, like a creature's last cry; in my legs which twitch with the desire to be off, off to the spot where the thing will take place; in my hands that itch with the need to kill. How splendid it must be, how rare a delight, one worthy of a free man high above lesser men, who is master of his heart and who seeks strange, new sensations!

Aug. 22.—I could not resist any longer. I killed a little bird to see how it was, to make a beginning.

John, my servant, had a goldfinch whose cage hung at the pantry window. I sent him off on an errand and I took the little bird in my hand . . . in my hand . . . and I felt its heart beat against it. It was warm to hold. I went up into my room. From moment to moment I squeezed it a little harder; its heart beat quicker—it was horrible and delicious. I almost suffocated it, but then I should not have seen any blood.

Then I took a pair of scissors, short nail-scissors, and slashed his throat in three cuts, quite gently. He opened his beak, tried to get away from me, but I held him fast, oh! I held him fast. I could have held on to a mad bulldog. And I saw his blood flow. How beautiful it was, red and bright and glistening—blood! I felt like drinking it. I wet the tip of my tongue with it. It was delicious.

But he had so little of it, poor little bird! There was not time enough to enjoy the sight as I should have liked to do. How splendid it must be to see a bull bled.

And then I did as real murderers do. I washed the scissors. I washed my hands. I threw out the water and I carried the body, the corpse, into the garden to bury it. I hid it under a strawberry-plant. It will never be found. Every day I shall eat a strawberry from that plant. Truly, how one can enjoy life when one knows how.

My servant wept; he thought his bird had flown away. How should anyone ever suspect me? Hah! Hah!

Aug. 25.—I must kill a man! I must!

Aug. 29.—It is done. How simple a thing it is.

I went to walk In the Vernes woods. I wasn't thinking of anything, of anything at all. Then I caught sight of a child in the road, a boy who was eating a piece of bread-and-butter. He stopped to watch me go by and said:

"How do you do, *M'sieu le President?*"

And the thought came into my head, suppose I kill him.

I replied, "Thou art alone, my boy?"

"Yes, *M'sieu.*"

"Quite alone In the woods?"

"Yes, *M'sieu.*"

The idea of killing him intoxicated me as if it were alcohol. I approached him quietly, certain that he would run away. And then I grabbed him by the throat. I choked It. I choked it with all my strength. He looked at me with frightened eyes. What eyes ! Round, dark, limpid, terrified. I have never experienced an emotion so brutal—but so short. He held my wrists in his little hands and his body shook like a feather thrown upon a flame. Then he ceased to move.

My heart beat! Oh, the heart of the bird! I threw the body In the ditch, then grass on top of it.

I went home again and dined well. How simple a thing it was! That evening I was very gay, light-hearted, rejuvenated, and I spent the evening with the prefect. Every one found me witty.

But I did not see the blood. I am tranquil.

Aug. 30.—They have discovered the corpse and are looking for the murderer. Hah! Hah!

Sept. 1.—They have arrested two tramps, but there is no proof.

Sept. 2.—The parents have been to see me. They wept. Hah! Hah!

Oct. 6.—Nothing has been discovered. Some straggling vagabond must have done the deed. Hah! Hah! If I had seen the blood flow I believe I should now be tranquil.

Oct. 18.—The desire to kill penetrates my very marrow. It can be compared to the rages of love which torture you when you are twenty.

Oct. 22.—Another one. I was walking along the river-bank after breakfast, and I caught sight of a sleeping fisherman under a willow-tree. It was noon.

A spade sticking up in a potato-field nearby seemed to have been left there for the express purpose. I took it; I came back; I raised it like a club, and in one blow I cut open with its edges the fisherman's head. Oh, he bled, he did! Red blood, full of his brains. It ran down into the water quite gently.

And I walked off slowly. If anyone had seen me.,..Hah! Hah! I should have made a fine assassin.

Oct. 25.—The case of the fisherman has made a great stir. They accuse his nephew, his nephew who was fishing with him, of the murder.

Oct. 26.— The examining magistrate declares the nephew is guilty. Everybody in the city believes it. Hah! Hah!

Oct. 27.—The nephew defends himself very badly. He declares that he had been to the village to buy bread and cheese. He swears that his uncle was killed during his absence. Who will believe him?

Oct. 28.—The nephew had to confess; they confused him so that he lost his head. Hah! Hah! There's justice for you.

Nov. 15.—They have overwhelming proofs against the nephew, who was his uncle's heir. I am to preside at the assizes.

Jan. 25.—To death! To death! I condemned him to death! Hah! Hah! The advocate-general spoke like an angel. Hah! Hah! Still another. I am going to see him executed.

March 18.—It is done. They guillotined him this morning. He died beautifully! Oh, beautifully! It gave me pleasure. How fine it was to see a man's head cut off. The blood spurted over like a jet, like a jet. Oh, if I could have bathed myself in it! What an intoxication to lie down under it, to let it drip on my hair, on to my face, and to get up all red, all red! Ah, if they knew!

Now I shall wait; I can wait. It would take so little for them to find me out.

The manuscript contained several more pages but did not disclose any other crime.

The alienists to whom it was confided declared that there are many unknown insane just as adroit and as dangerous as this monstrous madman.

The Englishman
A.k.a The Hand/The Flayed Hand

They made a circle around Judge Bermutier, who was giving his opinion of the mysterious affair that had happened at Saint-Cloud. For a month Paris had doted on this inexplicable crime. No one could understand it at all.

M. Bermutier, standing with his back to the chimney, talked about it, discussed the divers opinions, but came to no conclusions.

Many women had risen and come nearer, remaining standing, with eyes fixed upon the shaven mouth of the magistrate, whence issued these grave words. They shivered and vibrated, crisp through their curious fear, through that eager, insatiable need of terror which haunts their soul, torturing them like a hunger.

One of them, paler than the others, after a silence, said:

"It is frightful. It touches the supernatural. We shall never know anything about it."

The magistrate turned toward her, saying: "Yes, *Madame*, it is probable that we never shall know anything about it. As for the word 'supernatural' when you come to use that, it has no place here. We are in the presence of a crime skilfully conceived, very skilfully executed, and so well enveloped in mystery that we cannot separate the impenetrable circumstances which surround it. But, once in my life, I had to follow an affair which seemed truly to be mixed up with something very unusual. However, it was necessary to give it up, as there was no means of explaining it."

Many of the ladies called out at the same time, so quickly that their voices sounded as one:

"Oh! tell us about it."

M. Bermutier smiled gravely, as judges should, and replied:

"You must not suppose, for an instant, that I, at least, believed there was anything superhuman in the adventure. I believe only in normal causes. And, if in place of using the word 'supernatural' to express what we cannot comprehend we should simply use the word 'inexplicable,' it would be much better. In any case, the surrounding circumstances in the affair I am going to relate to you, as well as the preparatory circumstances, have affected me much. Here are the facts:

"I was then Judge of Instruction at Ajaccio, a little white town lying on the border of an admirable gulf that was surrounded on all sides by high mountains.

"What I particularly had to look after there was the affairs of vendetta. Some of them were superb; as dramatic as possible, ferocious, and heroic. We find there the most beautiful subjects of vengeance that one could dream of, hatred a century old, appeased for a moment but never extinguished, abominable plots, assassinations becoming massacres and almost glorious battles. For two years I heard of nothing but the price of blood, of the terribly prejudiced Corsican who is bound to avenge all injury upon the person of him who is the cause of it, or upon his nearest descendants. I saw old men and infants, cousins, with their throats cut, and my head was full of these stories.

"One day we learned that an Englishman had rented for some years a little villa at the end of the Gulf. He had brought with him a French domestic, picked up at Marseilles on the way.

"Soon everybody was occupied with this singular person, who lived alone in his house, only going out to hunt and fish. He spoke to no one, never came to the town, and, every morning, practiced shooting with a pistol and a rifle for an hour or two.

"Some legends about him were abroad. They pretended that

he was a high personage fled from his own country for political reasons; then they affirmed that he was concealing himself after having committed a frightful crime. They even cited some of the particularly horrible details.

"In my capacity of judge, I wished to get some information about this man. But it was impossible to learn anything. He called himself Sir John Rowell.

" I contented myself with watching him closely; although, in reality, there seemed nothing to suspect regarding him.

"Nevertheless, as rumours on his account continued, grew, and became general, I resolved to try and see this stranger myself, and for this purpose began to hunt regularly in the neighbourhood of his property.

"I waited long for an occasion. It finally came in the form of a partridge which I shot and killed before the very nose of the Englishman. My dog brought it to me; but, immediately taking it I went and begged Sir John Rowell to accept the dead bird, excusing myself for intrusion.

"He was a tall man with red hair and red beard, very large, a sort of placid, polite Hercules. He had none of the so-called British haughtiness, and heartily thanked me for the delicacy in French, with a beyond-the-Channel accent. At the end of a month we had chatted together five or six times.

"Finally, one evening, as I was passing by his door, I perceived him astride a chair in the garden, smoking his pipe. I saluted him and he asked me in to have a glass of beer. It was not necessary for him to repeat before I accepted.

"He received me with the fastidious courtesy of the English, spoke in praise of France and of Corsica, and declared that he loved that country and that shore.

"Then, with great precaution in the form of a lively interest, I put some questions to him about his life and his projects. He responded without embarrassment, told me that he had travelled much, in Africa, in the Indies, and in America. He added, laughing:

"'I have had many adventures, oh! yes.'

"I began to talk about hunting, and he gave me many curious details of hunting the hippopotamus, the tiger, the elephant, and even of hunting the gorilla.

"'I said: 'All these animals are very formidable.'

"He laughed: 'Oh! no. The worst animal is man.' Then he began to laugh, with the hearty laugh of a big contented Englishman. He continued:

"'I have often hunted man, also.'

"He spoke of weapons and asked me to go into his house to see his guns of various makes and kinds.

"His drawing-room was hung in black, in black silk embroidered with gold. There were great yellow flowers running over the sombre stuff, shining like fire.

"'It is Japanese cloth,' he said.

"But in the middle of a large panel, a strange thing attracted my eye. Upon a square of red velvet, a black object was attached. I approached and found it was a hand, the hand of a man. Not a skeleton hand, white and characteristic, but a black, desiccated hand, with yellow joints with the muscles bare and on them traces of old blood, of blood that seemed like a scale, over the bones sharply cut off at about the middle of the forearm, as with a blow of a hatchet. About the wrist was an enormous iron chain, riveted, soldered to this unclean member, attaching it to the wall by a ring sufficiently strong to hold an elephant.

"I asked: 'What is that?'

"The Englishman responded tranquilly:

"'It belonged to my worst enemy. It came from America. It was broken with a sabre, cut off with a sharp stone, and dried in the sun for eight days. Oh, very good for me, that was!'

"I touched the human relic, which must have belonged to a colossus. The fingers were immoderately long and attached by enormous tendons that held the straps of skin in place. This dried hand was frightful to see, making one think, naturally, of the vengeance of a savage.

"I said: 'This man must have been very strong.'

"With gentleness the Englishman answered:

"'Oh! yes; but I was stronger than he. I put this chain on him to hold him.'

"I thought he spoke in jest and replied:

"'The chain is useless now that the hand cannot escape.'

"Sir John Rowell replied gravely: 'It always wishes to escape. The chain is necessary.'

"With a rapid, questioning glance, I asked myself: 'Is he mad, or is that an unpleasant joke?'

"But the face remained impenetrable, tranquil, and friendly. I spoke of other things and admired the guns.

"Nevertheless, I noticed three loaded revolvers on the pieces of furniture, as if this man lived in constant fear of attack.

"I went there many times after that; then for some time I did not go. We had become accustomed to his presence; he had become indifferent to us.

"A whole year slipped away. Then, one morning, toward the end of November, my domestic awoke me with the announcement that Sir John Rowell had been assassinated in the night.

"A half hour later, I entered the Englishman's house with the central Commissary and the Captain of Police. The servant, lost in despair, was weeping at the door. I suspected him at first, but afterward found that he was innocent.

"The guilty one could never be found.

"Upon entering Sir John's drawing-room, I perceived his dead body stretched out upon its back, in the middle of the room. His waistcoat was torn, a sleeve was hanging, and it was evident that a terrible struggle had taken place.

"The Englishman had been strangled! His frightfully black and swollen face seemed to express an abominable fear; he held something between his set teeth; and his neck, pierced with five holes apparently done with a pointed iron, was covered with blood.

"A doctor joined us. He examined closely the prints of fingers in the flesh and pronounced these strange words:

"'One would think he had been strangled by a skeleton.'

"A shiver ran down my back and I cast my eyes to the place

on the wall where I had seen the horrible, torn-off hand. It was no longer there. The chain was broken and hanging.

"Then I bent over the dead man and found in his mouth a piece of one of the fingers of the missing hand, cut off, or rather sawed off by the teeth exactly at the second joint.

"Then they tried to collect evidence. They could find nothing. No door had been forced, no window opened, or piece of furniture moved. The two watchdogs on the premises had not been aroused.

"Here, in a few words, is the deposition of the servant:

"For a month, his master had seemed agitated. He had received many letters which he had burned immediately. Often, taking a whip, in anger which seemed like dementia, he had struck in fury, this dried hand, fastened to the wall and taken, one knew not how, at the moment of a crime.

"He had retired late and shut himself in with care. He always carried arms. Often in the night he talked out loud, as if he were quarrelling with someone. On that night, however, there had been no noise, and it was only on coming to open the windows that the servant had found Sir John assassinated. He suspected no one.

"I communicated what I knew of the death to the magistrates and public officers, and they made minute inquiries upon the whole island. They discovered nothing.

"One night, three months after the crime, I had a frightful nightmare. It seemed to me that I saw that hand, that horrible hand, running like a scorpion or a spider along my curtains and my walls. Three times I awoke, three times I fell asleep and again saw that hideous relic galloping about my room, moving its fingers like paws.

"The next day they brought it to me, found in the cemetery upon the tomb where Sir John Rowell was interred—for they had not been able to find his family. The index finger was missing.

"This, ladies, is my story. I know no more about it."

The ladies were terrified, pale, and shivering. One of them

cried:

"But that is not the end, for there was no explanation! We cannot sleep if you do not tell us what was your idea of the reason of it all."

The magistrate smiled with severity, and answered:

"Oh! certainly, ladies, but it will spoil all your terrible dreams. I simply think that the legitimate proprietor of the hand was not dead and that he came for it with the one that remained to him. But I was never able to find out how he did it. It was one kind of revenge."

One of the women murmured :

"No, it could not be thus."

And the Judge of Information, smiling still, concluded:

"I told you in the beginning that my explanation would not satisfy you."

The Englishman of Etretat

A great English poet has just crossed over to France in order
to greet Victor Hugo. All the newspapers are full of his name
and he is the great topic of conversation in all drawing-rooms.
Fifteen years ago I had occasion several times to meet Algernon
Charles Swinburne. I will attempt to show him just as I saw him
and to give an idea of the strange impression he made on me,
which will remain with me throughout time.

I believe it was in 1867 or in 1868 that an unknown young
Englishman came to Etretat and bought a little but hidden under great trees. It was said that he lived there, always alone, in a
strange manner; and he aroused the inimical surprise of the na-
tives, for the inhabitants were sullen and foolishly malicious, as
they always are in little towns.

They declared that this whimsical Englishman ate nothing
but boiled. roasted or stewed monkey; that he would see no one;
that he talked to himself hours at a time and many other surprising things that made people think that he was different from
other men. They were surprised that he should live alone with a
monkey. Had it been a cat or a dog they would have said nothing. But a monkey! Was that not frightful? What savage tastes the
man must have!

I knew this young man only from seeing him in the streets.
He was short, plump, without being fat, mild-looking, and he
wore a little blond moustache, which was almost invisible.

Chance brought us together. This savage had amiable and
pleasing manners, but he was one of those strange Englishmen

that one meets here and there throughout the world.

Endowed with remarkable intelligence, he seemed to live in a fantastic dream, as Edgar Poe must have lived. He had translated into English a volume of strange Icelandic legends, which I ardently desired to see translated into French. He loved the supernatural, the dismal and gruesome, but he spoke of the most marvellous things with a calmness that was typically English, to which his gentle and quiet voice gave a semblance of reality that was maddening.

Full of a haughty disdain for the world, with its conventions, prejudices and code of morality, he had nailed to his house a name that was boldly impudent. The keeper of a lonely inn who should write on his door: "*Travellers murdered here!*" could not make a more sinister jest. I never had entered his dwelling, when one day I received an invitation to luncheon, following an accident that had occurred to one of his friends, who had been almost drowned and whom I had attempted to rescue.

Although I was unable to reach the man until he had already been rescued, I received the hearty thanks of the two Englishmen, and the following day I called upon them.

The friend was a man about thirty years old. He bore an enormous head on a child's body—a body without chest or shoulders. An immense forehead, which seemed to have engulfed the rest of the man, expanded like a dome above a thin face which ended in a little pointed beard. Two sharp eyes and a peculiar mouth gave one the impression of the head of a reptile, while the magnificent brow suggested a genius.

A nervous twitching shook this peculiar being, who walked, moved, acted by jerks like a broken spring.

This was Algernon Charles Swinburne, son of an English admiral and grandson, on the maternal side, of the Earl of Ashburnham.

He strange countenance was transfigured when he spoke. I have seldom seen a man more impressive, more eloquent, incisive or charming in conversation. His rapid, clear, piercing and fantastic imagination seemed to creep into his voice and to lend life to his words. His brusque gestures enlivened his speech, which penetrated one like a dagger, and he had bursts of thought, just as lighthouses throw out flashes of fire, great, genial lights that seemed to illuminate a whole world of ideas.

The home of the two friends was pretty and by no means commonplace. Everywhere were paintings, some superb, some strange, representing different conceptions of insanity. Unless I am mistaken, there was a water-colour which represented the head of a dead man floating in a rose-colored shell on a boundless ocean, under a moon with a human face.

Here and there I came across bones. I clearly remember a flayed hand on which was hanging some dried skin and black muscles, and on the snow-white bones could be seen the traces of dried blood.

The food was a riddle which I could not solve. Was it good? Was it bad? I could not say. Some roast monkey took away all desire to make a steady diet of this animal, and the great monkey who roamed about among us at large and playfully pushed his head into my glass when I wished to drink cured me of any desire I might have to take one of his brothers as a companion for the rest of my days.

As for the two men, they gave me the impression of two strange, original, remarkable minds, belonging to that peculiar race of talented madmen from among whom have arisen Poe, Hoffmann and many others.

If genius is, as is commonly believed, a sort of aberration of great minds, then Algernon Charles Swinburne is undoubtedly a genius.

Great minds that are healthy are never considered geniuses, while this sublime qualification is lavished on brains that are often inferior but are slightly touched by madness.

At any rate, this poet remains one of the first of his time, through his originality and polished form. He is an exalted lyrical singer who seldom bothers about the good and humble truth, which French poets are now seeking so persistently and patiently. He strives to set down dreams, subtle thoughts, sometimes great, sometimes visibly forced, but sometimes magnificent.

Two years later I found the house closed and its tenants gone. The furniture was being sold. In memory of them I bought the hideous flayed hand. On the grass an enormous square block of granite bore this simple word: "*Nip.*" Above this a hollow stone offered water to the birds. It was the grave of the monkey, who had been hanged by a young, vindictive negro servant. It was said that this violent domestic had been forced to flee at the point of his exasperated master's revolver. After wandering about without home or food for several days, he returned and began to peddle barley-sugar in the streets. He was expelled from the country after he had almost strangled a displeased customer.

The world would be gayer if one could often meet homes like that.

The Inn

A.k.a. The Hostelry

Like all the little wooden inns in the higher Alps, tiny *auberges* situated in the bare and rocky gorges which intersect the white summits of the mountains, the inn of Schwarenbach is a refuge for travellers who are crossing the Gemmi.

It is open six months in the year, and is inhabited by the family of Jean Hauser. As soon as the snow begins to fall, and fills the valley so as to make the road down to Loëche impassable, the father, with mother, daughter, and the three sons depart, leaving the house in charge of the old guide, Gaspard Hari, with the young guide, Ulrich Kunsi, and Sam, the great mountain dog.

The two men and the dog remain till spring in their snowy prison, with nothing before their eyes except immense, white slopes of the Balmhorn, surrounded by light, glistening summits, and shut up, blocked up, and buried by the snow which rises around them, enveloping and almost burying the little house up to the eaves.

It was the day on which the Hauser family were going to return to Loëche, as winter was approaching, and the descent was becoming dangerous. Three mules started first, laden with baggage and led by the three sons. Then the mother, Jeanne Hauser, and her daughter Louise mounted a fourth mule, and set off in their turn. The father followed them, accompanied by the two men in charge, who were to escort the family as far as the brow of the descent. First of all they skirted the small lake, now frozen over, at the foot of the mass of rocks which stretched in front of

209

the inn; then they followed the valley, which was dominated on all sides by snow-covered peaks.

A ray of sunlight glinted into that little white, glistening, frozen desert, illuminating it with a cold and dazzling flame. No living thing appeared among this ocean of hills; there was no stir in that immeasurable solitude, no noise disturbed the profound silence.

By degrees the young guide, Ulrich Kunsi, a tall, long-legged Swiss, left daddy Hauser and old Gaspard behind, in order to catch up with the mule which carried the two women. The younger one looked at him as he approached, as if she would call him with her sad eyes. She was a young, light-haired peasant girl, whose milk-white cheeks and pale hair seemed to have lost their colour by long dwelling amid the ice. When Ulrich had caught up with the animal which carried the women, he put his hand on the crupper, and relaxed his speed. Mother Hauser began to talk to him, and enumerated with minutest detail all that he would have to attend to during the winter. It was the first winter he would spend up there, while old Hari had already spent fourteen winters amid the snow, at the inn of Schwarenbach.

Ulrich Kunsi listened, without appearing to understand, and looked incessantly at the girl. From time to time he replied: "Yes, Madame Hauser"; but his thoughts seemed far away, and his calm features remained unmoved.

They reached Lake Daube, whose broad, frozen surface reached to the bottom of the valley. On the right, the Daubenhorn showed its black mass, rising up in a peak above the enormous moraines of the Lömmeon glacier, which soared above the Wildstrubel. As they approached the neck of the Gemmi, where the descent to Loëche begins, the immense horizon of the Alps of the Valais, from which the broad, deep valley of the Rhône separated them, came in view.

In the distance, there was a group of white, unequal, flat or pointed mountain summits, which glistened in the sun; the Mischabel with its twin peaks, the huge group of the Weisshorn, the heavy Brunegghorn, the lofty and formidable pyramid of Mont Cervin, slayer of men, and the Dent Blanche, that terrible *coquette*.

Then beneath them, as at the bottom of a terrible abyss, they saw Loëche, its houses looking like grains of sand which had been thrown into that enormous crevice which finishes and closes the Gemmi, and which opens, down below, on to the Rhône.

The mule stopped at the edge of the path, which turns and twists continually, zigzagging fantastically and strangely along the steep side of the mountain, as far as the almost invisible little village at its feet. The women jumped into the snow, and the two old men joined them.

"Well," father Hauser said, "goodbye, and keep up your spirits till next year, my friends," and old Hari replied: "Till next year."

They embraced each other, and then Madame Hauser in her turn, offered her cheek, and the girl did the same. When Ulrich Kunsi's turn came, he whispered in Louise's ear:

"Do not forget those up yonder," and she replied: "No," in such a low voice, that he guessed what she had said, without hearing it.

"Well, *adieu*," Jean Hauser repeated, "and don't fall ill." Then, going before the two women, he commenced the descent, and soon all three disappeared at the first turn in the road, while the two men returned to the inn at Schwarenbach.

They walked slowly side by side, without speaking. The parting was over, and they would be alone together for four or five months. Then Gaspard Hari began to relate his life last winter. He had remained with Michael Canol, who was too old now to stand it; for an accident might happen during that long solitude. They had not been dull, however; the only thing was to be resigned to it from the first, and in the end one would find plenty of distraction, games and other means of whiling away the time.

Ulrich Kunsi listened to him with his eyes on the ground, for in thought he was with those who were descending to the village. They soon came in sight of the inn, which was scarcely visible, so small did it look, a mere black speck at the foot of that enormous billow of snow. When they opened the door, Sam, the great curly dog, began to romp round them.

"Come, my boy," old Gaspard said, "we have no women now, so we must get our own dinner ready. Go and peel the potatoes." And they both sat down on wooden stools, and began to put the bread into the soup.

The next morning seemed very long to Kunsi. Old Hari smoked and smoked beside the hearth, while the young man looked out of the window at the snow-covered mountain opposite the house. In the afternoon he went out, and going over the previous day's ground again, he looked for the traces of the mule that had carried the two women; then when he had reached the neck of the Gemmi, he laid himself down on his stomach, and looked at Loëche.

The village, in its rocky pit, was not yet buried under the snow, although the white masses came quite close to it, balked, however, of their prey by the pine woods which protected the hamlet. From his vantage point the low houses looked like paving-stones in a large meadow. Hauser's little daughter was there now in one of those gray-coloured houses. In which ? Ulrich Kunsi was too far away to be able to make them out separately. How he would have liked to go down while he was yet able!

But the sun had disappeared behind the lofty crest of the Wildstrubel, and the young man returned to the chalet. Daddy Hari was smoking, and, when he saw his mate come in, proposed a game of cards to him. They sat down opposite each other for a long time and played the simple game called *brisque*; then they had supper and went to bed.

The following days were like the first, bright and cold, without any more snow. Old Gaspard spent his afternoons in watching the eagles and other rare birds which ventured on to those frozen heights, while Ulrich journeyed regularly to the neck of the Gemmi to look at the village. In the evening they played at cards, dice, or dominoes, and lost and won trifling sums, just to create an interest in the game.

One morning Hari, who was up first, called his companion. A moving cloud of white spray, deep and light, was falling on them noiselessly, and burying them by degrees under a dark, thick coverlet of foam. This lasted four days and four nights. It was necessary to free the door and the windows, to dig out a passage, and to cut steps to get over this frozen powder, which a twelve-hours' frost had made as hard as the granite of the moraines.

They lived like prisoners, not venturing outside their abode. They had divided their duties and performed them regularly. Ulrich Kunsi undertook the scouring, washing, and everything that belonged to cleanliness. He also chopped up the wood, while Gaspard Hari did the cooking and attended to the fire. Their regular and monotonous work was relieved by long games at cards or dice, but they never quarrelled, and were always calm and placid. They were never even impatient or ill-humoured, nor did they ever use hard words, for they had laid in a stock of patience for this wintering on the top of the mountain.

Sometimes old Gaspard took his rifle and went after chamois, and occasionally killed one. Then there was a feast in the inn at Schwarenbach, and they revelled in fresh meat. One morning he went out as usual. The thermometer outside marked eighteen degrees of frost, and as the sun had not yet risen, the hunter hoped to surprise the animals at the approaches to the Wildstrubel. Ulrich, being alone, remained in bed until ten o'clock. He was of a sleepy nature, but would not have dared to give way like that to his inclination in the presence of the old guide, who was ever an early riser. He breakfasted leisurely with Sam, who also spent his days and nights in sleeping in front of the fire, then he felt low-spirited and even frightened at the solitude, and was seized by a longing for his daily game of cards, as one is by the domination of an invincible habit. So he went out to meet his companion, who was to return at four o'clock.

The snow had levelled the whole deep valley, filled up the crevasses, obliterated all signs of the two lakes and covered the rocks, so that between the high summits there was nothing but an immense, white, regular, dazzling, and frozen surface. For three weeks, Ulrich had not been to the edge of the precipice, from which he had looked down on to the village, and he wanted to go there before climbing the slopes which led to the Wildstrubel. Loëche was now covered by the snow, and the houses could scarcely be distinguished, hidden as they were by that white cloak.

Turning to the right, Ulrich reached the Lammern glacier. He strode along with a mountaineer's long swinging pace, striking the snow, which was as hard as a rock, with his iron-shod stick, and with piercing eyes looking for the little black, moving speck in the distance, on that enormous, white expanse.

When he reached the end of the glacier he stopped, and asked himself whether the old man had taken that road, and then he began to walk along the moraines with rapid and uneasy steps. The day was declining; the snow was assuming a rosy tint, and a dry, frozen wind blew in rough gusts over its crystal surface. Ulrich uttered a long, shrill, vibrating call. His voice sped through the deathlike silence in which the mountains were sleeping; it reached into the distance, over the profound and motionless waves of glacial foam, like the cry of a bird over the waves of the sea; then it died away and nothing answered him.

He started off again. The sun had sunk behind the mountain tops, which still were purpled with the reflection from the heavens; but the depths of the valley were becoming gray, and suddenly the young man felt frightened. It seemed to him as if the silence, the cold, the solitude, the wintry death of these mountains were taking possession of him, were stopping and freezing his blood, making his limbs grow stiff, and turning him into a motionless and frozen object; and he began to run rapidly toward the dwelling. The old man, he thought, would have returned during his absence. He had probably taken another road; and would, no doubt, be sitting before the fire, with a dead chamois at his feet.

He soon came in sight of the inn, but no smoke rose from it.

Ulrich ran faster. Opening the door he met Sam who ran up to him to greet him, but Gaspard Hari had not returned. Kunsi, in his alarm, turned round suddenly, as if he had expected to find his comrade hidden in a corner. Then he relighted the fire and made the soup; hoping every moment to see the old man come in. From time to time he went out to see if Gaspard were not in sight. It was night now, that wan night of the mountain, a livid night, with the crescent moon, yellow and dim, just disappearing behind the mountain tops, and shining faintly on the edge of the horizon.

Then the young man went in and sat down to warm his hands and feet, while he pictured to himself every possible sort of accident. Gaspard might have broken a leg, have fallen into a crevasse, have taken a false step and dislocated his ankle. Perhaps he was lying on the snow, overcome and stiff with the cold, in agony of mind, lost and perhaps shouting for help, calling with all his might, in the silence of the night.

But where ? The mountain was so vast, so rugged, so dangerous in places, especially at that time of the year, that it would have required ten or twenty guides walking for a week in all directions, to find a man in that immense space. Ulrich Kunsi, however, made up his mind to set out with Sam, if Gaspard did not return by one in the morning; and he made his preparations.

He put provisions for two days into a bag, took his steel climbing-irons, tied a long, thin, strong rope round his waist and looked to see that his iron-shod stick and his axe, which served to cut steps in the ice, were in order. Then he waited. The fire was burning on the hearth, the great dog was snoring in front of it, and the clock was ticking in its case of resounding wood, as regularly as a heart beating.

He waited, his ears on the alert for distant sounds, and shivered when the wind blew against the roof and the walls. It struck twelve, and he trembled. Then, as he felt frightened and shivery, he put some water on the fire, so that he might have hot coffee before starting. When the clock struck one he got up, woke Sam,

215

opened the door and went off in the direction of the Wildstrubel. For five hours he ascended, scaling the rocks by means of his climbing- irons, cutting into the ice, advancing continually, and occasionally hauling up the dog, who remained below at the foot of some slope that was too steep for him, by means of the rope. About six o'clock he reached one of the summits to which old Gaspard often came after chamois, and he waited till it should be daylight.

The sky was growing pale overhead, and suddenly a strange light, springing, nobody could tell whence, suddenly illuminated the immense ocean of pale mountain peaks, which stretched for many leagues around him. It seemed as if this vague brightness arose from the snow itself, in order to spread itself into space. By degrees the highest and most distant summits assumed a delicate, fleshlike rose colour, and the red sun appeared behind the ponderous giants of the Bernese Alps.

Ulrich Kunsi set off again, walking like a hunter, stooping and looking for any traces, and saying to his dog: "Seek old fellow, seek!"

He was descending the mountain now, scanning the depths closely, and from time to time shouting, uttering a loud, prolonged familiar cry which soon died away in that silent vastness. Then, he put his ear to the ground, to listen. He thought he could distinguish a voice, and so he began to run and shout again. But he heard nothing more and sat down, worn out and in despair. Toward midday he breakfasted and gave Sam, who was as tired as himself, something to eat also; then he recommenced his search.

When evening came he was still walking, having travelled more than thirty miles over the mountains. As he was too far away to return home, and too tired to drag himself along any further, he dug a hole in the snow and crouched in it with his dog, under a blanket which he had brought with him. The man and the dog lay side by side, warming themselves one against the other, but frozen to the marrow, nevertheless. Ulrich scarcely slept, his mind haunted by visions and his limbs shaking with cold.

Day was breaking when he got up. His legs were as stiff as iron bars, and his spirits so low that he was ready to weep, while his heart was beating so that he almost fell with excitement whenever he thought he heard a noise.

Suddenly he imagined that he also was going to die of cold in the midst of this vast solitude. The terror of such a death roused his energies and gave him renewed vigour. He was descending toward the inn, falling down and getting up again, and followed at a distance by Sam, who was limping on three legs. They did not reach Schwarenbach until four o'clock In the afternoon. The house was empty, and the young man made a fire, had something to eat, and went to sleep, so worn-out that he did not think of anything more.

He slept for a long time, for a very long time, the unconquerable sleep of exhaustion. But suddenly a voice, a cry, a name: "Ulrich," aroused him from his profound slumber, and made him sit up in bed. Had he been dreaming? Was it one of those strange appeals which cross the dreams of disquieted minds No, he heard it still, that reverberating cry, which had entered at his ears and remained in his brain, thrilling him to the tips of his sinewy fingers. Certainly, somebody had cried out, and called: "Ulrich!" There was somebody there, near the house, there could be no doubt of that, and he opened the door and shouted: "Is it you, Gaspard?" with all the strength of his lungs. But there was no reply, no murmur, no groan, nothing. It was quite dark, and the snow looked wan.

The wind had risen, that icy wind which cracks the rocks, and leaves nothing alive on those deserted heights. It came in sudden gusts, more parching and more deadly than the burning wind of the desert, and again Ulrich shouted: "Gaspard! Gaspard! Gaspard!" Then he waited again. Everything was silent on the mountain! Then he shook with terror, and with a bound he was inside the inn. He shut and bolted the door, and then fell into a chair, trembling all over, for he felt certain that his comrade had called him at the moment of dissolution.

He was certain of that, as certain as one is of conscious life or of taste when eating. Old Gaspard Han had been dying for two days and three nights somewhere, in some hole, in one of those deep, untrodden ravines whose whiteness is more sinister than subterranean darkness. He had been dying for two days and three nights and he had just then died, thinking of his comrade. His soul, almost before it was released, had taken its flight to the inn where Ulrich was sleeping, and it had called him by that terrible and mysterious power which the spirits of the dead possess. That voiceless soul had cried to the worn-out soul of the sleeper; it had uttered its last farewell, or its reproach, or its curse on the man who had not searched carefully enough.

And Ulrich felt that it was there, quite close to him, behind the wall, behind the door which he had just fastened. It was wandering about, like a night bird which skims a lighted window with his wings, and the terrified young man was ready to scream with horror. He wanted to run away, but did not dare go out; he did not dare, and would never dare in the future, for that phantom would remain there day and night, round the inn, as long as the old man's body was not recovered and deposited in the consecrated earth of a churchyard.

Daylight came, and Kunsi recovered some of his courage with the return of the bright sun. He prepared his meal, gave his dog some food, and then remained motionless on a chair, tortured at heart as he thought of the old man lying on the snow. Then, as soon as night once more covered the mountains, new terrors assailed him. He now walked up and down the dark kitchen, which was scarcely lighted by the flame of one candle. He walked from one end of it to the other with great strides, listening, listening to hear the terrible cry of the preceding night again break the dreary silence outside.

He felt himself alone, unhappy man, as no man had ever been alone before ! Alone in this immense desert of snow, alone five thousand feet above the inhabited earth, above human habitations, above that stirring, noisy, palpitating life, alone under an icy sky! A mad longing impelled him to run away, no matter where, to get down to Loëche by flinging himself over the precipice; but he did not even dare to open the door, as he felt sure that the other, the *dead*, man would bar his road, so that he might not be obliged to remain up there alone.

Toward midnight, tired with walking, worn-out by grief and fear, he fell into a doze in his chair, for he was afraid of his bed, as one is of a haunted spot. But suddenly the strident cry of the preceding evening pierced his ears, so shrill that Ulrich stretched out his arms to repulse the ghost, and he fell on to his back with his chair.

Sam, who was awakened by the noise, began to howl as frightened dogs do, and trotted all about the house trying to find out where the danger came from. When he got to the door, he sniffed beneath it, smelling vigorously, with his coat bristling and his tail stiff while he growled angrily. Kunsi, who was terrified, jumped up, and holding his chair by one leg, cried: "Don't come in, don't come in, or I shall kill you." And the dog, excited by this threat, barked angrily at that invisible enemy who defied his master's voice. By degrees, however, he quieted down, came back and stretched himself in front of the fire. But he was uneasy, and kept his head up, and growled between his teeth.

Ulrich, in turn, recovered his senses, but as he felt faint with terror, he went and got a bottle of brandy out of the sideboard, and drank off several glasses, one after another, at a gulp. His ideas became vague, his courage revived, and a feverish glow ran through his veins.

He ate scarcely anything the next day, and limited himself to alcohol; so he lived for several days, like a drunken brute. As soon as he thought of Gaspard Hari he began to drink again, and went on drinking until he fell on to the floor, overcome by intoxication. And there he remained on his face, dead drunk, his limbs benumbed, and snoring with his face to the ground. But scarcely had he digested the maddening and burning liquor, than the same cry, "Ulrich," woke him like a bullet piercing his brain, and he got up, still staggering, stretching out his hands to save himself from falling, and calling to Sam to help him. And the dog, who appeared to be going mad like his master, rushed to the door, scratched it with his claws, and gnawed it with his long white teeth, while the young man, his neck thrown back, and his head in the air, drank the brandy in gulps, as if it were cold water, so that it might by and by send his thoughts, his frantic terror, and his memory, to sleep again.

In three weeks he had consumed all his stock of ardent spirits. But his continual drunkenness only lulled his terror, which awoke more furiously than ever, as soon as it was impossible for him to calm it by drinking. His fixed idea, which had been intensified by a month of drunkenness, and which was continually increasing in his absolute solitude, penetrated him like a gimlet. He now walked about his house like a wild beast in its cage, putting his ear to the door to listen if the other were there, and defying him through the wall. Then as soon as he dozed, overcome by fatigue, he heard the voice which made him leap to his feet.

At last one night, as cowards do when driven to extremity, he sprang to the door and opened it, to see who was calling him, and to force him to keep quiet. But such a gust of cold wind blew into his face that it chilled him to the bone. He closed and bolted the door again immediately, without noticing that Sam had rushed out. Then, as he was shivering with cold, he threw some wood on the fire, and sat down in front of it to warm himself. But suddenly he started, for somebody was scratching at the wall, and crying. In desperation he called out: "Go away!" but was answered by another long, sorrowful wail.

Then all his remaining senses forsook him, from sheer fright. He repeated: "Go away!" and turned round to find some corner in which to hide, while the other person went round the house still crying, and rubbing against the wall. Ulrich went to the oak sideboard, which was full of plates and dishes and of provisions, and lifting it up with superhuman strength, he dragged it to the door, so as to form a barricade. Then piling up all the rest of the furniture, the mattresses, *paillasses*, and chairs, he stopped up the windows as men do when assailed by an enemy.

But the person outside now uttered long, plaintive, mournful groans, to which the young man replied by similar groans, and thus days and nights passed without their ceasing to howl at each other. The one was continually walking round the house and scraped the walls with his nails so vigorously that it seemed as if he wished to destroy them, while the other, inside, followed all his movements, stooping down, and holding his ear to the walls, and replying to all his appeals with terrible cries. One evening, however, Ulrich heard nothing more, and he sat down, so overcome by fatigue that he went to sleep immediately, and awoke in the morning without a thought, without any recollection of what had happened, just as if his head had been emptied during his heavy sleep. But he felt hungry, and he ate.

The winter was over, and the Gemmi pass was practicable again, so the Hauser family started off to return to their inn. As soon as they had reached the top of the ascent, the women mounted their mule, and spoke about the two men who they would meet again shortly. They were, indeed, rather surprised that neither of them had come down a few days before, as soon as the road became passable, in order to tell them all about their long winter sojourn. At last, however, they saw the inn, still covered with snow, like a quilt. The door and the windows were closed, but a little smoke was coming out of the chimney, which reassured old Hauser; on going up to the door, however, he saw the skeleton of an animal which had been torn to pieces by the eagles, a large skeleton lying on its side.

They all looked closely at it, and the mother said: "That must be Sam." Then she shouted: "Hi! Gaspard!" A cry from the interior of the house answered her, so sharp a cry that one might have thought some animal uttered it. Old Mauser repeated: "Hi! Gaspard!" and they heard another cry, similar to the first.

Then the three men, the father and the two sons, tried to open the door, but it resisted their efforts. From the empty cow-stall they took a beam to serve as a battering-ram, and hurled it against the door with all their might. The wood gave way, and the boards flew into splinters; then the house was shaken by a loud voice, and inside, behind the sideboard which was overturned, they saw a man standing upright, his hair falling on to his shoulders and a beard descending to his breast, with shining eyes and nothing but rags to cover him. They did not recognize him, but Louise Hauser exclaimed: "It is Ulrich, mother." And her mother declared that it was Ulrich, although his hair was white.

He allowed them to go up to him, and to touch him, but he did not reply to any of their questions, and they were obliged to take him to Loëche, where the doctors found that he was mad. Nobody ever knew what had become of his companion.

Little Louise Hauser nearly died that summer of decline, which the medical men attributed to the cold air of the mountains.

The Mad Woman

"I can tell you a terrible story about the Franco-Prussian war," Monsieur d'Endolin said to some friends assembled in the smoking-room of Baron de Ravot's *château*. "You know my house in the Faubourg de Cormeil. I was living there when the Prussians came, and I had for a neighbour a kind of mad woman, who had lost her senses in consequence of a series of misfortunes. At the age of seven and twenty she had lost her father, her husband, and her newly born child, all in the space of a month.

"When death has once entered into a house, it almost invariably returns immediately, as if it knew the way, and the young woman, overwhelmed with grief, took to her bed and was delirious for six weeks. Then a species of calm lassitude succeeded that violent crisis, and she remained motionless, eating next to nothing, and only moving her eyes. Every time they tried to make her get up, she screamed as if they were about to kill her, and so they ended by leaving her continually in bed, and only taking her out to wash her, to change her linen, and to turn her mattress.

"An old servant remained with her, to give her something to drink, or a little cold meat, from time to time. What passed in that despairing mind? No one ever knew, for she did not speak at all now. Was she thinking of the dead? Was she dreaming sadly, without any precise recollection of anything that had happened? Or was her memory as stagnant as water without any current? But however this may have been, for fifteen years she remained thus inert and secluded.

"The war broke out, and in the beginning of December the Germans came to Cormeil. I can remember it as if it were but yesterday. It was freezing hard enough to split the stones, and I myself was lying back in an armchair, being unable to move on account of the gout, when I heard their heavy and regular tread, and could see them pass from my window.

"They defiled past interminably, with that peculiar motion of a puppet on wires, which belongs to them. Then the officers billeted their men on the inhabitants, and I had seventeen of them. My neighbour, the crazy woman, had a dozen, one of whom was the Commandant, a regular violent, surly swashbuckler.

"During the first few days, everything went on as usual. The officers next door had been told that the lady was ill, and they did not trouble themselves about that in the least, but soon that woman whom they never saw irritated them. They asked what her illness was, and were told that she had been in bed for fifteen years, in consequence of terrible grief. No doubt they did not believe it, and thought that the poor mad creature would not leave her bed out of pride, so that she might not come near the Prussians, or speak to them or even see them.

"The Commandant insisted upon her receiving him. He was shown into the room and said to her roughly: 'I must beg you to get up, *Madame*, and to come downstairs so that we may all see you.' But she merely turned her vague eyes on him, without replying, and so he continued: 'I do not intend to tolerate any insolence, and if you do not get up of your own accord, I can easily find means to make you walk without any assistance.'

"But she did not give any signs of having heard him, and remained quite motionless. Then he got furious, taking that calm silence for a mark of supreme contempt; so he added: 'If you do not come downstairs tomorrow—' And then he left the room.

"The next day the terrified old servant wished to dress her, but the mad woman began to scream violently, and resisted with all her might. The officer ran upstairs quickly, and the servant threw herself at his feet and cried: 'She will not come down, *Monsieur*, she will not. Forgive her, for she is so unhappy.'

"The soldier was embarrassed, as in spite of his anger, he did not venture to order his soldiers to drag her out. But suddenly he began to laugh, and gave some orders in German, and soon a party of soldiers was seen coming out supporting a mattress as if they were carrying a wounded man. On that bed, which had not been unmade, the mad woman, who was still silent, was lying quite quietly, for she was quite indifferent to anything that went on, as long as they let her lie. Behind her, a soldier was carrying a parcel of feminine attire, and the officer said, rubbing his hands: 'We will just see whether you cannot dress yourself alone, and take a little walk.'

"And then the procession went off in the direction of the forest of Imauville; in two hours the soldiers came back alone, and nothing more was seen of the mad woman. What had they done with her? Where had they taken her to? No one knew.

"The snow was falling day and night, and enveloped the plain and the woods in a shroud of frozen foam, and the wolves came and howled at our very doors.

"The thought of that poor lost woman haunted me, and I made several applications to the Prussian authorities in order to obtain some information, and was nearly shot for doing so. When spring returned, the army of occupation withdrew, but my neighbour's house remained closed, and the grass grew thick in the garden walks. The old servant had died during the winter, and nobody troubled any longer about the occurrence; I alone thought about it constantly. What had they done with the woman? Had she escaped through the forest? Had somebody found her, and taken her to a hospital, without being able to obtain any information from her? Nothing happened to relieve my doubts; but by degrees, time assuaged my fears.

"Well, in the following autumn the woodcock were very plentiful, and as my gout had left me for a time, I dragged myself as far as the forest. I had already killed four or five of the long-billed birds, when I knocked over one which fell into a ditch full of branches, and I was obliged to get into it, in order to pick it up, and I found that it had fallen close to a dead, human body.

Immediately the recollection of the mad woman struck me like a blow in the chest. Many other people had perhaps died in the wood during that disastrous year, but though I do not know why, I was sure, sure, I tell you, that I should see the head of that wretched maniac.

"And suddenly I understood, I guessed everything. They had abandoned her on that mattress in the cold, deserted wood; and, faithful to her fixed idea, she had allowed herself to perish under that thick and light counterpane of snow, without moving either arms or legs.

"Then the wolves had devoured her, and the birds had built their nests with the wool from her torn bed, and I took charge of her bones. I only pray that our sons may never see any wars again."

"The Terror"

You say you cannot possibly understand it, and I believe you. You think I am losing my mind? Perhaps I am, but for other reasons than those you imagine, my dear friend.

Yes, I am going to be married, and will tell you what has led me to take that step.

I may add that I know very little of the girl who is going to become my wife tomorrow; I have only seen her four or five times. I know that there is nothing unpleasing about her, and that is enough for my purpose. She is small, fair, and stout; so, of course, the day after tomorrow I shall ardently wish for a tall, dark, thin woman.

She is not rich, and belongs to the middle classes. She is a girl such as you may find by the gross, well adapted for matrimony, without any apparent faults, and with no particularly striking qualities. People say of her:

"Mlle. Lajolle is a very nice girl," and tomorrow they will say: "What a very nice woman Madame Raymon is." She belongs, in a word, to that immense number of girls whom one is glad to have for one's wife, till the moment comes when one discovers that one happens to prefer all other women to that particular woman whom one has married.

"Well," you will say to me, "what on earth did you get married for?"

I hardly like to tell you the strange and seemingly improbable reason that urged me on to this senseless act; the fact, however, is that I am afraid of being alone.

I don't know how to tell you or to make you understand me, but my state of mind is so wretched that you will pity me and despise me.

I do not want to be alone any longer at night. I want to feel that there is someone close to me, touching me, a being who can speak and say something, no matter what it be.

I wish to be able to awaken somebody by my side, so that I may be able to ask some sudden question, a stupid question even, if I feel inclined, so that I may hear a human voice, and feel that there is some waking soul close to me, some one whose reason is at work; so that when I hastily light the candle I may see some human face by my side—because—because—I am ashamed to confess it—because I am afraid of being alone.

Oh, you don't understand me yet.

I am not afraid of any danger; if a man were to come into the room, I should kill him without trembling. I am not afraid of ghosts, nor do I believe in the supernatural. I am not afraid of dead people, for I believe in the total annihilation of every being that disappears from the face of this earth.

Well—yes, well, it must be told: I am afraid of myself, afraid of that horrible sensation of incomprehensible fear.

You may laugh, if you like. It is terrible, and I cannot get over it. I am afraid of the walls, of the furniture, of the familiar objects; which are animated, as far as I am concerned, by a kind of animal life. Above all, I am afraid of my own dreadful thoughts, of my reason, which seems as if it were about to leave me, driven away by a mysterious and invisible agony.

At first I feel a vague uneasiness in my mind, which causes a cold shiver to run all over me. I look round, and of course nothing is to be seen, and I wish that there were something there, no matter what, as long as it were something tangible. I am frightened merely because I cannot understand my own terror.

If I speak, I am afraid of my own voice. If I walk, I am afraid of I know not what, behind the door, behind the curtains, in the cupboard, or under my bed, and yet all the time I know there is nothing anywhere, and I turn round suddenly because I am afraid of what is behind me, although there is nothing there, and I know it.

I become agitated. I feel that my fear increases, and so I shut myself up in my own room, get into bed, and hide under the clothes; and there, cowering down, rolled into a ball, I close my eyes in despair, and remain thus for an indefinite time, remembering that my candle is alight on the table by my bedside, and that I ought to put it out, and yet—I dare not do it.

It is very terrible, is it not, to be like that?

Formerly I felt nothing of all that. I came home quite calm, and went up and down my apartment without anything disturbing my peace of mind. Had any one told me that I should be attacked by a malady—for I can call it nothing else—of most improbable fear, such a stupid and terrible malady as it is, I should have laughed outright. I was certainly never afraid of opening the door in the dark. I went to bed slowly, without locking it, and never got up in the middle of the night to make sure that everything was firmly closed.

It began last year in a very strange manner on a damp autumn evening. When my servant had left the room, after I had dined, I asked myself what I was going to do. I walked up and down my room for some time, feeling tired without any reason for it, unable to work, and even without energy to read. A fine rain was falling, and I felt unhappy, a prey to one of those fits of despondency, without any apparent cause, which make us feel inclined to cry, or to talk, no matter to whom, so as to shake off our depressing thoughts.

I felt that I was alone, and my rooms seemed to me to be more empty than they had ever been before. I was in the midst of infinite and overwhelming solitude. What was I to do? I sat down, but a kind of nervous impatience seemed to affect my legs, so I got up and began to walk about again. I was, perhaps, rather feverish, for my hands, which I had clasped behind me, as one often does when walking slowly, almost seemed to burn one another. Then suddenly a cold shiver ran down my back, and I thought the damp air might have penetrated into my rooms, so

I lit the fire for the first time that year, and sat down again and looked at the flames. But soon I felt that I could not possibly remain quiet, and so I got up again and determined to go out, to pull myself together, and to find a friend to bear me company.

I could not find anyone, so I walked to the boulevard to try and meet some acquaintance or other there.

It was wretched everywhere, and the wet pavement glistened in the gaslight, while the oppressive warmth of the almost impalpable rain lay heavily over the streets and seemed to obscure the light of the lamps.

I went on slowly, saying to myself: "I shall not find a soul to talk to."

I glanced into several cafes, from the Madeleine as far as the Faubourg Poissoniere, and saw many unhappy-looking individuals sitting at the tables who did not seem even to have enough energy left to finish the refreshments they had ordered.

For a long time I wandered aimlessly up and down, and about midnight I started for home. I was very calm and very tired. My janitor opened the door at once, which was quite unusual for him, and I thought that another lodger had probably just come in.

When I go out I always double-lock the door of my room, and I found it merely closed, which surprised me; but I supposed that some letters had been brought up for me in the course of the evening.

I went in, and found my fire still burning so that it lighted up the room a little, and, while in the act of taking up a candle, I noticed somebody sitting in my armchair by the fire, warming his feet, with his back toward me.

I was not in the slightest degree frightened. I thought, very naturally, that some friend or other had come to see me. No doubt the porter, to whom I had said I was going out, had lent him his own key. In a moment I remembered all the circumstances of my return, how the street door had been opened immediately, and that my own door was only latched and not locked.

I could see nothing of my friend but his head, and he had evidently gone to sleep while waiting for me, so I went up to him to rouse him. I saw him quite distinctly; his right arm was hanging down and his legs were crossed; the position of his head, which was somewhat inclined to the left of the armchair, seemed to indicate that he was asleep. "Who can it be?" I asked myself. I could not see clearly, as the room was rather dark, so I put out my hand to touch him on the shoulder, and it came in contact with the back of the chair. There was nobody there; the seat was empty.

I fairly jumped with fright. For a moment I drew back as if confronted by some terrible danger; then I turned round again, impelled by an imperious standing upright, panting with fear, so upset that I could not collect my thoughts, and ready to faint.

But I am a cool man, and soon recovered myself. I thought: "It is a mere hallucination, that is all," and I immediately began to reflect on this phenomenon. Thoughts fly quickly at such moments.

I had been suffering from an hallucination, that was an incontestable fact. My mind had been perfectly lucid and had acted regularly and logically, so there was nothing the matter with the brain. It was only my eyes that had been deceived; they had had a vision, one of those visions which lead simple folk to believe in miracles. It was a nervous seizure of the optical apparatus, nothing more; the eyes were rather congested, perhaps.

I lit my candle, and when I stooped down to the fire in doing so I noticed that I was trembling, and I raised myself up with a jump, as if somebody had touched me from behind.

I was certainly not by any means calm.

I walked up and down a little, and hummed a tune or two. Then I double-locked the door and felt rather reassured; now, at any rate, nobody could come in.

I sat down again and thought over my adventure for a long time; then I went to bed and blew out my light.

For some minutes all went well; I lay quietly on my back, but presently an irresistible desire seized me to look round the room, and I turned over on my side.

My fire was nearly out, and the few glowing embers threw a faint light on the floor by the chair, where I fancied I saw the man sitting again.

I quickly struck a match, but I had been mistaken; there was nothing there. I got up, however, and hid the chair behind my bed, and tried to get to sleep, as the room was now dark; but I had not forgotten myself for more than five minutes, when in my dream I saw all the scene which I had previously witnessed as clearly as if it were reality. I woke up with a start, and having lit the candle, sat up in bed, without venturing even to try to go to sleep again.

Twice, however, sleep overcame me for a few moments in spite of myself, and twice I saw the same thing again, till I fancied I was going mad. When day broke, however, I thought that I was cured, and slept peacefully till noon.

It was all past and over. I had been feverish, had had the nightmare. I know not what. I had been ill, in fact, but yet thought I was a great fool.

I enjoyed myself thoroughly that evening. I dined at a restaurant and afterward went to the theatre, and then started for home. But as I got near the house I was once more seized by a strange feeling of uneasiness. I was afraid of seeing him again. I was not afraid of him, not afraid of his presence, in which I did not believe; but I was afraid of being deceived again. I was afraid of some fresh hallucination, afraid lest fear should take possession of me.

For more than an hour I wandered up and down the pavement; then, feeling that I was really too foolish, I returned home. I breathed so hard that I could hardly get upstairs, and remained standing outside my door for more than ten minutes; then suddenly I had a courageous impulse and my will asserted itself. I inserted my key into the lock, and went into the apartment with a candle in my hand. I kicked open my bedroom door, which was partly open, and cast a frightened glance toward the fireplace. There was nothing there. A-h! What a relief and what a delight!

What a deliverance! I walked up and down briskly and boldly, but I was not altogether reassured, and kept turning round with a jump; the very shadows in the corners disquieted me.

I slept badly, and was constantly disturbed by imaginary noises, but did not see him; no, that was all over.

Since that time I have been afraid of being alone at night. I feel that the spectre is there, close to me, around me; but it has not appeared to me again.

And supposing it did, what would it matter, since I do not believe in it, and know that it is nothing?

However, it still worries me, because I am constantly thinking of it. His right arm hanging down and his head inclined to the left like a man who was asleep—I don't want to think about it!

Why, however, am I so persistently possessed with this idea? His feet were close to the fire!

He haunts me; it is very stupid, but who and what is he? I know that he does not exist except in my cowardly imagination, in my fears, and in my agony. There—enough of that!

Yes, it is all very well for me to reason with myself, to stiffen my backbone, so to say; but I cannot remain at home because I know he is there. I know I shall not see him again; he will not show himself again; that is all over. But he is there, all the same, in my thoughts. He remains invisible, but that does not prevent his being there. He is behind the doors, in the closed cupboard, in the wardrobe, under the bed, in every dark corner. If I open the door or the cupboard, if I take the candle to look under the bed and throw a light on the dark places he is there no longer, but I feel that he is behind me. I turn round, certain that I shall not see him, that I shall never see him again; but for all that, he is behind me.

It is very stupid, it is dreadful; but what am I to do? I cannot help it.

But if there were two of us in the place I feel certain that he would not be there any longer, for he is there just because I am alone, simply and solely because I am alone!

The Unknown

We were speaking of adventures, and each one of us was relating his story of delightful experiences, surprising meetings, on the train, in a hotel, at the seashore. According to Roger des Annettes, the seashore was particularly favourable to the little blind god.

Gontran, who was keeping mum, was asked what he thought of it.

"I guess Paris is about the best place for that," he said. "Woman is like a precious trinket, we appreciate her all the more when we meet her in the most unexpected places; but the rarest ones are only to be found in Paris."

He was silent for a moment, and then continued:

"By Jove, it's great! Walk along the streets on some spring morning. The little women, daintily tripping along, seem to blossom out like flowers. What a delightful, charming sight! The dainty perfume of violet is everywhere. The city is gay, and everybody notices the women. By Jove, how tempting they are in their light, thin dresses, which occasionally give one a glimpse of the delicate pink flesh beneath!

"One saunters along, head up, mind alert, and eyes open. I tell you it's great! You see her in the distance, while still a block away; you already know that she is going to please you at closer quarters. You can recognize her by the flower on her hat, the toss of her head, or her gait. She approaches, and you say to yourself: 'Look out, here she is!' You come closer to her and you devour her with your eyes.

"Is it a young girl running errands for some store, a young woman returning from church, or hastening to see her lover? What do you care? Her well-rounded bosom shows through the thin waist. Oh, if you could only take her in your arms and fondle and kiss her! Her glance may be timid or bold, her hair light or dark. What difference does it make? She brushes against you, and a cold shiver runs down your spine. Ah, how you wish for her all day! How many of these dear creatures have I met this way, and how wildly in love I would have been had I known them more intimately.

"Have you ever noticed that the ones we would love the most distractedly are those whom we never meet to know? Curious, isn't it? From time to time we barely catch a glimpse of some woman, the mere sight of whom thrills our senses. But it goes no further. When I think of all the adorable creatures that I have elbowed in the streets of Paris, I fairly rave. Who are they! Where are they? Where can I find them again? There is a proverb which says that happiness often passes our way; I am sure that I have often passed alongside the one who could have caught me like a linnet in the snare of her fresh beauty."

Roger des Annettes had listened smilingly. He answered: "I know that as well as you do. This is what happened to me: About five years ago, for the first time I met, on the Pont de la Concorde, a young woman who made a wonderful impression on me. She was dark, rather stout, with glossy hair, and eyebrows which nearly met above two dark eyes. On her lip was a scarcely perceptible down, which made one dream-dream as one dreams of beloved woods, on seeing a bunch of wild violets. She had a small waist and a well-developed bust, which seemed to present a challenge, offer a temptation.

Her eyes were like two black spots on white enamel. Her glance was strange, vacant, unthinking, and yet wonderfully beautiful. "I imagined that she might be a Jewess. I followed her, and then turned round to look at her, as did many others. She walked with a swinging gait that was not graceful, but somehow attracted one. At the Place de la Concorde she took a carriage, and I stood there like a fool, moved by the strongest desire that had ever assailed me.

"For about three weeks I thought only of her; and then her memory passed out of my mind.

"Six months later I descried her in the Rue de la Paix again. On seeing her I felt the same shock that one experiences on seeing a once dearly loved woman. I stopped that I might better observe her. When she passed close enough to touch me I felt as though I were standing before a red hot furnace. Then, when she had passed by, I noticed a delicious sensation, as of a cooling breeze blowing over my face. I did not follow her. I was afraid of doing something foolish. I was afraid of myself.

"She haunted all my dreams.

"It was a year before I saw her again. But just as the sun was going down on one beautiful evening in May I recognized her walking along the Avenue des Champs-Elysees. The Arc de Triomphe stood out in bold relief against the fiery glow of the sky. A golden haze filled the air; it was one of those delightful spring evenings which are the glory of Paris. "I followed her, tormented by a desire to address her, to kneel before her, to pour forth the emotion which was choking me. Twice I passed by her only to fall back, and each time as I passed by I felt this sensation, as of scorching heat, which I had noticed in the Rue de la Paix.

"She glanced at me, and then I saw her enter a house on the Rue de Presbourg. I waited for her two hours and she did not come out. Then I decided to question the janitor. He seemed not to understand me. 'She must be visiting someone,' he said.

"The next time I was eight months without seeing her. But one freezing morning in January, I was walking along the Boulevard Malesherbes at a dog trot, so as to keep warm, when at the corner I bumped into a woman and knocked a small package out of her hand. I tried to apologize. It was she!

"At first I stood stock still from the shock; then having returned to her the package which she had dropped, I said abruptly:

"'I am both grieved and delighted, *madame*, to have jostled you. For more than two years I have known you, admired you, and had the most ardent wish to be presented to you; nevertheless I have been unable to find out who you are, or where you live. Please excuse these foolish words. Attribute them to a passionate desire to be numbered among your acquaintances. Such sentiments can surely offend you in no way! You do not know me. My name is Baron Roger des Annettes. Make inquiries about me, and you will find that I am a gentleman. Now, if you refuse my request, you will throw me into abject misery. Please be good to me and tell me how I can see you.'

"She looked at me with her strange vacant stare, and answered smilingly:

"'Give me your address. I will come and see you.'

"I was so dumfounded that I must have shown my surprise. But I quickly gathered my wits together and gave her a visiting card, which she slipped into her pocket with a quick, deft movement.

"Becoming bolder, I stammered:

"'When shall I see you again?'

"She hesitated, as though mentally running over her list of engagements, and then murmured:

"'Will Sunday morning suit you?'

"'I should say it would!'

"She went on, after having stared at me, judged, weighed and analyzed me with this heavy and vacant gaze which seemed to leave a quieting and deadening impression on the person towards whom it was directed.

"Until Sunday my mind was occupied day and night trying to guess who she might be and planning my course of conduct towards her. I finally decided to buy her a jewel, a beautiful little jewel, which I placed in its box on the mantelpiece, and left it there awaiting her arrival.

"I spent a restless night waiting for her.

"At ten o'clock she came, calm and quiet, and with her hand outstretched, as though she had known me for years. Drawing up a chair, I took her hat and coat and furs, and laid them aside.

And then, timidly, I took her hand in mine; after that all went on without a hitch.

"Ah, my friends! what a bliss it is, to stand at a discreet distance and watch the hidden pink and blue ribbons, partly concealed, to observe the hazy lines of the beloved one's form, as they become visible through the last of the filmy garments! What a delight it is to watch the ostrich-like modesty of those who are in reality none too modest. And what is so pretty as their motions!

"Her back was turned towards me, and suddenly, my eyes were irresistibly drawn to a large black spot right between her shoulders. What could it be? Were my eyes deceiving me? But no, there it was, staring me in the face! Then my mind reverted to the faint down on her lip, the heavy eyebrows almost meeting over her coal-black eyes, her glossy black hair — I should have been prepared for some surprise.

"Nevertheless I was dumfounded, and my mind was haunted by dim visions of strange adventures. I seemed to see before me one of the evil *genii* of the Thousand and One Nights, one of these dangerous and crafty creatures whose mission it is to drag men down to unknown depths. I thought of Solomon, who made the Queen of Sheba walk on a mirror that he might be sure that her feet were not cloven.

"And when the time came for me to sing of love to her, my voice forsook me. At first she showed surprise, which soon turned to anger; and she said, quickly putting on her wraps:

"'It was hardly worthwhile for me to go out of my way to come here.'

"I wanted her to accept the ring which I had bought for her, but she replied haughtily: 'For whom do you take me, sir?' I blushed to the roots of my hair. She left without saying another word.

"There is my whole adventure. But the worst part of it is that I am now madly in love with her. I can't see a woman without thinking of her. All the others disgust me, unless they remind me of her. I cannot kiss a woman without seeing her face before me, and without suffering the torture of unsatisfied desire. She is always with me, always there, dressed or nude, my true love. She is there, beside the other one, visible but intangible. I am almost willing to believe that she was bewitched, and carried a talisman between her shoulders.

"Who is she? I don't know yet. I have met her once or twice since. I bowed, but she pretended not to recognize me. Who is she? An Oriental? Yes, doubtless an oriental Jewess! I believe that she must be a Jewess! But why? Why? I don't know!"

The White Wolf

A.k.a. The Wolf

This is the story the old Marquis d'Arville told us after a dinner honour of Saint-Hubert, at the house of Baron des Ravels. They had run down a stag that day. The Marquis was the only one of the guests who had not taken part in the chase. He never hunted. During the whole of the long repast, they had talked of scarcely anything but the massacre of animals. Even the ladies interested themselves in the sanguinary and often unlikely stories, while the orators mimicked the attacks and combats between man and beast, raising their arms and speaking in thunderous tones. M. d'Arville talked much, with a certain poesy, a little flourish, but full of effect. He must have related this story often, it ran so smoothly, never halting at a choice of words in which to clothe an image.

"Gentlemen, I never hunt, nor did my father, nor my grandfather, nor my great-great-grandfather. The last named was the son of a man who hunted more than all of you. He died in 1764. I will tell you how. He was named John, and was married, and became the father of the man who was my great-great-grandfather. He lived with his younger brother, Francis d'Arville, in our castle, in the midst of a deep forest in Lorraine.

"Francis d'Arville always remained a boy through his love for hunting. They both hunted from one end of the year to the other without cessation or weariness. They loved nothing else, understood nothing else, talked only of this, and lived for this alone.

"They were possessed by this terrible, inexorable passion. It consumed them, having taken entire control of them, leaving no place for anything else. They had agreed not to put off the chase for any reason whatsoever. My great-great-grandfather was born while his father was following a fox, but John d'Arville did not interrupt his sport, and swore that the little beggar might have waited until after the death-cry! His brother Francis showed himself still more hot-headed than he. The first thing on rising, he would go to see the dogs, then the horses; then he would shoot some birds about the place, even when about to set out hunting big game.

"They were called in the country *Monsieur* the Marquis and *Monsieur* the Cadet, noblemen then not acting as do those of our time, who wish to establish in their titles a descending scale of rank, for the son of a marquis is no more a count, or the son of a viscount a baron, than the son of a general is a colonel by birth. But the niggardly vanity of the day finds profit in this arrangement To return to my ancestors:

"They were, it appears, immoderately large, bony, hairy, violent, and vigorous. The younger one was taller than the elder, and had such a voice that, according to a legend he was very proud of, all the leaves of the forest moved when he shouted.

"And when mounted, ready for the chase, it must have been a superb sight to see these two giants astride their great horses.

"Toward the middle of the winter of that year, 1764, the cold was excessive and the wolves became ferocious.

"They even attacked belated peasants, roamed around houses at night, howled from sunset to sunrise, and ravaged the stables.

"At one time a rumour was circulated. It was said that a colossal wolf, of grayish-white colour, which had eaten two children, devoured the arm of a woman, strangled all the watchdogs of the country, was now coming without fear into the house inclosures and smelling around the doors. Many inhabitants affirmed that they had felt his breath, which made the lights flicker. Shortly a panic ran through all the province. No one dared to go out after night- fall. The very shadows seemed haunted by the image of this beast.

"The brothers D'Arville resolved to find and slay him. So they called together for a grand chase all the gentlemen of the country.

"It was in vain. They had beaten the forests and scoured the thickets, but had seen nothing of him. They killed wolves, but not that one. And each night after such a chase, the beast, as if to avenge himself, attacked some traveler, or devoured some cattle, always far from the place where they had sought him.

"Finally, one night he found a way into the swine-house of the castle D'Arville and ate two beauties of the best breed.

"The two brothers were furious, interpreting the attack as one of bravado on the part of the monster — a direct injury, a defiance. Therefore, taking all their best-trained hounds, they set out to run down the beast, with courage excited by anger.

"From dawn until the sun descended behind the great nut-trees, they beat about the forests with no result.

"At last, both of them, angry and disheartened, turned their horses' steps into a bypath bordered by brushwood. They were marvelling at the baffling power of this wolf, when suddenly they were seized with a mysterious fear.

"The elder said:

"'This can be no ordinary beast. One might say he can think like a man.'

"The younger replied:

"'Perhaps we should get our cousin, the Bishops to bless a bullet for him, or ask a priest to pronounce some words to help us.'

"Then they were silent

"John continued: 'Look at the sun, how red it is. The great wolf will do mischief tonight.'

"He had scarcely finished speaking when his horse reared. Francis's horse started to run at the same time. A large bush covered with dead leaves rose before them, and a colossal beast, grayish-white, sprang out, scampering away through the wood.

"Both gave a grunt of satisfaction, and bending to the necks

242

of their heavy horses, they urged them on with the weight of their bodies, exciting them, hastening with voice and spur, until these strong riders seemed to carry the weight of their beasts between their knees, carrying them by force as if they were flying.

"Thus they rode, crashing through forests, crossing ravines, climbing up the sides of steep gorges, and sounding the horn, at frequent intervals, to arouse the people and the dogs of the neighbourhood.

"But suddenly, in the course of this breakneck ride, my ancestor struck his forehead against a large branch and fractured his skull. He fell to the ground as if dead, while his frightened horse disappeared in the surrounding thicket

"The younger D'Arville stopped short, sprang to the ground, seized his brother in his arms, and saw that he had lost consciousness.

"He sat down beside him, took his disfigured head upon his knees, looking earnestly at the lifeless face. Little by little a fear crept over him, a strange fear that he had never before felt, fear of the shadows, of the solitude, of the lonely woods, and also of the chimerical wolf, which had now come to be the death of his brother.

"The shadows deepened, the branches of the trees crackled in the sharp cold. Francis arose shivering, incapable of remaining there longer, and already feeling his strength fail. There was nothing to be heard, neither the voice of dogs nor the sound of a horn; all within this invisible horizon was mute. And in this gloomy silence and the chill of evening there was something strange and frightful.

"With his powerful hands he seized John's body and laid it across the saddle to take it home; then mounted gently behind it, his mind troubled by horrible, supernatural images, as if he were possessed.

"Suddenly, in the midst of these fears, a great form passed. It was the wolf. A violent fit of terror seized upon the hunter; something cold, like a stream of ice-water seemed to glide through his veins, and he made the sign of the cross, like a monk haunted with devils, so dismayed was he by the reappearance of the frightful wanderer. Then, his eyes falling upon the inert body before him, his fear was quickly changed to anger, and he trembled with inordinate rage.

"He pricked his horse and darted after him.

"He followed him through copses, over ravines, and around great forest trees, traversing woods that he no longer recognized, his eye fixed upon a white spot, which was ever flying from him as night covered the earth.

"His horse also seemed moved by an unknown force. He galloped on with neck extended, crashing over small trees and rocks, with the body of the dead stretched across him on the saddle. Brambles caught in his mane; his head, where it had struck the trunks of trees, was spattered with blood; the marks of the spurs were over his flanks.

"Suddenly the animal and its rider came out of the forest, rushing through a valley as the moon appeared above the hills. This valley was stony and shut in by enormous rocks, over which it was impossible to pass; there was no other way for the wolf but to turn on his steps.

"Francis gave such a shout of joy and revenge that the echo of it was like the roll of thunder. He leaped from his horse, knife in hand.

"The bristling beast, with rounded back, was awaiting him; his eyes shining like two stars. But before joining in battle, the strong hunter, grasping his brother, seated him upon a rock, supporting his head, which was now but a mass of blood, with stones, and cried aloud to him, as to one deaf: 'Look, John! Look here!'

"Then he threw himself upon the monster. He felt himself strong enough to overthrow a mountain, to crush the very rocks in his hands. The beast meant to kill him by sinking his claws in his vitals; but the man had seized him by the throat, without even making use of his weapon, and strangled him gently, waiting until his breath stopped and he could hear the death-rattle at his heart. And he laughed, with the joy of dismay, clutching more and more with a terrible hold, and crying out in his delirium: 'Look, John! Look!' All resistance ceased. The body of the wolf was limp. He was dead.

"Then Francis, taking him in his arms, threw him down at the feet of his elder brother, crying out in expectant voice: 'Here, here, my little John, here he is!'

"Then he placed upon the saddle the two bodies, the one above the other, and started on his way.

"He returned to the castle laughing and weeping, like Gargantua at the birth of Pantagruel, shouting in triumph and stamping with delight in relating the death of the beast, and moaning and tearing at his beard in calling the name of his brother.

"Often, later, when he recalled this day, he would declare, with tears in his eyes: 'If only poor John had seen me strangle the beast, he would have died content, I am sure!'

"The widow of my ancestor inspired in her son a horror of the chase, which was transmitted from father to son down to myself."

The Marquis d'Arville was silent. Someone asked: "Is the story a legend or not?"

And the narrator replied:

"I swear to you it is true from beginning to end."

Then a lady, in a sweet little voice, declared:

"It is beautiful to have passions like that"

A Fishing Excursion
A.k.a. Two Friends

Paris was blockaded, desolate, famished. The sparrows were few, and anything that was to be had was good to eat.

On a bright morning in January, Mr. Morissot, a watchmaker by trade, but idler through circumstances, was walking along the *boulevard*, sad, hungry, with his hands in the pockets of his uniform trousers, when he came face to face with a brother-in-arms whom he recognized as an old-time friend. Before the war, Morissot could be seen at daybreak every Sunday, trudging along with a cane in one hand and a tin box on his back. He would take the train to Colombes and walk from there to the Isle of Marante where he would fish until dark. It was there he had met Mr. Sauvage who kept a little notion store in the Rue Notre Dame de Lorette, a jovial fellow and passionately fond of fishing like himself. A warm friendship had sprung up between these two and they would fish side by side all day, very often without saying a word. Some days, when everything looked fresh and new and the beautiful spring sun gladdened every heart, Mr. Morissot would exclaim:

"How delightful!" and Mr. Sauvage would answer:

"There is nothing to equal it."

Then again on a fall evening, when the glorious setting sun, spreading its golden mantle on the already tinted leaves, would throw strange shadows around the two friends, Sauvage would say:

"What a grand picture!"

"It beats the *boulevard!*" would answer Morissot. But they understood each other quite as well without speaking.

The two friends had greeted each other warmly and had resumed their walk side by side, both thinking deeply of the past and present events. They entered a *café*, and when a glass of *absinthe* had been placed before each Sauvage sighed:

"What terrible events, my friend!"

"And what weather!" said Morissot sadly; "this is the first nice day we have had this year. Do you remember our fishing excursions?"

"Do I! Alas! when shall we go again!"

After a second *absinthe* they emerged from the *café*, feeling rather dizzy — that light-headed effect which alcohol has on an empty stomach. The balmy air had made Sauvage exuberant and he exclaimed:

"Suppose we go!"

"Where?"

"Fishing."

"Fishing! Where?"

"To our old spot, to Colombes. The French soldiers are stationed near there and I know Colonel Dumoulin will give us a pass."

"It's a go; I am with you."

An hour after, having supplied themselves with their fishing tackle, they arrived at the colonel's villa. He had smiled at their request and had given them a pass in due form.

At about eleven o'clock they reached the advance-guard, and after presenting their pass, walked through Colombes and found themselves very near their destination. Argenteuil, across the way, and the great plains toward Nanterre were all deserted. Solitary the hills of Orgemont and Sannois rose clearly above the plains; a splendid point of observation.

"See," said Sauvage pointing to the hills, "the Prussians are there."

Prussians! They had never seen one, but they knew that they were all around Paris, invisible and powerful; plundering, devastating, and slaughtering. To their superstitious terror they added a deep hatred for this unknown and victorious people.

"What if we should meet some?" said Morissot.

"We would ask them to join us," said Sauvage in true Parisian style.

Still they hesitated to advance. The silence frightened them. Finally Sauvage picked up courage.

"Come, let us go on cautiously."

They proceeded slowly, hiding behind bushes, looking anxiously on every side, listening to every sound. A bare strip of land had to be crossed before reaching the river. They started to run. At last, they reached the bank and sank into the bushes; breathless, but relieved.

Morissot thought he heard someone walking. He listened attentively, but no, he heard no sound. They were indeed alone! The little island shielded them from view. The house where the restaurant used to be seemed deserted; feeling reassured, they settled themselves for a good day's sport.

Sauvage caught the first fish, Morissot the second; and every minute they would bring one out which they would place in a net at their feet. It was indeed miraculous! They felt that supreme joy which one feels after having been deprived for months of a pleasant pastime. They had forgotten everything; even the war!

Suddenly, they heard a rumbling sound and the earth shook beneath them. It was the cannon on Mont Vaterien. Morissot looked up and saw a trail of smoke, which was instantly followed by another explosion. Then they followed in quick succession.

"They are at it again," said Sauvage shrugging his shoulders. Morissot, who was naturally peaceful, felt a sudden, uncontrollable anger.

"Stupid fools! What pleasure can they find in killing each other!"

"They are worse than brutes!"

"It will always be thus as long as we have governments."

"Well, such is life!"

"You mean death!" said Morissot laughing.

They continued to discuss the different political problems, while the cannon on Mont Valerien sent death and desolation among the French.

Suddenly they started. They had heard a step behind them. They turned and beheld four big men in dark uniforms, with guns pointed right at them. Their fishing-lines dropped out of their hands and floated away with the current.

In a few minutes, the Prussian soldiers had bound them, cast them into a boat, and rowed across the river to the island which our friends had thought deserted. They soon found out their mistake when they reached the house, behind which stood a score or more of soldiers. A big burly officer, seated astride a chair, smoking an immense pipe, addressed them in excellent French:

"Well, gentlemen, have you made a good haul?"

Just then, a soldier deposited at his feet the net full of fish which he had taken good care to take along with him. The officer smiled and said:

"I see you have done pretty well; but let us change the subject. You are evidently sent to spy upon me. You pretended to fish so as to put me off the scent, but I am not so simple. I have caught you and shall have you shot. I am sorry, but war is war. As you passed the advance-guard you certainly must have the password; give it to me, and I will set you free."

The two friends stood side by side, pale and slightly trembling, but they answered nothing.

"No one will ever know. You will go back home quietly and the secret will disappear with you. If you refuse, it is instant death! Choose!"

They remained motionless; silent. The Prussian officer calmly pointed to the river.

"In five minutes you will be at the bottom of this river! Surely, you have a family, friends waiting for you?"

Still they kept silent. The cannon rumbled incessantly. The officer gave orders in his own tongue, then moved his chair away from the prisoners. A squad of men advanced within twenty feet of them, ready for command.

"I give you one minute; not a second more!"

Suddenly approaching the two Frenchmen, he took Morissot aside and whispered:

"Quick; the password. Your friend will not know; he will think I have changed my mind." Morissot said nothing.

Then taking Sauvage aside he asked him the same thing, but he also was silent. The officer gave further orders and the men levelled their guns. At that moment, Morissot's eyes rested on the net full of fish lying in the grass a few feet away. The sight made him feel faint and, though he struggled against it, his eyes filled with tears. Then turning to his friend:

"Farewell! Mr. Sauvage!"

"Farewell! Mr. Morissot."

They stood for a minute, hand in hand, trembling with emotion which they were unable to control.

"Fire!" commanded the officer.

The squad of men fired as one. Sauvage fell straight on his face. Morissot, who was taller, swayed, pivoted, and fell across his friend's body, his face to the sky; while blood flowed freely from the wound in his breast. The officer gave further orders and his men disappeared.

They came back presently with ropes and stones, which they tied to the feet of the two friends, and four of them carried them to the edge of the river. They swung them and threw them in as far as they could. The bodies weighted by stones sank immediately. A splash, a few ripples and the water resumed its usual calmness. The only thing to be seen was a little blood floating on the surface. The officer calmly retraced his steps toward the house muttering:

"The fish will get even now."

He perceived the net full of fish, picked it up, smiled, and called:

"Wilhelm!"

A soldier in a white apron approached. The officer handed him the fish saying:

"Fry these little things while they are still alive; They will make a delicious meal."

And having resumed his position on the chair, he puffed away at his pipe."

Was it a Dream?

"I had loved her madly!

"Why does one love? Why does one love? How queer it is to see only one being in the world, to have only one thought in one's mind, only one desire in the heart, and only one name on the lips—a name which comes up continually, rising, like the water in a spring, from the depths of the soul to the lips, a name which one repeats over and over again, which one whispers ceaselessly, everywhere, like a prayer.

"I am going to tell you our story, for love only has one, which is always the same. I met her and loved her; that is all. And for a whole year I have lived on her tenderness, on her caresses, in her arms, in her dresses, on her words, so completely wrapped up, bound, and absorbed in everything which came from her, that I no longer cared whether it was day or night, or whether I was dead or alive, on this old earth of ours.

"And then she died. How? I do not know; I no longer know anything. But one evening she came home wet, for it was raining heavily, and the next day she coughed, and she coughed for about a week, and took to her bed. What happened I do not remember now, but doctors came, wrote, and went away. Medicines were brought, and some women made her drink them. Her hands were hot, her forehead was burning, and her eyes bright and sad. When I spoke to her, she answered me, but I do not remember what we said. I have forgotten everything, everything, everything! She died, and I very well remember her slight, feeble sigh. The nurse said: 'Ah!' and I understood, I understood!

"I knew nothing more, nothing. I saw a priest, who said: 'Your mistress?' and it seemed to me as if he were insulting her. As she was dead, nobody had the right to say that any longer, and I turned him out. Another came who was very kind and tender, and I shed tears when he spoke to me about her.

"They consulted me about the funeral, but I do not remember anything that they said, though I recollected the coffin, and the sound of the hammer when they nailed her down in it. Oh! God, God!

"She was buried! Buried! She! In that hole! Some people came—female friends. I made my escape and ran away. I ran, and then walked through the streets, went home, and the next day started on a journey.

★ ★ ★ ★ ★ ★ ★

"Yesterday I returned to Paris, and when I saw my room again—our room, our bed, our furniture, everything that remains of the life of a human being after death—I was seized by such a violent attack of fresh grief, that I felt like opening the window and throwing myself out into the street. I could not remain any longer among these things, between these walls which had inclosed and sheltered her, which retained a thousand atoms of her, of her skin and of her breath, in their imperceptible crevices. I took up my hat to make my escape, and just as I reached the door, I passed the large glass in the hall, which she had put there so that she might look at herself every day from head to foot as she went out, to see if her *toilette* looked well, and was correct and pretty, from her little boots to her bonnet.

"I stopped short in front of that looking-glass in which she had so often been reflected—so often, so often, that it must have retained her reflection. I was standing there. trembling, with my eyes fixed on the glass—on that flat, profound, empty glass—which had contained her entirely, and had possessed her as much as I, as my passionate looks had. I felt as if I loved that glass. I touched it; it was cold. Oh! the recollection! sorrowful mirror, burning mirror, horrible mirror, to make men suffer such torments! Happy is the man whose heart forgets everything that it has contained, everything that has passed before it, everything that has looked at itself in it, or has been reflected in its affection, in its love! How I suffer!

"I went out without knowing it, without wishing it, and toward the cemetery. I found her simple grave, a white marble cross, with these few words:

"'*She loved, was loved, and died.*'

"She is there, below, decayed! How horrible! I sobbed with my forehead on the ground, and I stopped there for a long time, a long time. Then I saw that it was getting dark, and a strange, mad wish, the wish of a despairing lover, seized me. I wished to pass the night, the last night, in weeping on her grave. But I should be seen and driven out. How was I to manage? I was cunning, and got up and began to roam about in that city of the dead. I walked and walked.

"How small this city is, in comparison with the other, the city in which we live. And yet, how much more numerous the dead are than the living. We want high houses, wide streets, and much room for the four generations who see the daylight at the same time, drink water from the spring, and wine from the vines, and eat bread from the plains.

"And for all the generations of the dead, for all that ladder of humanity that has descended down to us, there is scarcely anything, scarcely anything! The earth takes them back, and oblivion effaces them. *Adieu!*

"At the end of the cemetery, I suddenly perceived that I was in its oldest part, where those who had been dead a long time are mingling with the soil, where the crosses themselves are decayed, where possibly newcomers will be put to-morrow. It is full of untended roses, of strong and dark cypress-trees, a sad and beautiful garden, nourished on human flesh.

"I was alone, perfectly alone. So I crouched in a green tree and hid myself there completely amid the thick and sombre branches. I waited, clinging to the stem, like a shipwrecked man does to a plank.

"When it was quite dark, I left my refuge and began to walk

softly, slowly, inaudibly, through that ground full of dead people. I wandered about for a long time, but could not find her tomb again. I went on with extended arms, knocking against the tombs with my hands, my feet, my knees, my chest, even with my head, without being able to find her. I groped about like a blind man finding his way, I felt the stones, the crosses, the iron railings, the metal wreaths, and the wreaths of faded flowers! I read the names with my fingers, by passing them over the letters. What a night! What a night! I could not find her again!

"There was no moon. What a night! I was frightened, horribly frightened in these narrow paths, between two rows of graves. Graves! graves! graves! nothing but graves! On my right, on my left, in front of me, around me, everywhere there were graves! I sat down on one of them, for I could not walk any longer, my knees were so weak. I could hear my heart beat! And I heard something else as well. What? A confused, nameless noise. Was the noise in my head, in the impenetrable night, or beneath the mysterious earth, the earth sown with human corpses? I looked all around me, but I cannot say how long I remained there; I was paralyzed with terror, cold with fright, ready to shout out, ready to die.

"Suddenly, it seemed to me that the slab of marble on which I was sitting, was moving. Certainly it was moving, as if it were being raised. With a bound, I sprang on to the neighbouring tomb, and I saw, yes, I distinctly saw the stone which I had just quitted rise upright. Then the dead person appeared, a naked skeleton, pushing the stone back with its bent back. I saw it quite clearly, although the night was so dark. On the cross I could read:

"'*Here lies Jacques Olivant, who died at the age of fifty-one. He loved his family, was kind and honourable, and died in the grace of the Lord.*'

"The dead man also read what was inscribed on his tombstone; then he picked up a stone off the path, a little, pointed stone and began to scrape the letters carefully. He slowly effaced them, and with the hollows of his eyes he looked at the places where they had been engraved. Then with the tip of the bone that had been his forefinger, he wrote in luminous letters, like those lines which boys trace on walls with the tip of a lucifer match:

Here reposes Jacques Olivant, who died at the age of fifty-one. He hastened his father's death by his unkindness, as he wished to inherit his fortune, he tortured his wife, tormented his children, deceived his neighbours, robbed everyone he could, and died wretched.

"When he had finished writing, the dead man stood motionless, looking at his work. On turning round I saw that all the graves were open, that all the dead bodies had emerged from them, and that all had effaced the lies inscribed on the gravestones by their relations, substituting the truth instead.

"And I saw that all had been the tormentors of their neighbours—malicious, dishonest, hypocrites, liars, rogues, calumniators, envious; that they had stolen, deceived, performed every disgraceful, every abominable action, these good fathers, these faithful wives, these devoted sons, these chaste daughters, these honest tradesmen, these men and women who were called irreproachable.

They were all writing at the same time, on the threshold of their eternal abode, the truth, the terrible and the holy truth of which everybody was ignorant, or pretended to be ignorant, while they were alive.

"I thought that SHE also must have written something on her tombstone, and now running without any fear among the half-open coffins, among the corpses and skeletons, I went toward her, sure that I should find her immediately. I recognized her at once, without seeing her face, which was covered by the winding-sheet, and on the marble cross, where shortly before I had read:

She loved, was loved, and died.

I now saw:

Having gone out in the rain one day, in order to deceive her lover, she caught cold and died.

★ ★ ★ ★ ★ ★ ★

"It appears that they found me at daybreak, lying on the grave unconscious."

Who Knows?

My God! My God! I am going to write down at last what has happened to me. But how can I? How dare I? The thing is so bizarre, so inexplicable, so incomprehensible, so silly!

If I were not perfectly sure of what I have seen, sure that there was 'not in my reasoning any defect, any error in my declarations, any lacuna in the inflexible sequence of my observations, I should believe myself to be the dupe of a simple hallucination, the sport of a singular vision. After all, who knows? Yesterday I was in a private asylum, but I went there voluntarily, out of prudence and fear. Only one single human being knows my history, and that is the doctor of the said asylum. I am going to write to him. I really do not know why. To disembarrass myself? Yea, I feel as though weighed down by an intolerable nightmare. Let me explain.

I have always been a recluse, a dreamer, a kind of isolated philosopher, easy-going, content with but little, harbouring ill-feeling against no man, and without even a grudge against heaven. I have constantly lived alone; consequently, a kind of torture takes hold of me when I find myself in the presence of others. How is this to be explained? I do not know. I am not averse to going out into the world, to conversation, to dining with friends, but when they are near me for any length of time, even the most intimate of them, they bore me, fatigue me, enervate me, and I experience an overwhelming, torturing desire to see them get up and go, to take themselves away, and to leave me by myself.

That desire is more than a craving; it is an irresistible necessity. And if the presence of people with whom I find myself were to be continued; if I were compelled, not only to listen, but also to follow, for any length of time, their conversation, a serious accident would assuredly take place. What kind of accident? Ah! who knows? Perhaps a slight paralytic stroke? Probably!

I like solitude so much that I cannot even endure the vicinage of other beings sleeping under the same roof. I cannot live in Paris, because there I suffer the most acute agony. I lead a moral life, and am therefore tortured in body and in nerves by that immense crowd which swarms and lives even when it sleeps. Ah! the sleeping of others is more painful still than their conversation. And I can never find repose when I know and feel that on the other side of a wall several existences are undergoing these regular eclipses of reason.

Why am I thus? Who knows? The cause of it is very simple perhaps. I get tired very soon of everything that does not emanate from me. And there are many people in similar case.

We are, on earth, two distinct races. Those who have need of others, whom others amuse, engage, soothe, whom solitude harasses, pains, stupefies, like the movement of a terrible glacier or the traversing of the desert; and those, on the contrary, whom others weary, tire, bore, silently torture, whom isolation calms and bathes in the repose of independency, and plunges into the humours of their own thoughts. In fine, there is here a normal, physical phenomenon. Some are constituted to live a life outside of themselves, others, to live a life within themselves. As for me, my exterior associations are abruptly and painfully short-lived, and, as they reach their limits, I experience in my whole body and in my whole intelligence an intolerable uneasiness.

As a result of this, I became attached, or rather had become much attached, to inanimate objects, which have for me the importance of beings, and my house has or had become a world in which I lived an active and solitary life, surrounded by all manner of things, furniture, familiar knickknacks, as sympathetic in my eyes as the visages of human beings. I had filled my mansion with them; little by little, I had adorned it with them, and I felt an inward content and satisfaction, was more happy than if I had been in the arms of a beloved girl, whose wonted caresses had become a soothing and delightful necessity.

I had had this house constructed in the centre of a beautiful garden, which hid it from the public highways, and which was near the entrance to a city where I could find, on occasion, the resources of society, for which, at moments, I had a longing. All my domestics slept in a separate building, which was situated at some considerable distance from my house, at the far end of the kitchen garden, which in turn was surrounded by a high wall. The obscure envelopment of night, in the silence of my concealed habitation, buried under the leaves of great trees, was so reposeful and so delicious, that before retiring to my couch I lingered every evening for several hours in order to enjoy the solitude a little longer.

One day *Signad* had been played at one of the city theatres. It was the first time that I had listened to that beautiful, musical, and fairy-like drama, and I had derived from it the liveliest pleasures.

I returned home on foot with a light step, my head full of sonorous phrases, and my mind haunted by delightful visions. It was night, the dead of night, and so dark that I could hardly distinguish the broad highway, and consequently I stumbled into the ditch more than once. From the custom-house, at the barriers, to my house, was about a mile,—perhaps a little more a leisurely walk of about twenty minutes. It was one o'clock in the morning, one o'clock or maybe half-past one; the sky had by this time cleared somewhat and the crescent appeared, the gloomy crescent of the last quarter of the moon. The crescent of the first quarter is that which rises about five or six o'clock in the evening and is clear, gay, and fretted with silver; but the one which rises after midnight is reddish, sad, and desolating—it is the true Sabbath crescent Every prowler by night has made the same observation. The first, though slender as a thread, throws a faint, joyous light which rejoices the heart and lines the ground with distinct shadows; the last sheds hardly a dying glimmer, and is so wan that it occasions hardly any shadows.

In the distance, I perceived the sombre mass of my garden, and, I know not why, was seized with a feeling of uneasiness at the idea of going inside. I slackened my pace, and walked very softly, the thick cluster of trees having the appearance of a tomb in which my house was buried.

I opened my outer gate and entered the long avenue of sycamores which ran in the direction of the house, arranged vault-wise like a high tunnel, traversing opaque masses, and winding round the turf lawns, on which baskets of flowers, in the pale darkness, could be indistinctly discerned.

While approaching the house, I was seized by a strange feeling. I could hear nothing, I stood still. Through the trees there was not even a breath of air stirring. "What is the matter with me?" I said to myself. For ten years I had entered and re-entered in the same way, without ever experiencing the least inquietude. I never had any fear at nights. The sight of a man, a marauder, or a thief would have thrown me into a fit of anger, and I would have rushed at him without any hesitation. Moreover, I was armed—I had my revolver. But I did not touch it, for I was anxious to resist that feeling of dread with which I was seized.

What was it? Was it a presentiment—that mysterious presentiment which takes hold of the senses of men who have witnessed something which, to them, is inexplicable? Perhaps? Who knows?

In proportion as I advanced, I felt my skin quiver more and more, and when I was close to the wall, near the outhouses of my large residence, I felt that it would be necessary for me to wait a few minutes before opening the door and going inside. I sat down, then, on a bench, under the windows of my drawing-room. I rested there, a little disturbed, with my head leaning against the wall, my eyes wide open, under the shade of the foliage. For the first few minutes, I did not observe anything unusual around me; I had a humming noise in my ears, but that has happened often to me. Sometimes it seemed to me that I heard trains passing, that I heard clocks striking, that I heard a multitude on the march.

Very soon, those humming noises became more distinct, more concentrated, more determinable, I was deceiving myself. It was not the ordinary tingling of my arteries which transmitted to my ears these rumbling sounds, but it was a very distinct, though confused, noise which came, without any doubt whatever, from the interior of my house. Through the walls I distinguished this continued noise,—I should rather say agitation than noise,—an indistinct moving about of a pile of things, as if people were tossing about, displacing, and carrying away surreptitiously all my furniture.

I doubted, however, for some considerable time yet, the evidence of my ears. But having placed my ear against one of the outhouses, the better to discover what this strange disturbance was, inside my house, I became convinced, certain, that something was taking place in my residence which was altogether abnormal and incomprehensible. I had no fear, but I was—how shall I express it—paralyzed by astonishment. I did not draw my revolver, knowing very well that there was no need of my doing so.

I listened a long time, but could come to no resolution, my mind being quite clear, though in myself I was naturally anxious. I got up and waited, listening always to the noise, which gradually increased, and at intervals grew very loud, and which seemed to become an impatient, angry disturbance, a mysterious commotion.

Then, suddenly, ashamed of my timidity, I seized my bunch of keys. I selected the one I wanted, guided it into the lock, turned it twice, and pushing the door with all my might, sent it banging against the partition.

The collision sounded like the report of a gun, and there responded to that explosive noise, from roof to basement of my residence, a formidable tumult. It was so sudden, so terrible, so deafening, that I recoiled a few steps, and though I knew it to be wholly useless, I pulled my revolver out of its case.

I continued to listen for some time longer. I could distinguish now an extraordinary pattering upon the steps of my grand staircase, on the waxed floors, on the carpets, not of boots, or of naked feet, but of iron and wooden crutches, which resounded like cymbals. Then I suddenly discerned, on the threshold of my door, an armchair, my large reading easy-chair, which set off waddling. It went away through my garden. Others followed it, those of my drawing-room, then my sofas, dragging themselves along like crocodiles on their short paws; then all my chairs, bounding like goats, and the little footstools, hopping like rabbits.

Oh! what a sensation! I slunk back into a clump of bushes where I remained crouched up, watching, meanwhile, my furniture defile past—for everything walked away, the one behind the other, briskly or slowly, according to its weight or size. My piano, my grand piano, bounded past with the gallop of a horse and a murmur of music in its sides; the smaller articles slid along the gravel like snails, my brushes, crystal, cups and saucers, which glistened in the moonlight. I saw my writing desk appear, a rare curiosity of the last century, which contained all the letters I had ever received, all the history of my heart, an old history from which I have suffered so much! Besides, there were inside of it a great many cherished photographs.

Suddenly—I no longer had any fear—I threw myself on it, seized it as one would seize a thief, as one would seize a wife about to run away; but it pursued its irresistible course, and despite my efforts and despite my anger, I could not even retard its pace. As I was resisting in desperation that insuperable force, I was thrown to the ground. It then rolled me over, trailed me along the gravel, and the rest of my furniture, which followed it, began to march over me, tramping on my legs and injuring them. When I loosed my hold, other articles had passed over my body, just as a charge of cavalry does over the body of a dismounted soldier.

Seized at last with terror, I succeeded in dragging myself out of the main avenue, and in concealing myself again among the shrubbery, so as to watch the disappearance of the most cherished objects, the smallest, the least striking, the least unknown which had once belonged to me.

I then heard, in the distance, noises which came from my apartments, which sounded now as if the house were empty, a loud noise of shutting of doors. They were being slammed from top to bottom of my dwelling, even the door which I had just opened myself unconsciously, and which had closed of itself, when the last thing had taken its departure. I took flight also, running toward the city, and only regained my self-composure, on reaching the *boulevards*, where I met belated people. I rang the bell of a hotel where I was known. I had knocked the dust off my clothes with my hands, and I told the porter that I had lost my bunch of keys, which included also that to the kitchen garden, where my servants slept in a house standing by itself, on the other side of the wall of the inclosure which protected my fruits and vegetables from the raids of marauders.

I covered myself up to the eyes in the bed which was assigned to me, but could not sleep; and I waited for the dawn listening to the throbbing of my heart. I had given orders that my servants were to be summoned to the hotel at daybreak, and my *valet de chambre* knocked at my door at seven o'clock in the morning.

His countenance bore a woeful look.

"A great misfortune has happened during the night, *Monsieur*," said he.

"What is it?"

"Somebody has stolen the whole of *Monsieur's* furniture, all, everything, even to the smallest articles."

This news pleased me. Why? Who knows? I was complete master of myself, bent on dissimulating, on telling no one of anything I had seen; determined on concealing and in burying in my heart of hearts a terrible secret. I responded:

"They must then be the same people who have stolen my keys. The police must be informed immediately. I am going to get up, and I will join you in a few moments."

The investigation into the circumstances under which the

robbery might have been committed lasted for five months. Nothing was found, not even the smallest of my knick-knacks, nor the least trace of the thieves. Good gracious! If I had only told them what I knew—If I had said—I should have been locked up—I, not the thieves—for I was the only person who had seen everything from the first.

Yes! but I knew how to keep silence. I shall never refurnish my house. That were indeed useless. The same thing would happen again. I had no desire even to re-enter the house, and I did not re-enter it; I never visited it again. I moved to Paris, to the hotel, and consulted doctors in regard to the condition of my nerves, which had disquieted me a good deal ever since that awful night.

They advised me to travel, and I followed their counsel.

2

I began by making an excursion into Italy. The sunshine did me much good. For six months I wandered about from Genoa to Venice, from Venice to Florence, from Florence to Rome, from Rome to Naples. Then I travelled over Sicily, a country celebrated for its scenery and its monuments, relics left by the Greeks and the Normans. Passing over into Africa, I traversed at my ease that immense desert, yellow and tranquil, in which camels, gazelles, and Arab vagabonds roam about—where, in the rare and transparent atmosphere, there hover no vague hauntings, where there is never any night, but always day.

I returned to France by Marseilles, and in spite of all its Provencal gaiety, the diminished clearness of the sky made me sad. I experienced, in returning to the Continent, the peculiar sensation of an illness which I believed had been cured, and a dull pain which predicted that the seeds of the disease had not been eradicated.

I then returned to Paris. At the end of a month I was very dejected. It was in the autumn, and I determined to make, before winter came, an excursion through Normandy, a country with which I was unacquainted.

I began my journey, in the best of spirits, at Rouen, and for eight days I wandered about, passive, ravished, and enthusiastic, in that ancient city, that astonishing museum of extraordinary Gothic monuments.

But one afternoon, about four o'clock, as I was sauntering slowly through a seemingly unattractive street, by which there ran a stream as black as the ink called "*Eau de Robec*," my attention, fixed for the moment on the quaint, antique appearance of some of the houses, was suddenly attracted by the view of a series of second-hand furniture shops, which followed one another, door after door.

Ah! they had carefully chosen their locality, these sordid traffickers in antiquities, in that quaint little street, overlooking the sinister stream of water, under those tile and slate-pointed roofs on which still grinned the vanes of bygone days.

At the end of these grim storehouses you saw piled up sculptured chests, Rouen, Sevres, and Moustier's pottery, painted statues, others of oak, Christs, Virgins, Saints, church ornaments, chasubles, capes, even sacred vases, and an old gilded wooden tabernacle, where a god had hidden himself away. What singular caverns there are in those lofty houses, crowded with objects of every description, where the existence of things seems to be ended, things which have survived their original possessors, their century, their times, their fashions, in order to be bought as curiosities by new generations.

My affection for antiques was awakened in that city of antiquaries. I went from shop to shop, crossing in two strides, the rotten four plank bridges thrown over the nauseous current of the "*Eau de Robec*."

Heaven protect me! What a shock! At the end of a vault, which was crowded with articles of every description and which seemed to be the entrance to the catacombs of a cemetery of ancient furniture, I suddenly descried one of my most beautiful wardrobes. I approached it, trembling in every limb, trembling to such an extent that I dared not touch it. I put forth my hand, I hesitated. Nevertheless it was indeed my wardrobe; a unique wardrobe of the time of Louis XIII., recognizable by anyone who had seen it only once. Casting my eyes suddenly a little farther, toward the more sombre depths of the gallery, I perceived three of my tapestry covered chairs; and farther on still, my two Henry II. tables, such rare treasures that people came all the way from Paris to see them.

Think! only think in what a state of mind I now was! I advanced, haltingly, quivering with emotion, but I advanced, for I am brave—I advanced like a knight of the dark ages.

At every step I found something that belonged to me; my brushes, my books, my tables, my silks, my arms, everything, except the *bureau* full of my letters, and that I could not discover.

I walked on, descending to the dark galleries, in order to ascend next to the floors above. I was alone; I called out, nobody answered, I was alone; there was no one in that house—a house as vast and tortuous as a labyrinth.

Night came on, and I was compelled to sit down in the darkness on one of my own chairs, for I had no desire to go away. From time to time I shouted, "Hallo, hallo, somebody."

I had sat there, certainly, for more than an hour when I heard steps, steps soft and slow, I knew not where. I was unable to locate them, but bracing myself up, I called out anew, whereupon I perceived a glimmer of light in the next chamber.

"Who is there?" said a voice.

"A buyer," I responded.

"It is too late to enter thus into a shop."

"I have been waiting for you for more than an hour," I answered.

"You can come back tomorrow."

"Tomorrow I must quit Rouen."

I dared not advance, and he did not come to me. I saw always the glimmer of his light, which was shining on a tapestry on which were two angels flying over the dead on a field of battle. It belonged to me also. I said:

"Well, come here."

"I am at your service," he answered.

I got up and went toward him.

Standing in the centre of a large room, was a little man, very short, and very fat, phenomenally fat, a hideous phenomenon.

He had a singular straggling beard, white and yellow, and not a hair on his head—not a hair!

As he held his candle aloft at arm's length in order to see me, his cranium appeared to me to resemble a little moon, in that vast chamber encumbered with old furniture. His features were wrinkled and blown, and his eyes could not be seen.

I bought three chairs which belonged to myself, and paid at once a large sum for them, giving him merely the number of my room at the hotel. They were to be delivered the next day before nine o'clock.

I then started off. He conducted me, with much politeness, as far as the door.

I immediately repaired to the *commissaire's* office at the central police depot, and told the *commissaire* of the robbery which had been perpetrated and of the discovery I had just made. He required time to communicate by telegraph with the authorities who had originally charge of the case, for information, and he begged me to wait in his office until an answer came back. An hour later, an answer came back, which was in accord with my statements.

"I am going to arrest and interrogate this man, at once," he said to me, "for he may have conceived some sort of suspicion, and smuggled away out of sight what belongs to you. Will you go and dine and return in two hours: I shall then have the man here, and I shall subject him to a fresh interrogation in your presence."

"Most gladly, *Monsieur*. I thank you with my whole heart."

I went to dine at my hotel and I ate better than I could have believed. I was quite happy now, thinking that man was in the hands of the police.

Two hours later I returned to the office of the police functionary, who was waiting for me.

"Well, *Monsieur*," said he, on perceiving me, "we have not

been able to find your man. My agents cannot put their hands on him."

Ah! I felt my heart sinking.

"But you have at least found his house?" I asked.

"Yes, certainly; and what is more, it is now being watched and guarded until his return. As for him, he has disappeared."

"Disappeared?"

"Yes, disappeared. He ordinarily passes his evenings at the house of a female neighbour, who is also a furniture broker, a queer sort of sorceress, the widow Bidoin. She has not seen him this evening and cannot give any information in regard to him. We must wait until tomorrow."

I went away. Ah! how sinister the streets of Rouen seemed to me, now troubled and haunted!

I slept so badly that I had a fit of nightmare every time I went off to sleep.

As I did not wish to appear too restless or eager, I waited till ten o'clock the next day before reporting myself to the police.

The merchant had not reappeared. His shop remained closed.

The commissary said to me:

"I have taken all the necessary steps. The court has been made acquainted with the affair. We shall go together to that shop and have it opened, and you shall point out to me all that belongs to you."

We drove there in a cab. Police agents were stationed round the building; there was a locksmith, too, and the door of the shop was soon opened.

On entering, I could not discover my wardrobes, my chairs, my tables; I saw nothing, nothing of that which had furnished my house, no, nothing, although on the previous evening, I could not take a step without encountering something that belonged to me.

The chief commissary, much astonished, regarded me at first with suspicion.

"My God, *Monsieur*," said I to him, "the disappearance of

these articles of furniture coincides strangely with that of the merchant."

He laughed.

"That is true. You did wrong in buying and paying for the articles which were your own property, yesterday. It was that which gave him the cue."

"What seems to me incomprehensible," I replied, "is that all the places that were occupied by my furniture are now filled by other furniture."

"Oh!" responded the commissary, "he has had all night, and has no doubt been assisted by accomplices. This house must communicate with its neighbours. But have no fear, *Monsieur*; I will have the affair promptly and thoroughly investigated. The brigand shall not escape us for long, seeing that we are in charge of the den."

★★★★★★★

Ah! My heart, my heart, my poor heart, how it beats!

I remained a fortnight at Rouen. The man did not return. Heavens! good heavens! That man, what was it that could have frightened and surprised him!

But, on the sixteenth day, early in the morning, I received from my gardener, now the keeper of my empty and pillaged house, the following strange letter:

"*Monsieur*:

"I have the honour to inform *Monsieur* that something happened, the evening before last, which nobody can understand, and the police no more than the rest of us. The whole of the furniture has been returned, not one piece is missing—everything is in its place, up to the very smallest article. The house is now the same in every respect as it was before the robbery took place. It is enough to make one lose one's head. The thing took place during the night Friday—Saturday. The roads are dug up as though the whole fence had been dragged from its place up to the door. The same thing was observed the day after the disappearance of the furniture.

"We are anxiously expecting *Monsieur*, whose very humble

and obedient servant,

I am,

Phillipe Raudim."

"Ah! no, no, ah! never, never, ah! no. I shall never return there!"

I took the letter to the commissary of police.

"It is a very clever restitution," said he. "Let us bury the hatchet. We shall nip the man one of these days."

★★★★★★★

But he has never been nipped. No. They have not nipped him, and I am afraid of him now, as of some ferocious animal that has been let loose behind me.

Inexplicable! It is inexplicable, this chimera of a moonstruck skull! We shall never solve or comprehend it. I shall not return to my former residence. What does it matter to me? I am afraid of encountering that man again, and I shall not run the risk.

And even if he returns, if he takes possession of his shop, who is to prove that my furniture was on his premises? There is only my testimony against him; and I feel that that is not above suspicion.

Ah! no! This kind of existence has become unendurable. I have not been able to guard the secret of what I have seen. I could not continue to live like the rest of the world, with the fear upon me that those scenes might be re-enacted.

So I have come to consult the doctor who directs this lunatic asylum, and I have told him everything.

After questioning me for a long time, he said to me:

"Will you consent, *Monsieur*, to remain here for some time?"

"Most willingly, *Monsieur*."

"You have some means?"

"Yes, *Monsieur*."

"Will you have isolated apartments?"

"Yes, *Monsieur*."

"Would you care to receive any friends?"

"No, *Monsieur*, no, nobody. The man from Rouen might take it into his head to pursue me here, to be revenged on me."

★★★★★★★

I have been alone, alone, all, all alone, for three months. I am growing tranquil by degrees. I have no longer any fears. If the antiquary should become mad . . . and if he should be brought into this asylum! Even prisons themselves are not places of security.

A Strange Traffic

A.k.a. A Mother of Monsters

I am reminded of this horrible story and this horrible woman by seeing at a watering-place much loved by the rich, a well-known Parisian lady, young, elegant, charming, adored and re-spected by everyone. My story dates far back, but one never forgets these things. I had been invited by a friend to spend some time in his house in a small provincial town. In order to do me the honours, he took me to walk in every direction, showed me the much-praised peasants, the villas, the industries, and the ruins. He pointed out the monuments, the churches, the carved old gates, trees that were enormous or strange in form, the oak of Saint Andrew and the yew-tree of Roqueboise. When I had examined all the curiosities of the country with enthusiastic delight, my friend declared, with a sorry countenance, that there was nothing more to be seen. I took a long breath. I should then be able to rest a little under the shadow of the trees. But sud-denly he uttered a cry:

"Oh! yes, we have a mother of monsters; you must make her acquaintance without fail."

I asked: "Who is she, this mother of monsters?"

He replied:

"She is an abominable woman, a veritable demon, a being who brings into the world each year, voluntarily, a deformed, hideous, frightful infant, in short, a monster which she sells to exhibitors of phenomena. These atrocious dealers come from time to time to see if she has produced any new abortion and, if the object pleases them, to buy it, paying the mother a stated income. She has had eleven offshoots of this nature, and she is rich. You believe that I am joking, or that I am inventing or exaggerating. No, no, my friend. I am telling you the truth, the exact truth."

He took me into the suburbs. She lived in a pretty little house near the street. It was genteel and very well kept. The garden was full of fragrant flowers; one would have said that it was the residence of a retired notary. A maid showed us into a kind of country parlour, and the miserable woman appeared. She seemed about forty years old. She was a large person, vigorous and healthy, with a hard countenance, the veritable type of robust peasant, half brute and half woman. She understood the reproach that was put upon her and received all with a hateful humility.

She asked: "What is it you want, sirs?"

My friend replied: "I was told that your last infant was like any other, that it resembled in no way its brothers. I wished to be assured if this was true."

She cast a sullen, furious look at us and replied: "Oh, no! oh, no! my poor sir! It is perhaps a little uglier still than the others. I had no chance, no chance. They are all alike, all alike my good sir. It seems hard on a poor woman alone in the world, a little hard, don't you think?" She spoke quickly, with lowered eyes and the air of a hypocrite, or a ferocious beast when frightened. She softened the sharp tone of her voice, so that one could but be astonished at the flow of tearful words that came out in high treble from that great bony body, strong and angular, which seemed made for vehement gestures and hurling out sounds, after the fashion of wolves.

My friend asked: "Could we see your little one?" She appeared to me to blush. Perhaps I was mistaken.

After some moments of silence, she asked in a high voice: "Of what use is it to you?" And she raised her head, looking straight at us, with fierce glances and fire in her eye.

My companion replied: "Why do you not wish to let us see

it? There must be some people to whom you have shown it. You know whom I mean!"

She gave a start, and raising her voice and rising in anger she cried: "That is what you have come for is it? To insult me, and for what reason? Because my children are like beasts, you say! You shall not see it, no! no! Go away, now, go away! I know you; you all want to make trouble for me, don't you?" She walked toward us, her hands on her hips. At the sound of her brutal voice, a kind of wail, or rather meowing, the lamentable cry of an idiot came from the next room. I shivered to the marrow. We recoiled before her.

My friend said in a severe tone: "Take care, Devil [they called her Devil among the people], take care, some day harm will overtake you!" She trembled with fury, shaking her doubled-up fists and shouting:

"Go away, you! Why should it bring me harm? Go away, bunch of beggars!"

She was about to jump at our faces. We fled, with shrivelled hearts. When we were outside the door, my friend said to me: "Well, you have seen her! What have you to say of her?"

I replied: "Tell me the history of this brute." And this is what he related to me, passing along the great white road, bordered with mulberry-trees, already harvested, through which a light wind passed, making them undulate like a calm sea:

"This girl was formerly a servant on a farm, and was strong, orderly, and economical. They never thought of her having a lover, or suspected her of weakness. She committed an error, as they all do, one evening in harvest time, among the sheafs, under a cloudy sky, when the air, heavy and lifeless, seemed full of the heat of an oven, which soaked in sweat the brown bodies of the lads and girls. She soon found herself with child and was tortured with shame and fear. Wishing to conceal her misfortune at any cost, she bound her body violently by some system of her own, with some strong corset made of boards and cords. The more her form swelled under the effort of the growing child, the more she bound herself with this instrument of torture, suffering martyrdom, but courageous in her grief, not allowing anything to be seen or suspected.

"She maimed the little being in her body, cramping him with that frightful machine. She compressed and deformed him; she made a monster of him. His head was lengthened, coming to a point with two great eyes almost starting from the sockets. The limbs, pressed against the body, tortured like a tree with clinging vines, lengthened out of all proportion, terminated with fingers like those on the foot of a spider. The back remained round and small as a nut. She was confined in an open field one morning in spring. When the weeders that came to her aid saw the beast that she had brought forth, they cried in alarm and fled. And the rumour spread in the country that she had given birth to a demon.

"Since that time they have called her the Devil. She was driven from her place. She lived on charity, and perhaps on love under the shadow, for she was a pretty girl, and all men are not in fear of the lower regions. She brought up her monster that she hated with a savage hate, and which she would have strangled, perhaps, had not the curate, foreseeing this crime, frightened her with threats of the law. Then one day, some showmen heard, in passing, about the frightful abortion and asked to see it in order to take it away if it pleased them. They were pleased and turning to the mother counted out five hundred *francs*. She, ashamed at first, had refused to let them see such an animal; but when she discovered that it was worth money, that it excited the greed of these people, she began to bargain and to discuss *sou* by *sou*, inciting them by reciting the deformities of her child, raising her price with the tenacity of a peasant.

"In order not to be robbed, she drew up a paper with them. And they bound themselves further to give her four hundred *francs* a year, when they had this beast in their service. This unexpected gain excited the mother, and the desire never left her of producing another phenomenon, in order to have an income of the middle class. As she was still young, she succeeded in her wish and became skilful, it appears, in varying the form of her monsters, according to the pressure that she subjected them to before birth. She had long and short ones, some that resembled crabs and some lizards. Many died and she was desolate. The law tried to intervene, but they could prove nothing. They then left her in peace to fabricate her phenomena. At this moment she possesses eleven living beings, which bring in, good years and bad, an income of from five to six thousand *francs* a year. One alone is not yet placed, the one she was not willing to show us. But she will not keep it long, because she is known today by all the mountebanks of the world, and they come from time to time to see if she has anything new.

"She even asks for bids among them when there is any difficulty in settling a matter."

My friend was silent. A profound disgust rose in my heart, and a tumultuous anger and regret at not having strangled this beast when I had her under my hand. I asked: "But who is the father?"

He answered: "They do not know. He or they have a certain shame. He or they conceal themselves. Perhaps they share in the benefits."

I had not thought of this far-off adventure until the other day when I saw on a fashionable beach an elegant, charming, *coquettish*, much liked woman surrounded by men who respected her. I was walking along the shore, arm in arm with a friend, a physician of distinction. Ten minutes later I saw a nursemaid taking care of three children rolling in the sand. A pair of little crutches lay on the ground and touched my sympathies. I then perceived that these three children were all deformed, humpbacked, crooked, and hideous. The doctor said to me: "These are the product of that charming woman we just met."

A profound pity for her and for them entered my soul. I cried:

"Oh! the poor mother! How can she ever laugh again?"

My friend replied: "Do not pity her, my dear. It is the poor little ones that merit your pity. These are the result of preserving a good figure up to the last day. These monsters are the work of the corset. She well knows that she risks her life at that game. What does that matter, so long as she is beautiful and beloved!"

And then I recalled the other one, the country woman, the Devil who sold her phenomena.

A New Year's Gift

Jacques de Randal, having dined at home alone, told his valet he might go out, and he sat down at his table to write some letters.

He ended every year in this manner, writing and dreaming. He reviewed the events of his life since last New Year's Day, things that were now all over and dead; and, in proportion as the faces of his friends rose up before his eyes, he wrote them a few lines, a cordial New Year's greeting on the first of January.

So he sat down, opened a drawer, took out of it a woman's photograph, gazed at it a few moments, and kissed it. Then, having laid it beside a sheet of notepaper, he began:

My Dear Irene: You must by this time have received the little souvenir I sent you addressed to the maid. I have shut myself up this evening in order to tell you ——

The pen here ceased to move. Jacques rose up and began walking up and down the room.

For the last ten months he had had a sweetheart, not like the others, a woman with whom one engages in a passing intrigue, of the theatrical world or the *demi-monde*, but a woman whom he loved and won. He was no longer a young man, although he was still comparatively young for a man, and he looked on life seriously in a positive and practical spirit.

Accordingly, he drew up the balance sheet of his passion, as he drew up every year the balance sheet of friendships that were ended or freshly contracted, of circumstances and persons that had entered into his life.

His first ardour of love having grown calmer, he asked himself with the precision of a merchant making a calculation what was the state of his heart with regard to her, and he tried to form an idea of what it would be in the future.

He found there a great and deep affection; made up of tenderness, gratitude and the thousand subtleties which give birth to long and powerful attachments.

A ring at the bell made him start. He hesitated. Should he open the door? But he said to himself that one must always open the door on New Year's night, to admit the unknown who is passing by and knocks, no matter who it may be.

So he took a wax candle, passed through the antechamber, drew back the bolts, turned the key, pulled the door back, and saw his sweetheart standing pale as a corpse, leaning against the wall.

He stammered:

"What is the matter with you?"

She replied:

"Are you alone?"

"Yes."

"Without servants?"

"Yes."

"You are not going out?"

"No."

She entered with the air of a woman who knew the house. As soon as she was in the drawing-room, she sank down on the sofa, and, covering her face with her hands, began to weep bitterly.

He knelt down at her feet, and tried to remove her hands from her eyes, so that he might look at them, and exclaimed:

"Irene, Irene, what is the matter with you? I implore you to tell me what is the matter with you?"

Then, amid her sobs, she murmured:

"I can no longer live like this."

"Live like this? What do you mean?"

"Yes. I can no longer live like this. I have endured so much.

He struck me this afternoon."

"Who? Your husband?"

"Yes, my husband."

"Ah!"

He was astonished, having never suspected that her husband could be brutal. He was a man of the world, of the better class, a clubman, a lover of horses, a theatregoer and an expert swordsman; he was known, talked about, appreciated everywhere, having very courteous manners, a very mediocre intellect, an absence of education and of the real culture needed in order to think like all well-bred people, and finally a respect for conventionalities.

He appeared to devote himself to his wife, as a man ought to do in the case of wealthy and well-bred people. He displayed enough of anxiety about her wishes, her health, her dresses, and, beyond that, left her perfectly free.

Randal, having become Irene's friend, had a right to the affectionate hand-clasp which every husband endowed with good manners owes to his wife's intimate acquaintance. Then, when Jacques, after having been for some time the friend, became the lover, his relations with the husband were more cordial, as is fitting.

Jacques had never dreamed that there were storms in this household, and he was bewildered at this unexpected revelation.

He asked:

"How did it happen? Tell me."

Thereupon she related a long story, the entire history of her life since the day of her marriage, the first disagreement arising out of a mere nothing, then becoming accentuated at every new difference of opinion between two dissimilar dispositions.

Then came quarrels, a complete separation, not apparent, but real; next, her husband showed himself aggressive, suspicious, violent. Now, he was jealous, jealous of Jacques, and that very day, after a scene, he had struck her.

She added with decision:"I will not go back to him. Do with

me what you like."

Jacques sat down opposite to her, their knees touching. He took her hands:

"My dear love, you are going to commit a gross, an irreparable folly. If you want to leave your husband, put him in the wrong, so that your position as a woman of the world may be saved."

She asked, as she looked at him uneasily:

"Then, what do you advise me?"

"To go back home and to put up with your life there till the day when you can obtain either a separation or a divorce, with the honours of war."

"Is not this thing which you advise me to do a little cowardly?"

"No; it is wise and sensible. You have a high position, a reputation to protect, friends to preserve and relations to deal with. You must not lose all these through a mere caprice."

She rose up, and said with violence:

"Well, no! I cannot stand it any longer! It is at an end! it is at an end!"

Then, placing her two hands on her lover's shoulders, and looking him straight in the face, she asked:

"Do you love me?"

"Yes."

"Really and truly?"

"Yes."

"Then take care of me."

He exclaimed:

"Take care of you? In my own house? Here? Why, you are mad. It would mean losing you forever; losing you beyond hope of recall! You are mad!"

She replied, slowly and seriously, like a woman who feels the weight of her words:

"Listen, Jacques. He has forbidden me to see you again, and I will not play this comedy of coming secretly to your house. You must either lose me or take me."

"My dear Irene, in that case, obtain your divorce, and I will marry you."

"Yes, you will marry me in—two years at the soonest. Yours is a patient love."

"Look here! Reflect! If you remain here he'll come to-morrow to take you away, seeing that he is your husband, seeing that he has right and law on his side."

"I did not ask you to keep me in your own house, Jacques, but to take me anywhere you like. I thought you loved me enough to do that. I have made a mistake. Goodbye!"

She turned round and went toward the door so quickly that he was only able to catch hold of her when she was outside the room:

"Listen, Irene."

She struggled, and would not listen to him. Her eyes were full of tears, and she stammered:

"Let me alone! let me alone! let me alone!"

He made her sit down by force, and once more falling on his knees at her feet, he now brought forward a number of arguments and counsels to make her understand the folly and terrible risk of her project. He omitted nothing which he deemed necessary to convince her, finding even in his very affection for her incentives to persuasion.

As she remained silent and cold as ice, he begged of her, implored of her to listen to him, to trust him, to follow his advice.

When he had finished speaking, she only replied:

"Are you disposed to let me go away now? Take away your hands, so that I may rise to my feet."

"Look here, Irene."

"Will you let me go?"

"Irene—is your resolution irrevocable?"

"Will you let me go."

"Tell me only whether this resolution, this mad resolution of yours, which you will bitterly regret, is irrevocable?"

"Yes—let me go!"

"Then stay. You know well that you are at home here. We

shall go away tomorrow morning."

She rose to her feet in spite of him, and said in a hard tone:

"No. It is too late. I do not want sacrifice; I do not want devotion."

"Stay! I have done what I ought to do; I have said what I ought to say. I have no further responsibility on your behalf. My conscience is at peace. Tell me what you want me to do, and I will obey."'

She resumed her seat, looked at him for a long time, and then asked, in a very calm voice:

"Well, then, explain."

"Explain what? What do you wish me to explain?"

"Everything—everything that you thought about before changing your mind. Then I will see what I ought to do."

"But I thought about nothing at all. I had to warn you that you were going to commit an act of folly. You persist; then I ask to share in this act of folly, and I even insist on it."

"It is not natural to change one's mind so quickly."

"Listen, my dear love. It is not a question here of sacrifice or devotion. On the day when I realized that I loved you, I said to myself what every lover ought to say to himself in the same case: 'The man who loves a woman, who makes an effort to win her, who gets her, and who takes her, enters into a sacred contract with himself and with her. That is, of course, in dealing with a woman like you, not a woman with a fickle heart and easily impressed.'

"Marriage which has a great social value, a great legal value, possesses in my eyes only a very slight moral value, taking into account the conditions under which it generally takes place.

"Therefore, when a woman, united by this lawful bond, but having no attachment to her husband, whom she cannot love, a woman whose heart is free, meets a man whom she cares for, and gives herself to him, when a man who has no other tie, takes a woman in this way, I say that they pledge themselves toward each other by this mutual and free agreement much more than by the 'Yes' uttered in the presence of the mayor.

"I say that, if they are both honourable persons, their union must be more intimate, more real, more wholesome, than if all the sacraments had consecrated it.

"This woman risks everything. And it is exactly because she knows it, because she gives everything, her heart, her body, her soul, her honour, her life, because she has foreseen all miseries, all dangers all catastrophes, because she dares to do a bold act, an intrepid act, because she is prepared, determined to brave every-thing—her husband, who might kill her, and society, which may cast her out. This is why she is worthy of respect in the midst of her conjugal infidelity; this is why her lover, in taking her, should also foresee everything, and prefer her to everyone else whatever may happen. I have nothing more to say. I spoke in the beginning like a sensible man whose duty it was to warn you; and now I am only a man—a man who loves you—Command, and I obey."

Radiant, she closed his mouth with a kiss, and said in a low tone:

"It is not true, darling! There is nothing the matter! My hus-band does not suspect anything. But I wanted to see, I wanted to know, what you would do I wished for a New Year's gift—the gift of your heart—another gift besides the necklace you sent me. You have given it to me. Thanks! thanks! God be thanked for the happiness you have given me!"

A Sister's Confession

A.k.a. The Confession

Marguerite de Therelles was dying. Although she was only fifty-six years old she looked at least seventy-five. She gasped for breath, her face whiter than the sheets, and had spasms of violent shivering, with her face convulsed and her eyes haggard as though she saw a frightful vision.

Her elder sister, Suzanne, six years older than herself, was sobbing on her knees beside the bed. A small table close to the dying woman's couch bore, on a white cloth, two lighted candles, for the priest was expected at any moment to administer extreme unction and the last communion.

The apartment wore that melancholy aspect common to death chambers; a look of despairing farewell. Medicine bottles littered the furniture; linen lay in the corners into which it had been kicked or swept. The very chairs looked, in their disarray, as if they were terrified and had run in all directions. Death— terrible Death—was in the room, hidden, awaiting his prey.

This history of the two sisters was an affecting one. It was spoken of far and wide; it had drawn tears from many eyes.

Suzanne, the elder, had once been passionately loved by a young man, whose affection she returned. They were engaged to be married, and the wedding day was at hand, when Henry de Sampierre suddenly died.

The young girl's despair was terrible, and she took an oath never to marry. She faithfully kept her vow and adopted widow's weeds for the remainder of her life.

But one morning her sister, her little sister Marguerite, then only twelve years old, threw herself into Suzanne's arms, sobbing: "Sister, I don't want you to be unhappy. I don't want you to mourn all your life. I'll never leave you—never, never, never! I shall never marry, either. I'll stay with you always—always!"

Suzanne kissed her, touched by the child's devotion, though not putting any faith in her promise.

But the little one kept her word, and, despite her parents' remonstrances, despite her elder sister's prayers, never married. She was remarkably pretty and refused many offers. She never left her sister.

They spent their whole life together, without a single day's separation. They went everywhere together and were inseparable. But Marguerite was pensive, melancholy, sadder than her sister, as if her sublime sacrifice had undermined her spirits. She grew older more quickly; her hair was white at thirty; and she was often ill, apparently stricken with some unknown, wasting malady.

And now she would be the first to die.

She had not spoken for twenty-four hours, except to whisper at daybreak:

"Send at once for the priest."

And she had since remained lying on her back, convulsed with agony, her lips moving as if unable to utter the dreadful words that rose in her heart, her face expressive of a terror distressing to witness.

Suzanne, distracted with grief, her brow pressed against the bed, wept bitterly, repeating over and over again the words:

"Margot, my poor Margot, my little one!"

She had always called her "my little one," while Marguerite's name for the elder was invariably "sister."

A footstep sounded on the stairs. The door opened. An acolyte appeared, followed by the aged priest in his surplice. As soon as she saw him the dying woman sat up suddenly in bed, opened her lips, stammered a few words and began to scratch the bedclothes, as if she would have made hole in them.

Father Simon approached, took her hand, kissed her on the forehead and said in a gentle voice:

"May God pardon your sins, my daughter. Be of good courage. Now is the moment to confess them—speak!"

Then Marguerite, shuddering from head to foot, so that the very bed shook with her nervous movements, gasped:

"Sit down, sister, and listen."

The priest stooped toward the prostrate Suzanne, raised her to her feet, placed her in a chair, and, taking a hand of each of the sisters, pronounced:

"Lord God! Send them strength! Shed Thy mercy upon them."

And Marguerite began to speak. The words issued from her lips one by one—hoarse, jerky, tremulous.

"Pardon, pardon, sister! pardon me! Oh, if only you knew how I have dreaded this moment all my life!"

Suzanne faltered through her tears:

"But what have I to pardon, little one? You have given me everything, sacrificed all to me. You are an angel."

But Marguerite interrupted her:

"Be silent, be silent! Let me speak! Don't stop me! It is terrible. Let me tell all, to the very end, without interruption. Listen. You remember—you remember—Henry —"

Suzanne trembled and looked at her sister. The younger one went on:

"In order to understand you must hear everything. I was twelve years old—only twelve—you remember, don't you? And I was spoilt; I did just as I pleased. You remember how everybody spoilt me? Listen. The first time he came he had on his riding boots; he dismounted, saying that he had a message for father. You remember, don't you? Don't speak. Listen. When I saw him I was struck with admiration. I thought him so handsome, and I stayed in a corner of the drawing-room all the time he was talking. Children are strange—and terrible. Yes, indeed, I dreamt of him.

"He came again—many times. I looked at him with all my

eyes, all my heart. I was large for my age and much more preco-cious than—anyone suspected. He came often. I thought only of him. I often whispered to myself:

"'Henry-Henry de Sampierre!'

"Then I was told that he was going to marry you. That was a blow! Oh, sister, a terrible blow—terrible! I wept all through three sleepless nights.

"He came every afternoon after lunch. You remember, don't you? Don't answer. Listen. You used to make cakes that he was very fond of—with flour, butter and milk. Oh, I know how to make them. I could make them still, if necessary. He would swal-low them at one mouthful and wash them down with a glass of wine, saying: 'Delicious!' Do you remember the way he said it?

"I was jealous—jealous! Your wedding day was drawing near. It was only a fortnight distant. I was distracted. I said to myself: 'He shall not marry Suzanne—no, he shall not! He shall mar-ry me when I am old enough! I shall never love any one half so much.' But one evening, ten days before the wedding, you went for a stroll with him in the moonlight before the house—and yonder—under the pine tree, the big pine tree—he kissed you—kissed you—and held you in his arms so long—so long! You remember, don't you? It was probably the first time. You were so pale when you came back to the drawing-room!

"I saw you. I was there in the shrubbery. I was mad with rage! I would have killed you both if I could!

"I said to myself: 'He shall never marry Suzanne—never! He shall marry no one! I could not bear it.' And all at once I began to hate him intensely.

"Then do you know what I did? Listen. I had seen the gar-dener prepare pellets for killing stray dogs. He would crush a bottle into small pieces with a stone and put the ground glass into a ball of meat.

"I stole a small medicine bottle from mother's room. I ground it fine with a hammer and hid the glass in my pocket. It was a glistening powder. The next day, when you had made your little cakes; I opened them with a knife and inserted the glass. He ate three. I ate one myself. I threw the six others into the pond. The two swans died three days later. You remember? Oh, don't speak! Listen, listen. I, I alone did not die. But I have always been ill. Listen—he died—you know—listen—that was not the worst. It was afterward, later—always—the most terrible—listen.

"My life, all my life—such torture! I said to myself: 'I will never leave my sister. And on my deathbed I will tell her all.' And now I have told. And I have always thought of this moment—the moment when all would be told. Now it has come. It is terrible—oh!—sister—

"I have always thought, morning and evening, day and night: 'I shall have to tell her some day!' I waited. The horror of it! It is done. Say nothing. Now I am afraid—I am afraid! Oh! Supposing I should see him again, by and by, when I am dead! See him again! Only to think of it! I dare not—yet I must. I am going to die. I want you to forgive me. I insist on it. I cannot meet him without your forgiveness. Oh, tell her to forgive me, Father! Tell her. I implore you! I cannot die without it."

She was silent and lay back, gasping for breath, still plucking at the sheets with her fingers.

Suzanne had hidden her face in her hands and did not move. She was thinking of him whom she had loved so long. What a life of happiness they might have had together! She saw him again in the dim and distant past—that past forever lost. Beloved dead! how the thought of them rends the heart! Oh! that kiss, his only kiss! She had retained the memory of it in her soul. And, after that, nothing, nothing more throughout her whole existence!

The priest rose suddenly and in a firm, compelling voice said:

"Mademoiselle Suzanne, your sister is dying!"

Then Suzanne, raising her tear-stained face, put her arms round her sister, and kissing her fervently, exclaimed:

"I forgive you, I forgive you, little one!"

Abandoned

"I really think you must be mad, my dear, to go for a country walk in such weather as this. You have had some very strange notions for the last two months. You drag me to the seaside in spite of myself, when you have never once had such a whim during all the forty-four years that we have been married. You chose Fecamp, which is a very dull town, without consulting me in the matter, and now you are seized with such a rage for walking, you who hardly ever stir out on foot, that you want to take a country walk on the hottest day of the year. Ask d'Apreval to go with you, as he is ready to gratify all your whims. As for me, I am going back to have a nap."

Madame de Cadour turned to her old friend and said:

"Will you come with me, Monsieur d'Apreval?"

He bowed with a smile, and with all the gallantry of former years:

"I will go wherever you go," he replied.

"Very well, then, go and get a sunstroke," Monsieur de Cadour said; and he went back to the Hotel des Bains to lie down for an hour or two.

As soon as they were alone, the old lady and her old companion set off, and she said to him in a low voice, squeezing his hand:

"At last! at last!"

"You are mad," he said in a whisper. "I assure you that you are mad. Think of the risk you are running. If that man—"

She started.

"Oh! Henri, do not say that man, when you are speaking of him."

"Very well," he said abruptly, "if our son guesses anything, if he has any suspicions, he will have you, he will have us both in his power. You have got on without seeing him for the last forty years. What is the matter with you to-day?"

They had been going up the long street that leads from the sea to the town, and now they turned to the right, to go to Etretat. The white road stretched in front of him, then under a blaze of brilliant sunshine, so they went on slowly in the burning heat. She had taken her old friend's arm, and was looking straight in front of her, with a fixed and haunted gaze, and at last she said:

"And so you have not seen him again, either?"

"No, never."

"Is it possible?"

"My dear friend, do not let us begin that discussion again. I have a wife and children and you have a husband, so we both of us have much to fear from other people's opinion."

She did not reply; she was thinking of her long past youth and of many sad things that had occurred. How well she recalled all the details of their early friendship, his smiles, the way he used to linger, in order to watch her until she was indoors. What happy days they were, the only really delicious days she had ever enjoyed, and how quickly they were over!

And then—her discovery—of the penalty she paid! What anguish!

Of that journey to the South, that long journey, her sufferings, her constant terror, that secluded life in the small, solitary house on the shores of the Mediterranean, at the bottom of a garden, which she did not venture to leave. How well she remembered those long days which she spent lying under an orange tree, looking up at the round, red fruit, amid the green leaves. How she used to long to go out, as far as the sea, whose fresh breezes came to her over the wall, and whose small waves she could hear lapping on the beach. She dreamed of its immense blue expanse sparkling under the sun, with the white sails of the small vessels, and a mountain on the horizon. But she did not dare to go outside the gate. Suppose anybody had recognized her!

And those days of waiting, those last days of misery and expectation! The impending suffering, and then that terrible night! What misery she had endured, and what a night it was! How she had groaned and screamed! She could still see the pale face of her lover, who kissed her hand every moment, and the clean-shaven face of the doctor and the nurse's white cap.

And what she felt when she heard the child's feeble cries, that wail, that first effort of a human's voice!

And the next day! the next day! the only day of her life on which she had seen and kissed her son; for, from that time, she had never even caught a glimpse of him.

And what a long, void existence hers had been since then, with the thought of that child always, always floating before her. She had never seen her son, that little creature that had been part of herself, even once since then; they had taken him from her, carried him away, and had hidden him. All she knew was that he had been brought up by some peasants in Normandy, that he had become a peasant himself, had married well, and that his father, whose name he did not know, had settled a handsome sum of money on him.

How often during the last forty years had she wished to go and see him and to embrace him! She could not imagine to herself that he had grown! She always thought of that small human atom which she had held in her arms and pressed to her bosom for a day.

How often she had said to M. d'Apreval: "I cannot bear it any longer; I must go and see him."

But he had always stopped her and kept her from going. She would be unable to restrain and to master herself; their son would guess it and take advantage of her, blackmail her; she would be lost.

"What is he like?" she said.

"I do not know. I have not seen him again, either."

"Is it possible? To have a son and not to know him; to be afraid of him and to reject him as if he were a disgrace! It is horrible."

They went along the dusty road, overcome by the scorching sun, and continually ascending that interminable hill.

"One might take it for a punishment," she continued; "I have never had another child, and I could no longer resist the longing to see him, which has possessed me for forty years. You men cannot understand that. You must remember that I shall not live much longer, and suppose I should never see him, never have seen him! . . . Is it possible? How could I wait so long? I have thought about him every day since, and what a terrible existence mine has been! I have never awakened, never, do you understand, without my first thoughts being of him, of my child. How is he? Oh, how guilty I feel toward him! Ought one to fear what the world may say in a case like this? I ought to have left everything to go after him, to bring him up and to show my love for him. I should certainly have been much happier, but I did not dare, I was a coward. How I have suffered! Oh, how those poor, abandoned children must hate their mothers!"

She stopped suddenly, for she was choked by her sobs. The whole valley was deserted and silent in the dazzling light and the overwhelming heat, and only the grasshoppers uttered their shrill, continuous chirp among the sparse yellow grass on both sides of the road.

"Sit down a little," he said.

She allowed herself to be led to the side of the ditch and sank down with her face in her hands. Her white hair, which hung in curls on both sides of her face, had become tangled. She wept, overcome by profound grief, while he stood facing her, uneasy and not knowing what to say, and he merely murmured: "Come, take courage."

She got up.

"I will," she said, and wiping her eyes, she began to walk again with the uncertain step of an elderly woman.

A little farther on the road passed beneath a clump of trees, which hid a few houses, and they could distinguish the vibrating and regular blows of a blacksmith's hammer on the anvil; and presently they saw a wagon standing on the right side of the road in front of a low cottage, and two men shoeing a horse under a shed.

Monsieur d' Apreval went up to them.

"Where is Pierre Benedict's farm?" he asked.

"Take the road to the left, close to the inn, and then go straight on; it is the third house past Poret's. There is a small spruce fir close to the gate; you cannot make a mistake."

They turned to the left. She was walking very slowly now, her legs threatened to give way, and her heart was beating so violently that she felt as if she should suffocate, while at every step she murmured, as if in prayer:

"Oh! Heaven! Heaven!"

Monsieur d'Apreval, who was also nervous and rather pale, said to her somewhat gruffly:

"If you cannot manage to control your feelings, you will betray yourself at once. Do try and restrain yourself."

"How can I?" she replied. "My child! When I think that I am going to see my child."

They were going along one of those narrow country lanes between farmyards, that are concealed beneath a double row of beech trees at either side of the ditches, and suddenly they found themselves in front of a gate, beside which there was a young spruce fir.

"This is it," he said.

She stopped suddenly and looked about her. The courtyard, which was planted with apple trees, was large and extended as far as the small thatched dwelling house. On the opposite side were the stable, the barn, the cow house and the poultry house, while the gig, the wagon and the manure cart were under a slated outhouse. Four calves were grazing under the shade of the trees and black hens were wandering all about the enclosure.

All was perfectly still; the house door was open, but nobody was to be seen, and so they went in, when immediately a large black dog came out of a barrel that was standing under a pear tree, and began to bark furiously.

There were four bee-hives on boards against the wall of the house.

Monsieur d'Apreval stood outside and called out:

"Is anybody at home?"

Then a child appeared, a little girl of about ten, dressed in a chemise and a linen, petticoat, with dirty, bare legs and a timid and cunning look. She remained standing in the doorway, as if to prevent any one going in.

"What do you want?" she asked.

"Is your father in?"

"No."

"Where is he?"

"I don't know."

"And your mother?"

"Gone after the cows."

"Will she be back soon?"

"I don't know."

Then suddenly the lady, as if she feared that her companion might force her to return, said quickly:

"I shall not go without having seen him."

"We will wait for him, my dear friend."

As they turned away, they saw a peasant woman coming toward the house, carrying two tin pails, which appeared to be heavy and which glistened brightly in the sunlight.

She limped with her right leg, and in her brown knitted jacket, that was faded by the sun and washed out by the rain, she looked like a poor, wretched, dirty servant.

"Here is mamma," the child said.

When she got close to the house, she looked at the strangers angrily and suspiciously, and then she went in, as if she had not seen them. She looked old and had a hard, yellow, wrinkled face, one of those wooden faces that country people so often have.

Monsieur d'Apreval called her back.

"I beg your pardon, *madame*, but we came in to know whether you could sell us two glasses of milk."

She was grumbling when she reappeared in the door, after putting down her pails.

"I don't sell milk," she replied.

"We are very thirsty," he said, "and *madame* is very tired. Can we not get something to drink?"

The peasant woman gave them an uneasy and cunning glance and then she made up her mind.

"As you are here, I will give you some," she said, going into the house, and almost immediately the child came out and brought two chairs, which she placed under an apple tree, and then the mother, in turn, brought out two bowls of foaming milk, which she gave to the visitors. She did not return to the house, however, but remained standing near them, as if to watch them and to find out for what purpose they had come there.

"You have come from Fecamp?" she said.

"Yes," Monsieur d'Apreval replied, "we are staying at Fecamp for the summer."

And then, after a short silence, he continued:

"Have you any fowls you could sell us every week?"

The woman hesitated for a moment and then replied:

"Yes, I think I have. I suppose you want young ones?"

"Yes, of course."

"'What do you pay for them in the market?"

D'Apreval, who had not the least idea, turned to his companion:

"What are you paying for poultry in Fecamp, my dear lady?"

"Four *francs* and four *francs* fifty *centimes*," she said, her eyes full of tears, while the farmer's wife, who was looking at her askance, asked in much surprise

"Is the lady ill, as she is crying?"

He did not know what to say, and replied with some hesitation:

"No—no—but she lost her watch as we came along, a very handsome watch, and that troubles her. If anybody should find

297

it, please let us know."

Mother Benedict did not reply, as she thought it a very equivocal sort of answer, but suddenly she exclaimed:

"Oh, here is my husband!"

She was the only one who had seen him, as she was facing the gate. D'Apreval started and Madame de Cadour nearly fell as she turned round suddenly on her chair.

A man bent nearly double, and out of breath, stood there, ten-yards from them, dragging a cow at the end of a rope. Without taking any notice of the visitors, he said:

"Confound it! What a brute!"

And he went past them and disappeared in the cow house.

Her tears had dried quickly as she sat there startled, without a word and with the one thought in her mind, that this was her son, and D'Apreval, whom the same thought had struck very unpleasantly, said in an agitated voice:

"Is this Monsieur Benedict?"

"Who told you his name?" the wife asked, still rather suspiciously.

"The blacksmith at the corner of the highroad," he replied, and then they were all silent, with their eyes fixed on the door of the cow house, which formed a sort of black hole in the wall of the building. Nothing could be seen inside, but they heard a vague noise, movements and footsteps and the sound of hoofs, which were deadened by the straw on the floor, and soon the man reappeared in the door, wiping his forehead, and came toward the house with long, slow strides. He passed the strangers without seeming to notice them and said to his wife:

"Go and draw me a jug of cider; I am very thirsty."

Then he went back into the house, while his wife went into the cellar and left the two Parisians alone.

"Let us go, let us go, Henri," Madame de Cadour said, nearly distracted with grief, and so d'Apreval took her by the arm, helped her to rise, and sustaining her with all his strength, for he felt that she was nearly fainting, he led her out, after throwing five *francs* on one of the chairs.

As soon as they were outside the gate, she began to sob and said, shaking with grief:

"Oh! oh! is that what you have made of him?"

He was very pale and replied coldly:

"I did what I could. His farm is worth eighty thousand *francs*, and that is more than most of the sons of the middle classes have."

They returned slowly, without speaking a word. She was still crying; the tears ran down her cheeks continually for a time, but by degrees they stopped, and they went back to Fecamp, where they found Monsieur de Cadour waiting dinner for them. As soon as he saw them, he began to laugh and exclaimed:

"So my wife has had a sunstroke, and I am very glad of it. I really think she has lost her head for some time past!"

Neither of them replied, and when the husband asked them, rubbing his hands:

"Well, I hope that, at least, you have had a pleasant walk?"

Monsieur d'Apreval replied:

"A delightful walk, I assure you; perfectly delightful."

Bellflower

A.k.a. Clochette

How strange are those old recollections which haunt us, without our being able to get rid of them!

This one is so very old that I cannot understand how it has clung so vividly and tenaciously to my memory. Since then I have seen so many sinister things, either affecting or terrible, that I am astonished at not being able to pass a single day without the face of Mother Bellflower recurring to my mind's eye, just as I knew her formerly, long, long ago, when I was ten or twelve years old.

She was an old seamstress who came to my parents' house once a week, every Thursday, to mend the linen. My parents lived in one of those country houses called *chateaux*, which are merely old houses with pointed roofs, to which are attached three or four adjacent farms.

The village, a large village, almost a small market town, was a few hundred yards off, and nestled round the church, a red brick church, which had become black with age.

Well, every Thursday Mother Bellflower came between half past six and seven in the morning, and went immediately into the linen-room and began to work. She was a tall, thin, bearded or rather hairy woman, for she had a beard all over her face, a surprising, an unexpected beard, growing in improbable tufts, in curly bunches which looked as if they had been sown by a madman over that great face, the face of a gendarme in petticoats. She had them on her nose, under her nose, round her nose, on her chin, on her cheeks; and her eyebrows, which were extraordinarily thick and long, and quite gray, bushy and bristling, looked exactly like a pair of moustaches stuck on there by mistake.

She limped, but not like lame people generally do, but like a ship pitching. When she planted her great, bony, vibrant body on her sound leg, she seemed to be preparing to mount some enormous wave, and then suddenly she dipped as if to disappear in an abyss, and buried herself in the ground. Her walk reminded one of a ship in a storm, and her head, which was always covered with an enormous white cap, whose ribbons fluttered down her back, seemed to traverse the horizon from North to South and from South to North, at each limp.

I adored Mother Bellflower. As soon as I was up I used to go into the linen-room, where I found her installed at work, with a foot-warmer under her feet. As soon as I arrived, she made me take the foot-warmer and sit upon it, so that I might not catch cold in that large, chilly room under the roof.

"That draws the blood from your head," she would say to me.

She told me stories, while mending the linen with her long, crooked, nimble fingers; behind her magnifying spectacles, for age had impaired her sight, her eyes appeared enormous to me, strangely profound, double.

As far as I can remember from the things which she told me and by which my childish heart was moved, she had the large heart of a poor woman. She told me what had happened in the village, how a cow had escaped from the cowhouse and had been found the next morning in front of Prosper Malet's mill, looking at the sails turning, or about a hen's egg which had been found in the church belfry without anyone being able to understand what creature had been there to lay it, or the queer story of Jean Pila's dog, who had gone ten leagues to bring back his master's breeches which a tramp had stolen while they were hanging up to dry out of doors, after he had been caught in the rain. She told me these simple adventures in such a man-

301

ner that in my mind they assumed the proportions of never-to-be-forgotten dramas, of grand and mysterious poems; and the ingenious stories invented by the poets, which my mother told me in the evening, had none of the flavour, none of the fullness or of the vigour of the peasant woman's narratives.

Well, one Thursday when I had spent all the morning in listening to Mother Clochette, I wanted to go upstairs to her again during the day, after picking hazelnuts with the manservant in the wood behind the farm. I remember it all as clearly as what happened only yesterday.

On opening the door of the linen-room, I saw the old seamstress lying on the floor by the side of her chair, her face turned down and her arms stretched out, but still holding her needle in one hand and one of my shirts in the other. One of her legs in a blue stocking, the longer one no doubt, was extended under her chair, and her spectacles glistened by the wall, where they had rolled away from her.

I ran away uttering shrill cries. They all came running, and in a few minutes I was told that Mother Clochette was dead.

I cannot describe the profound, poignant, terrible emotion which stirred my childish heart. I went slowly down into the drawing-room and hid myself in a dark corner, in the depths of a great, old armchair, where I knelt and wept. I remained there for a long time no doubt, for night came on. Suddenly someone came in with a lamp—without seeing me, however—and I heard my father and mother talking with the medical man, whose voice I recognized.

He had been sent for immediately, and he was explaining the cause of the accident, of which I understood nothing, however. Then he sat down and had a glass of liqueur and a biscuit.

He went on talking, and what he then said will remain engraved on my mind until I die! I think that I can give the exact words which he used.

"Ah!" said he, "the poor woman! she broke her leg the day of my arrival here. I had not even had time to wash my hands after getting off the diligence before I was sent for in all haste, for it was a bad case, very bad.

"She was seventeen, and a pretty girl, very pretty! Would anyone believe it? I have never told her story before, in fact no one but myself and one other person, who is no longer living in this part of the country, ever knew it. Now that she is dead, I may be less discreet.

"A young assistant teacher had just come to live in the village; he was good-looking and had the bearing of a soldier. All the girls ran after him, but he was disdainful. Besides that, he was very much afraid of his superior, the schoolmaster, old Grabu, who occasionally got out of bed the wrong foot first.

"Old Grabu already employed pretty Hortense, who has just died here, and who was afterward nicknamed Clochette. The assistant master singled out the pretty young girl, who was no doubt flattered at being chosen by this disdainful conqueror; at any rate, she fell in love with him, and he succeeded in persuading her to give him a first meeting in the hayloft behind the school, at night, after she had done her day's sewing.

"She pretended to go home, but instead of going downstairs when she left the Grabus', she went upstairs and hid among the hay, to wait for her lover. He soon joined her, and he was beginning to say pretty things to her, when the door of the hayloft opened and the schoolmaster appeared, and asked: 'What are you doing up there, Sigisbert?' Feeling sure that he would be caught, the young schoolmaster lost his presence of mind and replied stupidly: 'I came up here to rest a little among the bundles of hay, Monsieur Grabu.'

"The loft was very large and absolutely dark. Sigisbert pushed the frightened girl to the further end and said: 'Go there and hide yourself. I shall lose my situation, so get away and hide yourself.'

"When the schoolmaster heard the whispering, he continued: 'Why, you are not by yourself?'

"'Yes I am, Monsieur Grabu!'

"'But you are not, for you are talking.'

"'I swear I am, Monsieur Grabu.'

"'I will soon find out,' the old man replied, and double-locking the door, he went down to get a light.

"Then the young man, who was a coward such as one sometimes meets, lost his head, and he repeated, having grown furious all of a sudden: 'Hide yourself, so that he may not find you. You will deprive me of my bread for my whole life; you will ruin my whole career! Do hide yourself!'

"They could hear the key turning in the lock again, and Hortense ran to the window which looked out on to the street, opened it quickly, and then in a low and determined voice said: 'You will come and pick me up when he is gone,' and she jumped out.

"Old Grabu found nobody, and went down again in great surprise. A quarter of an hour later, Monsieur Sigisbert came to me and related his adventure. The girl had remained at the foot of the wall unable to get up, as she had fallen from the second story, and I went with him to fetch her. It was raining in torrents, and I brought the unfortunate girl home with me, for the right leg was broken in three places, and the bones had come out through the flesh. She did not complain, and merely said, with admirable resignation: 'I am punished, well punished!'

"I sent for assistance and for the workgirl's friends and told them a made-up story of a runaway carriage which had knocked her down and lamed her, outside my door. They believed me, and the *gendarmes* for a whole month tried in vain to find the author of this accident.

"That is all! Now I say that this woman was a heroine, and had the fibre of those who accomplish the grandest deeds in history.

"That was her only love affair, and she died a virgin. She was a martyr, a noble soul, a sublimely devoted woman! And if I did not absolutely admire her, I should not have told you this story, which I would never tell anyone during her life: you understand why."

The doctor ceased; mamma cried and papa said some words which I did not catch; then they left the room, and I remained on my knees in the armchair and sobbed, while I heard a strange noise of heavy footsteps and something knocking against the side of the staircase.

They were carrying away Clochette's body.

Denis

To Leon Chapron.

Marambot opened the letter which his servant Denis gave him and smiled.

For twenty years Denis has been a servant in this house. He was a short, stout, jovial man, who was known throughout the countryside as a model servant. He asked:

"Is *monsieur* pleased? Has *monsieur* received good news?"

M. Marambot was not rich. He was an old village druggist, a bachelor, who lived on an income acquired with difficulty by selling drugs to the farmers. He answered:

"Yes, my boy. Old man Malois is afraid of the law-suit with which I am threatening him. I shall get my money to-morrow. Five thousand *francs* are not liable to harm the account of an old bachelor."

M. Marambot rubbed his hands with satisfaction. He was a man of quiet temperament, more sad than gay, incapable of any prolonged effort, careless in business.

He could undoubtedly have amassed a greater income had he taken advantage of the deaths of colleagues established in more important centres, by taking their places and carrying on their business. But the trouble of moving and the thought of all the preparations had always stopped him. After thinking the matter over for a few days, he would be satisfied to say:

"Bah! I'll wait until the next time. I'll not lose anything by the delay. I may even find something better."

Denis, on the contrary, was always urging his master to new

enterprises. Of an energetic temperament, he would continually repeat:

"Oh! If I had only had the capital to start out with, I could have made a fortune! One thousand *francs* would do me."

M. Marambot would smile without answering and would go out in his little garden, where, his hands behind his back, he would walk about dreaming.

All day long, Denis sang the joyful refrains of the folk-songs of the district. He even showed an unusual activity, for he cleaned all the windows of the house, energetically rubbing the glass, and singing at the top of his voice.

M. Marambot, surprised at his zeal, said to him several times, smiling:

"My boy, if you work like that there will be nothing left for you to do tomorrow."

The following day, at about nine o'clock in the morning, the postman gave Denis four letters for his master, one of them very heavy. M. Marambot immediately shut himself up in his room until late in the afternoon. He then handed his servant four letters for the mail. One of them was addressed to M. Malois; it was undoubtedly a receipt for the money.

Denis asked his master no questions; he appeared to be as sad and gloomy that day as he had seemed joyful the day before.

Night came. M. Marambot went to bed as usual and slept.

He was awakened by a strange noise. He sat up in his bed and listened. Suddenly the door opened, and Denis appeared, holding in one hand a candle and in the other a carving knife, his eyes staring, his face contracted as though moved by some deep emotion; he was as pale as a ghost.

M. Marambot, astonished, thought that he was sleep-walking, and he was going to get out of bed and assist him when the servant blew out the light and rushed for the bed. His master stretched out his hands to receive the shock which knocked him over on his back; he was trying to seize the hands of his servant, whom he now thought to be crazy, in order to avoid the blows which the latter was aiming at him.

He was struck by the knife; once in the shoulder, once in the forehead and the third time in the chest. He fought wildly, waving his arms around in the darkness, kicking and crying:

"Denis! Denis! Are you mad? Listen, Denis!"

But the latter, gasping for breath, kept up his furious attack always striking, always repulsed, sometimes with a kick, sometimes with a punch, and rushing forward again furiously.

M. Marambot was wounded twice more, once in the leg and once in the stomach. But, suddenly, a thought flashed across his mind, and he began to shriek:

"Stop, stop, Denis, I have not yet received my money!"

The man immediately ceased, and his master could hear his laboured breathing in the darkness.

M. Marambot then went on:

"I have received nothing. M. Malois takes back what he said, the law-suit will take place; that is why you carried the letters to the mail. Just read those on my desk."

With a final effort, he reached for his matches and lit the candle.

He was covered with blood. His sheets, his curtains, and even the walls, were spattered with red. Denis, standing in the middle of the room, was also bloody from head to foot.

When he saw the blood, M. Marambot thought himself dead, and fell unconscious.

At break of day he revived. It was some time, however, before he regained his senses, and was able to understand or remember. But, suddenly, the memory of the attack and of his wounds returned to him, and he was filled with such terror that he closed his eyes in order not to see anything. After a few minutes he grew calmer and began to think. He had not died immediately, therefore he might still recover. He felt weak, very weak; but he had no real pain, although he noticed an uncomfortable smarting sensation in several parts of his body. He also felt icy cold, and all wet, and as though wrapped up in bandages. He thought that this dampness came from the blood which he had lost; and he shivered at the dreadful thought of this red liquid which had come from his veins and covered his bed. The idea of seeing this terrible spectacle again so upset him that he kept his eyes closed with all his strength, as though they might open in spite of himself.

What had become of Denis? He had probably escaped.

But what could he, Marambot, do now? Get up? Call for help? But if he should make the slightest motions, his wounds would undoubtedly open up again and he would die from loss of blood.

Suddenly he heard the door of his room open. His heart almost stopped. It was certainly Denis who was coming to finish him up. He held his breath in order to make the murderer think that he had been successful.

He felt his sheet being lifted up, and then someone feeling his stomach. A sharp pain near his hip made him start. He was being very gently washed with cold water. Therefore, someone must have discovered the misdeed and he was being cared for. A wild joy seized him; but prudently, he did not wish to show that he was conscious. He opened one eye, just one, with the greatest precaution.

He recognized Denis standing beside him, Denis himself! Mercy! He hastily closed his eye again.

Denis! What could he be doing? What did he want? What awful scheme could he now be carrying out?

What was he doing? Well, he was washing him in order to hide the traces of his crime! And he would now bury him in the garden, under ten feet of earth, so that no one could discover him! Or perhaps under the wine cellar! And M. Marambot began to tremble like a leaf. He kept saying to himself: "I am lost, lost!" He closed his eyes so as not to see the knife as it descended for the final stroke. It did not come. Denis was now lifting him up and bandaging him. Then he began carefully to dress the wound on his leg, as his master had taught him to do.

There was no longer any doubt. His servant, after wishing to kill him, was trying to save him.

Then M. Marambot, in a dying voice, gave him the practical

piece of advice:

"Wash the wounds in a dilute solution of carbolic acid!"

Denis answered:

"This is what I am doing, *monsieur.*"

M. Marambot opened both his eyes. There was no sign of blood either on the bed, on the walls, or on the murderer. The wounded man was stretched out on clean white sheets.

The two men looked at each other.

Finally M. Marambot said calmly:

"You have been guilty of a great crime."

Denis answered:

"I am trying to make up for it, *monsieur.* If you will not tell on me, I will serve you as faithfully as in the past."

This was no time to anger his servant. M. Marambot murmured as he closed his eyes:

"I swear not to tell on you."

Denis saved his master. He spent days and nights without sleep, never leaving the sick room, preparing drugs, broths, potions, feeling his pulse, anxiously counting the beats, attending him with the skill of a trained nurse and the devotion of a son.

He continually asked:

"Well, *monsieur,* how do you feel?"

M. Marambot would answer in a weak voice:

"A little better, my boy, thank you."

And when the sick man would wake up at night, he would often see his servant seated in an armchair, weeping silently.

Never had the old druggist been so cared for, so fondled, so spoiled. At first he had said to himself:

"As soon as I am well I shall get rid of this rascal."

He was now convalescing, and from day to day he would put off dismissing his murderer. He thought that no one would ever show him such care and attention, for he held this man through fear; and he warned him that he had left a document with a lawyer denouncing him to the law if any new accident should occur.

This precaution seemed to guarantee him against any future

attack; and he then asked himself if it would not be wiser to keep this man near him, in order to watch him closely.

Just as formerly, when he would hesitate about taking some larger place of business, he could not make up his mind to any decision.

"There is always time," he would say to himself.

Denis continued to show himself an admirable servant. M. Marambot was well. He kept him.

One morning, just as he was finishing breakfast, he suddenly heard a great noise in the kitchen. He hastened in there. Denis was struggling with two *gendarmes*. An officer was taking notes on his pad.

As soon as he saw his master, the servant began to sob, exclaiming:

"You told on me, *monsieur*, that's not right, after what you had promised me. You have broken your word of honour, Monsieur Marambot; that is not right, that's not right!"

M. Marambot, bewildered and distressed at being suspected, lifted his hand:

"I swear to you before the Lord, my boy that I did not tell on you. I haven't the slightest idea how the police could have found out about your attack on me."

The officer started:

"You say that he attacked you, M. Marambot?"

The bewildered druggist answered:

"Yes—but I did not tell on him—I haven't said a word—I swear it—he has served me excellently from that time on —"

The officer pronounced severely:

"I will take down your testimony. The law will take notice of this new action, of which it was ignorant, Monsieur Marambot. I was commissioned to arrest your servant for the theft of two ducks surreptitiously taken by him from M. Duhamel of which act there are witnesses. I shall make a note of your information."

Then, turning toward his men, he ordered:

"Come on, bring him along!"

The two gendarmes dragged Denis out.

The lawyer used a plea of insanity, contrasting the two misdeeds in order to strengthen his argument. He had clearly proved that the theft of the two ducks came from the same mental condition as the eight knife-wounds in the body of Maramlot. He had cunningly analyzed all the phases of this transitory condition of mental aberration, which could, doubtless, be cured by a few months' treatment in a reputable sanatorium. He had spoken in enthusiastic terms of the continued devotion of this faithful servant, of the care with which he had surrounded his master, wounded by him in a moment of alienation.

Touched by this memory, M. Marambot felt the tears rising to his eyes.

The lawyer noticed it, opened his arms with a broad gesture, spreading out the long black sleeves of his robe like the wings of a bat, and exclaimed:

"Look, look, gentleman of the jury, look at those tears. What more can I say for my client? What speech, what argument, what reasoning would be worth these tears of his master? They, speak louder than I do, louder than the law; they cry: 'Mercy, for the poor wandering mind of a while ago! They implore, they pardon, they bless!'"

He was silent and sat down.

Then the judge, turning to Marambot, whose testimony had been excellent for his servant, asked him:

"But, *monsieur*, even admitting that you consider this man insane, that does not explain why you should have kept him. He was none the less dangerous."

Marambot, wiping his eyes, answered:

"Well, your honour, what can you expect? Nowadays it's so hard to find good servants—I could never have found a better one."

Denis was acquitted and put in a sanatorium at his master's expense.

The Horla

May 8. What a lovely day! I have spent all the morning lying on the grass in front of my house, under the enormous plantain tree which covers and shades and shelters the whole of it. I like this part of the country; I am fond of living here because I am attached to it by deep roots, the profound and delicate roots which attach a man to the soil on which his ancestors were born and died, to their traditions, their usages, their food, the local expressions, the peculiar language of the peasants, the smell of the soil, the hamlets, and to the atmosphere itself.

I love the house in which I grew up. From my windows I can see the Seine, which flows by the side of my garden, on the other side of the road, almost through my grounds, the great and wide Seine, which goes to Rouen and Havre, and which is covered with boats passing to and fro.

On the left, down yonder, lies Rouen, populous Rouen with its blue roofs massing under pointed, Gothic towers. Innumerable are they, delicate or broad, dominated by the spire of the cathedral, full of bells which sound through the blue air on fine mornings, sending their sweet and distant iron clang to me, their metallic sounds, now stronger and now weaker, according as the wind is strong or light.

What a delicious morning it was! About eleven o'clock, a long line of boats drawn by a steam-tug, as big a fly, and which scarcely puffed while emitting its thick smoke, passed my gate.

After two English schooners, whose red flags fluttered toward the sky, there came a magnificent Brazilian three-master; it was perfectly white and wonderfully clean and shining. I saluted it, I hardly know why, except that the sight of the vessel gave me great pleasure.

May 12. I have had a slight feverish attack for the last few days, and I feel ill, or rather I feel low-spirited.

Whence come those mysterious influences which change our happiness into discouragement, and our self-confidence into diffidence? One might almost say that the air, the invisible air, is full of unknowable Forces, whose mysterious presence we have to endure. I wake up in the best of spirits, with an inclination to sing in my heart. Why? I go down by the side of the water, and suddenly, after walking a short distance, I return home wretched, as if some misfortune were awaiting me there. Why? Is it a cold shiver which, passing over my skin, has upset my nerves and given me a fit of low spirits? Is it the form of the clouds, or the tints of the sky, or the colours of the surrounding objects which are so changeable, which have troubled my thoughts as they passed before my eyes? Who can tell?

Everything that surrounds us, everything that we see without looking at it, everything that we touch without knowing it, everything that we handle without feeling it, everything that we meet without clearly distinguishing it, has a rapid, surprising, and inexplicable effect upon us and upon our organs, and through them on our ideas and on our being itself.

How profound that mystery of the Invisible is! We cannot fathom it with our miserable senses: our eyes are unable to perceive what is either too small or too great, too near to or too far from us; we can see neither the inhabitants of a star nor of a drop of water; our ears deceive us, for they transmit to us the vibrations of the air in sonorous notes. Our senses are fairies who work the miracle of changing that movement into noise, and by that metamorphosis give birth to music, which makes the mute agitation of nature a harmony. So with our sense of smell, which is weaker than that of a dog, and so with our sense of taste, which can scarcely distinguish the age of a wine!

Oh! If we only had other organs which could work other

miracles in our favour, what a number of fresh things we might discover around us!

May 16. I am ill, decidedly! I was so well last month! I am feverish, horribly feverish, or rather I am in a state of feverish enervation, which makes my mind suffer as much as my body. I have without ceasing the horrible sensation of some danger threatening me, the apprehension of some coming misfortune or of approaching death, a presentiment which is no doubt, an attack of some illness still unnamed, which germinates in the flesh and in the blood.

May 18. I have just come from consulting my medical man, for I can no longer get any sleep. He found that my pulse was high, my eyes dilated, my nerves highly strung, but no alarming symptoms. I must have a course of shower baths and of bromide of potassium.

May 25. No change! My state is really very peculiar. As the evening comes on, an incomprehensible feeling of disquietude seizes me, just as if night concealed some terrible menace toward me. I dine quickly, and then try to read, but I do not understand the words, and can scarcely distinguish the letters. Then I walk up and down my drawing-room, oppressed by a feeling of confused and irresistible fear, a fear of sleep and a fear of my bed.

About ten o'clock I go up to my room. As soon as I have entered I lock and bolt the door. I am frightened—of what? Up till the present time I have been frightened of nothing. I open my cupboards, and look under my bed; I listen—I listen—to what? How strange it is that a simple feeling of discomfort, of impeded or heightened circulation, perhaps the irritation of a nervous centre, a slight congestion, a small disturbance in the imperfect and delicate functions of our living machinery, can turn the most light-hearted of men into a melancholy one, and make a coward of the bravest?

Then, I go to bed, and I wait for sleep as a man might wait for the executioner. I wait for its coming with dread, and my heart beats and my legs tremble, while my whole body shivers beneath the warmth of the bedclothes, until the moment when I suddenly fall asleep, as a man throws himself into a pool of stagnant water in order to drown. I do not feel this perfidious sleep coming over me as I used to, but a sleep which is close to me and watching me, which is going to seize me by the head, to close my eyes and annihilate me.

I sleep—a long time—two or three hours perhaps—then a dream—no—a nightmare lays hold on me. I feel that I am in bed and asleep—I feel it and I know it—and I feel also that somebody is coming close to me, is looking at me, touching me, is getting on to my bed, is kneeling on my chest, is taking my neck between his hands and squeezing it—squeezing it with all his might in order to strangle me.

I struggle, bound by that terrible powerlessness which paralyzes us in our dreams; I try to cry out—but I cannot; I want to move—I cannot; I try, with the most violent efforts and out of breath, to turn over and throw off this being which is crushing and suffocating me—I cannot!

And then suddenly I wake up, shaken and bathed in perspiration; I light a candle and find that I am alone, and after that crisis, which occurs every night, I at length fall asleep and slumber tranquilly till morning.

June 2. My state has grown worse. What is the matter with me? The bromide does me no good, and the shower-baths have no effect whatever. Sometimes, in order to tire myself out, though I am fatigued enough already, I go for a walk in the forest of Roumare. I used to think at first that the fresh light and soft air, impregnated with the odour of herbs and leaves, would instil new life into my veins and impart fresh energy to my heart. One day I turned into a broad ride in the wood, and then I diverged toward La Bouille, through a narrow path, between two rows of exceedingly tall trees, which placed a thick, green, almost black roof between the sky and me.

A sudden shiver ran through me, not a cold shiver, but a shiver of agony, and so I hastened my steps, uneasy at being alone in the wood, frightened stupidly and without reason, at the profound solitude. Suddenly it seemed as if I were being followed, that somebody was walking at my heels, close, quite close to me, near enough to touch me.

I turned round suddenly, but I was alone. I saw nothing behind me except the straight, broad ride, empty and bordered by high trees, horribly empty; on the other side also it extended until it was lost in the distance, and looked just the same—terrible.

I closed my eyes. Why? And then I began to turn round on one heel very quickly, just like a top. I nearly fell down, and opened my eyes; the trees were dancing round me and the earth heaved; I was obliged to sit down. Then, ah! I no longer remembered how I had come! What a strange idea! What a strange, strange idea! I did not the least know. I started off to the right, and got back into the avenue which had led me into the middle of the forest.

June 3. I have had a terrible night. I shall go away for a few weeks, for no doubt a journey will set me up again.

July 2. I have come back, quite cured, and have had a most delightful trip into the bargain. I have been to Mont Saint-Michel, which I had not seen before.

What a sight, when one arrives as I did, at Avranches toward the end of the day! The town stands on a hill, and I was taken into the public garden at the extremity of the town. I uttered a cry of astonishment. An extraordinarily large bay lay extended before me, as far as my eyes could reach, between two hills which were lost to sight in the mist; and in the middle of this immense yellow bay, under a clear, golden sky, a peculiar hill rose up, sombre and pointed in the midst of the sand. The sun had just disappeared, and under the still flaming sky stood out the outline of that fantastic rock which bears on its summit a picturesque monument.

At daybreak I went to it. The tide was low, as it had been the night before, and I saw that wonderful abbey rise up before me as I approached it. After several hours' walking, I reached the enormous mass of rock which supports the little town, dominated by the great church. Having climbed the steep and narrow street, I entered the most wonderful Gothic building that has ever been erected to God on earth, large as a town, and full of low rooms which seem buried beneath vaulted roofs, and of lofty galleries supported by delicate columns.

I entered this gigantic granite jewel, which is as light in its effect as a bit of lace and is covered with towers, with slender belfries to which spiral staircases ascend. The flying buttresses raise strange heads that bristle with chimeras. with devils, with fantastic animals, with monstrous flowers, are joined together by finely carved arches, to the blue sky by day, and to the black sky by night.

When I had reached the summit. I said to the monk who accompanied me: "Father, how happy you must be here!" And he replied: "It is very windy, *Monsieur*"; and so we began to talk while watching the rising tide, which ran over the sand and covered it with a steel *cuirass*.

And then the monk told me stories, all the old stories belonging to the place—legends, nothing but legends.

One of them struck me forcibly. The country people, those belonging to the Mornet, declare that at night one can hear talking going on in the sand, and also that two goats bleat, one with a strong, the other with a weak voice. Incredulous people declare that it is nothing but the screaming of the sea birds, which occasionally resembles bleatings, and occasionally human lamentations; but belated fishermen swear that they have met an old shepherd, whose cloak covered head they can never see, wandering on the sand, between two tides, round the little town placed so far out of the world. They declare he is guiding and walking before a he-goat with a man's face and a she-goat with a woman's face, both with white hair, who talk incessantly, quarrelling in a strange language, and then suddenly cease talking in order to bleat with all their might.

"Do you believe it?" I asked the monk. "I scarcely know," he replied; and I continued: "If there are other beings besides ourselves on this earth, how comes it that we have not known it for so long a time, or why have you not seen them? How is it that I have not seen them?"

He replied: "Do we see the hundred-thousandth part of what exists? Look here; there is the wind, which is the strongest force in nature. It knocks down men, and blows down buildings, uproots trees, raises the sea into mountains of water, destroys cliffs and casts great ships on to the breakers; it kills, it whistles, it sighs, it roars. But have you ever seen it, and can you see it? Yet it exists for all that."

I was silent before this simple reasoning. That man was a philosopher, or perhaps a fool; I could not say which exactly, so I held my tongue. What he had said had often been in my own thoughts.

July 3. I have slept badly; certainly there is some feverish influence here, for my coachman is suffering in the same way as I am. When I went back home yesterday, I noticed his singular paleness, and I asked him: "What is the matter with you, Jean?"

"The matter is that I never get any rest, and my nights devour my days. Since your departure, *Monsieur*, there has been a spell over me."

However, the other servants are all well, but I am very frightened of having another attack, myself.

July 4. I am decidedly taken again; for my old nightmares have returned. Last night I felt somebody leaning on me who was sucking my life from between my lips with his mouth. Yes, he was sucking it out of my neck like a leech would have done. Then he got up, satiated, and I woke up, so beaten, crushed, and annihilated that I could not move. If this continues for a few days, I shall certainly go away again.

July 5. Have I lost my reason? What has happened? What I saw last night is so strange that my head wanders when I think of it!

As I do now every evening, I had locked my door; then, being thirsty, I drank half a glass of water, and I accidentally noticed that the water-bottle was full up to the cut-glass stopper.

Then I went to bed and fell into one of my terrible sleeps, from which I was aroused in about two hours by a still more terrible shock.

Picture to yourself a sleeping man who is being murdered, who wakes up with a knife in his chest, a gurgling in his throat, is covered with blood, can no longer breathe, is going to die and does not understand anything at all about it—there you have it.

Having recovered my senses, I was thirsty again, so I lighted a candle and went to the table on which my water-bottle was. I lifted it up and tilted it over my glass, but nothing came out. It was empty! It was completely empty! At first I could not understand it at all; then suddenly I was seized by such a terrible feeling that I had to sit down, or rather fall into a chair! Then I sprang up with a bound to look about me; then I sat down again, overcome by astonishment and fear, in front of the transparent crystal bottle!

I looked at it with fixed eyes, trying to solve the puzzle, and my hands trembled! Somebody had drunk the water, but who? I? I without any doubt. It could surely only be I? In that case I was a somnambulist—was living, without knowing it, that double, mysterious life which makes us doubt whether there are not two beings in us—whether a strange, unknowable, and invisible being does not, during our moments of mental and physical torpor, animate the inert body, forcing it to a more willing obedience than it yields to ourselves.

Oh! Who will understand my horrible agony? Who will understand the emotion of a man sound in mind, wide-awake, full of sense, who looks in horror at the disappearance of a little water while he was asleep, through the glass of a water-bottle! And I remained sitting until it was daylight, without venturing to go to bed again.

July 6. I am going mad. Again all the contents of my water-bottle have been drunk during the night; or rather I have drunk it!

But is it I? Is it I? Who could it be? Who? Oh! God! Am I

going mad? Who will save me?

July 10. I have just been through some surprising ordeals. Undoubtedly I must be mad! And yet!

On July 6, before going to bed, I put some wine, milk, water, bread, and strawberries on my table. Somebody drank—I drank—all the water and a little of the milk, but neither the wine, nor the bread, nor the strawberries were touched.

On the seventh of July I renewed the same experiment, with the same results, and on July 8 I left out the water and the milk and nothing was touched.

Lastly, on July 9 I put only water and milk on my table, taking care to wrap up the bottles in white muslin and to tie down the stoppers. Then I rubbed my lips, my beard, and my hands with pencil lead, and went to bed.

Deep slumber seized me, soon followed by a terrible awakening. I had not moved, and my sheets were not marked. I rushed to the table. The muslin round the bottles remained intact; I undid the string, trembling with fear. All the water had been drunk, and so had the milk! Ah! Great God! I must start for Paris immediately.

July 12. Paris. I must have lost my head during the last few days! I must be the plaything of my enervated imagination, unless I am really a somnambulist, or I have been brought under the power of one of those influences—hypnotic suggestion, for example—which are known to exist, but have hitherto been inexplicable. In any case, my mental state bordered on madness, and twenty-four hours of Paris sufficed to restore me to my equilibrium.

Yesterday after doing some business and paying some visits, which instilled fresh and invigorating mental air into me, I wound up my evening at the *Theatre Francais*. A drama by Alexander Dumas the Younger was being acted, and his brilliant and powerful play completed my cure. Certainly solitude is dangerous for active minds. We need men who can think and can talk, around us. When we are alone for a long time, we people space with phantoms.

I returned along the boulevards to my hotel in excellent spirits. Amid the jostling of the crowd I thought, not without irony, of my terrors and surmises of the previous week, because I believed, yes, I believed, that an invisible being lived beneath my roof. How weak our mind is; how quickly it is terrified and unbalanced as soon as we are confronted with a small, incomprehensible fact. Instead of dismissing the problem with: "We do not understand because we cannot find the cause," we immediately imagine terrible mysteries and supernatural powers.

July 14. Fête of the Republic. I walked through the streets, and the crackers and flags amused me like a child. Still, it is very foolish to make merry on a set date, by Government decree. People are like a flock of sheep, now steadily patient, now in ferocious revolt. Say to it: "Amuse yourself," and it amuses itself. Say to it: "Go and fight with your neighbour," and it goes and fights. Say to it: "Vote for the Emperor," and it votes for the Emperor; then say to it: "Vote for the Republic," and it votes for the Republic.

Those who direct it are stupid, too; but instead of obeying men they obey principles, a course which can only be foolish, ineffective, and false, for the very reason that principles are ideas which are considered as certain and unchangeable, whereas in this world one is certain of nothing, since light is an illusion and noise is deception.

July 16. I saw some things yesterday that troubled me very much. I was dining at my cousin's, Madame Sable, whose husband is colonel of the Seventy-sixth Chasseurs at Limoges. There were two young women there, one of whom had married a medical man, Dr. Parent, who devotes himself a great deal to nervous diseases and to the extraordinary manifestations which just now experiments in hypnotism and suggestion are producing.

He related to us at some length the enormous results obtained by English scientists and the doctors of the medical school at Nancy, and the facts which he adduced appeared to me so strange, that I declared that I was altogether incredulous.

"We are," he declared, "on the point of discovering one of the most important secrets of nature, I mean to say, one of its most important secrets on this earth, for assuredly there are some up in the stars, yonder, of a different kind of importance. Ever since man has thought, since he has been able to express and write down his thoughts, he has felt himself close to a mystery which is impenetrable to his coarse and imperfect senses, and he endeavours to supplement the feeble penetration of his organs by the efforts of his intellect.

As long as that intellect remained in its elementary stage, this intercourse with invisible spirits assumed forms which were commonplace though terrifying. Thence sprang the popular belief in the supernatural, the legends of wandering spirits, of fairies, of gnomes, of ghosts, I might even say the conception of God, for our ideas of the Workman-Creator, from whatever religion they may have come down to us, are certainly the most mediocre, the stupidest, and the most unacceptable inventions that ever sprang from the frightened brain of any human creature. Nothing is truer than what Voltaire says: *If God made man in His own image, man has certainly paid Him back again.*

"But for rather more than a century, men seem to have had a presentiment of something new. Mesmer and some others have put us on an unexpected track, and within the last two or three years especially, we have arrived at results really surprising."

My cousin, who is also very incredulous, smiled, and Dr. Parent said to her: "Would you like me to try and send you to sleep, *Madame?*"

"Yes, certainly."

She sat down in an easy-chair, and he began to look at her fixedly, as if to fascinate her. I suddenly felt myself somewhat discomposed; my heart beat rapidly and I had a choking feeling in my throat. I saw that Madame Sable's eyes were growing heavy, her mouth twitched, and her bosom heaved, and at the end of ten minutes she was asleep.

"Go behind her," the doctor said to me; so I took a seat behind her. He put a visiting-card into her hands, and said to her: "This is a looking-glass; what do you see in it?"

She replied: "I see my cousin."

"What is he doing?"

"He is twisting his moustache."

"And now?"

"He is taking a photograph out of his pocket."

"Whose photograph is it?"

"His own."

That was true, for the photograph had been given me that same evening at the hotel.

"What is his attitude in this portrait?"

"He is standing up with his hat in his hand."

She saw these things in that card, in that piece of white paste-board, as if she had seen them in a looking-glass.

The young women were frightened, and exclaimed: "That is quite enough! Quite, quite enough!"

But the doctor said to her authoritatively: "You will get up at eight o'clock tomorrow morning; then you will go and call on your cousin at his hotel and ask him to lend you the five thousand *francs* which your husband asks of you, and which he will ask for when he sets out on his coming journey."

Then he woke her up.

On returning to my hotel, I thought over this curious *séance* and I was assailed by doubts, not as to my cousin's absolute and undoubted good faith, for I had known her as well as if she had been my own sister ever since she was a child, but as to a possible trick on the doctor's part. Had not he, perhaps, kept a glass hidden in his hand, which he showed to the young woman in her sleep at the same time as he did the card? Professional conjurers do things which are just as singular.

However, I went to bed, and this morning, at about half past eight, I was awakened by my footman, who said to me: "Madame Sable has asked to see you immediately, *Monsieur.*" I dressed hastily and went to her.

She sat down in some agitation, with her eyes on the floor,

and without raising her veil said to me: "My dear cousin, I am going to ask a great favour of you."

"What is it, cousin?"

"I do not like to tell you, and yet I must. I am in absolute want of five thousand *francs*."

"What, you?"

"Yes, I, or rather my husband, who has asked me to procure them for him."

I was so stupefied that I hesitated to answer. I asked myself whether she had not really been making fun of me with Dr. Parent, if it were not merely a very well-acted farce which had been got up beforehand. On looking at her attentively, however, my doubts disappeared. She was trembling with grief, so painful was this step to her, and I was sure that her throat was full of sobs.

I knew that she was very rich and so I continued: "What! Has not your husband five thousand *francs* at his disposal? Come, think. Are you sure that he commissioned you to ask me for them?"

She hesitated for a few seconds, as if she were making a great effort to search her memory, and then she replied: "Yes—yes, I am quite sure of it."

"He has written to you?"

She hesitated again and reflected, and I guessed the torture of her thoughts. She did not know. She only knew that she was to borrow five thousand *francs* of me for her husband. So she told a lie.

"Yes, he has written to me."

"When, pray? You did not mention it to me yesterday."

"I received his letter this morning."

"Can you show it to me?"

"No; no—no—it contained private matters, things too personal to ourselves. I burned it."

"So your husband runs into debt?"

She hesitated again, and then murmured: "I do not know."

Thereupon I said bluntly: "I have not five thousand *francs* at my disposal at this moment, my dear cousin."

She uttered a cry, as if she were in pain and said: "Oh! oh! I beseech you, I beseech you to get them for me."

She got excited and clasped her hands as if she were praying to me! I heard her voice change its tone; she wept and sobbed, harassed and dominated by the irresistible order that she had received.

"Oh! oh! I beg you to—if you knew what I am suffering—I want them today."

I had pity on her: "You shall have them by and by, I swear to you."

"Oh! thank you! thank you! How kind you are."

I continued: "Do you remember what took place at your house last night?"

"Yes."

"Do you remember that Dr. Parent sent you to sleep?"

"Yes."

"Oh! Very well then; he ordered you to come to me this morning to borrow five thousand *francs*, and at this moment you are obeying that suggestion."

She considered for a few moments, and then replied: "But as it is my husband who wants them—"

For a whole hour I tried to convince her, but could not succeed, and when she had gone I went to the doctor. He was just going out, and he listened to me with a smile, and said: "Do you believe now?"

"Yes, I cannot help it."

"Let us go to your cousin's."

She was already resting on a couch, overcome with fatigue. The doctor felt her pulse, looked at her for some time with one hand raised toward her eyes, which she closed by degrees under the irresistible power of this magnetic influence. When she was asleep, he said:

"Your husband does not require the five thousand *francs* any longer! You must, therefore, forget that you asked your cousin to lend them to you, and, if he speaks to you about it, you will not understand him."

Then he woke her up, and I took out a pocket-book and said: "Here is what you asked me for this morning, my dear cousin." But she was so surprised, that I did not venture to persist; nevertheless, I tried to recall the circumstance to her, but she denied it vigorously, thought that I was making fun of her, and in the end, very nearly lost her temper.

There! I have just come back, and I have not been able to eat any lunch, for this experiment has altogether upset me.

July 19. Many people to whom I have told the adventure have laughed at me. I no longer know what to think. The wise man says: Perhaps?

July 21. I dined at Bougival, and then I spent the evening at a boatmen's ball. Decidedly everything depends on place and surroundings. It would be the height of folly to believe in the supernatural on the Ile de la Grenouilliere. But on the top of Mont Saint-Michel or in India, we are terribly under the influence of our surroundings. I shall return home next week.

July 30. I came back to my own house yesterday. Everything is going on well.

August 2. Nothing fresh; it is splendid weather, and I spend my days in watching the Seine flow past.

August 4. Quarrels among my servants. They declare that the glasses are broken in the cupboards at night. The footman accuses the cook, she accuses the needlewoman, and the latter accuses the other two. Who is the culprit? It would take a clever person to tell.

August 6. This time, I am not mad. I have seen—I have seen—I have seen!—I can doubt no longer—I have seen it!

I was walking at two o'clock among my rose-trees, in the full sunlight—in the walk bordered by autumn roses which are beginning to fall. As I stopped to look at a *Geant de Bataille*, which had three splendid blooms, I distinctly saw the stalk of one of the roses bend close to me, as if an invisible hand had bent it, and then break, as if that hand had picked it! Then the flower raised itself, following the curve which a hand would have described in carrying it toward a mouth, and remained suspended in the transparent air, alone and motionless, a terrible red spot, three yards from my eyes. In desperation I rushed at it to take it! I found nothing; it had disappeared. Then I was seized with furious rage against myself, for it is not wholesome for a reasonable and serious man to have such hallucinations.

But was it a hallucination? I turned to look for the stalk, and I found it immediately under the bush, freshly broken, between the two other roses which remained on the branch. I returned home, then, with a much disturbed mind; for I am certain now, certain as I am of the alternation of day and night, that there exists close to me an invisible being who lives on milk and on water, who can touch objects, take them and change their places; who is, consequently, endowed with a material nature, although imperceptible to sense, and who lives as I do, under my roof—

August 7. I slept tranquilly. He drank the water out of my decanter, but did not disturb my sleep.

I ask myself whether I am mad. As I was walking just now in the sun by the riverside, doubts as to my own sanity arose in me; not vague doubts such as I have had hitherto, but precise and absolute doubts. I have seen mad people, and I have known some who were quite intelligent, lucid, even clear-sighted in every concern of life, except on one point. They could speak clearly, readily, profoundly on everything; till their thoughts were caught in the breakers of their delusions and went to pieces there, were dispersed and swamped in that furious and terrible sea of fogs and squalls which is called *madness*.

I certainly should think that I was mad, absolutely mad, if I were not conscious that I knew my state, if I could not fathom it and analyze it with the most complete lucidity. I should, in fact, be a reasonable man labouring under a hallucination. Some unknown disturbance must have been excited in my brain, one of those disturbances which physiologists of the present day try to note and to fix precisely, and that disturbance must have caused a profound gulf in my mind and in the order and logic of my ideas.

Similar phenomena occur in dreams, and lead us through the most unlikely phantasmagoria, without causing us any surprise, because our verifying apparatus and our sense of control have gone to sleep, while our imaginative faculty wakes and works. Was it not possible that one of the imperceptible keys of the cerebral finger-board had been paralyzed in me? Some men lose the recollection of proper names, or of verbs, or of numbers, or merely of dates, in consequence of an accident. The localization of all the avenues of thought has been accomplished nowadays; what, then, would there be surprising in the fact that my faculty of controlling the unreality of certain hallucinations should be destroyed for the time being?

I thought of all this as I walked by the side of the water. The sun was shining brightly on the river and made earth delight-ful, while it filled me with love for life, for the swallows, whose swift agility is always delightful in my eyes, for the plants by the riverside, whose rustling is a pleasure to my ears.

By degrees, however, an inexplicable feeling of discomfort seized me. It seemed to me as if some unknown force were numbing and stopping me, were preventing me from going fur-ther and were calling me back. I felt that painful wish to return which comes on you when you have left a beloved invalid at home, and are seized by a presentiment that he is worse.

I, therefore, returned despite of myself, feeling certain that I should find some bad news awaiting me, a letter or a telegram. There was nothing, however, and I was surprised and uneasy, more so than if I had had another fantastic vision.

August 8. I spent a terrible evening, yesterday. He does not show himself any more, but I feel that He is near me, watching me, looking at me, penetrating me, dominating me, and more terrible to me when He hides himself thus than if He were to manifest his constant and invisible presence by supernatural phenomena. However, I slept.

August 9. Nothing, but I am afraid.

August 10. Nothing; but what will happen tomorrow?

August 11. Still nothing. I cannot stop at home with this fear hanging over me and these thoughts in my mind; I shall go away.

August 12. Ten o'clock at night. All day long I have been trying to get away, and have not been able. I contemplated a simple and easy act of liberty, a carriage ride to Rouen—and I have not been able to do it. What is the reason?

August 13. When one is attacked by certain maladies, the springs of our physical being seem broken, our energies destroyed, our muscles relaxed, our bones to be as soft as our flesh, and our blood as liquid as water. I am experiencing the same in my moral being, in a strange and distressing manner. I have no longer any strength, any courage, any self-control, nor even any power to set my own will in motion. I have no power left to *will* anything, but someone does it for me and I obey.

August 14. I am lost! Somebody possesses my soul and governs it! Somebody orders all my acts, all my movements, all my thoughts. I am no longer master of myself, nothing except an enslaved and terrified spectator of the things which I do. I wish to go out; I cannot. *He* does not wish to; and so I remain, trembling and distracted in the armchair in which he keeps me sitting. I merely wish to get up and to rouse myself, so as to think that I am still master of myself: I cannot! I am riveted to my chair, and my chair adheres to the floor in such a manner that no force of mine can move us.

Then suddenly, I must, I *must* go to the foot of my garden to pick some strawberries and eat them—and I go there. I pick the strawberries and I eat them! Oh! my God! my God! Is there a God? If there be one, deliver me! save me! succour me! Pardon! Pity! Mercy! Save me! Oh! what sufferings! what torture! what horror!

August 15. Certainly this is the way in which my poor cousin was possessed and swayed, when she came to borrow five thousand *francs* of me. She was under the power of a strange will which had entered into her, like another soul, a parasitic and ruling soul. Is the world coming to an end?

But who is he, this invisible being that rules me, this unknowable being, this rover of a supernatural race?

Invisible beings exist, then! how is it, then, that since the beginning of the world they have never manifested themselves in such a manner as they do to me? I have never read anything that resembles what goes on in my house. Oh! If I could only leave it, if I could only go away and flee, and never return, I should be saved; but I cannot.

August 16. I managed to escape today for two hours, like a prisoner who finds the door of his dungeon accidentally open. I suddenly felt that I was free and that He was far away, and so I gave orders to put the horses in as quickly as possible, and I drove to Rouen. Oh! how delightful to be able to say to my coachman: "Go to Rouen!"

I made him pull up before the library, and I begged them to lend me Dr. Herrmann Herestauss's treatise on the unknown inhabitants of the ancient and modern world.

Then, as I was getting into my carriage, I intended to say: "To the railway station!" but instead of this I shouted—I did not speak; but I shouted—in such a loud voice that all the passers-by turned round: "Home!" and I fell back on to the cushion of my carriage, overcome by mental agony. He had found me out and regained possession of me.

August 17. Oh! What a night! what a night! And yet it seems to me that I ought to rejoice. I read until one o'clock in the morning! Herestauss, Doctor of Philosophy and Theogony, wrote the history and the manifestation of all those invisible beings which hover around man, or of whom he dreams. He describes their origin, their domains, their power; but none of them resembles the one which haunts me. One might say that man, ever since he has thought, has had a foreboding and a fear of a new being, stronger than himself, his successor in this world, and that, feeling him near, and not being able to foretell the nature of the unseen one, he has, in his terror, created the whole race of hidden beings, vague phantoms born of fear.

Having, therefore, read until one o'clock in the morning, I went and sat down at the open window, in order to cool my forehead and my thoughts in the calm night air. It was very pleasant and warm! How I should have enjoyed such a night formerly!

There was no moon, but the stars darted out their rays in the dark heavens. Who inhabits those worlds? What forms, what living beings, what animals are there yonder? Do those who are thinkers in those distant worlds know more than we do? What can they do more than we? What do they see which we do not? Will not one of them, some day or other, traversing space, appear on our earth to conquer it, just as formerly the Norsemen crossed the sea in order to subjugate nations feebler than themselves?

We are so weak, so powerless, so ignorant, so small—we who live on this particle of mud which revolves in liquid air.

I fell asleep, dreaming thus in the cool night air, and then, having slept for about three quarters of an hour, I opened my eyes without moving, awakened by an indescribably confused and strange sensation. At first I saw nothing, and then suddenly it appeared to me as if a page of the book, which had remained open on my table, turned over of its own accord. Not a breath of air had come in at my window, and I was surprised and waited. In about four minutes, I saw, I saw—yes I saw with my own eyes—another page lift itself up and fall down on the others, as if a finger had turned it over.

My armchair was empty, appeared empty, but I knew that He was there, He, and sitting in my place, and that He was reading. With a furious bound, the bound of an enraged wild beast that wishes to disembowel its tamer, I crossed my room to seize him, to strangle him, to kill him! But before I could reach it, my chair fell over as if somebody had run away from me. My table rocked, my lamp fell and went out, and my window closed as if some thief had been surprised and had fled out into the night, shutting it behind him.

So He had run away; He had been afraid; He, afraid of me!

So tomorrow, or later—some day or other, I should be able to hold him in my clutches and crush him against the ground! Do not dogs occasionally bite and strangle their masters?

August 18. I have been thinking the whole day long. Oh! yes, I will obey Him, follow His impulses, fulfil all His wishes, show myself humble, submissive, a coward. He is the stronger; but an hour will come.

August 19. I know, I know, I know all! I have just read the following in the *Revue du Monde Scientifique*:

A curious piece of news comes to us from Rio de Janeiro. Madness, an epidemic of madness, which may be compared to that contagious madness which attacked the people of Europe in the Middle Ages, is at this moment raging in the Province of San-Paulo. The frightened inhabitants are leaving their houses, deserting their villages, abandoning their land, saying that they are pursued, possessed, governed like human cattle by invisible, though tangible beings, by a species of vampire, which feeds on their life while they are asleep, and which, besides, drinks water and milk without appearing to touch any other nourishment.

Professor Don Pedro Henriques, accompanied by several medical savants, has gone to the Province of San-Paulo, in order to study the origin and the manifestations of this surprising madness on the spot, and to propose such measures to the Emperor as may appear to him to be most fitted to restore the mad population to reason.

Ah! Ah! I remember now that fine Brazilian three-master which passed in front of my windows as it was going up the Seine, on the eighth of last May! I thought it looked so pretty, so white and bright! That Being was on board of her, coming from there, where its race sprang from. And it saw me! It saw my house, which was also white, and He sprang from the ship on to the land. Oh! Good heavens!

Now I know, I can divine. The reign of man is over, and he has come. He whom disquieted priests exorcised, whom sorcerers evoked on dark nights, without seeing him appear, He to whom the imaginations of the transient masters of the world lent all the monstrous or graceful forms of gnomes, spirits, genii, fairies, and familiar spirits. After the coarse conceptions of primitive fear, men more enlightened gave him a truer form. Mesmer divined him, and ten years ago physicians accurately discovered the nature of his power, even before He exercised it himself.

They played with that weapon of their new Lord, the sway of a mysterious will over the human soul, which had become enslaved. They called it mesmerism, hypnotism, suggestion, I know not what? I have seen them diverting themselves like rash children with this horrible power! Woe to us! Woe to man! He has come, the—the—what does He call himself—the—I fancy that he is shouting out his name to me and I do not hear him—the—yes—He is shouting it out—I am listening—I cannot—repeat—it—Horla—I have heard—the Horla—it is He—the Horla—He has come!—

Ah! the vulture has eaten the pigeon, the wolf has eaten the lamb; the lion has devoured the sharp-horned buffalo; man has killed the lion with an arrow, with a spear, with gunpowder; but the Horla will make of man what man has made of the horse and of the ox: his chattel, his slave, and his food, by the mere power of his will. Woe to us!

But, nevertheless, sometimes the animal rebels and kills the man who has subjugated it. I should also like—I shall be able to—but I must know Him, touch Him, see Him! Learned men say that eyes of animals, as they differ from ours, do not distinguish as ours do. And my eye cannot distinguish this newcomer who is oppressing me.

Why? Oh! Now I remember the words of the monk at Mont Saint-Michel: "Can we see the hundred-thousandth part of what exists? Listen; there is the wind which is the strongest force in nature; it knocks men down, blows down buildings, uproots trees, raises the sea into mountains of water, destroys cliffs, and casts great ships on to the breakers; it kills, it whistles, it sighs, it roars,—have you ever seen it, and can you see it? It exists for all that, however!"

And I went on thinking: my eyes are so weak, so imperfect, that they do not even distinguish hard bodies, if they are as transparent as glass! If a glass without quicksilver behind it were to bar my way, I should run into it, just like a bird which has flown into a room breaks its head against the windowpanes. A thousand things, moreover, deceive a man and lead him astray. How then is it surprising that he cannot perceive a new body which is penetrated and pervaded by the light?

A new being! Why not? It was assuredly bound to come! Why should we be the last? We do not distinguish it, like all the others created before us? The reason is, that its nature is more delicate, its body finer and more finished than ours. Our makeup is so weak, so awkwardly conceived; our body is encumbered with organs that are always tired, always being strained like locks that are too complicated; it lives like a plant and like an animal nourishing itself with difficulty on air, herbs, and flesh; it is a brute machine which is a prey to maladies, to malformations, to decay; it is broken-winded, badly regulated, simple and eccentric, ingeniously yet badly made, a coarse and yet a delicate mechanism, in brief, the outline of a being which might become intelligent and great.

There are only a few—so few—stages of development in this world, from the oyster up to man. Why should there not be one more, when once that period is accomplished which separates the successive products one from the other?

Why not one more? Why not, also, other trees with immense, splendid flowers, perfuming whole regions? Why not other elements beside fire, air, earth, and water? There are four, only four, nursing fathers of various beings! What a pity! Why should not there be forty, four hundred, four thousand! How poor everything is, how mean and wretched—grudgingly given, poorly invented, clumsily made! Ah! the elephant and the hippopotamus, what power! And the camel, what suppleness!

But the butterfly, you will say, a flying flower! I dream of one that should be as large as a hundred worlds, with wings whose shape, beauty, colours, and motion I cannot even express. But I see it—it flutters from star to star, refreshing them and perfuming them with the light and harmonious breath of its flight! And the people up there gaze at it as it passes in an ecstasy of delight!

What is the matter with me? It is He, the Horla who haunts me, and who makes me think of these foolish things! He is within me, He is becoming my soul; I shall kill him!

August 20. I shall kill Him. I have seen Him! Yesterday I sat down at my table and pretended to write very assiduously. I knew quite well that He would come prowling round me, quite close to me, so close that I might perhaps be able to touch him, to seize him. And then—then I should have the strength of desperation; I should have my hands, my knees, my chest, my forehead, my teeth to strangle him, to crush him, to bite him, to tear him to pieces. And I watched for him with all my overexcited nerves.

I had lighted my two lamps and the eight wax candles on my mantelpiece, as if, by this light I should discover Him.

My bed, my old oak bed with its columns, was opposite to me; on my right was the fireplace; on my left the door, which was carefully closed, after I had left it open for some time, in order to attract Him; behind me was a very high wardrobe with a looking-glass in it, which served me to dress by every day, and in which I was in the habit of inspecting myself from head to foot every time I passed it.

So I pretended to be writing in order to deceive Him, for He also was watching me, and suddenly I felt, I was certain, that He was reading over my shoulder, that He was there, almost touching my ear.

I got up so quickly, with my hands extended, that I almost

fell. Horror! It was as bright as at midday, but I did not see myself in the glass! It was empty, clear, profound, full of light! But my figure was not reflected in it—and I, I was opposite to it! I saw the large, clear glass from top to bottom, and I looked at it with unsteady eyes. I did not dare advance; I did not venture to make a movement; feeling certain, nevertheless, that He was there, but that He would escape me again, He whose imperceptible body had absorbed my reflection.

How frightened I was! And then suddenly I began to see myself through a mist in the depths of the looking-glass, in a mist as it were, or through a veil of water; and it seemed to me as if this water were flowing slowly from left to right, and making my figure clearer every moment. It was like the end of an eclipse. Whatever hid me did not appear to possess any clearly defined outlines, but was a sort of opaque transparency, which gradually grew clearer.

At last I was able to distinguish myself completely, as I do every day when I look at myself.

I had seen Him! And the horror of it remained with me, and makes me shudder even now.

August 21. How could I kill Him, since I could not get hold of Him? Poison? But He would see me mix it with the water; and then, would our poisons have any effect on His impalpable body? No—no—no doubt about the matter. Then?—then?

August 22. I sent for a blacksmith from Rouen and ordered iron shutters of him for my room, such as some private hotels in Paris have on the ground floor, for fear of thieves, and he is going to make me a similar door as well. I have made myself out a coward, but I do not care about that!

September 10. Rouen, Hotel Continental. It is done; it is done—but is He dead? My mind is thoroughly upset by what I have seen.

Well then, yesterday, the locksmith having put on the iron shutters and door, I left everything open until midnight, although it was getting cold.

Suddenly I felt that He was there, and joy, mad joy took possession of me. I got up softly, and I walked to the right and left for some time, so that He might not guess anything; then I took off my boots and put on my slippers carelessly; then I fastened the iron shutters and going back to the door quickly I double-locked it with a padlock, putting the key into my pocket.

Suddenly I noticed that He was moving restlessly round me, that in his turn He was frightened and was ordering me to let Him out. I nearly yielded, though I did not quite, but putting my back to the door, I half opened it, just enough to allow me to go out backward, and as I am very tall, my head touched the lintel. I was sure that He had not been able to escape, and I shut Him up quite alone, quite alone. What happiness! I had Him fast. Then I ran downstairs into the drawing-room which was under my bedroom. I took the two lamps and poured all the oil on to the carpet, the furniture, everywhere; then I set fire to it and made my escape, after having carefully double locked the door.

I went and hid myself at the bottom of the garden, in a clump of laurel bushes. How long it was! how long it was! Everything was dark, silent, motionless, not a breath of air and not a star, but heavy banks of clouds which one could not see, but which weighed, oh! so heavily on my soul.

I looked at my house and waited. How long it was! I already began to think that the fire had gone out of its own accord, or that He had extinguished it, when one of the lower windows gave way under the violence of the flames, and a long, soft, caressing sheet of red flame mounted up the white wall, and kissed it as high as the roof. The light fell on to the trees, the branches, and the leaves, and a shiver of fear pervaded them also! The birds awoke; a dog began to howl, and it seemed to me as if the day were breaking!

Almost immediately two other windows flew into fragments, and I saw that the whole of the lower part of my house was nothing but a terrible furnace. But a cry, a horrible, shrill, heart-rending cry, a woman's cry, sounded through the night, and two garret windows were opened! I had forgotten the servants! I saw the terror-struck faces, and the frantic waving of their arms!

Then, overwhelmed with horror, I ran off to the village, shouting: "Help! help! fire! fire!" Meeting some people who were already coming on to the scene, I went back with them to see!

By this time the house was nothing but a horrible and magnificent funeral pile, a monstrous pyre which lit up the whole country, a pyre where men were burning, and where He was burning also, He, He, my prisoner, that new Being, the new Master, the Horla!

Suddenly the whole roof fell in between the walls, and a volcano of flames darted up to the sky. Through all the windows which opened on to that furnace, I saw the flames darting, and I reflected that He was there, in that kiln, dead.

Dead? Perhaps? His body? Was not his body, which was transparent, indestructible by such means as would kill ours?

If He were not dead? Perhaps time alone has power over that Invisible and Redoubtable Being. Why this transparent, unrecognizable body, this body belonging to a spirit, if it also had to fear ills, infirmities, and premature destruction?

Premature destruction? All human terror springs from that! After man the Horla. After him who can die every day, at any hour, at any moment, by any accident, He came, He who was only to die at his own proper hour and minute, because He had touched the limits of his existence!

No—no—there is no doubt about it—He is not dead. Then—then—I suppose I must kill *myself!*

The Parrot

1

Everybody in Fecamp knew Mother Patin's story. She had certainly been unfortunate with her husband, for in his lifetime he used to beat her, just as wheat is threshed in the barn.

He was master of a fishing bark and had married her, formerly, because she was pretty, although poor.

Patin was a good sailor, but brutal. He used to frequent Father Auban's inn, where he would usually drink four or five glasses of brandy, on lucky days eight or ten glasses and even more, according to his mood. The brandy was served to the customers by Father Auban's daughter, a pleasing brunette, who attracted people to the house only by her pretty face, for nothing had ever been gossiped about her.

Patin, when he entered the inn, would be satisfied to look at her and to compliment her politely and respectfully. After he had had his first glass of brandy he would already find her much nicer; at the second he would wink; at the third he would say. "If you were only willing, Mam'zelle Desiree——" without ever finishing his sentence; at the fourth he would try to hold her back by her skirt in order to kiss her; and when he went as high as ten it was Father Auban who brought him the remaining drinks.

The old innkeeper, who knew all the tricks of the trade, made Desiree walk about between the tables in order to increase the consumption of drinks; and Desiree, who was a worthy daughter of Father Auban, flitted around among the benches and joked with them, her lips smiling and her eyes sparkling.

Patin got so well accustomed to Desiree's face that he thought of it even while at sea, when throwing out his nets, in storms or in calms, on moonlit or dark evenings. He thought of her while holding the tiller in the stern of his boat, while his four companions were slumbering with their heads on their arms. He always saw her, smiling, pouring out the yellow brandy with a peculiar shoulder movement and then exclaiming as she turned away: "There, now; are you satisfied?"

He saw her so much in his mind's eye that he was overcome by an irresistible desire to marry her, and, not being able to hold out any longer, he asked for her hand.

He was rich, owned his own vessel, his nets and a little house at the foot of the hill on the Retenue, whereas Father Auban had nothing. The marriage was therefore eagerly agreed upon and the wedding took place as soon as possible, as both parties were desirous for the affair to be concluded as early as convenient.

Three days after the wedding Patin could no longer understand how he had ever imagined Desiree to be different from other women. What a fool he had been to encumber himself with a penniless creature, who had undoubtedly inveigled him with some drug which she had put in his brandy!

He would curse all day long, break his pipe with his teeth and maul his crew. After he had sworn by every known term at everything that came his way he would rid himself of his remaining anger on the fish and lobsters, which he pulled from the nets and threw into the baskets amid oaths and foul language. When he returned home he would find his wife, Father Auban's daughter, within reach of his mouth and hand, and it was not long before he treated her like the lowest creature in the world. As she listened calmly, accustomed to paternal violence, he grew exasperated at her quiet, and one evening he beat her. Then life at his home became unbearable.

For ten years the principal topic of conversation on the Retenue was about the beatings that Patin gave his wife and his manner of cursing at her for the least thing. He could, indeed, curse with a richness of vocabulary in a roundness of tone unequalled by any other man in Fecamp. As soon as his ship was sighted at the entrance of the harbour, returning from the fishing expedition, every one awaited the first volley he would hurl from the bridge as soon as he perceived his wife's white cap.

Standing at the stern he would steer, his eye fixed on the bows and on the sail, and, notwithstanding the difficulty of the narrow passage and the height of the turbulent waves, he would search among the watching women and try to recognize his wife, Father Auban's daughter, the wretch!

Then, as soon as he saw her, notwithstanding the noise of the wind and waves, he would let loose upon her with such power and volubility that everyone would laugh, although they pitied her greatly. When he arrived at the dock he would relieve his mind, while unloading the fish, in such an expressive manner that he attracted around him all the loafers of the neighbourhood. The words left his mouth sometimes like shots from a cannon, short and terrible, sometimes like peals of thunder, which roll and rumble for five minutes, such a hurricane of oaths that he seemed to have in his lungs one of the storms of the Eternal Father.

When he left his ship and found himself face to face with her, surrounded by all the gossips of the neighbourhood, he would bring up a new cargo of insults and bring her back to their dwelling, she in front, he behind, she weeping, he yelling at her.

At last, when alone with her behind closed doors, he would thrash her on the slightest pretext. The least thing was sufficient to make him raise his hand, and when he had once begun he did not stop, but he would throw into her face the true motive for his anger. At each blow he would roar: "There, you beggar! There, you wretch! There, you pauper! What a bright thing I did when I rinsed my mouth with your rascal of a father's apology for brandy."

The poor woman lived in continual fear, in a ceaseless trembling of body and soul, in everlasting expectation of outrageous thrashings.

This lasted ten years. She was so timorous that she would grow pale whenever she spoke to any one, and she thought of nothing but the blows with which she was threatened; and she became thinner, more yellow and drier than a smoked fish.

2

One night, when her husband was at sea, she was suddenly awakened by the wild roaring of the wind!

She sat up in her bed, trembling, but, as she hear nothing more, she lay down again; almost immediately there was a roar in the chimney which shook the entire house; it seemed to cross the heavens like a pack of furious animals snorting and roaring.

Then she arose and rushed to the harbour. Other women were arriving from all sides, carrying lanterns. The men also were gathering, and all were watching the foaming crests of the breaking wave.

The storm lasted fifteen hours. Eleven sailors never returned; Patin was among them.

In the neighbourhood of Dieppe the wreck of his *bark*, the *Jeune-Amelie,* was found. The bodies of his sailors were found near Saint-Valery, but his body was never recovered. As his vessel seemed to have been cut in two, his wife expected and feared his return for a long time, for if there had been a collision he alone might have been picked up and carried afar off.

Little by little she grew accustomed to the thought that she was rid of him, although she would start every time that a neighbour, a beggar or a peddler would enter suddenly.

One afternoon, about four years after the disappearance of her husband, while she was walking along the Rue aux Juifs, she stopped before the house of an old sea captain who had recently died and whose furniture was for sale. Just at that moment a parrot was at auction. He had green feathers and a blue head and was watching everybody with a displeased look. "Three *francs!*" cried the auctioneer. "A bird that can talk like a lawyer, three *francs!*"

A friend of the Patin woman nudged her and said:

"You ought to buy that, you who are rich. It would be good company for you. That bird is worth more than thirty *francs*. Anyhow, you can always sell it for twenty or twenty-five!"

Patin's widow added fifty *centimes*, and the bird was given her in a little cage, which she carried away. She took it home, and, as she was opening the wire door in order to give it something to drink, he bit her finger and drew blood.

"Oh, how naughty he is!" she said.

Nevertheless she gave it some hemp-seed and corn and watched it pruning its feathers as it glanced warily at its new home and its new mistress. On the following morning, just as day was breaking, the Patin woman distinctly heard a loud, deep, roaring voice calling: "Are you going to get up, carrion?"

Her fear was so great that she hid her head under the sheets, for when Patin was with her as soon as he would open his eyes he would shout those well-known words into her ears.

Trembling, rolled into a ball, her back prepared for the thrashing which she already expected, her face buried in the pillows, she murmured: "Good Lord! he is here! Good Lord! he is here! Good Lord! he has come back!"

Minutes passed; no noise disturbed the quiet room. Then, trembling, she stuck her head out of the bed, sure that he was there, watching, ready to beat her. Except for a ray of sun shining through the window, she saw nothing, and she said to herself: "He must be hidden."

She waited a long time and then, gaining courage, she said to herself: "I must have dreamed it, seeing there is nobody here."

A little reassured, she closed. her eyes, when from quite near a furious voice, the thunderous voice of the drowned man, could be heard crying: "Say! when in the name of all that's holy are you going to get up, you b——?"

She jumped out of bed, moved by obedience, by the passive obedience of a woman accustomed to blows and who still re-members and always will remember that voice! She said: "Here I am, Patin; what do you want?"

Put Patin did not answer. Then, at a complete loss, she looked around her, then in the chimney and under the bed and finally sank into a chair, wild with anxiety, convinced that Patin's soul alone was there, near her, and that he had returned in order to torture her.

Suddenly she remembered the loft, in order to reach which one had to take a ladder. Surely he must have hidden there in order to surprise her. He must have been held by savages on some distant shore, unable to escape until now, and he had returned, worse than ever. There was no doubting the quality of that voice. She raised her head and asked: "Are you up there, Patin?"

Patin did not answer. Then, with a terrible fear which made her heart tremble, she climbed the ladder, opened the skylight, looked, saw nothing, entered, looked about and found nothing. Sitting on some straw, she began to cry, but while she was weeping, overcome by a poignant and supernatural terror, she heard Patin talking in the room below.

He seemed less angry and he was saying: "Nasty weather! Fierce wind! Nasty weather! I haven't eaten, damn it!"

She cried through the ceiling: "Here I am, Patin; I am getting your meal ready. Don't get angry."

She ran down again. There was no one in the room. She felt herself growing weak, as if death were touching her, and she tried to run and get help from the neighbours, when a voice near her cried out: "I haven't had my breakfast, by G—!"

And the parrot in his cage watched her with his round, knowing, wicked eye. She, too, looked at him wildly, murmuring: "Ah! so it's you!"

He shook his head and continued: "Just you wait! I'll teach you how to loaf."

What happened within her? She felt, she understood that it was he, the dead man, who had come back, who had disguised himself in the feathers of this bird in order to continue to torment her; that he would curse, as formerly, all day long, and bite her, and swear at her, in order to attract the neighbours and make them laugh. Then she rushed for the cage and seized the bird, which scratched and tore her flesh with its claws and beak.

But she held it with all her strength between her hands. She threw it on the ground and rolled over it with the frenzy of one possessed. She crushed it and finally made of it nothing but a little green, flabby lump which no longer moved or spoke. Then she wrapped it in a cloth, as in a shroud, and she went out in her nightgown, barefoot; she crossed the dock, against which the choppy waves of the sea were beating, and she shook the cloth and let drop this little, dead thing, which looked like so much grass. Then she returned, threw herself on her knees before the empty cage, and, overcome by what she had done, kneeled and prayed for forgiveness, as if she had committed some heinous crime.

The Man With The Dogs

His wife, even when talking to him, always called him Monsieur Bistaud, but in all the country round, within a radius of ten leagues, in France and Belgium, he was known as *Cet homme aux chiens*, (That man with the dogs.) It was not a very valuable reputation, however, and "That man with the dogs," became a sort of pariah.

In Thierache they are not very fond of the custom-house officers, for everybody, high or low, profits by smuggling; thanks to which many articles, and especially coffee, gunpowder, and tobacco, are to be had cheap. It may here be stated that on that wooded, broken country, where the meadows are surrounded by brushwood, and the lanes are dark and narrow, smuggling is carried on chiefly by means of sporting dogs, who are broken in to become smuggling dogs. Scarcely an evening passes without some of them being seen, loaded with contraband, trotting silently along, pushing their nose through a hole in a hedge, with furtive and uneasy looks, and sniffing the air to scent the custom-house officers and their dogs. These dogs also are specially trained, and are very ferocious, and can easily kill their unfortunate congeners, who become the game instead of hunting for it.

Now, nobody was capable of imparting this unnatural education to them so well as the man with the dogs, whose business consisted in breaking in dogs for the custom-house authorities. Everybody looked upon it as a dirty business, a business which could only be performed by a man without any proper feeling.

"He is a men's robber," the women said, "to take honest dogs in to nurse, and to make a lot of traitors out of them."

While the boys shouted insulting verses behind his back, and the men and the women abused him, no one ventured to do it to his face, for he was not very patient, and was always accompanied by one of his huge dogs, and that served to make him respected.

Certainly without that bodyguard, he would have had a bad time of it, especially at the hands of the smugglers, who had a deadly hatred for him. By himself, and in spite of his quarrelsome looks, he did not appear very formidable. He was short and thin, his back was round, his legs were bandy, and his arms were as long and as thin as spiders' legs, and he could easily have been knocked down by a backhanded blow or a kick. But then, he had those confounded dogs, which intimidated even the bravest smugglers. How could they risk even a blow when he had those huge brutes, with their fierce and bloodshot eyes, and their square heads, with jaws like a vise, and enormous white teeth, sharp as daggers, and with huge molars which crunched up beef-bones to a pulp? They were wonderfully broken in, were always by him, obeyed him by signs, and were taught not only to worry the smugglers' dogs, but also to fly at the throats of the smugglers themselves.

The consequence was that both he and his dogs were left alone, and people were satisfied with calling them names and sending them all to Coventry. No peasant ever set foot in his cottage, although Bistaud's wife kept a small shop and was a handsome woman, and the only persons who went there were the custom-house officers. The others took their revenge on them all by saying that the man with the dogs sold his wife to the custom-house officers, like he did his dogs.

"He keeps her for them, as well as his dogs," they said jeeringly. "You can see that he is a born cuckold with his yellow beard and eyebrows, which stick up like a pair of horns."

His hair was certainly red or rather yellow, his thick eyebrows were turned up in two points on his temples, and he used to twirl them mechanically as if they had been a pair of mous-taches. And certainly, with hair like that, and with his long beard and shaggy eyebrows, with his sallow face, blinking eyes, and dull looks, with his dogged mouth, thin lips, and his miserable, deformed body, he was not a pleasing object.

But he assuredly was not a complaisant cuckold, and those who said that of him had never seen him at home. On the con-trary, he was always jealous, and kept as sharp a lookout on his wife as he did on his dogs, and if he had broken her in at all, it was to be as faithful to him as they were.

She was a handsome and, what they call in the country, a fine body of a woman; tall, well-built, with a full bust and broad hips, and she certainly made more than one exciseman squint at her. But it was no use for them to come and sniff round her too closely, or else there would have been blows. At least, that is what the custom-house officers said, when anybody joked with them and said to them: "That does not matter; no doubt, you and she have hunted for your fleas together."

It was no use for them to defend Madame Bistaud's fierce virtue; nobody believed them, and the only answer they got, was: "You are hiding your game, and are ashamed of going to seduce a woman who belongs to such a wretched creature."

And, certainly, nobody would have believed that such a bux-om woman, who must have liked to be well attended to, could be satisfied with such a puny husband, with such an ugly, weak, red-headed fellow, who smelled of his dogs, and of the mustiness of the carrion which he gave to his hounds.

But they did not know that the man with the dogs had some years before given her, once for all, a lesson in fidelity, and that for a mere trifle, a venial sin! He had surprised her for allowing herself to be kissed by some gallant, that was all! He had not taken any notice, but when the man was gone, he brought two of his hounds into the room, and said:

"If you do not want them to tear your inside out as they would a rabbit's, go down on your knees so that I may thrash you!"

She obeyed in terror, and the man with the dogs had beaten her with a whip until his arm dropped with fatigue. And she did not venture to scream, although she was bleeding under the blows of the thong, which tore her dress, and cut into the flesh; all she dared to do was to utter low, hoarse groans; for while beating her, he kept on saying:

"Don't make a noise, by ——; don't make a noise, or I will let the dogs fly at you."

From that time she had been faithful to Bistaud, though she had naturally not told anyone the reason for it, or for her hatred either, not even Bistaud himself, who thought that she was subdued for all time, and always found her very submissive and respectful. But for six years she had nourished her hatred in her heart, feeding it on silent hopes and promises of revenge. And it was that flame of hope and that longing for revenge, which made her so *coquettish* with the custom-house officers, for she hoped to add a possible avenger among her inflammable admirers.

At last she came across the right man. He was a splendid sub-officer of the customs, built like a Hercules, with fists like a butcher's, and had long leased four of his ferocious dogs from her husband.

As soon as they had grown accustomed to their new master, and especially after they had tasted the flesh of the smugglers' dogs, they had, by degrees become detached from their former master, who had reared them. No doubt they still recognized him a little, and would not have sprung at his throat, as if he were a perfect stranger, but still, they did not hesitate between his voice and that of their new master, and they obeyed the latter only.

Although the woman had often noticed this, she had not hitherto been able to make much use of the circumstance. A custom-house officer, as a rule, only keeps one dog, and Bistaud always had half-a-dozen, at least, in training, without reckoning a personal guard which he kept for himself, which was the fiercest of all. Consequently, any duel between some lover assisted by only one dog, and the dog-breaker defended by his pack, was impossible.

But on that occasion, the chances were more equal, just then he had only five dogs in the kennel, and two of them were quite young, though certainly old *Bourreau* (executioner, hangman), counted for several. After all they could risk a battle against him and the other three, with the two couples of the custom-house officer, and they must profit by the occasion.

So one fine evening, as the brigadier of the custom-house officers was alone in the shop with Bistaud's wife and was squeezing her waist, she said to him abruptly:

"Do you really want to have something to do with me, *Môssieu* (vulgar for *Monsieu),* Fernand?"

He kissed her on the lips as he replied: "Do I really want to? I would give my stripes for it; so you see."

"Very well!" she replied, "do as I tell you, and upon my word, as an honest woman, I will be your commodity to do what you like with."

And laying a stress on that word *commodity*, which in that part of the country means strumpet, she whispered hotly into his ear:

"A commodity who knows her business, I can tell you, for my beast of a husband has trained me up in such a way that I am now absolutely disgusted with him."

Fernand, who was much excited, promised her everything that she wished, and feverishly, malignantly she told him how shamefully her husband had treated her a short time before, how her fair skin had been cut, and of her hatred and thirst for revenge. The brigadier acquiesced, and that same evening came to the cottage accompanied by his four hounds, with their spiked collars on.

"What are you going to do with them?" the man with the dogs asked.

"I have come to see whether you did not rob me, when you leased them to me," the brigadier replied.

"What do you mean by "robbed you?'"

351

"Well, robbed! I have been told that they could not tackle a dog like your Bourreau, and that many smugglers have dogs who are as good as he is."

"Impossible."

"Well, in case any of them should have one, I should like to see how the dogs that you sold me could tackle them."

The woman laughed an evil laugh, and her husband grew suspicious, when he saw that the brigadier replied to it by a wink. But his suspicions came too late. The breaker had no time to go to the kennel to let out his pack, for Bourreau had been seized by the custom-house officer's four dogs. At the same time, the woman locked the door; already her husband was lying motionless on the floor, while Bourreau could not go to his assistance, as he had enough to do to defend himself against the furious attack of the other dogs, who were almost tearing him to pieces, in spite of his strength and courage. Five minutes later two of the attacking hounds were totally disabled, with their bowels protruding, but Bourreau himself was dying, with his throat gaping.

Then the woman and the custom-house officer kissed each other before the breaker, whom they bound firmly. The two dogs of the custom-house officer that were still on their legs were panting for breath, and the other three were wallowing in their blood. And now the amorous couple were carrying on all sorts of capers, still further excited by the rage of the dog-breaker, who was forced to look at them, and who shouted in his despair:

"You wretches! you shall pay for this!" And the woman's only reply was, to say: "Cuckold! cuckold! cuckold!"

When she was tired of larking, her hatred was not yet satisfied, and she said to the brigadier:

"Fernand, go to the kennels and shoot the five other brutes, otherwise he will make them kill me tomorrow. Off you go, old fellow!"

The brigadier obeyed, and immediately five shots were heard in the darkness; it did not take long, but that short time had been enough for the man with the dogs to show what he could do. While he was tied, the two dogs of the custom-house officer had gradually recognized him, and came and fondled him, and as soon as he was alone with his wife, as she was insulting him, he said in his usual voice of command to the dogs:

"At her, Flanbard! at her, Garou!" The two dogs sprang at the wretched woman, and one seized her by the throat, while the other caught her by the side.

When the brigadier came back, she was dying on the ground in a pool of blood, and the man with the dogs said with a laugh:

"There you see, that is the way I break in my dogs!"

The custom-house officer rushed out in horror, followed by his hounds, who licked his hands as they ran, and made them quite red.

The next morning the man with the dogs was found still bound, but chuckling, in his hovel that was turned into a slaughter-house.

They were both arrested and tried; the man with the dogs was acquitted, and the brigadier sentenced to a term of imprisonment. The matter gave much food for talk in the district, and is indeed still talked about, for the man with the dogs returned there, and is more celebrated than ever under his nickname. But his celebrity is not of a bad kind, for he is now just as much respected and liked as he was despised and hated formerly. He is still, as a matter of fact, the man with the dogs, as he is rightly called, for he has not his equal as a dog-breaker, for leagues round. But now he no longer breaks in mastiffs, as he has given up teaching honest dogs to "act the part of Judas," as he says, for those dirty custom-house officers. He only devotes himself to dogs to be used for smuggling, and he is worth listening to, when he says:

"You may depend upon it, that I know how to punish such commodities as she, when they have sinned! I was glad to see my dogs tearing that strumpet's skin and her lying mouth."

Ghosts

Just at the time when the Concordat was in its most flourishing condition, a young man belonging to a wealthy and highly respectable middle-class family went to the office of the head of the police at P——, and begged for his help and advice, which was immediately promised him.

"My father threatens to disinherit me," the young man began, "although I have never offended against the laws of the State, of morality, or against his paternal authority, merely because I do not share his blind reverence for the Catholic Church and her clergy.

"On that account he looks upon me, not merely as Latitudinarian but as a perfect Atheist, and a faithful old manservant of ours, who is much attached to me, and who accidentally saw my father's will, told me in confidence that he had left all his property to the Jesuits. I think this is highly suspicious, and I fear that the priests have been maligning me to my father. Until less than a year ago, we used to live very quietly and happily together, but ever since he has had so much to do with the clergy, our domestic peace and happiness are at an end."

"What you have told me," replied the official, "is as likely as it is regrettable, but I fail to see how I can interfere in the matter. Your father is in full possession of all his mental faculties, and can dispose of all his property exactly as he pleases. I think that your protest is premature; you must wait until his will can legally take effect, and then you can invoke the aid of justice. I am sorry to say that just now I can do nothing for you."

"I think you will be able to," the young man replied; "for I believe that a very clever piece of deceit is being carried on."

"How? Please explain yourself more clearly."

"When I remonstrated with him, yesterday evening, he referred to my dead mother, and at last assured me, in a voice of the deepest conviction, that she had frequently appeared to him, had threatened him with all the torments of the damned, if he did not disinherit his son, who had fallen away from God, and leave all his property to the Church. Now I do not believe in ghosts."

"Neither do I," the police director replied, "but I cannot well do anything on such grounds, having nothing but superstitions to go upon. You know how the Church rules all our affairs since the Concordat with Rome, and if I investigate this matter and obtain no results, I am risking my post. It would be very different if you could adduce any proofs for your suspicions. I do not deny that I should like to see the clerical party, which will, I fear, be the ruin of Austria, receive a staggering blow; try, therefore, to get to the bottom of this business, and then we will talk it over again."

About a month passed, without the young Latitudinarian being heard of. Suddenly, he came one evening, in a great state of excitement, and told the Inspector that he was in a position to expose the priestly deceit which he had mentioned, if the authorities would assist him. The police director asked for further information.

"I have obtained a number of important clues," said the young man. "In the first place, my father confessed to me that my mother did not appear to him in our house, but in the churchyard where she is buried. My mother was consumptive for many years, and a few weeks before her death she went to the village of S——, where she died and was buried. In addition to this, I found out from our footman that my father has already left the house twice, late at night, in company of X——, the Jesuit priest, and that on both occasions he did not return till morning.

"Each time he was remarkably uneasy and low-spirited after his return, and had three masses said for my dead mother. He also told me just now that he has to leave home this evening on business, but, immediately after he told me that, our footman saw the Jesuit go out of the house. We may, therefore, assume that he intends this evening to consult the spirit of my dead mother again, and this would be an excellent opportunity to solve the matter, if you do not object to opposing the most powerful force in the Empire for the sake of such an insignificant individual as myself."

"Every citizen has an equal right to the protection of the State," the police director replied; "and I think that I have shown often enough that I am not wanting in courage to perform my duty, no matter how serious the consequences may be. But only very young men act without any prospects of success, because they are carried away by their feelings. When you came to me the first time, I was obliged to refuse your request for assistance, but today your request is just and reasonable. It is now eight o'clock; I shall expect you in two hours' time, here in my office. At present, all you have to do is to hold your tongue; everything else is my affair."

As soon as it was dark, four men got into a closed carriage in the yard of the police-office, and were driven in the direction of the village of S——. Their carriage, however, did not enter the village, but stopped at the edge of a small wood in the immediate neighbourhood. Here all four alighted: the police director, accompanied by the young Latitudinarian, a police sergeant, and an ordinary policeman, the latter however, dressed in plain clothes.

"The first thing for us to do is to examine the locality carefully," said the police director. "It is eleven o'clock and the exorcisers of ghosts will not arrive before midnight, so we have time to look round us, and to lay our plans."

The four men went to the churchyard, which lay at the end of the village, near the little wood. Everything was as still as death, and not a soul was to be seen. The sexton was evidently sitting in the public house, for they found the door of his cottage locked, as well as the door of the little chapel that stood in the middle of the churchyard.

"Where is your mother's grave?" the police director asked. As there were only a few stars visible, it was not easy to find it, but at last they managed it, and the police director surveyed the neighbourhood of it.

"The position is not a very favourable one for us," he said at last; "there is nothing here, not even a shrub, behind which we could hide."

But just then, the policeman reported that he had tried to get into the sexton's hut through the door or a window, and that at last he had succeeded in doing so by breaking open a square in a window which had been mended with paper, that he had opened it and obtained possession of the key, which he brought to the police director.

The plans were very quickly settled. The police director had the chapel opened and went in with the young Latitudinarian; then he told the police sergeant to lock the door behind him and to put the key back where he had found it, and to shut the window of the sexton's cottage carefully. Lastly, he made arrangements as to what they were to do, in case anything unforeseen should occur, whereupon the sergeant and the constable left the churchyard, and lay down in a ditch at some distance from the gate, but opposite to it.

Almost as soon as the clock struck half past eleven, they heard steps near the chapel, whereupon the police director and the young Latitudinarian went to the window in order to watch the beginning of the exorcism, and as the chapel was in total darkness, they thought that they should be able to see without being seen; but matters turned out differently from what they expected.

Suddenly, the key turned in the lock. They barely had time to conceal themselves behind the altar, before two men came in, one of whom was carrying a dark lantern. One was the young man's father, an elderly man of the middle class, who seemed very unhappy and depressed, the other the Jesuit father X——, a tall, lean, big-boned man, with a thin, bilious face, in which two large gray eyes shone restlessly under bushy, black eyebrows. He lit the tapers, which were standing on the altar, and began to say a "*Requiem Mass*"; while the old man knelt on the altar steps and served him.

When it was over, the Jesuit took the book of the Gospels and the holy-water sprinkler, and went slowly out of the chapel, the old man following him with the holy-water basin in one hand, and a taper in the other. Then the police director left his hiding place, and stooping down, so as not to be seen, crept to the chapel window, where he cowered down carefully; the young man followed his example. They were now looking straight at his mother's grave.

The Jesuit, followed by the superstitious old man, walked three times round the grave; then he remained standing before it, and by the light of the taper read a few passages from the Gospel. Then he dipped the holy-water sprinkler three times into the holy-water basin, and sprinkled the grave three times. Then both returned to the chapel, kneeled down outside it with their faces toward the grave, and began to pray aloud, until at last the Jesuit sprang up, in a species of wild ecstasy, and cried out three times in a shrill voice:

"*Exsurge! Exsurge! Exsurge!*" ("Arise!")

Scarcely had the last words of the exorcism died away, when thick, blue smoke rose out of the grave, rapidly grew into a cloud, and began to assume the outlines of a human body, until at last a tall, white figure stood behind the grave, and beckoned with its hand.

"Who art thou?" the Jesuit asked solemnly, while the old man began to cry.

"When I was alive, I was called Anna Maria B——," replied the ghost in a hollow voice.

"Will you answer all my questions?" the priest continued.

"As far as I can."

"Have you not yet been delivered from purgatory by our

prayers, and by all the Masses for your soul, which we have said for you?"

"Not yet, but soon, soon I shall be."

"When?"

"As soon as that blasphemer, my son, has been punished."

"Has that not already happened? Has not your husband disinherited his lost son, and in his place made the Church his heir?"

"That is not enough."

"What must he do besides?"

"He must deposit his will with the Judicial Authorities, as his last will and testament, and drive the reprobate out of his house."

"Consider well what you are saying; must this really be?"

"It must, or otherwise I shall have to languish in purgatory much longer," the sepulchral voice replied with a deep sigh; but the next moment the ghost yelled out in terror: "Oh! Good Lord!" and began to run away as fast as it could. A shrill whistle was heard, and then another, and the police director laid his hand on the shoulder of the exorciser with the remark:

"You are in custody."

Meanwhile, the police sergeant and the policeman, who had come into the churchyard, had caught the ghost, and dragged it forward. It was the sexton, who had put on a flowing, white dress, and wore a wax mask, which bore a striking resemblance to his mother, so the son declared.

When the case was heard, it was proved that the mask had been very skilfully made from a portrait of the deceased woman. The government gave orders that the matter should be investigated as secretly as possible, and left the punishment of Father X——to the spiritual authorities, which was a matter of necessity, at a time when priests were outside of the jurisdiction of the civil authorities. It is needless to say that Father X——was very comfortable during his imprisonment in a monastery, in a part of the country which abounded with game and trout.

The only valuable result of the amusing ghost story was that it brought about a reconciliation between father and son; the former, as a matter of fact, felt such deep respect for priests and their ghosts in consequence of the apparition, that a short time after his wife had left purgatory for the last time in order to talk with him, he turned Protestant.

The Spasm

A.k.a. From the Tomb

The hotel-guests slowly entered the dining-room, and sat down in their places. The waiters began to attend on them in a leisurely fashion so as to enable those who were late to arrive, and to avoid bringing back the dishes. The old bathers, the habitats, those whose season was advancing, gazed with interest toward the door, whenever it opened, with a desire to see new faces appearing. This is the principal distraction of health-resorts. People look forward to the dinner hour in order to inspect each day's new arrivals, to find out who they are, what they do, and what they think. A vague longing springs up in the mind, a longing for agreeable meetings, for pleasant acquaintances, perhaps for love-adventures. In this life of elbowings, strangers, as well as those with whom we have come into daily contact, assume an extreme importance. Curiosity is aroused, sympathy is ready to exhibit itself, and sociability is the order of the day.

We cherish antipathies for a week and friendships for a month; we see other people with different eyes, when we view them through the medium of the acquaintanceship that is brought about at health-resorts. We discover in men suddenly, after an hour's chat in the evening after dinner, or under the trees in the park where the generous spring bubbles up, a high intelligence and astonishing merits, and, a month afterward, we have completely forgotten these new friends, so fascinating when we first met them.

There also are formed lasting and serious ties more quickly than anywhere else. People see each other every day; they become acquainted very quickly; and with the affection thus originated is mingled something of the sweetness and self-abandonment of long-standing intimacies. We cherish in after years the dear and tender memories of those first hours of friendship, the memory of those first conversations through which we have been able to unveil a soul, of those first glances which interrogate and respond to the questions and secret thoughts which the mouth has not as yet uttered, the memory of that first cordial confidence, the memory of that delightful sensation of opening our hearts to those who are willing to open theirs to us.

And the melancholy of health-resorts, the monotony of days that are alike, help from hour to hour in this rapid development of affection.

★★★★★★★

Well, this evening, as on every other evening, we awaited the appearance of strange faces.

Only two appeared, but they were very remarkable looking! a man and a woman—father and daughter.

They immediately produced the same effect on my mind as some of Edgar Poe's characters; and yet there was about them a charm, the charm associated with misfortune. I looked upon them as the victims of fatality. The man was very tall and thin, rather stooping, with hair perfectly white, too white for his comparatively youthful physiognomy; and there was in his bearing and in his person that austerity peculiar to Protestants. The daughter, who was probably twenty-four or twenty-five, was small in stature, and was also very thin, very pale, and had the air of one worn out with utter lassitude.

We meet people like this from time to time, people who seem too weak for the tasks and the needs of daily life, too weak to move about, to walk, to do all that we do every day. This young girl was very pretty, with the diaphanous beauty of a phantom; and she ate with extreme slowness, as if she were almost incapable of moving her arms. It must have been she assuredly who had come to take the waters.

They found themselves facing me at the opposite side of the table; and I at once noticed that the father had a very singular nervous spasm. Every time he wanted to reach an object, his hand made a hook-like movement, a sort of irregular zigzag, before it succeeded in touching what it was in search of ; and, after a little while, this action was so wearisome to me that I turned aside my head in order not to see it. I noticed, too, that the young girl, during meals, wore a glove on her left hand.

After dinner, I went for a stroll in the park of the thermal establishment. This led toward the little Auvergnese station of Chatel Guyon, hidden in a gorge at the foot of the high mountain, of that mountain from which flow so many boiling springs, rising from the deep bed of extinct volcanoes. Over there, above us, the domes, which had once been craters, raised their mutilated heads on the summit of the long chain. For Chatel Guyon is situated at the spot where the region of domes begins. Beyond it stretches out the region of peaks, and, further on again, the region of precipices.

The Puy de Dome is the highest of the domes, the Peak of Sancy is the loftiest of the peaks, and Cantal is the most precipitous of these mountain heights.

This evening, it was very warm. I walked up and down a shady path, on the side of the mountain overlooking the park, listening to the opening strains of the Casino band. I saw the father and the daughter advancing slowly in my direction. I saluted them, as we are accustomed to salute our hotel-companions at health-resorts; and the man, coming to a sudden halt, said to me:

"Could you not, *Monsieur,* point out to us a short walk, nice and easy, if that is possible, and excuse my intrusion on you?"

I offered to show them the way toward the valley through which the little river flowed, a deep valley forming a gorge between two tall, craggy, wooded slopes. They gladly accepted my offer, and we talked naturally about the virtues of the waters.

"Oh!" he said, "my daughter has a strange malady, the seat of which is unknown. She suffers from incomprehensible nervous disorders. At one time, the doctors think she has an attack of heart disease, at another time, they imagine it is some affection of the liver, and at another time they declare it to be a disease of the spine. Today, her condition is attributed to the stomach, which is the great caldron and regulator of the body, the Protean source of diseases with a thousand forms and a thousand susceptibilities to attack. This is why we have come here. For my part, I am rather inclined to think it is the nerves. In any case it is very sad."

Immediately the remembrance of the violent spasmodic movement of his hand came back to my mind, and I asked him:

"But is this not the result of heredity? Are not your own nerves somewhat affected?"

He replied calmly:

"Mine? Oh! no—my nerves have always been very steady."

Then suddenly, after a pause, he went on:

"Ah! You were alluding to the spasm in my hand every time I want to reach for anything? This arises from a terrible experience which I had. Just imagine! this daughter of mine was actually buried alive!"

I could only give utterance to the word "Ah!" so great were my astonishment and emotion.

★★★★★★★

He continued:

"Here is the story. It is simple. Juliette had been subject for some time to serious attacks of the heart. We believed that she had disease of that organ and we were prepared for the worst.

"One day, she was carried into the house cold, lifeless, dead. She had fallen down unconscious in the garden. The doctor certified that life was extinct. I watched by her side for a day and two nights. I laid her with my own hands in the coffin, which I accompanied to the cemetery where she was deposited in the family vault. It is situated in the very heart of Lorraine.

"I wished to have her interred with her jewels, bracelets, necklaces, rings, all presents which she had got from me, and with her first ball-dress on.

"You may easily imagine the state of mind in which I was when I returned home. She was the only companion I had, for my wife has been dead for many years. I found my way to my own apartment in a half-distracted condition, utterly exhausted, and I sank into my easy-chair, without the capacity to think or the strength to move. I was nothing better now than a suffering, vibrating machine, a human being who had, as it were, been flayed alive; my soul was like a living wound.

"My old valet, Prosper, who had assisted me in placing Juliette in her coffin, and preparing her for her last sleep, entered the room noiselessly, and asked:

"'Does *Monsieur* want anything?'

"I merely shook my head, by way of answering 'No.'

"He urged: '*Monsieur* is wrong. He will bring some illness on himself. Would *Monsieur* like me to put him to bed?'

"I answered: 'No! let me alone!' And he left the room.

"I know not how many hours slipped away. Oh! what a night, what a night! It was cold. My fire had died out in the huge grate; and the wind, the winter wind, an icy wind, a hurricane accompanied by frost and snow, kept blowing against the window with a sinister and regular noise.

"How many hours slipped away? There I was without sleeping, powerless, crushed, my eyes wide open, my legs stretched out, my body limp, inanimate, and my mind torpid with despair. Suddenly, the great bell of the entrance gate, the bell of the vestibule, rang out.

"I got such a shock that my chair cracked under me. The solemn ponderous sound vibrated through the empty *chateau* as if through a vault. I turned round to see what the hour was by my clock. It was just two in the morning. Who could be coming at such an hour?

"And abruptly the bell again rang twice. The servants, without doubt, were afraid to get up, I took a wax-candle and descended the stairs. I was on the point of asking: 'Who is there?'

"Then, I felt ashamed of my weakness, and I slowly opened the huge door. My heart was throbbing wildly; I was frightened;

I hurriedly drew back the door, and in the darkness, I distinguished a white figure standing erect, something that resembled an apparition.

"I recoiled, petrified with horror, faltering:

"'Who—who—who are you?'

"A voice replied:

"'It is I, father.'

"It was my daughter. I really thought I must be mad, and I retreated backward before this advancing spectre. I kept moving away, making a sign with my hand, as if to drive the phantom away, that gesture which you have noticed, — that gesture of which since then I have never got rid.

"The apparition spoke again:

"'Do not be afraid, papa; I was not dead. Somebody tried to steal my rings, and cut one of my fingers, the blood began to flow, and this reanimated me.'

"And, in fact, I could see that her hand was covered with blood.

"I fell on my knees, choking with sobs and with a rattling in my throat.

"Then, when I had somewhat collected my thoughts, though I was still so much dismayed that I scarcely realized the gruesome good-fortune that had fallen to my lot, I made her go up to my room, and sit down in my easy-chair; then I rang excitedly for Prosper to get him to light up the fire again and to get her some wine and summon the rest of the servants to her assistance.

"The man entered, stared at my daughter, opened his mouth with a gasp of alarm and stupefaction, and then fell back, insensible.

"It was he who had opened the vault, and who had mutilated and then abandoned my daughter, for he could not efface the traces of the theft. He had not even taken the trouble to put back the coffin into its place, feeling sure, besides, that he would not be suspected by me, as I completely trusted him.

"You see, *Monsieur*, that we are very unhappy people."

★★★★★★★

He stopped.

The night had fallen, casting its shadows over the desolate, mournful vale, and a sort of mysterious fear possessed me at finding myself by the side of those strange beings, of this young girl who had come back from the tomb and this father with his uncanny spasm.

I found it impossible to make any comment on this dreadful story. I only murmured: "What a horrible thing!" Then, after a minute's silence, I added: "Suppose we go back, I think it is getting cold." And we made our way back to the hotel.

The Penguins' Rock

This is the season for penguins.

From April to the end of May, before the Parisian visitors arrive, one sees, all at once, on the little beach at Etretat several old gentlemen, booted and belted in shooting costume. They spend four or five days at the Hotel Hauville, disappear, and return again three weeks later. Then, after a fresh sojourn, they go away altogether.

One sees them again the following spring.

These are the last penguin hunters, what remain of the old set. There were about twenty enthusiasts thirty or forty years ago; now there are only a few of the enthusiastic sportsmen.

The penguin is a very rare bird of passage, with peculiar habits. It lives the greater part of the year in the latitude of Newfoundland and the islands of St. Pierre and Miquelon. But in the breeding season a flight of emigrants crosses the ocean and comes every year to the same spot to lay their eggs, to the Penguins' Rock near Etretat. They are found nowhere else, only there. They have always come there, have always been chased away, but return again, and will always return. As soon as the young birds are grown they all fly away, and disappear for a year.

Why do they not go elsewhere? Why not choose some other spot on the long white, unending cliff that extends from the Pas-de-Calais to Havre? What force, what invincible instinct, what custom of centuries impels these birds to come back to this place? What first migration, what tempest, possibly, once cast their ancestors on this rock? And why do the children, the grandchildren, all the descendants of the first parents always return here?

There are not many of them, a hundred at most, as if one single family, maintaining the tradition, made this annual pilgrimage.

And each spring, as soon as the little wandering tribe has taken up its abode on the rock, the same sportsmen also reappear in the village. One knew them formerly when they were young; now they are old, but constant to the regular appointment which they have kept for thirty or forty years. They would not miss it for anything in the world.

It was an April evening in one of the later years. Three of the old sportsmen had arrived; one was missing—M. d'Arnelles.

He had written to no one, given no account of himself. But he was not dead, like so many of the rest; they would have heard of it. At length, tired of waiting for him, the other three sat down to table. Dinner was almost over when a carriage drove into the yard of the hotel, and the late corner presently entered the dining room.

He sat down, in a good humour, rubbing his hands, and ate with zest. When one of his comrades remarked with surprise at his being in a frock-coat, he replied quietly:

"Yes, I had no time to change my clothes."

They retired on leaving the table, for they had to set out before daybreak in order to take the birds unawares.

There is nothing so pretty as this sport, this early morning expedition.

At three o'clock in the morning the sailors awoke the sportsmen by throwing sand against the windows. They were ready in a few minutes and went down to the beach. Although it was still dark, the stars had paled a little. The sea ground the shingle on the beach. There was such a fresh breeze that it made one shiver slightly in spite of one's heavy clothing.

Presently two boats were pushed down the beach, by the sailors, with a sound as of tearing cloth, and were floated on the nearest waves. The brown sail was hoisted, swelled a little, fluttered, hesitated and swelling out again as round as a paunch, carried the boats towards the large arched entrance that could be faintly distinguished in the darkness.

The sky became clearer, the shadows seemed to melt away. The coast still seemed veiled, the great white coast, perpendicular as a wall.

They passed through the Manne-Porte, an enormous arch beneath which a ship could sail; they doubled the promontory of La Courtine, passed the little valley of Antifer and the cape of the same name; and suddenly caught sight of a beach on which some hundreds of seagulls were perched.

That was the Penguins' Rock. It was just a little protuberance of the cliff, and on the narrow ledges of rock the birds' heads might be seen watching the boats.

They remained there, motionless, not venturing to fly off as yet. Some of them perched on the edges, seated upright, looked almost like bottles, for their little legs are so short that when they walk they glide along as if they were on rollers. When they start to fly they cannot make a spring and let themselves fall like stones almost down to the very men who are watching them.

They know their limitation and the danger to which it subjects them, and cannot make up their minds to fly away.

But the boatmen begin to shout, beating the sides of the boat with the wooden boat pins, and the birds, in affright, fly one by one into space until they reach the level of the waves. Then, moving their wings rapidly, they scud, scud along until they reach the open sea; if a shower of lead does not knock them into the water.

For an hour the firing is kept up, obliging them to give up, one after another. Sometimes the mother birds will not leave their nests, and are riddled with shot, causing drops of blood to spurt out on the white cliff, and the animal dies without having deserted her eggs.

The first day M. d'Arnelles fired at the birds with his habitual zeal; but when the party returned toward ten o'clock, beneath a brilliant sun, which cast great triangles of light on the white cliffs along the coast he appeared a little worried, and absent-minded, contrary to his accustomed manner.

As soon as they got on shore a kind of servant dressed in black came up to him and said something in a low tone. He seemed to reflect, hesitate, and then replied:

"No, tomorrow."

The following day they set out again. This time M, d'Arnelles frequently missed his aim, although the birds were close by. His friends teased him, asked him if he were in love, if some secret sorrow was troubling his mind and heart. At length he confessed.

"Yes, indeed, I have to leave soon, and that annoys me."

"What, you must leave? And why?"

"Oh, I have some business that calls me back. I cannot stay any longer."

They then talked of other matters.

As soon as breakfast was over the valet in black appeared. M. d'Arnelles ordered his carriage, arid the man was leaving the room when the three sportsmen interfered, insisting, begging, and praying their friend to stay. One of them at last said:

"Come now, this cannot be a matter of such importance, for you have already waited two days."

M. d'Arnelles, altogether perplexed, began to think, evidently baffled, divided between pleasure and duty, unhappy and disturbed.

After reflecting for some time he stammered:

"The fact is—the fact is—I am not alone here. I have my son-in-law."

There were exclamations and shouts of "Your son-in-law! Where is he?"

He suddenly appeared confused and his face grew red.

"What! do you not know? Why—why—he is in the coach house. He is dead."

They were all silent in amazement.

M. d'Arnelles continued, more and more disturbed:

"I had the misfortune to lose him; and as I was taking the body to my house, in Briseville, I came round this way so as not to miss our appointment. But you can see that I cannot wait any longer."

Then one of the sportsmen, bolder than the rest said:

"Well, but—since he is dead—it seems to me that he can wait a day longer."

The others chimed in:

"That cannot be denied."

M. d'Arnelles appeared to be relieved of a great weight, but a little uneasy, nevertheless, he asked:

"But, frankly—do you think—"

The three others, as one man, replied:

"*Parbleu!* my dear boy, two days more or less can make no difference in his present condition."

And, perfectly calmly, the father-in-law turned to the under-taker's assistant, and said:

"Well, then, my friend, it will be the day after tomorrow."

The White Lady

Fortuna, the goddess of chance and good luck, has always been Cupid's best ally and Arnold T., who was a lieutenant in a hussar regiment, was evidently a special favourite of both those roguish deities.

This good-looking, well-bred young officer had been an enthusiastic admirer of the two Countesses W., mother and daughter, during a tolerably long leave of absence, which he spent with his relations in Vienna. He had admired them in the *Prater*, and worshiped them at the opera, but he had never had an opportunity of making their acquaintance, and when he was back at his dull quarters in Galicia, he liked to think about those two aristocratic beauties. Last summer his regiment was transferred to Bohemia, to a wildly romantic district, that had been made illustrious by a talented writer. It abounds in magnificent woods, lofty mountain-forests and castles, and which is a favourite summer resort of the neighbouring aristocracy.

Who can describe his joyful surprise, when he and his men were quartered in an old, weather-beaten castle in the middle of a wood, and he learnt from the house-steward who received him that the owner of the castle was the husband, and, consequently, also the father of his Viennese ideals. An hour after he had taken possession of his old-fashioned, but beautifully furnished, room in a side-wing of the castle, he put on his full-dress uniform, and throwing his *dolman* over his shoulders, he went to pay his respects to the Count and the ladies.

He was received with the greatest cordiality. The Count was

delighted to have a companion when he went out shooting, and the ladies were no less pleased at having someone to accompany them on their walks in the forests, or on their rides, so that he felt only half on the earth, and half in the seventh heaven of Mohammedan bliss. Before supper he had time to inspect the house more closely, and even to take a sketch of the large, gloomy building from a favourable point.

The ancient seat of the Counts of W. was really very gloomy; in fact it gave one a sinister, uncomfortable feeling. The walls, which were crumbling away here and there, were covered with dark ivy; the round towers harboured jackdaws, owls, and hawks; the Æolian harp, which complained and sighed and wept in the wind; the stones in the castle yard were overgrown with grass; the cloisters re-echoed to every footstep; great ancestral portraits which hung on the walls, coated as it were with dark, mysterious veils by the centuries which had passed over them. All this recalled to him the legends and fairy tales of his youth, and he involuntarily thought of the *Sleeping Beauty in the Wood*, and of *Blue Beard*, of the cruel mistress of the Kynast (see note), and that aristocratic tigress of the Carpathians, who obtained the unfading charms of eternal youth by bathing in human blood.

(*Note*: Kynast, a castle, now a well-preserved ruin, in the Giant Mountains in N. Germany. The legend is that its mistress, Kunigerude, vowed to marry nobody except the knight who should ride round the parapet of the castle, and many perished in the attempt. At last one of them succeeded in performing the feat, but he merely sternly rebuked her, and took his leave. He was accompanied by his wife, disguised as his page, according to some versions of the legend.)

He came in to supper where he found himself for the first time in the company of all the members of the family, just in the frame of mind that was suitable for ghost stories, and was not a little surprised when his host told him, half smiling and half seriously, that the "White Lady" was disturbing the castle again, and that she had latterly been seen very often.

"Yes, indeed," Countess Ida exclaimed; "You must take care,

Baron, for she haunts the very wing where your room is."

The hussar was just in the frame of mind to take the matter seriously, but, on the other hand, when he saw the dark, ardent eyes of the Countess, and then the merry blue eyes of her daughter fixed on him, any real fear of ghosts was quite out of the question with him. For Baron T. feared nothing in this world, but he possessed a very lively imagination, which could conjure up threatening forms from another world so plainly that sometimes he felt very uncomfortable at his own fancies. But on the present occasion that malicious apparition had no power over him; the ladies took care of that, for both of them were beautiful and amiable.

The Countess was a mature Venus of thirty-six, of middle height, with bright eyes, thick dark hair, beautiful white teeth, and with the voluptuous figure of a true Viennese, while her daughter Ida, who was seventeen, had light hair and the pert little nose of the china figures of shepherdesses in the dress of the period of Louis XIV., and was short, slim, and full of French grace. Besides them and the Count, a son of twelve and his tutor were present at supper. It struck the hussar as strange that the tutor, who was a strongly-built young man, with a winning face and those refined manners which the greatest plebeian quickly acquires when brought into close and constant contact with the aristocracy, was treated with great consideration by all the family except the Countess, who treated him very haughtily. She assumed a particularly imperious manner towards her son's tutor, and she either found fault with, or made fun of, everything that he did, while he put up with it all with smiling humility.

Before supper was over their conversation again turned on to the ghost, and Baron T. asked whether they did not possess a picture of the White Lady.

"Of course we have one," they all replied at once; whereupon Baron T. begged to be allowed to see it.

"I will show it you tomorrow," the Count said.

"No, Papa, now, immediately," the younger lady said mockingly; "just before the ghostly hour, such a thing creates a much greater impression."

All who were present, not excepting the boy and his tutor, took a candle. Then they walked, as if in a torchlight procession, to the wing of the house where the hussar's room was. There was a life-size picture of the White Lady hanging in a Gothic passage near his room, among other ancestral portraits, and it by no means made a terrible impression on anyone who looked at it, but rather the contrary. The ghost, dressed in stiff, gold brocade and purple velvet, and with a hawk on her wrist, looked like one of those seductive Amazons of the fifteenth century, who exercised the art of laying men and game at their feet with equal skill.

"Don't you think that the White Lady is very like mamma?" Countess Ida said, interrupting the Baron's silent contemplation of the picture.

"There is no doubt of it," the hussar replied, while the Countess smiled and the tutor turned red. They were still standing before the picture, when a strong gust of wind suddenly extinguished all the lights, and they all uttered a simultaneous cry.

The White Lady, the little Count whispered, but she did not come, and as it was luckily a moonlight night, they soon recovered from their momentary shock. The family retired to their apartments, while the hussar and the tutor went to their own rooms, which were situated in the wing of the castle which was haunted by the White Lady; the officer's being scarcely thirty yards from the portrait, while the tutor's were rather further down the corridor.

The hussar went to bed, and was soon fast asleep, and though he had rather uneasy dreams nothing further happened. But while they were at breakfast the next morning, the Count's body-servant told them, with every appearance of real terror, that as he was crossing the courtyard at midnight, he had suddenly heard a noise like bats in the open cloisters, and when he looked he distinctly saw the White Lady gliding slowly through them; but they merely laughed at the poltroon, and though our hussar laughed also, he fully made up his mind, without saying a word about it, to keep a lookout for the ghost that night.

Again they had supper alone, without any company, had some music and pleasant talk and separated at half-past eleven. The hussar, however, only went to his room for form's sake; he loaded his pistols, and when all was quiet in the castle, he crept down into the courtyard and took up his position behind a pillar which was quite hidden in the shade, while the moon, which was nearly at the full, flooded the cloisters with its clear, pale light.

There were no lights to be seen in the castle except from two windows, which were those of the Countess's apartments, and soon they were also extinguished. The clock struck twelve, and the hussar could scarcely breathe from excitement; the next moment, however, he heard the noise which the Count's body-servant had compared to that of bats, and almost at the same instant a white figure glided slowly through the open cloisters and passed so close to him, that it almost made his blood curdle, and then it disappeared in the wing of the castle which he and the tutor occupied.

The officer who was usually so brave, stood as though he was paralyzed for a few moments, but then he took heart, and feeling determined to make the nearer acquaintance of the spectral beauty, he crept softly up the broad staircase and took up his position in a deep recess in the cloisters, where nobody could see him.

He waited for a long time; he heard every quarter strike, and at last, just before the close of the "witching hour," he heard the same noise like the rustling of bats, and then she came. He felt the flutter of her white dress, and she stood before him—it was indeed the Countess.

He presented his pistol at her as he challenged her, but she raised her hand menacingly.

"Who are you?" he exclaimed. "If you are really a ghost, prove it, for I am going to fire."

"For heaven's sake!" the White Lady whispered, and at the same instant two white arms were thrown round him, and he felt a full, warm bosom heaving against his own.

After that night the ghost appeared more frequently still. Not only did the White Lady make her appearance every night in the cloisters, only to disappear in the proximity of the hussar's rooms as long as the family remained at the castle, but she even followed them to Vienna.

Baron T., who went to that capital on leave of absence during the following winter, and who was the Count's guest at the express wish of his wife, was frequently told by the footman that although hitherto she had seemed to be confined to the old castle in Bohemia, she had shown herself now here, now there, in the mansion in Vienna, in a white dress and making a noise like the wings of a bat, and bearing a striking resemblance to the beautiful Countess.

Violated

"Really," Paul repeated, "really!"

"Yes, I who am here before you have been violated, and violated by—But if I were to tell you immediately by whom, there would be no story, eh? And as you want a story, I will tell you all about it from beginning to end. "I had been shooting for a week, over the waste lands in the heart of Brittany which border on the Black Mountains. It is a desolate and wild country, but it abounds in game. You can walk for hours without meeting a human being, and when you meet anybody, it is just the same as if you had not, for the people are absolutely ignorant of French. When I got to an inn at night, I had to employ signs to let the people know that I wanted supper and a bed.

"As I happened to be in a melancholy frame of mind at the time, the solitude delighted me, and my dog's companionship was quite enough for me. So you may guess my irritation when I perceived one morning that I was being followed, absolutely followed, by another sportsman, who seemed to wish to enter into conversation with me. On the previous day I had noticed him obstructing the horizon several times, and had attributed it to the chances of sport, which brought us both to the same likely spots for game, but now I could not be mistaken! The fellow was evidently following me, and was stretching his little pair of compasses as much as he could so as to keep up with my long strides, and was taking shortcuts, so as to catch up with me at the half circle.

"As he seemed bent upon the matter, I naturally grew obstinate, too. He spent his whole day in trying to catch up, while I spent mine in trying to baffle him. We seemed to be playing at hide-and-seek; the consequence was that when it was getting dark I had completely lost myself in the most deserted part of the moor. There was no cottage near, and not even a church spire in the distance. The only landmark was the hateful outline of that cursed man, about five hundred yards off.

"Of course he had won the game! I should have to put a good face on the matter and allow him to join me, or rather I should have to join him myself, if I did not wish to sleep in the open air with an empty stomach. So I went up to him and asked my way in a half-surly manner.

"He replied very affably that there was no inn in the neighbourhood, and that the nearest village was five leagues off, but that he lived only about an hour's walk off, and considered himself very fortunate in being able to offer me hospitality.

"I was utterly done up, and could not refuse. So we went off through the heather and furze; I walking slowly because I was so tired, and he tripping along merrily on legs like a basset-hound's, they seemed so untirable.

"And yet he was an old man, and not strongly built, for I could have knocked him over by blowing on him; but how he could walk, the beast!

"He was not a troublesome companion, as I imagined he would have been, and he did not seem to wish to enter into conversation with me, as I feared he would. When he had given his invitation, and I had accepted it and thanked him in a few words, he did not open his lips again, and we walked on in silence. Yet his glances worried me, for I felt them on me, as if he wished to force me into an intimacy which my closed lips refused. But on the whole, his constant looks, which I noticed furtively, appeared sympathetic and even admiring—yes, really admiring!

"But I could not give him the same, for he was certainly not handsome; his legs were short and rather bandy, and he was thin and narrow-chested. His face was like a bit of parchment, furrowed and wrinkled, without a hair on it to hide the folds in his skin. His hair resembled that of an *Ignorantin* brother, (a lay brother in a monastery who is devoted to the instruction of the poor) with its gray locks falling on to a greasy collar; he had a nose like a ferret and rat's eyes, but he was able to offer me food and quarters for the night, and it was not requisite that he should be handsome in order to do that.

"Capital food, and very comfortable quarters! A manorial dwelling, a real old, well-furnished manor-house; and in the large dining-room, in front of the huge fireplace, where a large fire was blazing, dinner was laid; I will say no more than that! There was a hotchpotch, which had been stewing since morning, no doubt; a *salmi* of woodcock, in defence of which angels would have taken up arms; buckwheat cakes in cream, flavoured with aniseed, and a cheese—which is a rare thing and hardly ever to be found in Brittany—a cheese to make anyone eat a four-pound loaf, if he only smelled the rind! The whole was washed down by Chambertin, and then by brandy distilled from cider, which was so good that it made a man fancy that he had swallowed a goddess in velvet. Then came cigars, pure, smuggled Havanas; large, strong, not dry but green, fragrant and soothing to smoke.

"And how the little old gentleman stuffed and drank and smoked! He was an ogre, a quicksand, a chimney, and so was I, I must confess. Upon my word, I cannot remember what we talked about during our Gargantuan feed! We certainly talked, but what about? About shooting, certainly, and about women most probably, as men do after drinking! Yes, yes, I am quite sure he told some funny stories about women, did the little old man! Especially about a portrait hanging over the large fireplace, which represented his grandmother, a Marchioness of the old regime. She was a woman who had certainly played some pranks, and they said that she was still frisky when she was seventy.

"'It is extraordinary,' I remarked, 'how like you are to that portrait.'

"'Yes,' the old man replied with a smile; and then he added

in his harsh, tremulous voice: 'I resemble her in everything. I am only sixty, and I feel as if I should have lusty, hot blood in me until I am seventy.'

"And then suddenly, very much moved, and looking at me admiringly, as he had done once before, he said to the portrait:

"'I say. Marchioness, what a pity that you did not know this handsome young fellow!'

"I remembered that apostrophe and that look very well, about an hour later, when I went to bed nearly drunk, in the large room papered in white and gold, to which I was shown by a tall, broad-shouldered footman, who wished me good night in Breton.

"Goodnight—yes! But that implied going to sleep, which was just what I could not do. The Chambertin, the cider brandy, and the cigars had certainly made me drunk, but not so as to overcome me altogether. On the contrary, I was excited, my nerves were highly strung, my blood was heated, and I was in a half-sleep in which I felt that I was very much alive, and that my whole being was in a vibration and expansion, just as if I had been smoking hashish.

"Of course! That was it; I was dreaming while I was awake; but I saw the door open and the Marchioness come in. She had stepped down out of her frame. She had taken off her furbelows, and was in her nightgown. Her high headdress was replaced by a simple knot of ribbon, which confined her powdered hair in a small *chignon*, but I recognized her quite plainly by the trembling light of the candle she was carrying. It was her face—with its piercing eyes, its pointed nose, and its smiling and sensual mouth. She did not look as young to me as she appeared in her portrait. Bah! Perhaps that was merely caused by the feeble, flickering light! But I had not even time to account for it, nor to reflect on the strangeness of the sight, nor to discuss the matter with myself and to say: 'Am I dead drunk, or is it a ghost?'

"No, I had no time, and that is the fact, for the candle was suddenly blown out and the Marchioness was in my bed and holding me in her arms.

"By Jove, yes! She did not speak. Oh, *Marchioness! Marchioness!* And suddenly, in spite of myself and to convince myself that it was not merely a fantastic dream, I exclaimed:

"'Why, good heavens! I am not dreaming!'

"'No, you are not dreaming,' two lips replied, trying to press themselves against mine.

"But, oh! horror! The mouth smelled of cigars and brandy! The voice was that of the little old man!

"With a bound I sent him flying on to the floor, and jumped out of bed, shouting:

"'Beast! beast!'

"Then I heard the door slam, and bare feet pattering on the stairs as he ran away. I dressed hastily in the dark and went downstairs, still shouting.

"In the hall below, where I could see through the upper windows that the dawn was breaking, I met the broad-shouldered footman, who was holding a great cudgel in his hand. He was shouting also, in Breton, and pointed to the open door, outside where my dog was waiting. What could I say to this savage who did not speak French? Should I face his cudgel? There was no reason for doing so; and besides, I was more ashamed than furious. So I hastily took up my gun and my game-bag, which were in the hall, and went off without looking back.

"Disgusted with sport in that part of the country, I returned to Brest the same day, and there, timidly and with many precautions, I tried to find out something about the little old man.

"'Oh, I know!' somebody replied at last to my question; 'you are speaking of the manor-house at Hervdnidozse, where the old Countess lives. She dresses like a man and sleeps with her coachman.'

"And with a deep sigh of relief, and much to the astonishment of my informant, I replied:

"'Oh! so much the better!'"

Minuet

Great misfortunes do not affect me very much, said John Bridelle, an old bachelor who passed for a sceptic. I have seen war at quite close quarters; I walked across corpses without any feeling of pity. The great brutal facts of nature, or of humanity, may call forth cries of horror or indignation, but do not cause us that tightening of the heart, that shudder that goes down your spine at sight of certain little heartrending episodes.

The greatest sorrow that anyone can experience is certainly the loss of a child, to a mother; and the loss of his mother, to a man. It is intense, terrible, it rends your heart and upsets your mind; but one is healed of these shocks, just as large bleeding wounds become healed. Certain meetings, certain things half perceived, or surmised, certain secret sorrows, certain tricks of fate which awake in us a whole world of painful thoughts, which suddenly unclose to us the mysterious door of moral suffering, complicated, incurable; all the deeper because they appear benign, all the more bitter because they are intangible, all the more tenacious because they appear almost factitious, leave in our souls a sort of trail of sadness, a taste of bitterness, a feeling of disenchantment, from which it takes a long time to free ourselves.

I have always present to my mind two or three things that others would surely not have noticed, but which penetrated my being like fine, sharp incurable stings.

You might not perhaps understand the emotion that I retained from these hasty impressions. I will tell you one of them.

She was very old, but as lively as a young girl. It may be that my imagination alone is responsible for my emotion.

I am fifty. I was young then and studying law. I was rather sad, somewhat of a dreamer, full of a pessimistic philosophy and did not care much for noisy *cafés*, boisterous companions, or stupid girls. I rose early and one of my chief enjoyments was to walk alone about eight o'clock in the morning in the nursery garden of the Luxembourg.

You people never knew that nursery garden. It was like a forgotten garden of the last century, as pretty as the gentle smile of an old lady. Thick hedges divided the narrow regular paths,— peaceful paths between two walls of carefully trimmed foliage. The gardener's great shears were pruning unceasingly these leafy partitions, and here and there one came across beds of flowers, lines of little trees looking like schoolboys out for a walk, companies of magnificent rose bushes, or regiments of fruit trees.

An entire corner of this charming spot was in habited by bees. Their straw hives skilfully arranged at distances on boards had their entrances—as large as the opening of a thimble—turned towards the sun, and all along the paths one encountered these humming and gilded flies, the true masters of this peaceful spot, the real promenaders of these quiet paths.

I came there almost every morning. I sat down on a bench and read. Sometimes I let my book fall on my knees, to dream, to listen to the life of Paris around me, and to enjoy the infinite repose of these old-fashioned hedges.

But I soon perceived that I was not the only one to frequent this spot as soon as the gates were opened, and I occasionally met face to face, at a turn in the path, a strange little old man.

He wore shoes with silver buckles, knee-breeches, a snuff-coloured frock coat, a lace jabot, and an outlandish gray hat with wide brim and long-haired surface that might have come out of the ark.

He was thin, very thin, angular, grimacing and smiling. His bright eyes were restless beneath his eyelids which blinked continuously. He always carried in his hand a superb cane with a gold knob, which must have been for him some glorious souvenir.

This good man astonished me at first, then caused me the intensest interest. I watched him through the leafy walls, I followed him at a distance, stopping at a turn in the hedge so as not to be seen.

And one morning when he thought he was quite alone, he began to make the most remarkable motions. First he would give some little springs, then make a bow; then, with his slim legs, he would give a lively spring in the air, clapping his feet as he did so, and then turn round cleverly, skipping and frisking about in a comical manner, smiling as if he had an audience, twisting his poor little puppet-like body, bowing pathetic and ridiculous little greetings into the empty air. He was dancing.

I stood petrified with amazement, asking myself which of us was crazy, he or I.

He stopped suddenly, advanced as actors do on the stage, then bowed and retreated with gracious smiles, and kissing his hand as actors do, his trembling hand, to the two rows of trimmed bushes.

Then he continued his walk with a solemn demeanour.

After that I never lost sight of him, and each morning he began anew his outlandish exercises.

I was wildly anxious to speak to him. I decided to risk it, and one day, after greeting him, I said:

"It is a beautiful day, *monsieur.*"

He bowed.

"Yes, sir, the weather is just as it used to be."

A week later we were friends and I knew his history. He had been a dancing master at the opera, in the time of Louis XV. His beautiful cane was a present from the Comte de Clermont. And when we spoke about dancing he never stopping talking.

One day he said to me:

"I married La Castris, *monsieur.* I will introduce you to her if you wish it, but she does not get here till later. This garden, you see, is our delight and our life. It is all that remains of former days. It seems as though we could not exist if we did not have it. It is old and *distingué*, is it not? I seem to breathe an air here that has not changed since I was young. My wife and I pass all our afternoons here, but I come in the morning because I get up early."

As soon as I had finished luncheon I returned to the Luxembourg, and presently perceived my friend offering his arm ceremoniously to a very old little lady dressed in black, to whom he introduced me. It was La Castris, the great dancer, beloved by princes, beloved by the king, beloved by all that century of gallantry that seems to have left behind it in the world an atmosphere of love.

We sat down on a bench. It was the month of May. An odour of flowers floated in the neat paths; a hot sun glided its rays between the branches and covered us with patches of light. The black dress of La Castris seemed to be saturated with sunlight.

The garden was empty. We heard the rattling of vehicles in the distance.

"Tell me," I said to the old dancer, "what was the *minuet?*"

He gave a start.

"The minuet, *monsieur,* is the queen of dances, and the dance of queens, do you understand? Since there is no longer any royalty, there is no longer any *minuet.*"

And he began in a pompous manner a long dithyrambic eulogy which I could not understand. I wanted to have the steps, the movements, the positions, explained to me. He became confused, was amazed at his inability to make me understand, became nervous and worried.

Then suddenly, turning to his old companion who had remained silent and serious, he said:

"Elise, would you like—say—would you like, it would be very nice of you, would you like to show this gentleman what it was?"

She turned eyes uneasily in all directions, then rose without saying a word and took her position opposite him.

Then I witnessed an unheard-of thing.

They advanced and retreated with childlike grimaces, smiling, swinging each other, bowing, skipping about like two automaton dolls moved by some old mechanical contrivance, somewhat damaged, but made by a clever workman according to the fashion of his time.

And I looked at them, my heart filled with extraordinary emotions, my soul touched with an indescribable melancholy. I seemed to see before me a pathetic and comical apparition, the out-of-date ghost of a former century.

They suddenly stopped. They had finished all the figures of the dance. For some seconds they stood opposite each other, smiling in an astonishing manner. Then they fell on each other's necks sobbing.

I left for the provinces three days later. I never saw them again. When I returned to Paris, two years later, the nursery had been destroyed. What became of them, deprived of the dear garden of former days, with its mazes, its odour of the past, and the graceful windings of its hedges?

Are they dead? Are they wandering among modern streets like hopeless exiles? Are they dancing—grotesque spectres—a fantastic *minuet* in the moonlight, amid the cypresses of a cemetery, along the pathways bordered by graves?

Their memory haunts me, obsesses me, torments me, remains with me like a wound. Why? I do not know.

No doubt you think that very absurd?

Am I Insane?

Am I insane or jealous? I know not which, but I suffer horribly. I committed a crime it is true, but is not insane jealousy, betrayed love, and the terrible pain I endure enough to make anyone commit crime, without actually being a criminal?

I have loved this woman to madness—and yet, is it true? Did I love her? No, no! She owned me body and soul, I was her plaything, she ruled me by her smile, her look, the divine form of her body. It was all those things that I loved, but the woman contained in that body, I despise her; hate her. I always have hated her, for she is but an impure, perfidious creature, in whom there was no soul; even less than that, she is but a mass of soft flesh in which dwells infamy!

The first few months of our union were deliciously strange. Her eyes were three different colours. No, I am not insane, I swear they were. They were gray at noon, shaded green at twilight, and blue at sunrise. In moments of love they were blue; the pupils dilated and nervous. Her lips trembled and often the tip of her pink tongue could be seen, as that of a reptile ready to hiss. When she raised her heavy lids and I saw that ardent look, I shuddered, not only for the unceasing desire to possess her, but for the desire to kill this beast.

When she walked across the room each step resounded in my heart. When she disrobed and emerged infamous but radiant from the white mass of linen and lace, a sudden weakness seized me, my limbs gave way beneath me, and my chest heaved; I was faint, coward that I was!

Each morning when she awakened I waited for that first look, my heart filled with rage, hatred, and disdain for this beast whose slave I was; but when she fixed those limpid blue eyes on me, that languishing look showing traces of lassitude, it was like a burning, unquenchable fire within me, inciting me to passion.

When she opened her eyes that day I saw a dull, indifferent look; a look devoid of desire, and I knew then she was tired of me. I saw it, knew it, felt right away that it was all over, and each hour and minute proved to me that I was right. When I beckoned her with my arms and lips she shrank from me.

"Leave me alone," she said. "You are horrid!"

Then I became suspicious, insanely jealous; but I am not insane, no indeed! I watched her slyly; not that she had betrayed me, but she was so cold that I knew another would soon take my place.

At times she would say:

"Men disgust me!" Alas! it was too true.

Then I became jealous of her indifference, of her thoughts, which I knew to be impure, and when she awakened sometimes with that same look of lassitude I suffocated with anger, and an irresistible desire to choke her and make her confess the shameful secrets of her heart took hold of me.

Am I insane? No.

One night I saw that she was happy. I felt, in fact I was convinced, that a new passion ruled her. As of old, her eyes shone, she was feverish and her whole self fluttered with love.

I feigned ignorance, but I watched her closely. I discovered nothing however. I waited a week, a month, almost a year. She was radiantly, ideally happy; as if soothed by some ephemeral caress.

At last I guessed. No, I am not insane, I swear I am not. How can I explain this inconceivable, horrible thing? How can I make myself understood? This is how I guessed.

She came in one night from a long ride on horseback and sank exhausted in a seat facing me. An unnatural flush tinted her cheeks and her eyes,—those eyes that I knew so well,—had such a look in them. 1 was not mistaken, I had seen her look like that; she loved! But whom? What? I almost lost my head, and so as not to look at her I turned to the window. A valet was leading her horse to the stable and she stood and watched him disappear; then she fell asleep almost immediately. I thought and thought all night. My mind wandered through mysteries too deep to conceive. Who can fathom the perversity and strange caprices of a sensual woman?

Every morning she rode madly through hills and dales and each time she came back languid; exhausted. At last I understood. It was of the horse I was jealous—of the wind which caressed her face, of the drooping leaves and of the dewdrops, of the saddle which carried her! It was all those things which made her so happy and brought her back to me satiated; exhausted! I resolved to be revenged. I became very attentive. Every time she came back from her ride I helped her down and the horse made a vicious rush at me. She would pat him on the neck, kiss his quivering nostrils, without even wiping her lips. I watched my chance.

One morning I got up before dawn and went to the path in the woods she loved so well. I carried a rope with me, and my pistols were hidden in my breast as if I were going to fight a duel. I drew the rope across the path, tying it to a tree on each side, and hid myself in the grass. Presently I heard her horse's hoofs, then I saw her coming at a furious pace; her cheeks flushed, an insane look in her eyes. She seemed enraptured; transported into another sphere.

As the animal approached the rope he struck it with his fore feet and fell. Before she had struck the ground I caught her in my arms and helped her to her feet. I then approached the horse, put my pistol close to his ear, and shot him—as I would a man.

She turned on me and dealt me two terrific blows across the face with her riding-whip which felled me, and as she rushed at me again, I shot her!

Tell me, Am I insane?

LEONAUR

ALSO FROM LEONAUR
AVAILABLE IN SOFTCOVER OR HARDCOVER WITH DUST JACKET

THE LONG PATROL by *George Berrie*—A Novel of Light Horsemen from Gallipoli to the Palestine campaign of the First World War.

NAPOLEONIC WAR STORIES by *Arthur Quiller-Couch*—Tales of soldiers, spies, battles & sieges from the Peninsular & Waterloo campaingns.

THE FIRST DETECTIVE by *Edgar Allan Poe*—The Complete Auguste Dupin Stories—The Murders in the Rue Morgue, The Mystery of Marie Rogêt & The Purloined Letter.

THE COMPLETE DR NIKOLA—MAN OF MYSTERY: 1 by *Guy Boothby*—*A Bid for Fortune* & *Dr Nikola Returns*—Guy Boothby's Dr.Nikola adventures continue to fascinate readers and enthusiasts of crime and mystery fiction because—in the manner of Raffles, the gentleman cracksman—here is character far removed from the uncompromising goodness of Holmes and Watson or the uncompromising evil of Professor Moriarty.

THE COMPLETE DR NIKOLA—MAN OF MYSTERY: 2 by *Guy Boothby*—*The Lust of Hate, Dr Nikola's Experiment* & *Farewell, Nikola*—Guy Boothby's Dr.Nikola adventures continue to fascinate readers and enthusiasts of crime and mystery fiction because—in the manner of Raffles, the gentleman cracksman—here is character far removed from the uncompromising goodness of Holmes and Watson or the uncompromising evil of Professor Moriarty.

THE CASEBOOKS OF MR J. G. REEDER: BOOK 1 by *Edgar Wallace*—*Room 13, The Mind of Mr J. Reeder* and *Terror Keep*—Edgar Wallace's sleuth—whose territory is the London of the 1920s—is an unlikely figure, more bank clerk than detective in appearance, ever wearing his square topped bowler, frock coat, cravat and muffler, Mr Reeder is usually inseparable from his umbrella.

THE CASEBOOKS OF MR J. G. REEDER: BOOK 2 by *Edgar Wallace*—*Red Aces, Mr J. G. Reeder Returns, The Guv'nor* and *The Man Who Passed*—Edgar Wallace's sleuth—whose territory is the London of the 1920s—is an unlikely figure, more bank clerk than detective in appearance, ever wearing his square topped bowler, frock coat, cravat and muffler, Mr Reeder is usually inseparable from his umbrella.

THE COMPLETE FOUR JUST MEN: VOLUME 1 by *Edgar Wallace*—*The Four Just Men, The Council of Justice* & *The Just Men of Cordova*—disillusioned with a world where the wicked and the abusers of power perpetually go unpunished, the Just Men set about to rectify matters according to their own standards, and retribution is dispensed on swift and deadly wings.

LEONAUR

ALSO FROM LEONAUR

AVAILABLE IN SOFTCOVER OR HARDCOVER WITH DUST JACKET

THE COMPLETE FOUR JUST MEN: VOLUME 2 *by Edgar Wallace—The Law of the Four Just Men & The Three Just Men*—disillusioned with a world where the wicked and the abusers of power perpetually go unpunished, the Just Men set about to rectify matters according to their own standards, and retribution is dispensed on swift and deadly wings.

THE COMPLETE RAFFLES: 1 *by E. W. Hornung—The Amateur Cracksman & The Black Mask*—By turns urbane gentleman about town and accomplished cricketer, life is just too ordinary for Raffles and that sets him on a series of adventures that have long been treasured as a real antidote to the 'white knights' who are the usual heroes of the crime fiction of this period.

THE COMPLETE RAFFLES: 2 *by E. W. Hornung—A Thief in the Night & Mr Justice Raffles*—By turns urbane gentleman about town and accomplished cricketer, life is just too ordinary for Raffles and that sets him on a series of adventures that have long been treasured as a real antidote to the 'white knights' who are the usual heroes of the crime fiction of this period.

THE COLLECTED SUPERNATURAL AND WEIRD FICTION OF WILKIE COLLINS: VOLUME 1 *by Wilkie Collins*—Contains one novel 'The Haunted Hotel', one novella 'Mad Monkton', three novelettes 'Mr Percy and the Prophet', 'The Biter Bit' and 'The Dead Alive' and eight short stories to chill the blood.

THE COLLECTED SUPERNATURAL AND WEIRD FICTION OF WILKIE COLLINS: VOLUME 2 *by Wilkie Collins*—Contains one novel 'The Two Destinies', three novellas 'The Frozen deep', 'Sister Rose' and 'The Yellow Mask' and two short stories to chill the blood.

THE COLLECTED SUPERNATURAL AND WEIRD FICTION OF WILKIE COLLINS: VOLUME 3 *by Wilkie Collins*—Contains one novel 'Dead Secret,' two novelettes 'Mrs Zant and the Ghost' and 'The Nun's Story of Gabriel's Marriage' and five short stories to chill the blood.

FUNNY BONES *selected by Dorothy Scarborough*—An Anthology of Humorous Ghost Stories.

MONTEZUMA'S CASTLE AND OTHER WEIRD TALES *by Charles B. Cory*—Cory has written a superb collection of eighteen ghostly and weird stories to chill and thrill the avid enthusiast of supernatural fiction.

SUPERNATURAL BUCHAN *by John Buchan*—Stories of Ancient Spirits, Uncanny Places & Strange Creatures.

www.ingramcontent.com/pod-product-compliance
Lightning Source LLC
Chambersburg PA
CBHW020932020726
47495CB00002B/453